the forest of Lost souLs

ANNE PLICHOTA
CENDRINE WOLF

Translated by Sue Rose

PUSHKIN
CHILDREN'S

Pushkin Children's Books
71–75 Shelton Street
London WC2H 9JQ

Translation © Sue Rose 2014

Oksa Pollock: The Forest of Lost Souls first published in French as
Oksa Pollock: La forêt des égarés by XO Editions in 2010

Original text © XO Editions, 2010. All Rights Reserved

First published by Pushkin Children's Books in 2014

ISBN 978-1-78269-031-3

Set in 12 on 16 Arno Pro by Tetragon, London

Printed in Great Britain by CPI Group (UK) Ltd, Croydon CR0 4YY

www.pushkinpress.com

For dearest, adorable, ever-patient Zoe

1

A Surprising Connection

Zoe kept rushing around the McGraws' house, frantically looking in every room. Orthon had disappeared and there was no sign of his wife Barbara or his son Mortimer. She was alone.

"Go to your room, Zoe, don't worry," Mortimer had told her two weeks ago. "I'll pop up and see you in a bit."

That was the last time she'd spoken to him. She'd waited all evening, then she'd fallen asleep, worn out with worry. The house was empty when she'd woken up. Horribly empty. Zoe had waited for hours for Orthon or Mortimer to come back, wandering from room to room and leaving worried messages on their mobiles, which had rung unanswered. Hours had turned into days. The cupboards and fridge gradually emptied, dust settled on the furniture, growing thicker by the day, and spiders' webs formed high up on the walls. With all hope gone, she'd finally had to face facts: she'd been abandoned. She was all alone in the world with nowhere to go and no one cared if she lived or died. The house felt as if it were closing in on her like a tomb.

This unpleasant sensation shocked her into action. She packed a small bag with her most treasured possessions: the photo album documenting special events in her short life, a few birthday cards, a pendant in the shape of a clover leaf and her gran's strange-looking flute. Then, with her bag slung over her shoulder, she walked to the Pollocks' house without looking back, her heart in pieces.

When Dragomira opened the door she was astounded to recognize a thin, grubby Zoe gazing at her with desperate, tear-filled eyes ringed with dark circles.

"Mrs Pollock, I'm so sorry for coming here—I didn't know where else to go…"

Then, overcome with emotion, she sank down onto the top step in front of the house. Dragomira, who was still bruised and battered from her final encounter with Orthon, summoned the Lunatrixes to help. Zoe didn't resist, too exhausted to show any fear of these remarkable creatures. They carried her up to their mistress's apartment and laid her on a sofa, where she immediately fell asleep.

"Misunderstanding is about to experience mending!" exclaimed the Lunatrix, even more enigmatically than ever.

"Oh, please, my Lunatrix," said Dragomira, rebuking the small creature. "This is no time to speak in riddles!"

"Beware of judgement overflowing with errors and grudges, Old Gracious," continued the small creature nonetheless. "Vast importance must be attributed to this girl because she contains Gracious blood…"

The Old Gracious frowned and slumped down onto the sofa opposite the one where the Lunatrixes had deposited Zoe. Despite her weakened condition and the scolding she'd just given her Lunatrix, she knew in her heart of hearts that this pitiable-looking girl was going to turn their lives upside down.

To Zoe's great embarrassment, Dragomira was watching her when she woke up, even though she could see no hostility in Baba Pollock's eyes.

"Hello, Zoe," Dragomira said softly. "Are you feeling any better?"

When Zoe replied "no" in an almost inaudible whisper, Dragomira leant towards her and, gently taking her hand, murmured kindly:

"I know you're scared. I would be too if I were in your shoes. I just want to say that I don't mean you any harm—quite the opposite, in fact. You can trust me."

Feeling somewhat reassured and more hopeful, Zoe glanced shyly at Dragomira.

"Why don't you tell me everything from the beginning?" suggested the old lady.

After a brief hesitation, Zoe made up her mind. The words poured from her, tumbling over each other to get out. She sobbed as the painful memories tore her apart, making her heart ache, but once she'd started, she couldn't stop. She kept talking through her tears while Dragomira stroked her hand, realizing the extent of the misunderstanding mentioned by the Lunatrix.

"So your father isn't Orthon-McGraw!" gasped Baba Pollock in amazement.

"No. He's my great-uncle, my gran was his twin sister. He took me in when she died."

She was now speaking in a tiny voice. Startled, Dragomira looked at her even more attentively and murmured:

"Reminiscens… Reminiscens was so near to us and we didn't realize."

"She told me you'd known each other when you were young and that you alone could help me if I was ever in trouble. She really admired you, you know. I've got some photos of her, if you'd like to see them…"

"I'd love to," whispered Dragomira.

Zoe took the photo album from her bag and handed it to Dragomira, who carefully opened it. The old lady turned the pages, her mind reeling. She kept looking from Zoe to the pictures and back again, her amazement increasing with every page.

"My gran knew a great deal about all kinds of things, particularly rocks and precious stones," continued Zoe. "She was a diamond-cutter. She'd always lived with me and my parents because she adored my dad. He was her only son. When he died, she focused all her energy and love on me. We both often held back tears to avoid upsetting each other. We had to be strong for each other and that was really hard. I'd lost my parents, but she'd lost her son."

"That's awful... Is that your dad in these photos?" asked the old lady, pointing to a page of the open album.

"Yes."

"He was very handsome."

Dragomira stared at the photos for a long while, her brow furrowed. Suddenly a thought struck her and the blood drained from her face.

"I'd like to ask you something, Zoe," she said, trembling. "What was your father's name? And do you know his date of birth?"

"My dad was born on 29th March 1953 and his name was Jan Evanvleck."

Dragomira sank back on the sofa. All these pieces of information came together in her mind, making her head spin and sucking her into a vortex of repressed grief and untold secrets. The truth erupted like lava from a volcano.

"Leomido..." murmured Dragomira.

She looked at Zoe, her eyes full of tears.

"You haven't lost everything, my child. When you knocked on my door, you found a family. Your own family."

"I... I don't understand!" stammered Zoe.

"My dear brother, Leomido, is your grandfather."

2

A Brief Respite

Four months later…

IT WAS THE END OF TERM AT LAST AND THE STUDENTS OF
St Proximus were letting off steam, racing around the courtyard
shouting and laughing, their uniforms in disarray and their ties unknotted. Oksa Pollock and Gus Bellanger were more than ready for the
holidays—they'd begun to think the school year would never end. So
much had happened… What with the revelation of Oksa's mysterious
origins and the vaporization of Orthon-McGraw, the last few months
had held more than their fair share of exciting discoveries and terrifying
ordeals. Oksa shook her head, determined not to let these dark thoughts
dampen her high spirits, and walked over to Zoe, once her sworn enemy,
now her second cousin and firm friend.

"Everyone's having a great time!"

Zoe smiled back at her. It hadn't been easy winning Oksa's friendship.
She'd held a deep-seated grudge against Zoe for the gift of the poisoned
soap which had made Marie so ill. It hadn't been long, though, before
the Young Gracious had realized that Zoe had been an unwitting pawn
in Orthon's hands. And when Dragomira had told her great-niece about
the magical origins she shared with the Pollocks and the Runaways,
Oksa had been extremely supportive, providing a shoulder to cry on

when necessary and helping her to master the powers which, until then, she'd had no idea she possessed... Now, the two cousins were virtually inseparable.

"Hey! Why don't we go and annoy Gus?" exclaimed Oksa suddenly.

"You go, Oksa. I'd rather stay here," replied Zoe.

Oksa gave her a worried look. Zoe tended to withdraw into her own shell when she felt sad, which was quite often, even though she tried hard to stay upbeat.

"I'm fine, honestly," she said, seeing Oksa's sceptical expression.

Oksa headed over to Gus and began dragging him towards the fountain in the middle of the paved courtyard. He struggled to free himself, laughing.

"It doesn't take a genius to guess what you're up to!"

"How could you say no to a refreshing dip in honour of this red-letter day?" exclaimed Oksa, pulling her friend by the arm with all her might.

"You're making a big mistake if you think you can use brute force. Perhaps you've forgotten that nothing and no one can make me do something against my will!"

He brushed back a strand of dark hair with pretend arrogance. Weak with laughter, Oksa let go, and, losing her balance, crashed into the edge of the fountain.

"Ouch," she yelped. "My elbow!"

A ring of blood appeared around the tear in her blouse.

"That really hurt," she grumbled. "Dammit! Look at the mess I've made of myself."

Gus held out his hand to help her to her feet. She twisted round to take off the little bag she wore slung over her shoulder and handed it to him.

"Would you look after this for me while I go and clean myself up?" she asked.

"Wow... the Young Gracious's magical accessories? What an honour!"

Oksa smiled at him and headed off in the direction of the grey stone cloister. Gus watched until she vanished into the shadowy staircase that led into the magnificent building.

※

Twenty minutes later Gus was still there.

"Come on, Gus!" yelled a fair-haired student. "We're going to play basketball."

"I'd better not, Merlin, I'm waiting for Oksa."

Sitting there patiently against a low wall with nothing much to do, Gus gently pressed the bag. Inside he could feel a soft, round shape—the Tumble-Bawler. He hoped it wouldn't make a fuss. As if it could read his mind, the Tumble-Bawler said:

"Don't worry, young Master, discretion is my middle name! It has to be, since high volume doesn't make for a low profile."

This quirky motto made Gus smile.

"Come on, Oksa… what on earth are you doing up there?" he grumbled after a few more moments.

"I can inform you that the Young Gracious is currently in the first-floor toilets, fifty-six yards north-north-west of here," the small creature volunteered in a muffled voice.

Gus shuddered at the thought of someone overhearing this bizarre conversation, but all the other students were having too much fun to pay attention to him. Tired of waiting, he finally stood up and headed over to the staircase.

Walking along the deserted corridor, all he could hear was the sound of his own footsteps and the hubbub from the courtyard. It was strange thinking back to the awful events that had taken place just four months earlier—Oksa injured, fiendish McGraw showing his true colours, Miss Heartbreak… He couldn't help glancing through the lab window as he walked past and, as he did, he heard someone singing a sad, slow song that sounded like a lament. Intrigued, he turned the door handle—the lab was unlocked. Gus walked in and looked around. He couldn't see anyone, but he could definitely hear someone as clearly as if they were standing right next to him. He opened Oksa's bag: the Tumble-Bawler hadn't made a sound.

"What's going on? What is that noise?"

He walked round the room, clutching Oksa's bag tightly. He looked under every desk and opened the door to the storeroom, then the large cupboard. Nothing. And yet he could still hear the soft, mournful weeping. He stopped searching and stood in the middle of the room listening hard, all his senses alert. He could now make out what sounded like faint words amongst the sobs.

"What are you saying? Where are you?" he asked falteringly, looking around despite his fear.

He heard a voice which sounded as though it were coming from a long way off and yet was very close, saying:

"I'm here, right in front of you. I need your help. Please come and set me free… *I'm begging you!*"

❋

Oksa was hurrying back to the courtyard, her shirt still damp, when the wail of a foghorn caught her attention.

"Hey, that sounds like Gus's mobile!"

The ringtone grew louder as she walked past the first-floor lab, then cut out. Oksa stopped and listened for a few seconds. With a smile, she heard what she'd been expecting to hear: Darth Vader's rasping voice saying that someone had just left a message. It was definitely Gus's phone. She pushed open the door and walked in.

"Gus! Are you in here?"

No answer. Oksa glanced around and looked under the desks. Her friend didn't usually play tricks like this, but you never knew what he might get up to. Suddenly she spotted his mobile on the floor.

16

"What's his phone doing there?" she muttered with a frown.

She picked it up and gazed around again with a puzzled expression, then walked out of the room and went to join the others.

⁂

"You haven't seen Gus, have you?"

Zoe looked up, an expression of concern on her pretty face. Annoyed with herself for needlessly worrying her friend, Oksa hurriedly continued:

"What an Incompetent he is. Look, he's lost his mobile! He must be around here somewhere. Let's go and find him."

She grabbed Zoe's hand and, as impulsive as ever, dragged her off to hunt for Gus.

⁂

"Just wait till he dares to show his face again…" grumbled Oksa.

After half an hour spent searching fruitlessly for him, the two girls were back where they'd started and were both feeling more concerned than they cared to admit. It was getting late and the other students were beginning to file out of the school.

"You'd better phone home," suggested Zoe, her forehead creased in an anxious frown, which only made Oksa feel more apprehensive.

⁂

By the time Pierre Bellanger and Pavel Pollock had arrived in the courtyard, the girls were beside themselves with worry. They had spent nearly an hour searching the school again from top to bottom with mounting desperation.

"He isn't at Bigtoe Square or at home," declared Pierre, sliding shut his mobile.

17

The caretaker locked St Proximus's heavy gates and they had to come to terms with the harsh fact that Gus was nowhere to be found. Oksa and Zoe gazed at each other, eyes brimming with tears. The peace and quiet of the last few months had obviously just been a brief respite.

※

The Runaways were in shock. Brune and Naftali Knut, the imposing Swedish couple, and Dragomira's brother, Leomido, had rushed over to the Pollocks' house in a show of solidarity. Night had fallen long ago, doing nothing to lighten the heavy mood. Pierre, his face furrowed with worry, had his arms around his wife, Jeanne, who couldn't stop crying. Dragomira walked over and gave them a hug, but couldn't think of anything comforting to say. Standing behind Marie's wheelchair, his eyes fixed on Oksa, Pavel felt paralysed by a creeping sense of anxiety.

"Perhaps we should inform the police?" suggested Oksa hoarsely.

"We can't do that, Oksa," replied Abakum, the protector of the Runaways. "Anyway, you know they'd just say he's run away."

"Gus wouldn't run away from anything. He's been kidnapped!" cried Jeanne, frantic with worry.

"But by whom?" they all wondered, though no one dared to voice their thoughts. Only Oksa plucked up enough courage to say what they were all thinking:

"You don't think it could be a Felon, do you? Orthon-McGraw can't have been the only one to have got out of Edefia; who's to say there weren't others?"

They looked at her with some degree of gratitude. This was the best-case scenario for all of them. It meant that Gus would be used as a bargaining counter by the mystery kidnapper and wouldn't be harmed while negotiations were under way. But what if the kidnapper wasn't a Felon? It didn't bear thinking about.

They sat there all night constructing theories and possibilities, mobiles in hand and eyes glued to the front door. Around five o'clock in the morning, slumped on a sofa next to Zoe, who was as devastated as she'd been the night before, Oksa suddenly discovered what was to be their first lead. She'd kept Gus's phone and was listening for the umpteenth time to the last message that had activated the voicemail alert she'd heard. It was from Jeanne. "Gus, I haven't been able to get hold of you. Your dad will pick you up in an hour. See you later!" Amazed that she hadn't thought of it before, Oksa carefully examined everything on her friend's mobile. There wasn't anything much of interest in his messages, but there was something weird in the phone's picture library: just before his mother had called—the clock on the phone confirmed it—Gus had taken an odd photo.

"Look!"

Oksa showed them the thumbnail on the screen of the mobile.

"What on earth is that?"

Pavel immediately switched on his computer to enlarge the image and everyone crowded round to take a look. As soon as the picture appeared, Zoe cried out:

"That's my gran, Reminiscens!"

"Are you sure?" exclaimed Dragomira.

"Of course I am!"

They all stared at the screen: the picture showed the upper half of a woman who looked around seventy. She was slim, dressed in dark colours and her drawn face aroused compassion. Her pale-blue eyes, wide with despair and fear, were gazing straight ahead.

"That's my gran…" repeated Zoe, her voice hoarse with tiredness and emotion.

Dragomira and Abakum exchanged surprised glances. Suddenly, understanding dawned and, still looking at each other, they chorused:

"Impicturement!"

3

An Unexpected Visitor

G US WAS WOBBLING PRECARIOUSLY ON THE CRUMBLING ledge inside the painting he'd been looking at a few seconds ago in the science room at St Proximus. A heart-rending voice full of pain and sorrow had seemed to be coming from the picture and then suddenly, unable to tear his gaze away from its strangely shimmering surface, he'd been sucked in... As remarkable as it seemed, that's exactly what had happened. And now he was on the other side of the canvas, paralysed with fear, standing on a wooden ledge which appeared to be disintegrating under his feet.

"The painting..." he muttered. "I'm inside the painting!"

All he could see was a terrifyingly dark, motionless mass. The painting's frame had grown to gigantic proportions, dwarfing Gus and making him feel really small. He carefully twisted round to touch the taut canvas. With a bit of luck, he'd pass right back through the painting and escape from this nightmare... His fingertips grazed what he thought was the canvas and he groaned in disappointment: it had become a curtain of icy vapour as intangible as the air in a cold room.

"Is anyone there?" he called, the words catching in his throat. "Can you hear me?"

His voice sounded odd, muffled, as if he were in a padded cell. He'd never experienced such total silence. He felt a chunk of the wooden ledge give way beneath his weight and drop off. He listened carefully, hoping to

20

hear the wood hitting the ground after its fall, which would give him an idea of how high he was. Long seconds ticked by, but he heard nothing. He seemed to be standing above a bottomless void… He gulped and an icy trickle of sweat ran down his back. Perspiration beaded his forehead and dripped into his eyes, blurring his vision. Instinctively, he lifted his hand to rub his eyes and lost his balance. In an instant his fears became reality: he tumbled through the air with a despairing yell, his arms flailing in a desperate attempt to catch hold of something.

❄

The fall seemed to last for ever, as if time had ceased to exist. He was plummeting through complete darkness towards an unknown destination, unable to control his movements. Although he knew he was falling, it didn't feel like it. He was in the grip of a powerful but buoyant gravity which had him floating as slowly and gently as a feather dropped from a great height. He couldn't even tell if he was falling head first, or whether he was vertical or horizontal—he couldn't feel his body at all. And, even though it was an amazing sensation, Gus couldn't help being terrified. Maybe he was dead? Perhaps he was lost in a black hole from which he'd never escape? His eyes widened with fear at that horrible thought.

At long last, he felt himself bouncing on a surface as soft as an eiderdown. Panic-stricken, he held his breath and narrowed his eyes. He couldn't see a thing in the dense, velvety darkness. It was so impenetrable that it looked solid. Gus nervously stretched out his hand, expecting his fingertips to come into contact with something at any moment. A wall. A door. A face! But there was nothing except pitch-black, terrifying emptiness. He peered fearfully into the dark and, before long, noticed some small blue phosphorescent bubbles escaping from his mouth, as though his breath had materialized. He breathed out more heavily than usual and the astonishing phenomenon happened again, confirming his theory. Gus continued examining his surroundings, feeling scared. After a few minutes he made out something pulsing slowly, each palpitation crackling with purple electrical discharges. Was that the heart of the darkness? This thought sent a shiver up his spine. "Don't think about it," he thought frantically. "Darkness doesn't have a heart!"

He looked around, but all he could see was what appeared to be veins throbbing in time to the palpitations. The darkness might not have a heart, but it definitely seemed to be alive! Mustering his courage, Gus stood up. With shaking legs and chattering teeth he plunged resolutely into the gloom.

✵

It definitely didn't look as dark as before. The peculiar mauve sky was lightening gradually, casting a pale glow over the forest in which Gus now stood. There wasn't a thing to be seen—no sign of life anywhere. He shook his head, disconcerted by the lack of movement. Not even the air seemed to stir. He rubbed his eyes and slid down to a sitting position against the trunk of a massive tree, putting his head in his hands.

"What's happened to me?" he groaned, his heart thumping. "What's going on?"

Gus irritably brushed some black hair out of his eyes and tucked it behind his ear. He felt as though a hot, sticky substance like tar was spreading through his veins, paralysing his body and mind. He barely dared move, or even breathe. Where was he? In another dimension? A parallel world? In the Lost Land of Edefia? The only thing he was sure about was that he'd fallen *into a painting* and that he wasn't dead, because he could feel his heart pounding in his chest.

A few minutes or hours went by—there was no way of telling—before he grew a little calmer. Ever since that secret mark had appeared around Oksa's belly button, Gus had been involved in one adventure after another, each more extraordinary than the last. His life had become a whirlwind of events filled with never-ending mysteries. He'd had to deal with a host of problems all with a common cause: Orthon-McGraw. That man had been a living nightmare, a public menace. But McGraw was dead—Abakum the Fairyman had dispatched him with a Crucimaphila Granok, pitilessly vaporizing him into several billion particles. Gus had seen it with his own eyes.

It had to be McGraw's fault that he'd fallen into this trap. Gus distinctly remembered their hateful teacher hanging this hideous painting on the wall in the science room at St Proximus. That was the day Oksa had gone way too far—not for the first time—and had used her gifts to send McGraw into a fury. Gus winced at the memory, then turned his thoughts back to the forest. Still leaning against the massive tree, which seemed to have moulded itself to the shape of his body, he began examining the frighteningly motionless forest around him. Towering trees inspected him from their lofty heights, soaring so high that it was impossible to see their tops. Feeling that these colossuses were about to crash down on him, Gus looked at the ground, his head reeling. A path lined with strange plants wound amongst the foot of the giant trees. The long stem of the plant nearest to him was covered in sticky hairs and crowned by an intricate flower with delicate fiery-red petals that seemed about to burst into flames. Beside it, another plant—an electric-blue sphere the size of a football—looked like an obese jellyfish with its eight waving stems. However, even more incredible than the size of the trees and the shape of the plants was the light filtering through the dense treetops. It was a light which looked… dark! Deep mauve rays seemed to be coming from a huge black sun. One of them hit the ground at Gus's feet. He held out his hand and the beam passed right through as if his palm were transparent.

"Whoa…" he murmured.

A delicate, sparkling powder trickled from his hand onto the moss with a barely audible patter. This was the first sound Gus had heard since he'd landed in this forest. Silence closed around him again, stilling the air and erasing all signs of life. Gus leant back against the tree and immediately jumped: the trunk had become *soft*! He carefully looked round to see that the bark seemed to be formed of thousands of petals in every shade of brown and gold. Intrigued, he stood up slowly, as if the trunk were an animal he didn't want to frighten, and ran his fingers lightly over it. Fascinating! Every inch of the trunk felt unusually soft, like flesh. Gus edged closer, fighting the irresistible temptation to plunge his face into this strange material.

At that moment the bark began vibrating and, with the faintest of rustling noises, a cloud of butterflies took to the air and fluttered around him. Gus couldn't believe what he was seeing: the whole trunk had been covered with thousands of butterflies! Although the circle of magnificent insects around him was terrifying, it also filled him with wonder. He couldn't take his eyes off the dancing butterflies and his head filled with the whisper of delicate wings beating in perfect time. However, it hadn't escaped his notice that the circle was spinning faster and faster and was closing in on him. A wave of panic swept over him and he fell back onto the springy moss, his last vestiges of courage gone.

"Stop!" he croaked, holding his hands in front of him in a futile attempt to ward off the butterflies.

An enormous pitch-black butterfly broke away from the circle and fluttered closer—so close, in fact, that he could feel its wings beating against his cheek. A few seconds later it rejoined the circle and they flew off into the mauve sky with a faint hum.

* * *

Overcoming his fear, Gus was just pushing himself into a sitting position with his hands when he felt something move. Something was squirming and wriggling; something was alive! What next?

"Hey! Watch what you're doing! Don't you realize you're squashing me?"

The voice had come from the ground. Gus jumped to his feet with a yell.

"Look at the state of me now!" continued the voice.

Gus panicked. All he wanted to do was run away, but as he tried to do so, he caught his foot in a root writhing on the ground—and this was no ordinary root, since the part protruding from the earth had a small head at the end of it. All around him the forest seemed to be coming to life after holding its breath. The leaves were quivering in the trees and the moss was rising and falling as if it had just started breathing. Gus didn't notice any of this activity, though, because the scene that greeted his eyes was so unexpected. The small head undulating on the end of the long root was glaring indignantly at Gus. Suddenly it gave a shrill whistle and several other roots, all equipped with a head, emerged swaying at the foot of the tree. The root Gus had squashed came nearer, allowing him to examine its strange face more closely: neither entirely human nor animal, it was the size of a fist and looked like a cross between a young girl covered in freckles and a squirrel with cunning eyes. The head studied him inquisitively but benevolently, then sniffed at him and pulled at the tails of his white shirt with its tiny teeth. Suddenly, it blurted out:

"Oh no! It's not going to be happy!"

The other heads fidgeted at the end of their roots and a nervous murmur arose, although Gus couldn't work out what they were saying. All the little eyes had turned towards the mauve sky and were watching the majestic approach of a bird. Then the roots and their heads sank into the ground as quickly as they'd appeared, leaving Gus struggling to believe his eyes. The bird, which was growing visibly larger, turned out to be a glossy black crow. When it reached him it shook its feathers and opened its golden beak to give a revolting splutter. Then, folding its long wings, it stared reproachfully at Gus, grumbling. Gus was so amazed that he allowed the crow to come within pecking distance. It examined him carefully, then recoiled in surprise.

"Who are you? What are you doing here?" it cawed harshly, plumes of black steam escaping from its beak.

"Um… I don't know," replied Gus.

"You don't know who you are?" snapped the crow. "Well, I know who you're not!"

"No! Well yes… I do know who I am! I'm Gus Bellanger," replied the boy, disconcerted by this hostile reception. "But I don't know what I'm doing here. Do you know why I'm here?"

"You've been Impictured, obviously!" replied the crow crossly. "But you're not the person we were expecting at all."

The crow sighed, emitting another puff of black steam.

"This is the worst thing that could have happened," it said miserably.

4

FRIGHTENING SECRETS

"I've been Impictured?" repeated Gus, flabbergasted. "What does that mean? What did I do?"

The crow groaned in annoyance and ruffled its feathers, spraying him with icy droplets.

"What did you do? You didn't do anything!" it replied irritably. "It's him! It's his fault!"

"Who do you mean?"

"I mean the one who should have been Impictured, of course!" retorted the crow. "He's the reason the Soul-Searcher is in a coma!"

"Impictured?" repeated Gus, bewildered. "The Soul-Searcher?"

The crow seemed to be in the grip of strong emotion. It looked away, close to tears.

"The Soul-Searcher has been held in thrall by the Wickedesses since the false Impicturement," it continued without answering Gus's question. "All reference points have disappeared and Impicturement can no longer fulfil its basic function."

"I have no idea what you're talking about," sighed Gus. "Please explain!"

"The Soul-Searcher is crucial to Impicturement," replied the crow, meeting his eyes. "Ever since the one who should have been Impictured corrupted the process, Evil has dominated my world, preying upon anything good. The Wickedesses were born from this Evil. Despite its wisdom, the Soul-Searcher was unable to prevent them from being spawned and from multiplying. They're spreading like an epidemic and gain strength by feeding on anything alive and mortal."

"What can be done about it?" asked Gus anxiously.

"The Evil that has descended on us can only be eradicated if he who should have been Impictured pays his debt, because this Impicturement was intended for him. If he doesn't come, one extreme solution remains: the destruction of the Soul-Searcher. This would be regrettable, because the Soul-Searcher isn't intrinsically evil. It also grieves me that I can't assist with this, but I have to hide from the Wickedesses. If I'm killed, none of you in here have any chance of surviving."

"What part do I play in all of this?"

"I'm afraid I have to ask you to brave great danger in order to return to your world. Only one type of magic is strong enough to send you home: that of the potion. I'll leave my Wayfinder with you," the crow added, jutting its beak at the black butterfly. "You must find the Soul-Searcher's Sanctuary. It has become the stronghold of the Wickedesses, somewhere within the Stonewall Territory, deep inside a fortress protected by spells, evil beyond imagining. Here's something to help you."

The crow unfastened the tiny phial around its neck with its talons and held it out to Gus.

"What is it?" murmured the boy, turning the phial between his fingers. "What do I have to do?"

"If you manage to reach the Soul-Searcher without being killed by the Wickedesses, you must use this potion made by the Ageless Fairies. It will unleash the Displacement Spell, which has the power to destroy the Soul-Searcher. One drop of blood mixed with the phial's magic will release you for ever from this trap."

"Why don't you destroy it yourself then?" asked Gus. "You seem to be much stronger than me!"

"Of course I'm stronger than you. But I'm not human and the spell

28

only works when mixed with human blood. May luck be with you, my young friend. Until we meet again…"

The crow exhaled one last puff of black steam and spread its wide wings to fly away, signalling that the conversation was over. For a few seconds Gus watched the bird departing, then, just as it was about to disappear into the mauve sky, he yelled:

"Please come back! Don't leave me like this!"

The crow seemed to slow down, then Gus realized it was returning. With just a few beats of its wings it was standing before him again. It cawed so loudly that Gus flinched.

"Give me a clue!" begged Gus. "Tell me what to do!"

"I've already told you a great deal," objected the crow. "The intrinsic mystery of Impicturement must be preserved. However, since this is such an unusual situation, I'll give you some additional information. Listen carefully, because this is all I can tell you:

> *To leave the Forest of No Return*
> *Each traveller through it has to yearn*
> *For one thing—all else must be forsworn.*
> *Then every innocent heart and mind*
> *Must stop the Void from claiming life—*
> *Escape will depend on speed and might.*
> *Lives will again come under threat*
> *From creatures truly merciless*
> *Who descend on you with airborne death.*
> *Then you'll have to risk a rout*
> *In the realm of heat and drought*
> *Where cruelty crawls from underground.*
> *At last, the Stonewall opens wide*
> *When you locate the catch inside*
> *Bringing you closer to home Outside.*
> *But there's no escape if you don't beware*

29

The Wickedesses which, with lethal brawn,
Hold sway over every creature born
For the power of life and death is theirs.

After reciting this, the crow swiftly took off again without waiting for Gus's reaction. Confused and concerned, Gus turned round to question the black butterfly, but it too had disappeared: Gus was alone again. He thought over what the crow had just told him. It sounded like he'd have to perform all kinds of *Mission: Impossible*-style feats to escape from the picture. In fact, none of that information seemed to be much help. It just implied that things were going to get a whole lot worse. A Void that claims life? Merciless creatures? The lethal brawn of the Wickedesses? He wasn't cut out for this kind of adventure! But what choice did he have? None at all, and he knew it. If he failed, he'd be devoured by the Wickedesses and lost for ever.

He looked around again. In other circumstances, he would have loved this place. Everything was so big! The peace and quiet of the forest was doing nothing to allay his fears, so he set off towards its dark interior, taking care not to step on a sleeping plant. He made his way through a maze of trees silhouetted against the sky like black stakes. The forest grew thicker as he walked between the giant trunks. Around him, the moss rose and fell with the rhythm of shallow breathing, accompanied by the gentle movement of the trees' foliage as it swayed in a strange breeze that seemed to come from the leaves themselves then rise into the sky. When Gus stopped walking, everything froze, becoming as motionless as a photo. The plants were so still that they seemed to be holding their breath to keep a better eye on him. He found that even more frightening than when they were speaking directly to him. "I'm becoming totally paranoid… Is anyone there?" he asked hesitantly.

There was total silence. Conversely, though, everything inside his body seemed to be amplified and was making a terrible racket, which further increased his anxiety: the sound of his blood flowing through his veins was as deafening as a motorway at rush hour. His heart had become a massive gong and his lungs were puffing like a steam engine. His empty stomach suddenly growled with a dull rumble that sounded like distant thunder. Gus jumped, upset by the unusual din made by his own body.

"Is anybody there?" he called again. "Please answer me!"

Exhausted and fraught with worry, Gus sank down onto the ground and stretched out. The ground was silky-soft like fur but, even though he was comfortable and bone-weary, Gus had absolutely no desire to risk falling asleep.

"I'm going to die here all alone," he groaned. "Of hunger, for a start," he added, rubbing his stomach. "I'd never have thought I'd end up like this. What a rubbish way to die…"

He lay there for a while, tortured by his thoughts. Just picturing his parents brought tears to his eyes. Would he ever see them again? They had to be out of their minds with worry. And what about Oksa? And the Runaways? They'd do their utmost to get him out of this mess… He had to keep his spirits up. Instinctively, he squeezed the bag he'd been wearing over his shoulder ever since Oksa had asked him to look after it. There was something wriggling inside. He opened the bag and the Tumble-Bawler—his best friend's personal *and* living alarm—looked out in bewilderment.

"Tumble!" cried Gus. "You have no idea how good it is to see a friendly face!" The Tumble-Bawler crawled out of the bag, its conical body swaying back and forth.

"The Young Gracious's friend is too kind…" it said, blushing.

"Do you know where we are?"

Since the Tumble-Bawler was an expert at pinpointing locations, Gus hoped it might have some idea.

"One thing is certain: we're in Great Britain, in London, Young Master. Centre-centre-west, to be exact, Bean Street, St Proximus College, first floor, third classroom from the main staircase, north wall, four feet and eleven inches up from the floor, seven feet and two inches from the west corner, twenty-one feet and one inch from the east corner."

"Um… right," muttered Gus in astonishment. "Do you think you could be even more precise? Where are we *exactly*?" he added, waving his arm at the strange forest around them.

"We're in the picture, of course, Young Master!" replied the Tumble-Bawler, rocking back and forth furiously. "We're in the picture, which is fourteen point nine inches long by nine point eight inches high. I can't be any more precise than that, but that's not my fault. I can't see any of the four cardinal points, and there's no indication of height or depth. Distances, time and measurements don't exist, but the atmosphere is breathable…"

"Yes, I had noticed," murmured Gus.

"…and there are several superimposed levels. No," continued the Tumble-Bawler, "the levels aren't superimposed: they're nested inside one another."

"Like Russian dolls?"

The small creature nodded, then turned and scuttled back into the shelter of the bag. Gus, feeling more sceptical and despairing than ever, said nothing for a moment, staring into the silent shadows of the undergrowth.

⁕

"Come on, son, don't lose hope…"

Gus jumped and looked up. He scanned the ground for the headed root which had so unexpectedly chatted to him earlier. Several plants in a clump at the foot of the tree seemed to be watching him. One of them, topped with an enormous downy ball, leant towards the quivering berries and whispered something that Gus didn't understand.

"If at first you don't succeed, then try, try, try again," repeated the voice.

Gus suddenly noticed a figure standing nearby in the gloom of the dense forest. He remembered that voice: he'd heard it before... but where?

"Don't be afraid," it continued. "Please don't be afraid."

Gus braced himself for the worst. As the indistinct figure slowly walked out of the forest, he stared wide-eyed. It was the woman from the portrait in the classroom, the woman who'd lured him into this awful trap. In no time at all she was standing right in front of him with an enigmatic smile on her face.

5

IMPICTUREMENT

OKSA AND ZOE EXCHANGED A LOOK OF MINGLED concern and amazement. Opposite them, Dragomira seemed about to faint. Pale and worried, she grabbed Abakum's hand and squeezed it hard.

"Impicturement..." she murmured miserably.

Abakum took a deep breath, stroked his short beard and closed his eyes. When he reopened them he looked intensely troubled, which did nothing to reassure the others, who had no idea what "Impicturement" might be. If the Fairyman was that worried, then things were serious.

"It's impossible," said Abakum emotionally. "I can accept that Reminiscens might have been Impictured, but not Gus!"

"You mean... my gran isn't dead?" broke in Zoe.

"She won't have had an easy time of it," whispered Leomido. "But, thank God, yes, she's alive." Despite the circumstances, Zoe closed her eyes, weak with relief.

"What about Gus?" ventured Oksa with a panicky glance at Pierre and Jeanne, who seemed to be rooted to the spot with horror.

The Runaways looked at each other in confusion. No one dared to say anything, as if the words might inflict unbearable pain. As usual, Oksa was the one who broke the silence:

"If Reminiscens is alive *inside* the picture, then Gus must be too, mustn't he?" she asked briskly. "It stands to reason! The picture in the science room at St Proximus is the last thing Gus saw. He took a photo of it, then disappeared!"

Everyone turned to look at Reminiscens's portrait on the screen.

"That's what Impicturement is, isn't it?" continued Oksa. "Gus is trapped in the picture with Reminiscens!" Jeanne groaned, and collapsed onto her chair. At her side, her husband clenched his fists in anger.

"Gus can't have been Impictured," he declared, shaking.

"But Reminiscens obviously has!" said Dragomira.

"There might have been a reason why she was…" continued Abakum. "But not Gus… It's impossible, I tell you!"

"Why?" cried Oksa forcefully. "You can see there can't be any other explanation!"

"The Young Gracious has truth in her mouth," said the Lunatrix, his eyes open wide. "The Runaways must absorb this certainty in their heart: the friend of the Young Gracious has sustained Impicturement, the revelation is crammed with tragedy, but it assumes a covering of indisputability."

"Thank you, my Lunatrix," said Dragomira, patting the small creature's fuzzy yellow head. "I'm very much afraid that we have to face facts. I'm stunned that such a thing could have happened. Can anyone explain it? Naftali? Brune? You were Servants of the High Enclave before the Great Chaos—do you know the laws governing Impicturement? I was so young when we had to flee our beloved Edefia… All I remember is that only those who've committed serious offences or crimes can be Impictured as a result of a court ruling. It's a kind of imprisonment, isn't it?"

"Yes, in principle," agreed Naftali Knut, the towering, bald-headed Swede. "But it's so much more than imprisonment. Impicturement is a powerful, highly complex spell—which is why it's generally so reliable. That's why I'm so astounded by what's happened, my friends."

"What do you mean?" asked Dragomira, narrowing her fierce blue eyes.

"I mean that the process is immediately stopped if there's any error of judgement."

"So there can't have been a judicial error?" asked Oksa.

"No," replied Naftali, in a throaty voice. "But let me explain… People sometimes commit serious crimes against others, through greed, despair or madness. In Edefia, society was based on notions of equality and harmony, which helped citizens to avoid these pitfalls. When we arrived on the Outside, we discovered a world that seemed much more inclined to indulge in criminal activities, a world where certain individuals were willing to risk their freedom for wealth, glory or love. Not to mention heads of state capable of tearing each other apart and endangering their populace for obscure political or religious reasons… We were all shocked at how little people valued life here because, in Edefia, nothing was more important, and this fundamental belief influenced how Edefians went about their daily business. Naturally, there was the odd individual who didn't value these convictions so highly. Edefia experienced acts of violence, conspiracy and murder, just like the Outside. The only difference is that those crimes were very rare…"

"Until the Great Chaos," broke in Oksa.

"That's right," agreed Naftali. "The Great Chaos resulted in a tidal wave of violence, worse than we'd ever experienced before. We weren't at all prepared for mayhem on such a grand scale. That was our main weakness and one of the worst contributory factors in our downfall: what was good and right couldn't triumph over evil."

The tall Swede fell silent for a moment, his emerald eyes fixed on his trembling hands. His wife, Brune, nervously fiddled with one of the many silver rings on her long fingers and looked encouragingly at her husband.

"It's possible that mankind is not as good as we'd have liked to believe," continued Naftali. "Some people are, certainly. But it would appear that goodness is not an innate quality: it's acquired over time, passed on from one person to another, maybe even learnt… My life on the Outside has provided me with ample food for thought on this subject: being good here isn't easy because there are so many temptations. Insiders have understood this from the dawn of time: Edefia was founded on charitable principles which formed the basis for people's behaviour and were handed down from generation to generation, all the more easily because society had been designed to promote these core values. But, as I said, being good doesn't come naturally to everyone and, despite the efforts of the vast majority, some individuals proved violent, and others even committed murder."

"Marpel," murmured Oksa. "The man who killed Gonzal to steal the Nontemporentas..."

"Yes, Marpel is a good example," remarked Naftali. "Or perhaps I should say a bad example! He had violent tendencies, even as a child. He rejected the concept of hard work, either to improve the stability of our society or to meet his own needs: he expected other people to do everything for him without giving anything back in return. He began stealing as an adult, first in secret, then openly, not thinking twice about taking down anyone in his way. The jewellery-factory owner was one of his last victims and that's what caused Marpel to be Impictured. And he would probably have been Impictured again for murdering old Gonzal. But that's another story... Impicturement, unlike imprisonment—which is what happens on the Outside—forces the Impictured individual to withdraw from the world in order to become a better person. In Edefia we don't pay for our mistakes, nor are we fined: we believe the only way for someone to make amends is to improve what can be improved."

"What if... someone is all bad?" asked Oksa. "What if there's no good in them at all?"

"Even the worst person on earth has room for improvement, darling!" insisted Dragomira. Naftali and Brune raised their eyebrows in obvious scepticism.

"I'm not as idealistic as your gran, Oksa," continued Brune. "But yes, in Edefia we were convinced that it was crucial to work on an individual's intrinsic qualities. That was the fundamental aim of Impicturement."

"So Marpel did have some qualities?" asked Oksa.

"Of course!"

"What were they? Can you give me some examples?"

"No," admitted Brune.

"Why? He was Impictured, so how come you don't know how he became a better person? That's such a cop-out!"

Despite the tense situation, everyone smiled at Oksa's annoyance.

"The criminal does not display his inner embellishment to others," said the Lunatrix. "Impicturement provides the ordeal and the Soul-Searcher produces the assessment."

Oksa clicked her tongue and frowned sceptically.

"I'm sorry, Lunatrix. I usually manage to follow what you're saying, but I didn't understand…"

"That's because, as we mentioned earlier, Impicturement is so complex," continued Naftali. "When someone is arrested for a serious offence, they're brought before the Gracious who decides whether to cast the Impicturement Spell; an Imagicon—a canvas with magical properties made by the Ageless Fairies—is unrolled, stretched taut and fixed to a frame. The offence is read out aloud and appears on the Imagicon. The criminal then blows on the words. His breath spreads through the material until it reaches the Soul-Searcher. The Soul-Searcher is the spirit of the Imagicon—its heart and mind. When the Soul-Searcher receives the criminal's breath and the statement of their crimes, it carefully searches the hidden recesses of their secret self. After careful consideration, it decides if they deserve Impicturement or not. If they do, then the Soul-Searcher creates a series of ordeals intended to encourage the criminal to improve what can be improved in their nature. These ordeals are noted indelibly within the Imagicon, which then prepares to welcome the criminal, whose portrait slowly forms on the fibres of the canvas. The criminal lets a drop of their blood fall onto the Imagicon as a guarantee of their identity and they are then Impictured or sucked into the picture in order to carry out the series of ordeals devised by the Soul-Searcher. If they can overcome these ordeals, thereby successfully mastering their own demons and giving the best of themselves, they will be released."

The room was filled with a stunned silence. They were all struggling to catch their breath and exchanging fearful glances. Once more, Oksa asked the question on everyone's lips:

"Can the Soul-Searcher get it wrong?"

She glanced anxiously at Gus's parents, who were more frightened to hear the answer than anyone else.

"It just isn't possible…" Naftali struggled to say. "The Soul-Searcher never Impictures an innocent person."

"How can you be so sure?" continued Oksa.

"I've attended several trials for offences punishable by Impicturement," replied Naftali. "The Soul-Searcher has never been wrong. Even when we were all convinced that someone was guilty, it turned out that we were mistaken. And there is one other important detail I should give you: in Edefia's history, only criminals guilty of attempted murder have been Impictured."

"But Gus has never killed anyone!" cried Oksa, in a panic. "So why has he been Impictured?"

Naftali looked at the Young Gracious, then Gus's parents, before whispering in a choked voice:

"I'm very much afraid that the Soul-Searcher has fallen victim to an evil spell."

6

A Tragic Mistake

B Y THE TIME DAWN BROKE OVER BIGTOE SQUARE, THE
Runaways had all faced the awful facts. No one could understand
how such a thing could have happened, but they all knew in their heart
of hearts that Gus had been Impictured. Jeanne and Pierre Bellanger
were devastated and their friends were trying hard to comfort them,
although it was Dragomira's Lunatrix who did the best job of reassuring them.

"The Lunatrix possesses knowledge of the mystery of life and death,"
he said, resting his plump hand on Jeanne's shoulder. "He has mastery
over the detection of who is living and who will never be living again.
The present moment is accompanied by utter certainty: the friend of
our Young Gracious is full of life and his presence honours the perilous
picture in the company of the ill-fated Reminiscens. You must fill up
your heart with this conviction."

"I hope you're right," whispered Pierre, wringing his hands.

"My Lunatrix is always right, as you know," said Dragomira, with
a sad smile. "But I think we might be able to find out more from the
Squoracle…" she added, rising to her feet.

Holding up her voluminous grey satin dress, she left the room to return
shortly with the tiny hen, which was shivering with cold.

"My dear girls," she said to Oksa and Zoe, as she stroked the Squoracle
nestling against her, "this delicate little creature not only has the gift of

determining where icy draughts come from or of gauging how many degrees the temperature is about to drop. It has quite another talent: it is able to divine the truth. If anyone can tell us what has happened, this creature can!"

Everyone looked at the little hen, which gave a violent shiver and snuggled even closer to Baba Pollock's mohair wrap-over top.

"Squoracle, Gus has been Impictured..." said the old lady.

"I know that!" snapped the creature irritably. "But can someone tell me why it's so cold when it's almost summer?"

"Do I need to remind you that we're in London, which means we're just above the 45th parallel, a long way from the tropics, and that the temperature is twenty-two degrees centigrade, after all," sighed Leomido wearily.

"That's as maybe!" retorted the Squoracle, flapping its small reddish-brown wings in resentment. "But I'd have expected slightly more satis-factory temperatures!"

Oksa pulled a wry face at Zoe: the Squoracle never missed an opportunity to complain about the English climate.

"Can you tell us what's going on with the picture?" asked Dragomira loudly, cutting short this conversation about the weather. "Has an evil spell been cast on the Soul-Searcher?"

"Obviously!" replied the Squoracle briskly. "The Soul-Searcher made a tragic mistake when it claimed Reminiscens instead of her twin brother, the Felon Orthon. He'd committed numerous crimes so he should have been Impictured, not her... Ever since that mistake, the Soul-Searcher has been spiralling out of control. It's gone insane, just like I will if someone doesn't shut that window!" squawked the little hen shrilly. "My feathers are like icicles!"

Leomido sighed and stood up to shut the window, which was letting in a trickle of balmy air.

"The Soul-Searcher's mistake wasn't a true mistake," continued the Squoracle. "Reminiscens and the Felon Orthon share the same DNA, so there was some kind of mix-up—who knows if it was an accident or a deliberate act of sabotage?"

"What about Gus? What can you tell us about him?" asked Dragomira.

"The Soul-Searcher was completely thrown off balance by its mistake over the twins," replied the Squoracle gravely. "The boy shouldn't have been Impictured: two people cannot coexist in the same picture."

The Squoracle shook its little head and pressed up against Dragomira, shivering as if frozen to the bone. The Runaways looked at each other in astonishment.

"The Young Gracious was the one who was summoned."

"Good Lord!" exclaimed Dragomira, with her hand over her heart.

"But how could the Soul-Searcher have got it so wrong?" asked Oksa indignantly. "I don't know if you've noticed, but Gus and I aren't exactly identical! You'd have to be totally barmy to mix the two of us up."

"Squoracle, you mentioned that Reminiscens and Orthon share the same DNA," continued Zoe, furiously pulling threads from the sleeve of her T-shirt. "That might explain why the Soul-Searcher made a mistake: they were identical, as far as it was concerned."

The Squoracle nodded, trembling with cold.

"What if Gus had some of Oksa's DNA on him? Would that be enough to confuse the Soul-Searcher?" continued Zoe.

"What do you mean?" asked the Squoracle sharply.

All the Runaways were listening intently and Zoe blushed at being the centre of attention.

"I think I can see where Zoe is going with this," said Naftali, coming to her aid. "You think Gus might have had one of Oksa's hairs on him, or…"

Everyone looked at Oksa, who frowned, lost in concentration. Suddenly, she smacked the palm of her hand against her forehead.

"OH NO!"

Everyone froze.

"Gus has my bag," the Young Gracious informed them flatly.

"And… what's in your bag?" said Pierre in a strangled voice.

"It couldn't be any worse," replied Oksa, finding it hard to catch her breath. "My Tumble-Bawler… my Caskinette… my Granok-Shooter…"

Dragomira looked at her in amazement. She was tempted to give vent to her sudden surge of anger, but didn't want to aggravate the situation, especially as things had just gone from bad to worse. She clasped her hands and tried to calm herself down, but she wasn't fooling the Runaways, who could see how upset she was. Oksa was beginning to realize the sheer magnitude of the disaster, which seemed to be all her fault. Her gran and Abakum had warned her: a Young Gracious should never hand over her tools to anyone, whatever the circumstances. Never. They could fall into the wrong hands and it wasn't hard to guess what the outcome might be. But how could she have anticipated this?

Her nose began prickling and her eyes brimmed with tears. A sob filled her chest, making it hard to breathe and she inhaled deeply, hoping to relieve the pressure. When she met Dragomira's gaze, which was blazing with anger—she would have staked her life on it—she felt even more choked.

"What have I done?" she whispered almost inaudibly.

"Do you understand now what we meant when we warned you? Even the smallest act of stupidity can cost us dearly," thundered Dragomira, struggling to control her temper.

"We're all in great danger," continued Abakum, sounding overwhelmed. "Every second. We have to remember that."

"Let's not waste time crying over spilt milk," said Naftali firmly. "We need to act, and quickly! We have to rescue the picture. If someone else gets their hands on it before us—"

Oksa looked up at the tall Swede. If someone else got their hands on the picture, they'd never see Gus again.

7

Ninja Father and Daughter

That evening, Oksa felt as though the night would never come. By the time the shadows had finally started to lengthen and the sky grow dark, the Young Gracious felt as though she was about to explode with impatience. She'd bitten off her last remaining nail and kept looking outside in exasperation.

"Is it time yet? Can we go?" she asked for the umpteenth time that evening.

Her father examined the sky again and looked gravely at Oksa. Then, to hide his emotion, he knelt down to lace his lightweight shoes. Pavel Pollock was a worrier. He'd always found it hard to accept his remarkable origins and, over the past few months, not a week had gone by without a reminder that he was the son of both Dragomira, the Old Gracious with amazing powers, and Vladimir, the Siberian shaman. But he was also Oksa's father, and his daughter was the Runaways' only means of returning to the Lost Land of Edefia. She was their Last Hope… After trying and failing to thwart the unalterable destiny of the Runaways— and, whether he liked it or not, he was one of them—he'd set himself one priority: to protect his wife and only daughter. Marie Pollock was still suffering the effects of the poisoned soap from their sworn enemy, Orthon-McGraw and, although it wasn't Pavel's fault that his wife's condition was deteriorating, it felt like a personal failure. The fact that he hadn't been able to help anyone up till now was festering in his heart like an open sore that wouldn't heal. Now it was time to prove to his family and friends that they could count on him as much as Abakum and Leomido.

"Get ready to leave, Oksa," he said flatly. "Let's go and get this picture."

✻

Although it was dark when they arrived at the imposing entrance to St Proximus College, a few streets away from Bigtoe Square, the street was brightly lit, which could jeopardize the Pollocks' mission. Unlike Oksa, Pavel was well aware of the risks they were running by entering the college uninvited in the middle of the night. He had no intention of breaking in, though—as far as he was concerned, this was just a little "visit", and the use of his special gifts should be enough. He pointed his index finger at the street lamps, which immediately winked out one after the other, plunging the street into protective darkness. Oksa gave a small cry of admiration.

"Brilliant!" she whispered. "I must learn how to do that."

"Come on…" murmured her father, adjusting his black scarf over his face.

"You look like a real ninja, Dad!" remarked Oksa, looking at her father dressed all in black from head to toe.

"So do you, Oksa-san," he replied in a whisper.

"I'm ready, Most Revered Master," she said, pulling on her own fabric mask.

She just had time to notice the amused yet deeply sad expression in her father's eyes, before he ran with feline grace towards the perimeter wall around the college. With his feet sticking to the stone, he scaled the wall with the agility of a spider. Watching her father in admiration, the Young Gracious rose in a perfect Vertiflight. Then, hand in hand, father and daughter descended on the other side.

St Proximus was dark and empty. There wasn't a soul about. The only movement came from the centre of the courtyard, where the steady play of water from the stone fountain glittered in the darkness. The gargoyles overlooking the courtyard from the roof were silhouetted against a sky bathed in the orangey glow of the city lights. Looking up at them, Oksa shivered, momentarily imagining that those stone monsters were about to slip their shackles to swoop down and devour her.

"Come on, let's not waste any time," murmured Pavel, pulling her towards the cloister bordering the courtyard.

Silently, they entered one of the four ground-floor corridors. The moon cast a cold radiance over the statues standing along this passageway paved with large polished flagstones. To her surprise, Oksa didn't feel any safer. She had the awful feeling she was being followed and looked back over her shoulder. Was it Abakum? Had the Fairyman turned into a shadow again so that he could go with them and protect them? No. There were no shadows. Just the impassive gaze of the statues lining the corridor. Oksa's heart was pounding so hard that she was starting to feel sick. What was going on? Was she afraid? It had to be the first time, if she was. If Gus had been there, he'd have looked at her in astonishment and nudged her in the ribs, saying: "Hey, Ninja-Oksa! Do I have to remind you that I'm the coward, not you!" Gus... She missed him so much. What if the Runaways didn't work out what to do? What if the evil spell cast on the Soul-Searcher was too strong to be broken? This horrible thought filled Oksa with dread. Her heart turned over at the idea that her loyal friend might be lost for ever in that fiendish picture. She stood there, breathless with panic, staring at one of the statues, which was eyeing her sternly. Picking up on its mistress's anxiety, the Curbita-Flatulo began undulating on her wrist. Oksa gave a shiver as feelings of reassurance immediately washed over her.

"Hang in there, Gus," she murmured resolutely. "Come on, Dad, it's this way."

They climbed the monumental staircase leading to the first floor and soon found themselves in the science room. The picture was a few yards away, gleaming with a strange shifting light. Surprised by the darkness in the room, Pavel bumped into a coat stand and sent it tumbling to the wooden floor with what sounded to the two intruders like a deafening crash.

"Idiot..." hissed Pavel, cursing his stupidity.

He took out his Granok-Shooter, muttered a few words and blew into it. A bright light appeared and floated in the middle of the room. Oksa dashed over to the picture.

"We're going to get you out of there, Gus!" she whispered, only a couple of inches away from the canvas.

"Careful!" warned her father, pulling her back. "Remember what Dragomira said: don't, under any circumstances, touch the Imagicon. Anyone who does so is in danger of being Impictured immediately."

He drew a fabric bag from his pocket, unfolded it and spread it out on one of the desks. Then, with the utmost care, he took hold of the picture by its wooden frame.

"Open the bag, Oksa!"

The girl obeyed, holding her breath. Pavel slipped the picture inside, then pulled the strings tight to fasten the bag and slung it over his shoulder.

"Excellent," he said. "Let's go."

But as he put his hand on the door handle, a blinding light flooded the corridor. Oksa bit her lip to stop herself screaming. Someone had heard them. And, what was worse, they were coming upstairs! The caretaker? McGraw's ghost? Petrified by such an awful thought, she wasted valuable time hesitating to follow her father, who was trying to pull her back into the science lab. The steps grew closer, sounding loud and threatening. Pavel dragged her inside the room and pushed her against the wall, thrusting a small capsule into her hand. Then he silently closed the door behind them.

Oksa thought she was going to pass out when the door handle was pressed down with a creak. The caretaker—since that was who it was—poked his head through the half-open door.

"Is anybody there?" he shouted, making the girl jump.

Oksa had hoped he wouldn't investigate any further, but the caretaker was a meticulous man with exceptionally keen hearing. The noise he'd heard from the ground-floor storeroom, where he was putting equipment away, had left him in no doubt: someone was inside the college. He'd been taken on a few days earlier to keep watch on the college during the summer holidays and to do some routine maintenance. This was his first night and there was already a problem—just his luck! He switched on the light in the science room. Pavel had seen to it that none of the bulbs were working. Only the light from the corridor illuminated a small section of the room.

"Oh dear, I'll have to change the light bulbs," he muttered, taking out his electric torch. He took a look around inside. A large coat stand was lying on the ground.

"That's strange…" said the caretaker, frowning.

He picked up the coat stand and began inspecting the room, determined to do his job properly. He looked everywhere, under the desks, in the cupboard, behind the door. Everywhere except the ceiling, where Oksa and Pavel were clinging like bats. The bemused caretaker finally walked out. A few minutes later, all the lights were switched off, plunging the corridors of St Proximus into darkness once more. Followed by her father, Oksa detached herself from the ceiling with a skilful somersault.

"This Ventosa Capacitor is amazing!" she whispered enthusiastically, her cheeks flushed.

"You can say that again," replied Pavel tersely. "Let's not hang around though. We won't get a second chance."

He opened one of the many leaded-glass windows and stepped over the frame.

"Dad!" exclaimed Oksa, her hand over her mouth.

"Don't tell me you're afraid of going down this way! The caretaker will be keeping an eye on the main entrance, so we don't have a choice."

With that, he dropped into the darkness. Oksa rushed over to the window overlooking the street. Her father was on the ground, signalling to her. She climbed onto the windowsill, stretched her foot into the air, steadied herself, then floated down to the ground.

8

A Fraught Reunion

THE GRAVITY OF THE SITUATION MEANT THAT EVERY single known Runaway was summoned to an urgent meeting. So the hard core—the Pollocks, Bellangers, Knuts and Abakum—contacted all the other Runaways who'd been identified throughout the world: Mercedica de La Fuente, the elegant Spanish woman, former Servant of the High Enclave and a close friend of Dragomira's; Cockerell, a Brit living in Japan, former Treasurer of the Gracious's family and now a banker; and Bodkin, a former industrialist, who'd retrained as a Master Goldsmith in South Africa. Three trustworthy people who'd been forced to become perfectly assimilated in the Outside world, and yet who were still desperate to return to Edefia one day. Another member of the group was Tugdual, the Knuts' moody grandson, who'd just arrived, once more wreaking havoc with Oksa's feelings.

"Hi there, Lil' Gracious!" he said, after greeting each of the Runaways with his customary off-handedness.

He walked over to her and, for one terrifying second, she thought he was going to kiss her on the cheeks. Instead he gazed at her with his steely blue eyes and she felt herself blushing foolishly. Tugdual smiled, which made her kick herself, and finally looked away.

"Well, if it's not one thing, it's another," he remarked.

"This really isn't the time or the place for sarcasm!" replied his grandfather, Naftali, icily.

Tugdual looked at him with an expression of mingled disillusionment and rebelliousness.

"I've always said we had to expect the worst," he retorted, casually flicking some dust off his black shirt. "But no one ever took me seriously. Or perhaps I should say: no one ever took *him* seriously... I mean Orthon-McGraw, of course."

"May I remind you that Orthon is dead!" snapped Mercedica curtly, favouring the sombre young man with a glare.

Tugdual glowered back with the arrogance of someone who wouldn't let himself be flustered by such a trivial point.

"Allow me to have my doubts," he replied to the haughty Spanish woman. "Evil can survive and continue to cause mayhem beyond death. Evil never dies, as we've seen today, haven't we?"

The question hung in the room, like a wisp of disquieting smoke floating just below the ceiling.

"That isn't the problem," said Mercedica, slicing through the heavy silence.

Abakum and Naftali shifted uneasily on their chairs, looking disapproving.

"That is *exactly* the problem, my dear Mercedica," said the imposing Swede, contradicting her. "Everything that's happening now is Orthon's fault. I'm convinced that Reminiscens was Impictured by her twin brother."

"How would that be possible?" asked Mercedica in amazement, pulling threads from her armrest with her red-lacquered nails. "The Soul-Searcher never makes a mistake!"

"Well, we have to believe that it can, my dear friend!" retorted Abakum. "But now, we must put ourselves in Orthon's shoes. Because we can only fight our enemies if we understand them..."

"How can you talk about fighting enemies?" snarled Tugdual. "Frankly, I find it hard to see you in the role of brave little soldiers enlisted in the very Young Gracious's army. None of you would even hurt a fly."

Surprised by this remark, the Runaways looked uneasily between Abakum and Tugdual.

"Flies have never tried to kill the people I love!" retorted Abakum, staying remarkably calm. "But if they decided to do so, they'd pay dearly for it, mark my words, my young friend. And as for Orthon—"

The elderly Watcher broke off, raising one hand in front of him in a gesture of surrender. It was better for all concerned if this futile conversation was stopped before it got out of hand. Oksa was furious, though. Despite the unsettling effect Tugdual had on her whenever he was near, she thought he was going too far with his provocative comments. She knew that Abakum's wise exterior concealed a formidable man, more formidable than the most battle-hardened soldier. After all, hadn't he been the only one capable of firing a Crucimaphila Granok at Orthon-McGraw? No one else could have done it. Oksa knew it hadn't been easy for him and that he'd be tormented by the memory until his dying day. But his tremendous loyalty made him the man he was: unquestionably the most powerful of all the Runaways. This loyalty to Dragomira, and to her entire family, was the source of his immense strength. A mental strength which enabled him to surmount any obstacle. But how could she say all that to Tugdual? Her irascible friend couldn't have known it was Abakum who'd vaporized Orthon-McGraw in the cellar of his house. Otherwise, he wouldn't have been so flippant about the old man's pacifist ideals.

"You forget that Abakum is the Fairyman," she whispered to him, her cheeks scarlet with annoyance and embarrassment.

"Hey, talking of fairies," continued Tugdual sarcastically, "it's been quite a while since we had a visit from the Ageless Ones! We could do with a helping hand from them, couldn't we?"

With a frown, Dragomira leant over to Naftali and Brune, who were glaring at their grandson.

"I thought he was getting better recently," she murmured to her two friends, looking at Tugdual. "I thought he was less..."

"Less morbid? Less neurotic?" continued Tugdual, rolling his eyes. "I'm fine, thank you very much, so don't worry your heads about me! Abakum, whom I respect more than you can possibly imagine, knows me better than anyone and I have absolutely no intention of insulting him. I just wanted to remind you what you yourselves said once about your lack of experience when it comes to dealing with danger. You saw yourselves as old folk, who weren't up to the task. So take a good look at yourselves and be honest: are you really ready to face your enemies' bloodthirsty attacks? You've always thought I was exaggerating when I described Orthon as Evil incarnate. But they weren't just the misguided fears of a neurotic. Do you see that now? We have to expect the worst. Always expect the worst…"

Some of the Runaways nodded in approval. The young man certainly had a tendency to blow things out of proportion, but there was a lot of truth in what he said and they all believed him now: the writing was on the wall—things were clearly going to get worse before they got better.

9

A Very Important Decision

T HE SQUORACLE WAS STANDING ON AN OCCASIONAL table, its tiny beak about an inch from the picture. The Imagicon, held taut by the wooden frame, was gleaming with dark shimmers in perpetual motion. Staring intently at this strange phenomenon, the Runaways waited impatiently for the miniature hen to make its diagnosis.

"The Squoracle possesses the veracity of the elements of the present," whispered the Lunatrix in Oksa's ear by way of an explanation. "It can go where the knowledge of others cannot venture. The truth is always complete in its comprehension of the world and it never encounters errors. We can develop a total confidence: the Squoracle will provide an explication of the problem that has affected the picture."

"Shhh!" spat the Squoracle, glaring furiously at the Lunatrix. "How do you expect me to concentrate if you keep yelling behind me?"

Oksa looked at the Lunatrix, who turned purple with embarrassment, and winked at him, trying hard not to laugh. The Squoracle was no novice when it came to over-reacting; the tiny creature tended to fly off the handle with disconcerting ease, and none of the Runaways could help smiling.

"The only creature yelling right now is that hysterical excuse for a hen!" remarked a small, long-haired creature.

"Be quiet, Getorix," scolded Oksa in amusement. "You'll land yourself in trouble."

After a few long minutes, the Squoracle finally turned round, fluffed up its feathers and shook itself.

"Your attention, please. Listen to me!" it told the Runaways, who were waiting eagerly to hear what the little hen had to say.

"About time…" grumbled the Getorix.

"We're all ears, Squoracle," confirmed Dragomira, settling back comfortably in her armchair. "Tell us what you know!"

"This is a complicated and unfortunate business," began the Squoracle gravely. "At the present time, the Soul-Searcher is no longer in control of the picture: Evil has seized power and is endeavouring to trap the heart of a Gracious. Was it a case of mistaken identity when it lured Gus into the picture? Is the boy a victim of yet another catastrophic mistake? Or did Evil trap him deliberately? I cannot be more precise because my senses are fuddled by so much turmoil. The only thing I'm certain of is a sense of urgency: the boy and the old lady have a lethal weapon in their possession, yet they have no chance of survival without the help of their friends. Some of you will have to be Impictured to rescue them."

The Squoracle shivered violently.

"What's the matter?" asked the old lady.

"That place is hellish!" it whispered.

"What do you see?"

"It's like nothing I've ever seen before. My vision is clouded by utter chaos and an unwholesome power."

Dragomira smoothed the tiny hen's feathers, her eyes brimming with tears as she realized the true scale of the disaster. The Squoracle's information took the Runaways' breath away like an icy wave crashing over them. They gazed at each other in consternation. None of them would have thought it would be so difficult to get back to Edefia. They'd been waiting for fifty-seven years, but they'd never faced so many dangers, particularly since they'd held all the keys: the Mark around Oksa's belly button, Dragomira's medallion inherited from her mother Malorane, Edefia's Landmark kept safe within the Lunatrix's heart. Pavel, who'd been one of the hardest to persuade that returning to their lost land was the right thing to do, felt bewildered. His recent resolve to take part in this extraordinary adventure was ebbing away by the second. Why run all these risks? Was it really worth it? Life on the Outside wasn't that bad...

"You spoke about the heart of a Gracious coveted by Evil," Abakum said to the Squoracle. "Can you tell us more?"

The Runaways looked at the Fairyman apprehensively, aware that this was a crucial question.

"The heart of a Gracious means the Young Gracious herself," declared the Squoracle.

"No worries!" cried Oksa, jumping up from her seat. "I'm ready!"

"Oksa, please!" said her father immediately, gazing at her anxiously. "There's no question of you entering that picture."

"But Dad..." continued the girl.

"Don't 'but Dad' me," retorted Pavel firmly. "You're not going into that picture and that's final."

"But you're forgetting that Gus is trapped inside!" she raged. "If we don't go and find him, he has no chance of being rescued. How can you be so... *inhuman*?"

With these words, she spun round and ran out of the room with an angry yell of frustration. A deathly silence descended on the embarrassed Runaways. Some of them glanced furtively at Pavel, others didn't try to hide the reproach in their eyes. Dragomira, taken aback by her son's reaction, placed her hand on his forearm in the hope of making him see sense. But Pavel shrugged her off and looked down, his expression even more tortured than ever. He felt completely isolated and didn't know what to do for the best. He was trying to see a way out of this dilemma, which held him in its grip like prey in a falcon's talons. He could sense the anxiety of his friends, Pierre and Jeanne, whose only son was trapped in the painting. It was awful to think of him being lost, probably terrified, and do nothing to rescue him. But if they went into the picture, there was a risk they'd never come out! He looked up, avoiding eye contact with Pierre and Jeanne, who were gazing at him with mingled horror and grief. His eyes strayed to the computer screen displaying the last photo Gus had taken before being Impictured: the portrait of Reminiscens, Zoe's gran. Behind it, the window showed a patch of summer sky darkening with thick purple clouds. Pavel put his head in his hands and withdrew into his own shell.

⁂

Upstairs, Oksa was sitting on the floor, hunched against the wall. Her attempts to calm down had failed and she was seething with anger. The Curbita-Flatulo was frantically undulating on her wrist, but the Young Gracious was impervious to its efforts. She ran her hands through her chestnut hair and sighed. Outside there was a rumble of thunder which seemed to be approaching at high speed. Oksa jumped as a thunderclap sounded just above Bigtoe Square. The wind began blowing with frightening violence, making passers-by cry out in terror. Suddenly a blinding flash of lightning split the sky, striking Oksa's window, which exploded into splinters of glass.

"Whoa..." she breathed, fascinated.

It wasn't the first time she'd unleashed a storm, but this was something else! The furious wind was sweeping aside everything in its way: rubbish bins were blown over and rolled noisily along the pavement, tiles were hurled from the roofs and smashed on the ground, and television aerials were broken and flattened by the strong gusts. Standing in front of her shattered window, Oksa gazed in amazement at this cataclysmic scene. Suddenly the wind changed direction. Instead of whipping around Bigtoe Square, all its fury was centred on the girl, who was hit full-on by its blast. An indescribably icy sensation doused the raging fire inside her. The pitch-black clouds raced towards her, obscuring her sight. Inside her body, wind and fire battled fiercely, making it impossible to catch her breath. A strangled cry struggled up from deep within. Feeling herself losing consciousness, she gripped the windowsill covered in broken glass with all her might, then fainted and fell to the floor with bloodied hands.

***

The first person she saw when she regained consciousness was Tugdual. The young man was watching her with an expression of mingled concern and admiration on his face.

"I reckon it might be better to avoid making you angry," he said softly with a slight smile.

Oksa pulled a face. She felt stiff all over and as exhausted as if she'd been lifting weights for hours. She glanced out of the window. The sky was blue, the sun was shining and everything looked... normal.

"I thought it was the end of the world!" she remarked, sitting up.

"It wasn't far off," added Tugdual with an amused grimace. "The neighbourhood is all but destroyed."

"Hey..." rebuked his grandfather Naftali.

The Runaways were standing around the sofa where she was lying, their anxiety visible in their tormented eyes. Pavel walked over and put his hand on her shoulder.

"Oh, Dad!" she cried, throwing her arms around his neck. "I'm sorry! It's so stupid losing my temper like that. But... what's wrong with my hands?"

She turned them over in front of her. They were covered in bandages.

"You cut yourself on the broken glass," replied her father, quietly. "Don't worry though, Dragomira has already done the necessary. In a few hours, your cuts will be nothing but a bad memory."

"Thanks, Baba! Er... did you use the Spinollias?" asked the girl, shivering at the memory of those clever little seamstress spiders.

"It's all done, Dushka!" replied Dragomira, with subdued enthusiasm.

"Was I unconscious for long then?"

"Exactly four hours and thirty minutes," confirmed her father, looking at his watch. "We spent the time having a long chat. About you, Gus and the picture. And we've come to a very important decision."

"A crucial decision…" added Tugdual, looking increasingly gloomy.

Pavel cleared his throat and wiped his forehead with his hand, as if trying to decide what to say—and how to say it.

"Like everyone here, I'm broken-hearted—" he began in a hollow voice.

"You don't want to go after Gus, is that it?" broke in Oksa, tears in her eyes.

"What I want doesn't matter, darling," replied her father bitterly.

"We are going to look for Gus and Reminiscens," announced Abakum. "We're taking an enormous risk, but we don't have a choice: we can't leave one of our company imprisoned in the picture. Despite Tugdual's fears," he continued, glancing sternly at the young man, "we're stronger than we look. We may have deep wrinkles and white hair, but we also have some real trumps up our sleeve. And I'm not just talking about you, sweetheart…"

"Are you implying that I'm going to be part of this adventure?" whispered Oksa, her large grey eyes wide with impatience.

"It's a totally ir-res-pon-sible decision!" thundered Mercedica.

Her heavy bun quivered with exasperation. She glared at Dragomira, who tugged at her long plaits and gazed blankly into the distance. Oksa held her breath, more anxious than ever.

"We have to take you with us… unfortunately," confirmed Pavel sadly.

"When you say 'us', do you mean everyone?" she asked, gazing at the Runaways standing in a circle around her.

"No, Oksa," said her father. "It would be crazy for us all to go, particularly as your mother is too weak to cope with this kind of… escapade. Dragomira, Naftali and Brune will stay with her, as will Jeanne, Zoe and Mercedica. Since there can be strength in numbers, Cockerell and Bodkin will take it on themselves to search the world for Runaways who might join forces with us. At their request and with our unanimous agreement…"

"What about the restaurant?" asked Oksa.

Pavel's eyes clouded with bitterness.

"Jeanne will manage it while we're gone."

"So I'm coming with you, am I? It's agreed?" continued the girl.

"I repeat that I'm dead against taking Oksa into the picture! It's such a rash decision," exclaimed Mercedica in annoyance. "You seem to be forgetting that she's the Young Gracious! It's crazy to put her in such danger… To put US in such danger! May I remind you that she's the only one who can activate the opening of the Portal, which will let us back into Edefia."

"As I was saying," continued Pavel, doing his utmost to ignore Mercedica's warnings, "virtually all of us have agreed that Leomido, Abakum, Pierre, you and I should be the ones who enter the picture to rescue Reminiscens and Gus."

Oksa was speechless with surprise. It was so unreal! She didn't know what to say, she was so overwhelmed by the contradictory feelings of fear, excitement and impatience churning inside her. Zoe looked at her sadly and gave her a weak smile of resignation and encouragement.

"You're forgetting someone!" said Tugdual fiercely.

"Yes… I'm sorry, Tugdual," murmured Pavel. "Tugdual is also coming with us," he told his daughter.

"Wow…" was all that Oksa managed to say in reply.

Feeling a complete fool, she was immediately furious at herself. But, despite the awful circumstances, she was glad he was going with them.

"I'm the very Young Gracious's Servant," declared Tugdual, his sapphire eyes gazing intently at Oksa, who blushed to the roots of her hair. "Don't ever forget that I'd do anything in the world for you."

10

The Decisive Argument

Although Pavel sat motionless in his armchair, there was a storm raging in his heart—an invisible hurricane laying waste to everything in its path. His eyes, though fixed on the play of shadows from the street on the ceiling, revealed nothing of his inner turmoil. Leaning against the window, Abakum watched him gravely.

"I'm well aware of your reservations, and the huge effort you're making in agreeing to be Impictured," he said.

"You left me no choice…" retorted Pavel.

"None of us had a choice," murmured Abakum. "The future of the Outside, our future and the future of everyone who follows us depend on it. And even if that's not enough for you, there's another reason preventing us from backing out."

"What are you talking about? Isn't being responsible for the future of the world enough?"

"The other reason is Marie," replied Abakum, looking suddenly weary.

Pavel was speechless. He felt weak as a sudden wave of dizziness washed over him. His pulse raced with panic as he waited for Abakum's explanation.

"Marie is dying," announced the old man in a cracked voice. "The Robiga-Nervosa poison is stronger than any of the remedies that Dragomira and I know. We've tried everything. I'm sorry, Pavel. I'm really sorry."

There was a frightening silence. Pavel felt as though the sky had come crashing down on his head.

"But... but..." he muttered desperately, "I thought the Vermicula were working well! And what about that remedy based on... what was its name... Lasonillia? It's been very effective, Marie has made incredible progress, you said so yourself. She's doing well! How can you say she's dying? How can you tell me that, Abakum?"

His voice broke as despair claimed him. He put his head in his hands. He hadn't felt such mind-numbing misery since his father had died. That had been in Siberia, eight years ago. Vladimir had been the grandson of the great shaman Metchkov, who'd given Dragomira, Leomido and Abakum a roof over their heads after they'd been ejected from Edefia. One icy day in December, shortly before Christmas, Vladimir had been dragged away by the KGB, the Soviet secret police. His arrest had been incredibly brutal. His wife and young son had seen him beaten up and insulted by the police before he'd been taken to a gulag where he'd been sentenced as an "enemy of the State". Apart from the kindly inhabitants of the small Siberian village, who'd all known about the Pollocks' "talents", this was the first time Pavel had come into contact with Outsiders. This was also the last time he'd seen his father. A few weeks later, Dragomira received the dreadful news that Vladimir had been killed by his jailers while trying to escape. Neither Abakum nor Dragomira, nor any of the people who'd known him, believed this version of events: if Vladimir had wanted to escape, he would have done. Wasn't he an accomplished shaman? Hadn't he proved that he could match his wife and best friend, the Fairyman, who had such vast powers, in many fields? The authorities were lying: it was obvious, given the condition he'd been in when they took him away, that he'd had no strength left to do anything much, let alone escape. The truth of the matter was that Vladimir had been executed: killed like a dog because of his great powers. Pavel had never managed to get over it. Life had gone on, relentless and unstoppable, but the wound had never properly healed.

The awful news about Marie reopened this old wound. Disbelief gave way to indescribable fury and a bitter feeling of outrage—this was so unfair. Why Marie? Why the most inoffensive member of the Runaways? He hadn't forgotten that Oksa had been the intended target of the poisoned soap, but she would have been able to defend herself against the effects of the Robiga-Nervosa despite being so young and inexperienced. Oksa... the Young Gracious watched over by the Ageless Ones... Oksa, so young and so determined, so vulnerable and yet so powerful. Oksa his only daughter and Marie his beloved wife. They were the most important people in his life. Pavel wanted to protect them so much and be a worthy father and husband. Instead, his paralysed wife was confined to bed and his daughter's fate lay in the hands of a group of foolish old fossils. But what choice did he have? Albeit unwillingly, Abakum had struck the fatal blow with his last argument—it was a real deal-breaker.

"You're right, Pavel," Abakum said, his grey eyes brimming with tears. "Lasonillia, or the Imperial Flower as we call it, has worked miracles on Marie. It's the antidote she needs."

"So what's the problem?" growled Pavel angrily.

"With the advent of the Great Chaos and before we were ejected into the Outside, I'd packed a selection of Edefia's most important plants and creatures in my Boximinus," continued the Fairyman, looking pale. "Among them was a young Lasonillia plant which I've struggled to keep alive. The care and attention Dragomira and I lavished on this specimen enabled us to obtain a few seedlings. But it wasn't easy, believe you me: growing Lasonillia is complicated and demanding work, simply because the soil composition on the Outside lacks all the nutrients found in Edefia. We've sent for soil samples from all over the world to try to cultivate more of them and we'd thought we'd succeeded with a blend from the eastern banks of the River Amazon and the orange groves of Cordoba. This soil encouraged the seedlings to flourish, so we were able to perfect the antidote which has done so much for Marie. Indeed, Pavel, Lasonillia is the only remedy that can save her."

"I don't understand... What's the problem? You and Dragomira have come up against some obstacle, haven't you? So what's wrong?"

At that moment he was more afraid of the old man's answer than anything else in the world. He knew Abakum was about to deliver an irrevocable verdict.

"Yes, we've found the remedy, Pavel. We're adamant about that—" Abakum broke off once more, overcome by emotion.

"Tell me!" roared Pavel. "Tell me, please!"

Abakum gazed at him for long moments before answering.

"Two weeks ago, Marie took a dose of Lasonillia, which considerably improved her condition. That dose was the last. We have no more Lasonillia left, Pavel. Despite our best efforts, the last seedling didn't survive. It died yesterday evening."

"But... what can be done about it?" stammered Pavel, his features drawn.

"I've searched all over the world, but I know only one place where Lasonillia can be found," explained the Fairyman. "A place where it grows abundantly, where you need only to stoop down and pick it."

"We have to go there immediately! What are we waiting for?" exclaimed Pavel. Abakum placed his hand on his friend's shoulder and, without breaking eye contact, said:

"That place is the Distant Reaches, situated in the remote plains of southern Edefia. Only there will we find the Lasonillia which can save Marie's life."

11

WILL THE REAL TUGDUAL
PLEASE STAND UP?

I T HADN'T ESCAPED OKSA'S NOTICE THAT ABAKUM AND Dragomira seemed very anxious. Although, in the circumstances, she supposed there were all kinds of reasons for them to be worried, her questioning nature made her suspect something even more serious and even more secret. She kept her ears open, trying to overhear snatches of the tense conversation they were having in the living room a few feet away. But, sensing they were under scrutiny, they spoke even more quietly, and she could only hear a few snippets. Feeling discouraged, the Young Gracious slumped lower in the crimson velvet sofa between her gran's two Lunatrixes, who'd quietly sat down next to her. The two creatures gazed at her with huge, bulging eyes, waiting for her to start a conversation, but Oksa didn't say a word. She just sat there, absent-mindedly stroking the downy forearm of the Lunatrix, her mind on other things. Their Impicturement was scheduled for the next morning. How strange that was… While some people were preparing to go on holiday, others were about to enter a bewitched painting.

"Each to his own destiny…" murmured Oksa, somewhat ironically.

"The words of the Young Gracious radiate sarcastic intent," remarked the podgy little creature.

"Very perceptive, Lunatrix!" sighed Oksa, glancing at him out of the corner of her eye. "Anyway, I'm glad the Lunatrixa will be travelling with us."

"The Lunatrixes must never experience separation from their mistresses. The Graciouses represent the reason for the existence of the Lunatrixes and their accompaniment is unfailing, whatever the conditions. The Lunatrix is the Guardian of the Definitive Landmark, he will therefore maintain surveillance over the presence of the Old Gracious here and the Lunatrixa will escort the Young Gracious into the picture. Death will be the representation of the only separation possible."

The mere mention of this possibility made Oksa shiver. There was no doubt it was all very exciting, but she was acutely aware of the dangers posed by this adventure and of what was at stake. The next morning, she'd be inside the bewitched picture with her father, Tugdual and a group of courageous Runaways on their way to rescue Gus. It wasn't exactly your common-or-garden variety of experience… Even with boundless confidence and optimism, she wasn't about to forget that there were no guarantees as to the probable outcome. But Gus's life was at stake. And so was her mother's. The constant treatment administered by Abakum and Dragomira—based on injections of Vermicula, which were working tirelessly on her nervous system—had successfully stabilized her condition, but the Robiga-Nervosa was relentless and the paralysis was spreading through her body like an unstoppable black tide. And now Oksa knew why. Lasonillia…

"Is the Young Gracious encountering anxiety?" asked the Lunatrixa, gazing inquisitively at her.

"Er… I'm just a tiny bit *terrified*, you know!" remarked Oksa with a tense laugh. "I hadn't planned on spending my school holidays inside a deranged picture. Still, I'm sure I'll get used to the idea. After all, we could have decided to go to Iraq or Chechnya for a complete rest. But no! That would have been far too ordinary for the Pollocks. Our tailor-made break is just what the doctor ordered! Anyway, it'll be child's play: we go into the schizo picture, we free Gus, then we pop over to Edefia to pick some Lasonillia. Oh yes! And while we're at it, we'll save the world... Nothing like a package holiday with a difference, is there?"

The Lunatrixes didn't say anything, they just looked bewildered by all this talk of a "package holiday with a difference".

"I'd really like to know what they're talking about," she continued, looking at Abakum and Dragomira, who were still chatting in low voices. "What are they up to?"

"Ahem, ahem..." said the Lunatrix.

Oksa turned towards him, her eyes sparkling as a thought struck her.

"Oh! You know something, don't you?" she said, tossing back her hair.

"The Lunatrix holds the knowledge of all kinds of things, the Young Gracious possesses that belief, is that not the truth?"

"I certainly do possess that belief!" said Oksa, nodding. "So tell me what you know... that I don't."

The Lunatrix looked around and then, reassured, leant towards the girl and rasped softly in her ear:

"The Young Gracious must receive the information that a traitor has given orders to begin surveillance of the Runaways."

"What's all this?" muttered Oksa, frowning.

"Treachery is at the heart of the activity, Young Gracious," continued the Lunatrix, watched fearfully by his mate. "Treachery works at the heart of the Runaways. Interior and exterior perform the surrounding. The need for warning is severe: the Felons, like friends, have no obligation to coincide with our belief."

"You know, Lunatrix, sometimes I find it really hard to follow what you're saying," remarked Oksa, scratching her head sceptically.

"But it's crystal clear!" said a loud voice behind her, making her jump.

She turned round to see Tugdual leaning against the living-room door jamb. A lock of black hair was hiding part of his face but even though he had his head down, Oksa could see that his blue eyes were gazing intently at her. Tugdual brushed his hair away from his thin, handsome face and gave a strange half-smile, as kind as it was unsettling. Without taking his eyes off her, he walked over and Oksa stiffened on the sofa. As for the Lunatrixes, they stood up with as much tact and discretion as they could muster and went over to curl up in the corner of the hearth.

"What the Lunatrix means is that friends and enemies are not always who you think they are," explained Tugdual, flopping down in an armchair opposite Oksa.

Unlike her, he looked completely relaxed. He swung a leg over the armrest and began running his pierced tongue over his teeth with an irritating grating noise. Oksa sighed, annoyed at feeling so confused every time she was in his company. He was so unreadable. She tried to think of something to say, but the words got muddled in her head.

"So you've gone back to wearing your piercings, have you?" was all she managed, cursing herself for such a lame comment.

Tugdual's eyes darkened briefly in surprise, then brightened again, reverting to that startling icy blue which—she suddenly realized—she found so attractive. She swallowed and gnawed at her lower lip, shocked by this discovery.

"Oh! You know," replied Tugdual, "a leopard never changes its spots…"

His voice was serious, melancholy and cold as the winter wind. Tugdual aroused such conflicting feelings in her: his catlike nature and strong instincts made her feel safe, but he had another side which she found scary, almost intimidating. The only thing she was sure of was that he made her heart race whenever he was near, and that she'd never felt so confused. Oksa studied him: dressed in black from head to toe, eyebrows, ears and nose pierced with countless tiny precious stones, Tugdual looked and acted the same as when she'd first met him on the evening she'd learnt the secret of the Runaways. The only difference now was that he was watching her much more searchingly than he had before. "Oksa-san, get a grip on yourself!" she rebuked herself. She folded her legs beneath her in a bid to conceal her embarrassment.

"The most important thing is to know who you are and to accept it," he continued.

"So who are you?" asked Oksa immediately, amazed at her own daring.

Tugdual shot her a half-surprised, half-amused glance, which made her feel as if her face was on fire. He thought for a few seconds before answering in a voice which was as throaty as that of his striking grandmother, Brune:

"Who am I? Do you want the official or unofficial version?"

"I want the real version," answered Oksa boldly. "I want to know who the real Tugdual is."

"You're very inquisitive, Lil' Gracious! I'm not sure you're ready for the truth…"

"You think I'm such a baby!" retorted Oksa angrily, clenching her fists. "It's so… *humiliating*!" Tugdual looked at her in astonishment, his lips twitching, as if about to burst out laughing. Which unexpectedly infuriated Oksa.

"You really get on my nerves," she muttered furiously, looking away so as not to see his blue eyes burning into her.

"You really want to know then?" asked Tugdual, after a few seconds of sheer torture.

"Of course I do," she mumbled, biting a nail.

"Well, I'm descended from two of the most eminent members of the Firmhand tribe exiled from Edefia. I have gifts which the most powerful men on this planet only dream of possessing. I could actually be the most powerful man in the world and yet I have to bury what I am deep inside because to show it would mean death for me and my family. But that also holds true for your father, your gran, Abakum or my grandparents… and for you, of course. Particularly for you… Apart from that, I'm a sixteen-year-old boy who's drawn to the dark, hidden side of all living creatures, human or animal. Some people call me neurotic and accuse me of having a morbid obsession but, the way I look at it, darkness and moral ambiguity are like food and drink to me. They're just a route to self-fulfilment. I can be just as good as I can be bad. I can be the most loyal friend and the vilest traitor, and I never do things by

69

halves. I thrive on danger and, of course, death, particularly when they allow us to transcend our mundane existence. And, since you want to know everything, meeting a certain Lil' Gracious rescued me from a terminal state of boredom. I was about to be carried off by the spectre of world-weariness when you appeared on the scene, like a little miracle. Basically, Lil' Gracious, it could be said that you saved me from a deadly dull demise..."

With these words, he stretched like a cat, the smug smile on his lips in sharp contrast to his icy stare. Fascinated but confused, Oksa had the unpleasant feeling that she was nothing but a plaything in his cruel claws. She thought for a couple of seconds, remembering the Lunatrix's words of warning, before demanding:

"You say that you can be the most loyal friend and the vilest traitor... so which one are you, right now?"

"What do you think?" mocked Tugdual, teasingly.

"Don't make yourself out to be worse than you are!" rang out Abakum's voice suddenly.

Oksa turned round and saw the Fairyman, standing ramrod stiff in the doorway to the living room. At his side, Dragomira was looking wearily at Tugdual.

"This is our young friend's favourite game," explained Abakum, walking over to join Oksa. "He likes to make people think he's on the wrong side when, deep down, he's probably the most fervent defender of our cause. Isn't that right, Tugdual?"

Tugdual's only reply was to aim a dazzling smile at Oksa, which almost knocked her off her feet. She clenched her fists so tight that it hurt and smiled back with an expression on her face which she hoped was as dispassionate as his. Although she knew that this perplexing boy wouldn't be so easily fooled...

12

THE STRANGER IN THE SQUARE

D RAGOMIRA AND ABAKUM COULD SEE THAT OKSA WAS
flustered by Tugdual, but they chose to ignore it because something had just come up which complicated what was already a very tricky situation.

"We have a problem, youngsters," said Dragomira, looking first at Oksa, then at Tugdual.

"There's a traitor in our midst, is that it?" immediately asked Oksa.

"What makes you say that?" asked her gran with a frown, glaring at Tugdual.

"Er... it's just that it's the worst thing that could happen to us now, isn't it?" replied Oksa, in order to shift the blame from her friend and protect the anonymity of her little informer curled up in the corner of the hearth.

Dragomira gave her a puzzled look, patted the crown of braided hair around her head and continued:

"We don't think we have a traitor in our group, but we are sure we're under surveillance. Ever since Gus's Impicturement, we've been followed, watched and spied on."

"How do you know?" broke in Tugdual.

"You're well aware, dear boy, that Abakum has a remarkable sense of smell. He's been detecting the scent of our spy continually for the past three days and we've seen a man leaning against one of the trees in Bigtoe

Square for hours. When you unleashed the storm, Oksa, that man didn't budge an inch, not even to run for shelter. That's a real giveaway, don't you think? A short time ago, Abakum went out to learn the truth. The man ran off as soon as he saw him. Two hours later, he was back in the same spot. Abakum then turned into a shadow to try to get closer. But the man must have been well informed, because he ran away again. And that convinced us once and for all that he was a Runaway."

"Or a Felon!" exclaimed Oksa.

"The Felons *are* Runaways, Dushka," reminded Dragomira.

"Yes, that's true," admitted Oksa. "But he could also be a secret agent, couldn't he? Or a policeman?"

Dragomira and Abakum exchanged a brief smile.

"An Outsider wouldn't have run away when Abakum's shadow came over," objected Baba Pollock. "He wouldn't have run away because he wouldn't even have noticed it! Only a well-informed Insider—in other words, a Runaway close to our family—would know about Abakum's gift."

"You're right," conceded Oksa, still thinking hard. "Couldn't it be a Runaway trying to get back in touch with us?"

"If that were the case, don't you think he might go about it a little differently?" objected Abakum. "For a start, he wouldn't run off. You know, Oksa, it's beginning to look like you don't want to accept that there might be a Runaway spy."

Oksa glanced down, disconcerted by this remark, and particularly by the fact that a stranger might be watching them.

"Well... I don't want it to be true!" she replied. "Things are complicated enough already, aren't they?"

"Do you think it could be Mortimer McGraw?" asked Tugdual suddenly.

"That's the first person I thought of," replied Dragomira.

"But why would Mortimer keep watch on us?" continued Oksa. "Because of Zoe? Maybe he wants to see her again? She is part of his family, after all... OH NO! Perhaps he wants to kidnap her!"

This possibility frightened her more than she would have imagined. Zoe was Leomido's and Reminiscens's granddaughter, Orthon-McGraw's niece, a descendant of the vicious Werewalls, Ocious and Temistocles, and of Malorane, the ill-advised Gracious. But she was also just a vulnerable girl with great powers and a tragic, chequered past.

"I don't think Zoe is the target of this spy," said Abakum. "Mortimer certainly has the same motives as his father, but I've always believed that Orthon wasn't the only Felon on the Outside. The one thing we're sure of is that the minute we're Impictured, the painting will be even more valuable, which is our main problem now. There are people who see you only as a key that will allow them to re-enter Edefia, Oksa, and they'll do anything to get their hands on the picture. If they did, they'd only have to wait until you came out to snatch you, so to speak. That's much easier than trying to abduct you!"

"Um... I don't want you to think I'm afraid of entering the picture, but if that's what you're concerned about, why don't I just stay here?" asked Oksa, dismayed.

"It's certainly true that being watched by this man complicates matters," continued Abakum. "There is danger outside the picture, as well as inside—who knows what we'll find there and, more importantly, how we're going to get out? This changes things and we did in fact think about leaving you here and taking Dragomira in your place."

"No!" protested Oksa. "That's out of the question. I'm coming with you!"

"No one wants to put you in danger. That's not in our interest, nor in that of the Felons. But of course you're coming with us," confirmed Abakum sadly. "You heard the Squoracle: you're our friends' only hope of rescue, there's no denying that."

"Let's imagine the worst," suggested Tugdual. "Say this Felon or someone else gets hold of the picture. With us inside, of course. And say that, for one reason or another, he destroys it. What happens to us? Are we condemned to wander for ever in an unknown and hostile dimension? Will we die an agonizing death?"

Dragomira sighed, shaking her head despondently.

"Are you trying to make Oksa even more scared?" she said. "Don't you think the situation is bad enough?"

"You really are *impossible*!" exclaimed Oksa, turning to Tugdual, who looked very pleased to see her lose her temper. "Of course we'd die... that would be the logical outcome, wouldn't it? And, I'll have you know it doesn't frighten me! One little bit! Well... perhaps a little," she admitted quietly.

Tugdual chuckled, which enraged the Young Gracious. Resisting the desire to hit him, she clenched her fists and her jaw, determined not to show how angry she was.

"That's why, despite the great help she could be if she let herself be Impictured with us, Dragomira will stay outside to protect the picture," concluded Abakum. "Anyway, don't forget your mother needs someone to look after her. Can you think of anyone better than your gran? An apothecary with magic powers: who could ask for anyone better?"

13

SETTING OFF FOR THE UNKNOWN

MARIE WAS SQUEEZING THE ARMRESTS OF HER WHEEL-chair with all her might, digging her nails into the thick leather. Oksa had put her arms around her mother from behind and was hugging her anxiously. Impicturement was imminent. Would they ever see each other again? Although Oksa didn't doubt it for a minute and was convinced they'd succeed, it didn't prevent her from being on edge and very nervous a few minutes before their departure. She could feel muffled sobs shaking her mother and making her breathe faster. Her own nostrils started prickling and she could do nothing to stop the tears. Around them, the Runaways stood in complete silence. An emotional Dragomira was clinging to Abakum's arm—this was the first time she'd ever been separated from her loyal Watcher. All day, in bleak silence, she'd worked alongside him in her private workroom making the final stocks of Granoks and Capacitors. They would certainly need them inside the bewitched picture! Her eyes bloodshot with tears and tiredness, Baba Pollock looked at her friend and murmured:

"Take care of yourself, my dear Watcher… and please bring them all back alive!" she added, her voice cracking.

"Everything will be fine," said the Fairyman reassuringly, although he didn't seem completely convinced by his own words. "We'll be back in no time, I promise. Nothing will happen to us. You know we have some formidable secret weapons: Pavel is stronger than he'd ever admit; Leomido combines experience with wisdom; Pierre is the embodiment of strength and Tugdual has subtle talents which we idealists lack sometimes. And, as for our Last Hope, she may not know it, but she's incredibly powerful."

"Keep her safe, I'm begging you!" broke in Marie, who'd been listening, as had all the Runaways. "I'll die if you don't."

Oksa felt her heart clench painfully. Hearing her ailing mother mention death broke down all her defences. Death was on the prowl like a merciless predator with an equally formidable hunter: time.

"Come on, let's go!" she said suddenly, afraid she wouldn't have the courage to leave if they didn't make a move soon.

Pierre was the first to say his farewells. He hugged his wife and everyone followed suit, embracing each other silently and lengthily, as the tears fell soundlessly. Zoe extricated herself from the arms of her grandfather, Leomido, while Pavel gave Marie one last kiss, followed by Oksa, who buried her face in her mother's neck. "I can't bear it," she thought sadly. Abakum gently rested his hand on her shoulder, upset by the Young Gracious's misery. It was time to go. Oksa ran her hand through her hair and, to hide her sadness, adopted a ninja pose, one leg stretched out behind her and hands pressed together in front.

"Here we come, picture!" she said, wiping away the tears with the back of her hand. "You'd better watch out... Hang in there, Gus! We're coming to get you."

As soon as Pavel had lightly touched the Imagicon, the six Runaways, hand in hand, felt themselves being sucked inside the strange mixture of slowly shifting iridescent colours. For a while they teetered on the edge of the wooden frame above the terrifying abyss below. Abakum was the first to give in to the urge to jump into the void, dragging his companions with him.

"Muuuuuuum!" screamed Oksa, clinging so hard to the hands she was holding—Abakum's and her father's—that for a second she was afraid she might break their bones.

Her cry was muffled, deadened by the walls of the long, wide vertical passageway through which they were falling, hanging on to each other. For a few minutes it felt as though they were floating like feathers in the middle of a strange, dark, frightening cloud. All they could make out was the dark purple fog which wreathed them as they fell. The deeper they plunged, the fainter the light grew; and the faster their hearts raced…

❋

Suddenly, they stopped. They held their breath in the unsettling silence. Sitting on the spongy ground, they opened their eyes so wide that it hurt. The darkness was total—as absolute as the silence.

"Are we all here?" came Abakum's subdued voice.

"I'm here," replied Pavel immediately, squeezing Oksa's hand, which he was still holding firmly. "Are you okay, Oksa?"

"Um… yes… I think so…" said the girl, trembling.

"I'm here," said Pierre.

"Me too!" added Leomido. "But I'm afraid I've lost Tugdual," he continued, sounding worried. "We let go of each other's hands just before we stopped falling, so he can't be far."

Oksa felt the blood drain from her face. Her nerves were at breaking point. She breathed deeply to try to calm herself, while her Curbita-Flatulo undulated more strenuously on her wrist than ever before.

"Tugdual! Where are you?" she cried at the top of her voice.

Following Oksa's example, the four men yelled as loudly as they could and the Lunatrixa, sitting in a harness tightly fastened to Pavel's back, added her rasping voice to theirs. This immediately reminded Abakum about another of their small companions:

"Incompetent? Are you there?"

From Leomido's back came a slow, groggy voice:

"Yes, I think I'm here, but I'm not completely sure because I can't see anything… What about you? Are you here? And who are you? Your voice sounds familiar… have we met before?"

"The Incompetent is on top form as usual!" observed Oksa, squeezing her father's hand. "Aaargh! What was that? Help!!!!" she screamed suddenly, kicking into empty space.

"Oh… sorry, Oksa! I think that was your leg I just touched."

"Tugdual, is that you?" enquired Leomido. "Thank God you're here… Are you okay?"

"Yes, I'm fine, don't worry," he drawled as offhandedly as usual. "You should come with me. I think I've found something… Oksa, give me your hand. Don't let go of each other, okay? I'm going to guide you."

Tugdual's fingers felt along Oksa's leg, then up her side until he found her hand and the girl was glad they were in complete darkness. At least no one could see how red her cheeks were. Holding hands, the Runaways carefully stood up. The darkness was still impenetrable, but their eyes were becoming gradually accustomed to it: soon they could make out velvety mauve and grey palpitations in the inky darkness, which made the shadows look monstrously alive. Oksa shivered fearfully.

"Isn't it beautiful?" asked Tugdual, realizing how frightened she was.

"Stop!" said Oksa. "I'm scared to death."

Tugdual squeezed the girl's hand and continued to guide the small group, moving confidently through the shadows that were pulsing as though animated by a heartbeat.

"Tugdual, may I ask you something?" murmured Oksa.

"Ask away, Lil' Gracious."

"Can you see in the dark?"

"Of course," he replied tersely. "Don't forget I'm of Firmhand descent! We have animalistic instincts, strength and senses. But I'm not the only one here with those gifts, am I, Pierre?"

The latter cleared his throat.

"No... but I have to admit that, as far as night vision is concerned, you appear to be much more gifted than I am, my young friend!" said the Viking.

"It's not far now, we're almost there," remarked Tugdual, pulling his companions along behind him.

They took another few steps on the springy ground, peering through the slowly dissipating gloom. Then, in a few seconds, the last wisps of darkness had vanished, revealing a dense, shadowy forest.

14

THE FOREST
OF NO RETURN

A PALE GLIMMER OF MOONLIGHT FILTERED THROUGH the thick foliage of the giant trees, shedding patches of strange mauve light over the undergrowth. The Runaways gazed at the silent forest in astonishment, finding it hard to believe they were actually there. The lack of movement was unsettling—they would have felt less intimidated if it had been teeming with life. Suddenly something stirred: a strange small head had just emerged from the ground, its freckled face tapered like a squirrel's. Its body was a long, thick root, which was waving about in the air, sending small clumps of earth flying. Turning to the Runaways, it extended until the tips of its silky eyelashes lightly brushed Oksa's face. The girl flinched and the head-root immediately drew back.

"Don't move," whispered Abakum. "It's just as frightened as we are."

Humans and head-root faced off for several minutes, when suddenly a spectacular black butterfly with a twelve-inch wingspan landed at their feet. It studied Oksa inquisitively with tiny eyes, its shimmering black wings vibrating faintly. Other heads popped up in their turn, forming an odd gathering, and began whispering to each other. Listening hard, the Runaways realized who the subject of conversation was.

"It's the Young Gracious!" one of the little half-human, half-plant creatures told the butterfly. "You can go and tell *it* she's arrived. But for pity's sake, try not to bump into the Wickedesses!"

"May luck be with me… What about those men? Who are they?" asked the butterfly.

Oksa cleared her throat. The butterfly turned to her, fluttering closer and caressing her with its velvety wings. Oksa held her breath, feeling defensive. She'd never much cared for insects, even when they were incredibly beautiful like the specimen stroking her skin. The slightest wrong move and she'd squash it between her hands. No mercy! But the butterfly turned round and silently disappeared into the forest, escaping a painful death.

"What was that?" murmured Pavel.

The first head-root replied in an outraged tone:

"What! You didn't recognize the Wayfinder of the Envoy of the Soul-Searcher?"

"Well, that is… we're not from around here, you know!" retorted Oksa, sarcastically.

At the sound of the Young Gracious's voice, the small head bowed so low that its long auburn hair brushed against the mossy ground.

"That's right—be rude, then grovel!" mocked the Squoracle, poking its tiny head out of Abakum's jacket. "Hey! It's rather nice here! The temperature is perfect and the rate of humidity ideal. A paradise on Earth…"

"Um… on Earth… I have my doubts about that, Squoracle," retorted Oksa, looking around at the strange landscape.

"I wish I could help you by telling you where we are, but I've been unable to locate any landmarks, it's very odd," said the tiny hen.

"The boy and the old lady will be glad to have some visitors," said the head-root in a shrill voice.

"You mean Gus?" asked Oksa, giving a start, her face suddenly lighting up. "Have you seen him?"

"I wouldn't exactly say I'd seen him," replied the creature. "More like felt him. Particularly when he was sitting on me!"

"That's brilliant!" exclaimed Oksa, her heart feeling lighter.

"Yeah, sure—if you like being squashed," remarked the head-root, clearly not sharing Oksa's view.

"Where is he?" asked Pierre in turn.

He scanned the gloomy forest eagerly for any reassuring sign that his son was still alive. Acting on impulse, he rushed headlong into the trees and disappeared from sight.

"Pierre!" called Abakum. "Don't do that! You'll get lost!"

"He can't get lost," informed the head-root.

"What do you mean?" asked Oksa in surprise, worried about her friend's father. "You can always get lost. Particularly in a forest like this!"

"He can't," insisted the head-root. "In the forest, your footsteps will lead wherever you want to go. The Forest of No Return chooses the path, but the traveller's will determines the destination, even though the route may not be the most direct."

"So if we all want to go to the same place, we're bound to find each other even though we've been taking the paths chosen by the forest. Is that what you mean?" enquired Abakum.

"You've understood perfectly!" confirmed the head-root.

"He's lucky," muttered the Incompetent, still in the harness on Leomido's back. "I didn't understand a thing."

"It doesn't matter," said Oksa kindly. "Shall we go then?" she added, curbing her impatience with difficulty.

"Yes, let's go!" echoed Abakum. "Let's all think very hard about Gus and, whatever happens, don't panic if we get separated. We all want to be wherever Gus is, and the forest will take us there."

"I'm not letting Oksa out of my sight," declared Pavel, taking his daughter's hand.

"As you wish, Pavel... but I fear the forest may be stronger than you," said Abakum. "If it has decided to separate you, you'll have no choice but to comply. Just keep your mind focused on our shared destination and we'll be together again, with Gus beside us."

Oksa set off first, Gus's face clear in her mind's eye. "Whatever you do, don't think," she told herself. "Act!" She smiled when she thought about what Gus would say: "Hell's bells, Oksa! You need to think before you act!" The complete opposite of what she was about to do... She glanced one last time at her father, who seemed beside himself with worry, then marched resolutely into the Forest of No Return.

❋

She was immediately plunged into semi-darkness. A narrow, winding path lay in front of her, dappled with patches of ghostly light that filtered through the leaves of the giant trees. She shivered nervously and looked round, tempted to turn back, but it looked as though the forest had closed behind her, true to its strange name... The only living thing was a magnificent hare with brown fur gazing at her in a kindly fashion.

"Abakum?" she murmured.

The hare nodded and Oksa could have sworn she saw it smile. She bent down and picked it up, comforted that she had such a trustworthy escort.

"Don't look round, my dear," whispered the hare. "Tugdual isn't far behind... let him think you don't know, okay?"

"Why?" asked Oksa in amazement, stopping herself from turning round.

"He needs to think he's your secret guardian."

"I understand," she said reluctantly. "But how did he manage to follow us, when Dad and Leomido became separated from us?"

"Oh..." sighed the hare. "Tugdual was just more single-minded. He set his sights on you, instead of focusing all his attention on Gus. Wherever you go, he goes, it's as simple as that."

Oksa blushed. Her morose friend never ceased to surprise her.

"Don't let your mind wander," reminded the hare. "Think about Gus."

Oksa drew herself up to her full height and forged ahead, her eyes fixed on the path leading deep into the forest, relishing the cool fragrance of the undergrowth. Ferns towered above her, arching in a vault over the path edged with dark-green moss. As she walked, the ferns closed behind her to form an impassable wall of vegetation—she had no choice but to keep going forward. Abakum the hare loped along nearby; she saw him leaping above the tall grass that carpeted the undergrowth. From time to time, she heard the crack of a twig breaking or the sound of leaves rustling, which made her think that Tugdual wasn't far away. A Fairyman and a Firmhand-Werewall—she couldn't ask for better protection! Comforted by this thought, she relaxed and began studying the forest as she walked. It was a magical place where everything seemed larger than life. The huge trees were so tall and beautiful that Oksa couldn't quite believe they were real. Even the tallest trees on earth—the giant North American sequoias—looked like shrubs compared to these colossuses. Oksa's thoughts turned to the Sylvabul Territory described by her gran and Abakum. She'd never dared admit that she'd found it hard to imagine whole cities built in the branches a hundred feet above ground, but at the sight of these giants, she no longer had any doubt it was possible. She shivered again, recognizing the signs of mounting anxiety. There was no denying that the forest was beautiful, but it was a freakish, almost intimidating type of beauty. The abnormal silence and stillness made her jittery. She felt spied upon, as though she was walking into an ambush. Cunning, hostile or dangerous creatures might be lurking behind every tree, fern and blade of grass, biding their time until the moment was ripe to attack and tear her limb from limb! She looked up: a glimpse of treetops and maybe a small patch of sky might alleviate this awful feeling of being trapped. However, she soon realized that the crests of those bark-covered giants were miles above the ground.

"That's insane," she murmured incredulously.

She continued walking, her head tilted up, spotting small patches of mauve sky through the dark leaves. The sensation of being caught in a trap grew stronger and her pace quickened in time with her racing heart, until she was running in a panic, although she managed not to scream so as not to alarm Abakum and make Tugdual think she was a wimp. She raced along the sharply twisting path which led deeper and deeper into the forest, until she came to an abrupt halt when she tripped over something snaking across the path and fell flat on her face. She cried out, irritated at herself for not paying enough attention. It was so dark though... Lying on the path, which was covered with black earth as fine and soft as ash, she levered herself up on her forearms and realized she was face to face with a hideous plant, a sort of hairy ball with aerial roots, which looked like a jellyfish. Oksa stood up to run away as fast as she could from this freak of nature, but hadn't reckoned on its desire for conversation. The plant stretched out one of its roots and grabbed Oksa's ankle, causing her to fall flat on her face again. The hare immediately bounded over to her side, looking warily at the plant.

"Stop!" said the plant in a strange voice. "I command you to calm down because I mean you no harm."

Her ankle still gripped tight, Oksa sat up and immediately adopted a ninja attack position. Infuriated rather than reassured by the jellyfish plant's warnings, she rose above the ground and began spinning in her famous "human top" manoeuvre in a bid to free herself. However, the plant wasn't caught out: it gripped Oksa's ankle with surprising force, and she was rolled up like a sausage by the root spooling from the plant as though on an endless reel. Oksa fell heavily, and was immediately joined by the hare, which was about to bite through the tendril.

"Let me go!" she screamed as she writhed, more angry than afraid.

Strangely enough, the plant obeyed immediately. It pulled on the root rope and Oksa rolled over and over on the ashy earth until she was free. She stood up, still fuming, and brushed her clothes, sending little clouds of fine dust into the air around her.

"Don't even think of trying that again!" she warned, threatening the jellyfish plant with her fist.

"Please accept my apologies," said the plant in its peculiar voice. "I may have been a little over-enthusiastic, but I only wanted to greet the Young Gracious," it added, rolling over to Oksa's feet.

"How do you know who I am?" exclaimed Oksa in amazement.

"Everyone here knows," replied the plant enigmatically. "But you should make haste to reach the young man and the old lady. Your arrival will put an end to despair, for them and for us too. Hurry! The forest isn't patient and the wilderness isn't kind. If you linger too long, the path will vanish. You and your guardians will be lost for ever, and nothing and no one will find you again—except for the Wickedesses. Hurry!"

So, listening only to her heart guiding her towards Gus, Oksa sprinted ahead as fast as she could.

15

Your Footsteps Will Lead Wherever You Want to Go

THE FASTER OKSA RAN, THE DENSER THE VEGETATION grew, as if the wilderness had suddenly changed its mind about allowing visitors. She had to concentrate hard to make out the path, which was becoming increasingly overgrown and more difficult to see with every stride. Fighting panic, the Young Gracious cursed herself for not having more self-control, sensing that her fear was undermining her judgement and making her waste valuable time. "This is no time for weakness, Oksa-san!" she scolded herself. "Gus is counting on you. They're all counting on you!" But the forest, impervious to her good resolutions, kept closing in on her. Oksa could now barely see the path: it was overrun with ferns, which scratched her face, and long grasses, which hindered her as she ran. With a strength born of desperation, she tried to throw a few random Knock-Bongs, then some Magnetuses, which flattened a few stalks, but didn't really help matters. These powers didn't seem to work as well on plants as they did on humans. She tried some Fireballisticos too, without much success, since the plants were far too green to burn. As a last resort, she stood by one of the massive trees and, trying to slow the beating of her heart, which felt as if it was trying to burst out of her chest, she scrambled up the trunk. Then, steadying herself by holding onto the rough bark, she lithely hurled herself towards the next tree, a good sixty feet away.

"Ya-haaaaaa!" she yelled furiously, grabbing a branch with all her might.

She continued like this, leaping from tree to tree with the agility of a small monkey, sparing only a fleeting thought for her two guardians.

"Abakum? Are you there?" she called anxiously, deliberately ignoring Tugdual, since she wasn't supposed to know he was following her.

"Keep going like that, Oksa!" she heard from the bushy ferns. "And don't stop thinking about Gus!"

She glanced down quickly and glimpsed the hare bounding through the almost black vegetation. Feeling relieved, she obeyed the Fairyman and concentrated on turning her thoughts back to Gus.

She pictured his handsome Eurasian face: his dark-blue eyes smiled at her, then misted over with fear. Oksa shivered and set off again, keeping her friend's frightened gaze firmly fixed in her mind's eye.

＊

She'd lost count of the number of trees she'd leapt from when she suddenly spotted something shimmering in the midst of the dark forest. At first barely visible, the twinkling light grew larger and brighter as she drew nearer. She reached it rapidly and felt herself being thrown sideways. She shut her eyes, gave a shrill scream and was suddenly rolling on earth as soft as the ash path in the forest.

"OKSA!"

"Gus? Is that really you?" she replied to the voice she'd just heard.

With her eyes still tight shut, she stayed there, curled in a ball on the ground, terrified of being disappointed.

"Yes, it's me!" continued the familiar voice. "Come on, relax! You look like a frightened hedgehog."

Oksa opened her eyes and, jumping up, found herself face to face with Gus, who was gazing at her as if she were a divine apparition.

"You took your time," he said, pretending to be cross to hide his joy.

He stared at her, breathing hard, with tears in his eyes. Just as emotional—and just as unable to show it—Oksa studied him. Although his face was shining with happiness, he looked awful: he had dark circles around his eyes and his face was haggard. His grubby shirt was torn and his hair was tangled. Grabbing his shoulders, she shook him like a plum tree.

"Is that all you have to say to me, you ungrateful wretch?" she spluttered. "I've just risked life and limb crossing a forest which seemed hell-bent on making mincemeat of me and that's all the welcome I get! Grrr. You selfish so-and-so! The next time you're Impictured, remind me to leave you to your own devices, okay?"

"Hey! Gently does it, young lady! Would you mind leaving my son's head on his neck?"

"Pierre!"

Gus's father was standing a few yards away, looking as if a huge weight had been lifted from his heart. Oksa threw herself into his enormous arms and all three laughed till their sides hurt, delighted at being reunited.

"A frightened hedgehog wants to take off the Young Gracious's friend's head? The inhabitants of this place are very violent, we ought to be careful."

As soon as the Incompetent, still harnessed to Pierre's back, had made this ridiculous remark, they exploded with laughter again, watched inquisitively by the slow-witted creature. It took them several minutes to regain their composure.

"Did you manage to get through the forest safely?" Oksa asked Pierre, wiping her eyes.

"Hmm… I've taken more relaxing strolls, but I had a real incentive," said the Viking, looking affectionately at his son.

"What about you, Gus? Are you… okay?" asked Oksa, looking carefully at her friend.

"I'm fine, now you're here," murmured Gus, focusing on a point somewhere behind Oksa. Oksa turned round and realized that Abakum was there. The Fairyman had changed back into human form and seemed exhausted by his long run through the forest. He untangled a piece of fern from his short beard and came over to Gus and hugged him.

"It's good to see you again, my boy."

Gus couldn't help hugging the old man back in relief and emotion.

"Hi, Gus!" came another voice which, although familiar, he was less pleased to hear.

"Hi, Tugdual," he muttered with a scowl. "You're here too, are you?"

"Tugdual!" cried Oksa, pretending to be surprised, and carefully avoiding Abakum's amused gaze. "So you managed to get through, did you?"

"Child's play, Lil' Gracious!" said the young man. "It's all about setting the right goals, you know…"

Oksa ignored this remark and turned to Gus, who was struggling to hide his irritation.

"Where are the others?" she asked, looking around for the first time since her vigorous exit from the forest.

Their surroundings were completely different. The forest had disappeared, along with all traces of greenery. Instead, rolling hills covered with dark-brown heather stretched as far as the eye could see. The sky, which had been glimpsed between the treetops, now glowed in all its mauve splendour. Pale rays emanated from an enormous hazy sun, casting a spectral light over the landscape. Behind Oksa and Gus was the entrance to a gloomy cave, which seemed to lead deep beneath the hills. A little farther away, Leomido was sitting on a rocky outcrop, his elbows on his knees, his head in his hands. His long silvery hair had come loose during the race through the forest and was hanging over his face. A woman was leaning over him, her hand on his shoulder. With a gentle movement, she lifted Leomido's chin and ran her fingertips over his features as if she wanted to commit them to memory. From where she was standing, Oksa could only see her back and white hair, which was arranged in a magnificent, complex hairstyle.

"Is that Reminiscens? Leomido's been reunited with her," she said quietly.

"I'll introduce you," said Gus.

They followed Gus quietly, feeling moved. Oksa glanced at Abakum. At that moment, he didn't look like Abakum, the powerful Shadow Man, magical hare and gifted Fairyman, but an ordinary old man, in the grip of deep emotion at being reunited with a loved one after years apart. He began walking hesitantly at first, then, struggling to catch his breath, he followed his three young friends. Reminiscens turned to look in their direction and Oksa was greeted by the most striking face she'd ever seen. She stopped in her tracks, stunned. Although the old lady's twin brother was none other than the terrible Orthon-McGraw, she didn't resemble him at all. She exuded a charismatic charm as she walked towards them with a wide smile. Gus took Oksa's arm and urged her closer, but it was Abakum who greeted her first.

"Reminiscens…" he said in hushed tones, bowing respectfully.

"Abakum?"

The old lady's voice was trembling. She looked overwhelmed. She covered the short distance between them with the grace of a dancer in her prime. Her delicate features were barely marred by a few faint wrinkles and her bright blue eyes lit up the pale, smooth skin of her face. Tall and slender, she was wearing a simple, almost severe, dress made of a soft, grey fabric which emphasized her figure. The only adornment she wore around her slender neck was a long necklace of tiny honey-coloured pearls.

"Abakum…" she repeated in a tremulous voice. "I'm so happy to see you again… after all these years… how can I thank you enough for coming?"

She bowed her head again—either from emotion or to avoid Abakum's penetrating gaze, it was impossible to tell—and the Fairyman put his hands on her shoulders, forcing her to look up at him.

"I'd given up hope of ever seeing you again," he murmured, almost inaudibly. Reminiscens stifled a sad cry and placed her hand on her heart. The scene, despite its great sense of decorum, moved Oksa to tears, which streamed down her cheeks.

"My friends! Oksa! You made it through!"

Leomido had come over to the little group, tactfully yet firmly interrupting Reminiscens and Abakum's reunion. The two men congratulated each other, relieved to see each other again after being separated in the forest.

"Oksa, I'd like you to meet Reminiscens," said Gus, taking his friend by the elbow. Oksa wiped away her tears and gave a noisy sniff.

"Reminiscens, may I introduce you to my friend Oksa…"

The elegant woman looked at her intently, with a mixture of surprise and curiosity.

"Here you are at last," she whispered, her eyes wide with exultation. "Oksa…"

And, much to the girl's amazement, Reminiscens deferentially sank down before her in an unexpected curtsey.

"Hello," she muttered in embarrassment. "Um… please get up!" Reminiscens obeyed, her eyes still fixed on Oksa.

"Your friend Gus has told me all about you, you know."

"Oh! I hope he didn't say anything incriminating!" said Oksa, to lighten the mood.

"Hey, what are you implying?" reacted Gus, nudging her vigorously as usual.

"No, nothing incriminating!" replied Reminiscens, laughing. "But he has told me a lot about you, your family and my darling Zoe," she added, her voice breaking suddenly. "I'm so glad you took her in."

"She's fine, don't worry," Oksa reassured her immediately. "If only you knew how relieved she was to find out that you weren't…"

Oksa hesitated.

"Dead?" added Reminiscens helpfully.

"Er… yes," admitted Oksa.

"No, I'm not dead, but I would have died of despair eventually if you hadn't solved the mystery of my Impicturement. Everyone, particularly my dear Zoe, would have believed me dead and gone."

"You'll see Zoe again soon!" said Oksa, enthusiastically.

"First we have to get out of this trap," added Reminiscens, her face clouding over.

She paused for a minute, her eyes brimming and her lips trembling.

"And who is this young man?" she continued, turning to Tugdual, who was watching the scene with his customary detachment.

"May I introduce you to Tugdual Knut," said Leomido. "Naftali and Brune's grandson."

"Delighted to meet you, Tugdual," said Reminiscens, bowing respectfully, one hand over her heart. "Thank you for having the courage to be Impictured. I knew your grandfather Naftali very well. An extraordinary man, a force of nature. He and your grandmother Brune made a truly striking couple."

Abakum and Leomido nodded in silence, touched by Reminiscens's excellent memory.

"What about Dad? Where's Dad?" asked Oksa suddenly, frantically looking around.

Everyone jumped in surprise. Oksa's mounting panic threatened to choke her and, eyes wild with terror, she stuttered.

"Has anyone seen Dad?" she cried. "Have any of you seen my dad?"

16

THE INK DRAGON AWAKES

A FEW HOURS EARLIER, PAVEL HAD RUSHED INTO THE
terrifying forest. Oksa had just disappeared into the trees, followed
by Abakum and Leomido, which suggested they wouldn't have gone far.

"Oksa!" he yelled, using his hands as a megaphone. "Oksa! Where
are you?"

But his voice didn't travel at all. It sounded flat, as if absorbed by the
dark, dense vegetation.

"She can't be far," he grumbled. "OK-SAAAA!"

He called out several times in every direction to increase his chances of
being heard. But it was no good. At some point, he also noticed that the
forest had closed behind him: there was no longer any trace of the path
leading back to the small clearing where he'd chatted with his daughter
and friends a short while ago.

"The father of the Young Gracious should digest the advice of the
head with the root body... there is no location for the Young Gracious
in this vicinity. She is pursuing another path."

These words, uttered by a small, shrill voice, had just come from the
Lunatrixa he was carrying on his back. Pavel stopped in surprise and
thought carefully. What had the creature said? "Your footsteps will lead
wherever you want to go. The Forest of No Return chooses the path,
but the traveller's will determines the destination, even though the route
may not be the most direct." He gave a deep sigh. It was stupid to keep

trying, he realized. That had been the story of his life: he'd set his mind on something and invest a great deal of time and effort in achieving it, only to end up feeling like a plaything of the gods. He clenched his fists with a bitter cry of rage. Looking down at his feet, he noticed that a winding path had formed in front of him. He followed it for a while, between tall ferns and colossal trees, distressed at being separated from his daughter. He didn't like their group being broken up one little bit, but there was nothing he could do about it. As soon as they'd been sucked into the picture, Pavel had realized that none of them was in control and this feeling of helplessness had been gnawing away at him, making him seethe. He was so blinded by anger, in fact, that it was a while before he noticed that the path had all but vanished.

"Focus, you fool," he snarled, causing the Lunatrixa to respond accordingly:

"The father of the Young Gracious trips into excess! Focusing is definitely a necessity, but foolishness is exempt from the plan. Do not be forgetful of the advice of the head with the root body: the friend of the Young Gracious is bound tightly to the goal that the father of the Young Gracious must keep in his sight and in his mind."

Pavel chuckled sadly and reached over his shoulder to pat the reassuring creature. She was right: if they all focused on Gus, they'd be reunited with the boy they'd come to save. Pavel closed his eyes and saw Gus's features in his mind's eye. When he opened them, the path had reappeared in front of him. Forcing himself to keep Gus at the forefront of his thoughts, he impatiently forged ahead with a determined stride.

※

He felt as if he'd been in this dark, silent forest for hours and had lost all notion of time and space. He'd begun walking faster and faster until he was running but it didn't seem as though he'd made any progress at all. He stopped for a moment to catch his breath and bent over with his hands on his thighs. The complete silence was unsettling. Suddenly, Pavel stiffened in the grip of an excruciating pain that made him whimper. He straightened up sharply and arched his back in agony, trying to reach behind him to release the Lunatrixa still harnessed to his back.

"Does the father of the Young Gracious experience torment? The weight of the Lunatrixa has caused exhaustion of his body. Ooohhhh! The regretful Lunatrixa is overcome with grief and makes requisition to give apology!"

The Lunatrixa twisted round, trying to struggle free from her harness, while Pavel groaned even louder, wracked by unbearable pain. He undid his Lunatrixa-carrier as best he could, and the little creature immediately came round to stand in front of him. Placing her two podgy hands on Pavel's hips, she hugged him, resting her chubby head against her master's stomach.

"Does the father of the Young Gracious have the will to bestow forgiveness on his heavy servant?" she groaned, pressing her cheek against Pavel.

"This has nothing to do with your weight, Lunatrixa," grimaced Pavel, straightening up again with difficulty. "My back was burning so badly I thought it was going to go up in flames!"

The pain gradually eased, leaving him weak and gasping for breath. With the Lunatrixa still clinging to his waist, he walked over to a giant tree and sat down against its trunk while he recovered.

"Did the Lunatrixa cause the burning of the back felt by the father of the Young Gracious?" asked the small creature in concern.

"No..." said Pavel quietly.

"So the father of the Young Gracious liberates the Lunatrixa from all responsibility?" asked the creature.

"I do," confirmed Pavel. "Shall we keep going? I have a feeling that we haven't seen the last of our troubles."

They set off again, following the path which led deeper and deeper into the dark heart of the Forest of No Return. Since the Lunatrixa had categorically refused to go back into the harness, Pavel was now carrying her on his shoulders so that he could run faster. The entire surface of his back was still painful—although not excruciating, it hurt as much as a bad dose of sunburn. He ran as fast as he could, maintaining a reckless pace. From time to time he gave a stifled moan, which alarmed the Lunatrixa who could do nothing to help. But although he was an excellent sprinter, his legs started to ache and the effort caused his muscles to cramp, which made it really hard to focus on Gus. He was exhausted by pain, impatience and anxiety and his thoughts kept turning to Oksa. He'd almost reached his limits—his strength was melting away like snow in the sun. Suddenly he spotted a movement through the thick foliage of the plants flanking the path. He stopped, his senses alert, and studied the vegetation. His heart missed a beat when he recognized a figure he hadn't dared hope to see.

"Oksa?" he called hesitantly. "Oksa? Is that you?"

Straying from the path, he pressed forward, parting the large leaves. Oksa was a few yards away, sitting beneath an enormous fern, smiling and stroking a magnificent hare.

"Oksa!" he exclaimed, overcome with joy at finding her again.

He walked closer, calling her name, but she didn't seem to hear him. She just continued stroking the hare, without taking any notice of him. Panic-stricken, Pavel pushed through the leaves in his way and continued towards Oksa. However, just when he was within touching distance, he was wracked by another red-hot spasm, even worse than the one before which had made him double over in agony. In despair he looked for his daughter, but she'd disappeared. He cried out in anger as the Lunatrixa jumped down. Pavel's back was on fire—it felt as if every inch of skin was being consumed by merciless flames.

"I'm burning up…" he wailed, grimacing with the pain.

The Lunatrixa took hold of her master's face and gazed at him, while massaging his temples and making her wide, protruding eyes spin round. A few seconds later the pain lessened and finally faded away, leaving Pavel exhausted.

"Thank you, Lunatrixa," he murmured gratefully to the little healer.

"Will the father of the Young Gracious give agreement to the Lunatrixa for inspection of his inflamed back?" Pavel's only reply was to pull up his T-shirt with a groan, his teeth clenched. The Lunatrixa released his temples and waddled round to stand behind him. There was a worrying silence, punctuated only by Pavel's moans.

"Well, Lunatrixa? What can you see?" he asked in a choked voice. The Lunatrixa paused for a few seconds before replying:

"The father of the Young Gracious is in possession of a mark on his back," she said finally.

"A mark? What mark?" said Pavel.

"The mark is that of a fantastic creature forgotten by time, but still feared by men. The father of the Young Gracious possesses the outline of this creature!"

"You mean my tattoo," remarked Pavel, feeling relieved.

"The tattoo is in existence," confirmed the Lunatrixa. "The Ink Dragon is visible. However, its border is receiving development. The Ink Dragon is invading the back, as well as the heart and veins of the father of the Young Gracious. The Ink Dragon is now experiencing the heat of life and is animated by the ambition to liberate itself from its master and allocate him the gift of strength." Looking stricken, Pavel put his head in his hands.

"The father of the Young Gracious has knowledge of the ability of his Ink Dragon, is that not so?" added the Lunatrixa, patting Pavel's shoulder. "The Ink Dragon has awoken."

"Yes," whispered Pavel. "I've always known this day might come. And I've always dreaded it."

"But the day of revelation is not dreadful!" continued the Lunatrixa. "The father of the Young Gracious will be filled with the strength of the Ink Dragon, which has been slumbering in his heart and experiences liberation from the power that has been suffocating it."

"The power that's been suffocating me," murmured Pavel, "the power that's been suffocating me..."

17

BITTERNESS

P AVEL STOPPED SUDDENLY, COMING FACE TO FACE WITH
a wall that rippled as if covered with water and that seemed to mark
the boundary of the silent forest. He looked round and saw that the path,
the trees and all the vegetation had disappeared. It was as if the forest had
vanished into thin air behind him as he'd penetrated deeper, leaving a vast,
gloomy nothingness. Fascinated, Pavel stretched his hand out towards
this void and felt an icy blast which appeared to be gaining on him. His
fingertips immediately turned blue with the cold, forming a striking
contrast to his burning back. He snatched his hand away in surprise.
Trusting to instinct, he plunged into the rippling wall with a warlike cry.
The shimmering surface sucked him in and he lost control of his limbs
for a few seconds, before landing in a ball on a thick carpet of vegetation.

"DAD!" cried Oksa, rushing towards her father lying on the ground.
"Dad! I was so worried!"

Pavel got to his feet, his heart filled with joy and relief, and opened
his arms wide so that Oksa could throw herself into them.

"My darling daughter!" he murmured, burying his face in Oksa's hair.
"I've found you at last."

He held back his tears as best he could, squeezing his eyes shut so
hard that he saw billions of flickering points of light.

"Are you hurt?" he whispered in Oksa's ear. "It was awful thinking of
you all alone in this terrible forest!"

"But I wasn't alone," replied the girl quietly. "Abakum was there, you know! At least... Abakum's animal self, if you know what I mean," she added teasingly. "And Tugdual was never far away either."

"Well, at least there were two people who were more reliable than your loser of a father," groused Pavel, hugging Oksa even closer.

"Oh, Dad, don't be such a drama queen!"

"Good to see you, Pavel!" broke in Abakum loudly.

"Good to see you too, Abakum," muttered Pavel. "Pierre, Leomido, Tugdual—I see I'm the last," he remarked bitterly, greeting each of his friends in turn.

"Who cares?" retorted Abakum. "The main thing is that we're all together again. And look who we've found."

With a big grin on his gaunt face, Gus walked over to Pavel, who gazed at him with genuine emotion.

"You gave us one hell of a fright, my boy," he said, giving him a bear hug. "Your father must be very happy!"

"Thank you, Pavel, thank you," said Pierre with a warm gaze. "I owe you, my friend."

Pavel looked silently at his friend, who was standing there with his hands on his son's shoulders. The gratitude in his eyes touched Pavel deeply.

"It's high time we introduced you to a new Runaway, our dear friend Reminiscens!" exclaimed Abakum.

The beautiful woman walked over gracefully and bowed, while keeping her eyes on Pavel.

"You look so much like Dragomira," she murmured.

Pavel greeted her respectfully, disconcerted at being face to face with a woman he'd heard so much about. He'd never have thought he would meet her one day. After all, as far as he knew, Reminiscens had remained in Edefia.

"I do look like my mother in some ways," he admitted stiffly, barely tolerating this comparison which he was determined not to take as a compliment. "But, if I may say so, you don't look at all like your brother, Orthon."

Reminiscens went pale and nervously crossed her hands over her stomach.

"Needless to say, my dear Reminiscens, what Pavel just said was meant as a compliment," explained Abakum, immediately reassuring her.

"Then I shall take it as intended," declared the old lady, with a dazzling smile for Pavel.

"Don't you want to relieve yourself of your small companion?" continued Abakum, motioning to the Lunatrixa who was waiting patiently in her harness.

"The mouth of the Fairyman contains kindness," admitted the creature. "The back of the father of the Young Gracious is already suffering from the flames of his Ink Dragon without the addition of the weight of his servant."

Abakum frowned, intrigued.

"What Ink Dragon do you mean, Lunatrixa?" he asked gently.

"My back was scratched, near my tattoo," said Pavel abruptly.

"You should show me," suggested Abakum, coming over.

"No point," Pavel replied, immediately twisting round to help the Lunatrixa clamber out of her harness. "It's just a scratch. I've had worse."

The Lunatrixa turned purple, a clear sign of bewilderment in creatures of her species.

"The father of the Young Gracious is attempting a reduction of the importance of the Ink Dragon," she murmured quietly.

"I'm fine, Lunatrixa!" snapped Pavel, sounding irritated. "Let's not make a mountain out of a molehill. It was just a tiny scratch… Well, Oksa?" he added suddenly, altering his tone. "Aren't you going to show me round this magnificent place? It's the perfect holiday resort, isn't it?"

Everyone laughed and followed him towards the top of the nearest hill to admire the strange landscape. The Lunatrixa took advantage of this distraction to attract Abakum's attention, as the Fairyman had expected.

Ever watchful, Oksa slowed down and listened, thrilled to be able to use the handy Volumiplus power.

"The Fairyman should receive the information that the father of the Young Gracious has not encountered a scratching," murmured the Lunatrixa.

"I thought as much," admitted Abakum, almost inaudibly. "What happened, Lunatrixa? You can trust me. I don't reveal my sources."

"The Lunatrixa does not have the habit of practising betrayal of her masters, but she knows the predicament of shrouding an event filled with importance in secrecy," confessed the little creature, her skin purple as an aubergine.

"Don't be afraid to tell me. What happened in the forest?"

The Lunatrixa glanced around in a panic, nervously rubbing her hands down the sides of her plump body. Then she gave a groan, which she stifled by putting her palm over her wide mouth.

"The father of the Young Gracious has experienced the liberation of his Ink Dragon," she confided, frightened by her own words.

"At last!" whispered Abakum. "It's finally happened…"

The Lunatrixa looked at him and gave another groan. The Fairyman gave a satisfied smile, which unsettled her so much that she fainted.

18

REMINISCENS

T HE SMALL GROUP CLIMBED THE GENTLE SLOPE, LED by Pavel, who was doing his utmost to divert attention from the Lunatrixa's words about his Ink Dragon. Only Oksa, who'd deliberately lagged behind, had managed to overhear the little creature's conversation with Abakum, and her mind was now working overtime. As the group made their way up the hill, the Young Gracious was seething with questions. Did her father really have a tattoo on his back? Did she remember seeing it? She didn't think so. Her father never went bare-chested, he was very modest. Too modest? Because of the tattoo? Was he ashamed of it? If so, why? No, there had to be a much more secret, personal reason for concealing the tattoo. The few words spoken by the Lunatrixa and the questions asked by Abakum had made that quite obvious.

"Grrrrr, it's so infuriating," she said angrily, rubbing her cheek.

"Is something wrong, Oksa?" asked Abakum, joining her, the Lunatrixa slumped in his arms.

The girl was bursting to ask all the questions whirling round her head, but thought better of it, preferring to watch, listen and learn by herself.

"No, everything's fine, thank you, Abakum," she replied, her tone more thoughtful than cheerful. "What's the matter with her?" she asked, stroking the Lunatrixa's cheek. "Too much excitement?"

"None of this is easy for her, you know," explained Abakum.

"That strange creature has a lot of psychological problems," said the Incompetent, which was also lagging behind, although not deliberately. "Look at the colour of her skin! She looks like she's suffered a stroke… Oh, now I understand," it exclaimed with delight. "She's had an emotional stroke!"

"You're right, Incompetent," said Oksa, chortling. "Excellent diagnosis!"

"That creature is the absolute limit," added Gus, who'd lost no time in joining his friend.

"Yes, I'm the absolute limit for diagnostics," agreed the Incompetent. "But would you remind me who you are? Your face looks familiar…"

Gus and Oksa burst out laughing, which helped dissipate the tension that had built up over the last few difficult hours—the fear of never seeing each other again and other such morbid thoughts. They cried with laughter at the Incompetent, who watched them incredulously, astonished to be the cause of such wild hilarity.

"You're very cheerful," it concluded candidly.

Oksa wiped her eyes and winked at Gus, sealing their renewed bond. Gus blushed and looked down. A long, dark strand of hair tumbled forward, hiding part of his face. He brushed it away and, as if to hide his emotion, declared in an unusually high voice:

"Look over there!"

Abakum and Oksa turned round: Leomido and Reminiscens had stopped some way off from the group and were deep in conversation. Oksa's great-uncle seemed very moved by whatever Reminiscens was saying to him.

"Amazing, isn't it?" exclaimed Gus, sounding more like his normal self. "They haven't seen each other for fifty-seven years."

"And she's still as beautiful," murmured Abakum, lost in thought.

Oksa and Gus exchanged looks, astonished by the Fairyman's wistful, nostalgic tone.

"That woman is fascinating," added Tugdual, who'd just joined them.

"Ocious's daughter, Orthon's twin sister and descendant of the genius Temistocles, the inventor of human shape-shifting."

"And you find that fascinating?" asked Gus.

"Of course I do!" retorted Tugdual. "It means she's a real powerhouse! Like the Graciouses, if I may say so, my Very Honourable Lil' Gracious… She used to frequent the Secret Society of the Werewalls and probably rubbed shoulders with Diaphans. It's not every day you meet someone like her. Have you thought about that?"

"No, we haven't thought about that. For a start, no one has such a twisted mind as you!" scoffed Gus. "Let's go over and join them, instead of listening to your stupid remarks."

Tugdual shrugged, without losing his ironic smile.

"Don't you two ever stop bickering?" asked Oksa quietly, with a worried glance.

"We're not bickering," answered Tugdual defensively, "it's just a frank and honest exchange of views."

"Frank and honest? Yeah, right!" retorted Oksa. "Is that what you call the relationship between two boys who can't stand each other and who systematically contradict whatever the other one says!"

"Hey, it's not my fault if your friend lacks my sparkling wit!" mocked Tugdual.

"You're impossible!" gasped Oksa.

"But that's what you like about me, isn't it?" replied the boy mischievously.

"Enough!" retorted Oksa. "You talk too much."

Tugdual laughed loudly, attracting the attention of the other Runaways standing in a circle around Leomido and Reminiscens on the heather. Gus looked furious.

"What's so funny, youngsters?" asked Reminiscens, smiling.

"Oh, Tugdual thinks he's funny, but unfortunately he's the only one laughing!" said Oksa, taking her revenge, avoiding both Gus's angry eyes and Tugdual's merry gaze.

"If only you knew how happy I am," continued Reminiscens. "Not only to meet you, but also, and especially, to be reunited with old friends I'd given up hope of ever seeing again."

"Can I ask you something?" suddenly broke in Oksa. "Um… it may be a bit nosy…"

"…but you're desperate to ask anyway!" continued Reminiscens, her eyes shining.

"Yes," replied Oksa with scarlet cheeks.

"I'm listening."

"Well, I'd like to know why you never tried to find Leomido when you arrived on the Outside."

Reminiscens looked down, upset.

"I knew one of you would ask me that some time. It's a long story…"

"We're in no hurry," replied Abakum quietly.

Reminiscens gazed sadly at him and slowly smoothed her dress. Then, with a faraway look in her eyes, she began:

"To answer your question, Oksa, I have to go back a long way into the past. Back to the time, years ago, when I was very much in love with your great-uncle Leomido. Our families had always been close; my twin brother Orthon, Leomido and I were practically raised together in the Glass Column under the watchful gaze of Malorane and her First Servant, my father Ocious. When I became a young woman, I realized my childhood friendship had turned into a deep, passionate love for the man who had, until then, been my best friend. And the day that Leomido confessed that his feelings had changed too was one of the happiest days of my life. Our love soon became obvious to everyone and that was the start of our problems…

"Malorane and Ocious did everything they could to break us up, although we couldn't understand why. Malorane introduced Leomido to a string of young women, each more attractive than the last, and my father presented me with all kinds of young men who professed to be madly in love with me. Leomido and I laughed about it at the time: we

106

thought these gambits were funny. We were so naïve… However, when we didn't take the bait, our parents resorted to more drastic measures. My family moved to the other side of Edefia, officially to make it easier for my father to govern Peak Ridge, the territory of the Firmhands. I didn't know then that this move was intended to keep us apart and, although I was upset at seeing the man I loved less often, I put up with it out of obedience to my father. He was a brilliant, austere man who was very strict. Many feared him, but he was my father and I stifled any questions I might have asked out of loyalty to my family. I was in love, though, and my heart hungered for Leomido, so we met in secret. The hours passed so quickly… we were miserable and it tore us apart to say goodbye. We didn't know why they were trying to stop us seeing each other.

"One day, my brother caught us together. I'd gone to see Leomido in one of the houses owned by the Gracious's family, a fine residence high in the forest of Green Mantle. We'd gone there to repeat our vows of fidelity and to encourage each other not to lose hope that things would work out, when Orthon turned up. I'd never seen him so angry. His words were full of a violent hatred that had never been directed at me before. Orthon had always looked up to Leomido. He regarded him as a brother whom he admired as much as envied. But, that day, I saw a different side to him. He was a savage, narrow-minded bully. I didn't understand what was going on: his reaction seemed so excessive, so absurd and pointless. I tried to have my say, telling Orthon that I loved Leomido and that I wanted to spend the rest of my life with him. He then dared to raise his hand to me. It hurt so much, but the physical pain was nothing compared to the wound in my heart. I may have lived through worse times in my life, but the memory of that day still upsets me because something was shattered for ever—my twin brother, the person to whom I'd always been so close, had hit me just because I loved someone against our father's will. Beside himself with rage, Orthon threw himself at Leomido, who might have been younger, but was much stronger. My brother ended up with a broken nose and some fine bruises, but it was the injury to his pride that really rankled and he never recovered from it.

"From that day onwards, my life was a living hell. My brother and father watched me all the time and used all kinds of cunning tricks to prove that Leomido wasn't the man I thought he was. They tried everything: persuasion, threats, blackmail... Leomido also received the same treatment from his mother. It was as if our parents had joined forces to separate us! It was a really difficult time for me. I couldn't understand why things had changed. But I wouldn't play ball with Orthon, Ocious and Malorane. I loved Leomido and that was all that mattered. We managed to continue meeting up with the help of some loyal friends. There weren't many of them left: our parents had done their best to cut us off from the world and isolate us—me more than Leomido. Most of the time, I was kept inside—at that time, we lived in a luxurious cave in the Firmhand mountains, its walls lined with precious stones. My mother, who was my guard, was powerless in the face of my misfortune: she was far too cowed by the threats made by my father, who'd become increasingly overbearing and vicious. She did all she could to dissuade me from loving Leomido, but none of her arguments won me over. Quite the opposite! The more I was kept away from him, the more I missed him and realized how much I loved him.

"I soon became a prisoner of my own family. I was like a caged lion and life lost all meaning. I was only allowed out under the close supervision of my father or brother. Orthon became increasingly hard-hearted—once so lacking in self-confidence, he became cruel, pitiless, almost inhuman in the space of a few months. He was under our father's thumb and I no longer recognized him. Leomido, whom he'd loved like a brother, had become his sworn enemy and the whispered conversations he had with my father led me to believe that I wasn't the only reason for this drastic change. I watched and listened—I was so bored in my cave—and I gradually formed the impression that I was nothing more than a grain of sand in the works and that they had far bigger fish to fry than my love affair with Leomido. It was around this time that I overheard a conversation which confirmed my suspicions: Orthon and Ocious were plotting to seize power! But they weren't interested in governing Edefia—Oh no! They were aiming much higher. Malorane had been foolish in screening her Dreamflights to the Outside, and these had awakened dark ambitions, as you all know. When I realized that the Felons who'd rallied to my father's cause were endangering our people, I Vertiflew to Leomido's house faster than I'd ever done in my life. He hid me in a secret house in Green Mantle for three days, until my father and his henchmen found me. The next day, Ocious dragged me to Retinburn where, in one of the caves owned by the terrible Secret Society of the Werewalls, I endured the worst punishment in the world."

19

Beloved Detachment

"One of the Diaphans inhaled every last drop of romantic love from my body. That foul creature gorged itself until it was sated and black tar flowed from its excuse for a nose. I've never seen anything so disgusting in my life… It felt like my soul had been sucked out of me. My heart froze, as if pierced by an arrow of ice, growing harder and harder as the life seemed to drain from my veins. The pain was gone—all I felt was a terrible sensation of coldness. I thought I was dying and that my life force was being consumed by the Diaphan. Even my brother looked upset by this vile act. I remember meeting his eyes… I was panic-stricken, terrified by the Diaphan, which was in a trance, while Orthon was standing in a corner of the cave, wringing his hands in dismay. Not far from him, my father was watching the scene with complete composure and I'll never forgive him for that. Only his eyes gleamed with the pitiless light of someone who had achieved his ends. He walked over to the Diaphan and collected the black tar trickling from what remained of its nostrils in a small phial, which he immediately pocketed. "Everything will be okay now, my dear," he said, caressing my cheek. My reaction was to spit in his face—which was all I could manage in my weakened state, even though I had a burning desire to kill him. He wiped his face slowly with his sleeve, looked me right in the eye and smiled cruelly, without saying a word.

"The next day, we moved back to the Glass Column and I was horrified to realize the consequences of what had been done to me: my love for Leomido had gone. When I met him in the corridors of the Glass Column, I was devastated by my own indifference. I knew that I'd loved him more than life itself. I knew that my heart had been beating for him alone the night before. And now my love for him had been stolen. I fainted, overcome with grief at my complete disinterest. I'd suffer from Beloved Detachment for the rest of my life because, after that fateful day, I'd never be able to fall in love again.

"My father had won. And Malorane, his accomplice in this gruesome business, had also scored a victory: I no longer loved Leomido. He soon realized this and began avoiding me. I should have told him, I should have talked to him about the torment I was suffering, but I couldn't. Deep down, I was ashamed. And more than that, I think I was afraid of his reaction: if he'd known the truth, blood would have been spilt, I'm sure, because Leomido wasn't the kind of man to allow such a barbaric act to go unpunished. So, retreating into silence, I sank into a deep depression, which only my mother saw. My father and brother were busy putting the finishing touches to the trap for Malorane. I was the least of their concerns and they no longer paid any attention to me. I could go wherever I wanted. I listened to their conversations and they made no attempt to hide what they were talking about, which made me realize that they'd soon escape from the Inside and then they'd rule the world.

"I tried to warn Leomido, but he fled as soon as he saw me coming. As for Malorane, I couldn't stand the sight of her, so there was no way I was going to speak to her. Her relationship with my father had deteriorated, but she was just as responsible for my unhappiness as he was. So I told my mother, who was also suffering at my father's hands, and I came up with the plan of travelling to the Outside at the same time as the Felons. Not to rule the world, as they wanted to do, but just to escape from a land where I could no longer be safe or happy. My mother was in two minds, when something persuaded her to come with me: I was pregnant! I was expecting Leomido's child! If my father had learnt about it, the child would have represented a powerful tool for him. Just imagine: the union of a Werewall woman descended from Temistocles with the son of Gracious Malorane! So we waited. The Great Chaos was unleashed a few weeks later, following the revelation of the Secret-Never-To-Be-Told. Our beautiful land was put to fire and sword by the Felons and, taking advantage of the prevailing pandemonium, my mother and I travelled to the Portal. I saw Leomido and the Young Gracious Dragomira pass through with a few others. The Portal was closing when we got there. I took my mother's hand, holding as tight as I could, and we raced forward, watched in amazement by my father, who screamed: "NO!" But it was too late! We were already on the other side, on the Outside…

"We were lucky enough to be ejected in the Netherlands, which was a peaceful, affluent country. Six months later, my son Jan was born. He didn't have the good fortune to know his grandmother: my poor mother died of a broken heart a few weeks after we arrived. This was a tough time for me. Without my son, who knows if I'd have coped with the loneliness of exile felt by any Insider at one time or another… My thoughts often strayed to Edefia and to those who passed through the Portal. And I felt so alone with my grief, my fears and, above all, that huge difference which sets us apart from the Outsiders and which meant that I was—like all of you—continually in danger. But I didn't give up, I adjusted and I grew accustomed to this life. I became a diamond-cutter and earned a decent reputation, which gave me confidence and strength. I raised my son as best I could and lived a quiet life, with no surprises, good or bad.

"Then one day, twenty years after the Great Chaos, a stroke of fate rekindled those distant memories. I was reading the newspaper, when I suddenly came upon an article about Leomido Fortensky, the brilliant conductor. I immediately recognized him from the photo printed alongside the article. How can I describe the rush of emotion? It was as if the ground had opened up under me. I'd spent more than twenty years trying to be like everyone else, and now the past had come back to haunt me, as if to say: "Don't forget who you are!" The article said that Leomido was giving a one-off concert at the Albert Hall that evening.

"I don't know what came over me: I rushed to the airport and caught the first plane to London. Once there, I met with disappointment: it was sold out! So I did what I hadn't done for twenty years and had promised myself I'd never to do again until my dying day: I used my gifts. I stole a ticket, taking it directly—and magically—from some poor woman's bag. Fortunately, it was for a seat in one of the secluded boxes which wouldn't be overlooked by other members of the audience, so I could study the auditorium without any fear of being seen. I didn't know what to expect, but I was so excited. When I recognized Naftali and Brune, I almost fainted. They were there, looking splendid, in the second row. Farther off, I saw Bodkin, my favourite jeweller in Edefia. What's more, by the greatest coincidence and despite the fabulous pieces I'd been working on for years, I was wearing one of his designs—a superb bracelet of emeralds shaped like tiny stars. Nervously I looked round the rest of the auditorium. Suddenly, the lights went out and the stage was illuminated. I thought my heart would stop when Leomido appeared. He greeted the audience and turned to face the orchestra. For two hours, I gazed at his profile. My feelings were almost unbearable. He hadn't changed much at all.

"At the end, a woman joined him on stage and kissed him—his wife, I thought with a twinge that was more painful than I would have imagined. So he'd married and made a life for himself. Naturally; why wouldn't he? I felt mingled relief and sorrow at the idea. I'd eventually stopped thinking about the fact that I'd never again experience the happiness of being in love but, at that moment, gazing at that handsome couple who looked so happy, I felt devastated by the realization. I remained sitting in the box with a heavy heart when a voice suddenly murmured behind me: 'Good evening, dear sister... It's so nice to see you again.' Twenty years had gone by, but I'd have recognized that voice anywhere. My brother Orthon was a few inches from me. I felt a mixture of emotions and hesitated to turn round. I didn't have to: Orthon came to sit beside me and covered my hand with his. I didn't stop him, I was so surprised and shocked. 'Our mutual friend is a magnet for Insiders, isn't he?' he said, rather ironically. 'I'm sure you'll have recognized, as I did, a few acquaintances. But the most important thing is that I've found you again. I was sure you wouldn't stay away.' When I finally turned round, I couldn't help crying out: he looked so young! And so heartless... I didn't remember him being kind, far from it. But I think, at that precise moment, I hated him. A feeling which only grew stronger when I understood the reasons behind his desire to return to Edefia: he'd devoted his life to opening the Portal and, for that, he needed the new Gracious. He was travelling the world, anonymously keeping his eye on any Insiders he'd located. Every girl born to them was carefully watched: one of them might be the new Gracious. When I told him I'd had a son, he was clearly disappointed and I have to confess that I felt relieved.

"My brother frightened me. I didn't want him back in my life. And yet, after that concert, he occasionally paid me a visit, not only to keep me informed about the progress of his search, but also to check that I hadn't met a potential Gracious. When my son and daughter-in-law gave birth to Zoe, he became more interested and visited more often. In view of her ancestry, there was a strong probability that Zoe might be the next Gracious. I knew it better than anyone and I trembled night and day at the thought. However, luckily the possibility never materialized and Orthon started focusing on Oksa, whom he'd just located.

"Despite this, my life was no easier: I was increasingly worried by Orthon's megalomania. I could no longer ignore the fact that he was dangerous and, what's more, he didn't hide it. I knew he wouldn't hesitate to kill anyone who stood in his way—he prided himself on being unscrupulous. So I made a fatal mistake: I threatened to warn Leomido if Orthon didn't abandon his plans. I was very worried for Oksa, whom I sensed was the new Gracious and I was about to go and tell Leomido everything. Unfortunately, something terrible happened, which prevented me from doing so: my son and daughter-in-law died in a plane crash, a tragedy I'll never get over."

The old lady broke off, with tears in her eyes and her lips trembling. She turned away and waited until her breathing steadied before continuing.

"After that, doubt crept into my heart: what if Orthon had killed them? I knew he was capable of it. That thought made my life a misery for several months, although I couldn't say anything. I had my hands full with young Zoe and our terrible grief. One day, Orthon turned up at my house. The conversation got out of hand, as it did every time he visited. I was on the verge of a breakdown and I blurted out my suspicions. I threatened to pay Leomido or Dragomira a visit and tell them everything. That was a few months ago. Since then, I've been Impictured."

20

THE MARITIME HILLS

REMINISCENS STOPPED SPEAKING. SHE STOOD THERE motionless, her hands crossed in front of her. The shocked Runaways gazed at her, deeply moved by her story. The Lunatrixa sniffled, breaking the heavy silence.

"My dear Reminiscens…" murmured Leomido, his face white. "I couldn't have acted any differently."

"Don't blame yourself."

"My hands were tied!" raged Leomido, clenching his fists.

"Let's not rake over the past," advised Reminiscens. "What's done is done. We have to learn to live with our unhappiness as best we can."

"I didn't know any of that. How terrible," muttered Oksa miserably. Reminiscens looked at her helplessly, then stood up, her head held high.

"Anyway, we should probably get going, shouldn't we?"

"There's an amazing view from up there—I'll bet you've never seen anything like it!" said Gus.

The Incompetent gazed at him vacantly as he took its hand, and they set off towards the rounded hilltop.

"Hey!" said the Incompetent, suddenly straightening up. "That means young Zoe is Reminiscens and Leomido's granddaughter!"

"Um… yes," confirmed Oksa. "And, to be honest, Incompetent, we've only known for the past four months!"

"Four months?" continued the creature in amazement. "Oh! So that's why I didn't know…"

"What a dope!" snorted Gus.

Oksa quickened her pace, and when she arrived at the top of the hill she realized what Gus had meant about the view: an endless desert of dark velvety hills stretched as far as the eye could see. What was incredible about this landscape, though, wasn't its immensity, but the fact that the hills were moving with a loud murmur. They were hypnotically undulating at regular intervals, like waves in a sea of vegetation, and their silky covering of heather shimmered with each ebb and flow.

"Wow," exclaimed Oksa in amazement, "it looks just like the sea! It makes you want to dive right in—"

"Don't!" urged Gus, holding her back by the arm as she started to head for the strange expanse. "I'm not sure what would happen, but I don't think you'd better try."

"He's right," agreed Tugdual, unable to tear his eyes away from the sight. "I have a nasty feeling that if you jumped in, you'd be swallowed like a fly by a carnivorous plant!"

Oksa shivered and stepped back in alarm. Gus glared at Tugdual, who gave him a deceptively innocent smile.

"Look, Oksa!" said Gus, pointing up. "Look at the sky!"

Oksa looked up and stared open-mouthed: the sky, which was as mauve as the patches she'd glimpsed in the Forest of No Return, was studded with planets spinning very fast around an enormous disc, which was radiating thousands of purple rays and seemed to serve as a sun.

"Where on earth are we?" murmured Oksa, fascinated.

"Would you like some precise details?" offered the Tumble-Bawler.

"I'll take anything you have!" replied Oksa, looking sceptical.

"We're still in Great Britain, in the west centre of London, of that I'm sure," continued the Tumble-Bawler. "But our location has changed: we're now in Bigtoe Square, top floor, in what is generally called the private workroom of the Old Gracious, south wall, three feet, eleven inches from the ground, ten feet, eight inches from the west corner, eleven feet, two inches from the east corner. I might also add that we're on a table and that three pairs of eyes are looking at us."

The Runaways followed the Tumble-Bawler's gaze, which was fixed on the mauve sky.

"How can it know that?" murmured Gus, narrowing his eyes.

"I don't know it, Young Master," replied the small conical creature, wobbling on the heather. "I can see it!"

"It's right!" shrieked Oksa suddenly. "Look! You can see shadows in the sky!"

They all looked up again, redoubling their attention. Shadows were moving across the strange sky, like shifting clouds scudding along or coming together, creating a growing sensation that there was someone there.

"The shadows aren't in the sky, Young Mistress," explained the Tumble-Bawler. "They're behind the sky. Look! One of them is examining us!"

Just above the small group, a dark, partial circle darkened the sky. Suddenly they could make out the outline of a face and they all recognized Dragomira.

"Baba!" Oksa began yelling. "BABA! WE'RE HERE!"

But Baba Pollock didn't notice anything as she examined the interior of the picture, and the Runaways' desperate cries and waves didn't reach Dragomira's eyes or ears. The old lady's face eventually disappeared from the mauve sky, leaving the occupants of the picture feeling disheartened.

"We're now rolled up in a tube three inches in diameter and tied by a leather cord seventeen inches long," announced the Tumble-Bawler, breaking the deathly silence. "The Old Gracious has put the picture in a wooden case, made of beech wood, I think. We're now concealed in a secret hiding place in the private workroom, behind the portrait of the Old Gracious's son."

"The Granok recess!" exclaimed Oksa. "That's good, we're safe. Hey, look over there! That could be the butterfly from the forest!"

Examining the sky, the Runaways spotted the magnificent black butterfly, which was growing larger with every second as it neared the hill.

"It's the Wayfinder of the Envoy of the Soul-Searcher!" explained Gus.

"Have you seen it before?" asked Oksa in surprise. "Do you know the Envoy?"

Gus explained to the Runaways how he'd met the crow and then relayed the valuable—and somewhat alarming—instructions the latter had given him.

"Well, at least we know we're not alone," remarked Oksa, after telling Gus what she knew about the mysterious process of Impicturement.

The butterfly had joined the group and was listening attentively to the two friends' conversation, nodding its head from time to time. All at once it began hovering in front of Oksa.

"You must flee, Young Gracious!" it boomed in a guttural voice. "Flee, Runaways!" it repeated. "Flee before the Void gets you. You must save the Young Gracious!"

"Look over there!" said Pavel suddenly, in a hollow voice. "What is that?"

"It's the Void!" replied the butterfly. "Hurry, it's coming!"

In the distance, an enormous dark mass was drawing closer with a terrifying roar, consuming everything in its path—sky, planets and rippling hills.

"Run!" shouted the butterfly, hastily fluttering towards the foot of the hill.

Realizing the danger they were in, the Runaways began racing down the hill in a panic. The butterfly flew in front of them, guiding them towards a cave at the foot of another hill, thirty or so yards away.

"Make for the cave!" boomed the Wayfinder's voice. "The Void won't enter the cave!"

"The Incompetent!" shrieked Oksa suddenly, glancing behind. "We forgot the Incompetent!"

Pavel stopped dead and, without a moment's hesitation, began running back up the hill he'd just come down.

"Dad!" screamed Oksa. "No! Don't go back!"

But Pavel had already gone. Abakum seized Oksa's hand and dragged her towards the cave as Pavel reached the top of the hill. The bone-idle Incompetent, true to form, hadn't budged an inch. Pavel snatched up the creature but, before retracing his steps, he couldn't help glancing at the landscape and blanched immediately at the alarming sight: the gently undulating Maritime Hills were now tossing wildly as if whipped up by a terrible storm. Waves of soil and vegetation were thrown against the sky, which turned frighteningly dark as the Void gained ground. It was as if the landscape wanted to muster all possible resistance against this unstoppable force. It was a futile battle though: the Void was inescapable, devouring every living thing with a monstrous roar.

"DAD! QUICK!"

Oksa's urgent tone distracted Pavel from this apocalyptic sight. Roused from his daze, he whirled round and raced down the hill, leaping over the heather, terror lending him strength. The Runaways were now all safe in the cave and were waiting for him at the entrance, distraught with anxiety.

"Dad! Hurry!" screamed Oksa, wringing her hands.

The Void was gaining on Pavel and the Incompetent. Oksa's father dashed forward in a final spurt of energy, his back burning so badly that it felt like it was about to burst into flame. Oksa kept her eyes on her father in an agony of fear, when suddenly she thought she was seeing things: long dragon wings had just sprouted from his back. It only took four beats of the outspread, blazing wings for Pavel to reach the cave, watched incredulously by his daughter, then his wings resumed their tattooed outline and he skidded uncontrollably inside. A few seconds later, the mouth of the cave was shrouded in darkness. The roar stopped and an icy breath of air invaded the refuge of the Runaways.

21

An Instructive Discussion

With a deep sigh, Dragomira carefully placed a wooden tube inside the small secret alcove in the wall and closed it. Two weeks before, Pavel and Oksa had allowed themselves to be Impictured with their loyal friends to help Gus. A risky undertaking whose outcome no one could predict.

"It's been so long," sighed Baba Pollock again. "I miss them so much…"

The Lunatrix came over and stood in front of his mistress, shifting from one foot to the other.

"The Old Gracious must preserve faith in her heart," he said in his shrill little voice. "The Young Gracious will experience extreme adventures, but the company of the Runaways will procure her protection and aid. And the father of the Young Gracious—alias the son of the Old Gracious—will be the one to beget the most unexpected and influential strength."

"Dear Pavel," whispered Dragomira, looking at her Lunatrix sceptically. "He was so reluctant to go along with our decision!"

"Reluctance does not prevent belief from being securely fastened," said the Lunatrix. Dragomira looked at him attentively and, with a sad smile, nodded.

"I like your comments, my dear Lunatrix. They're always enigmatic but, when you work out what they mean, you realize they're always accurate."

"The Lunatrixes possess the awareness of the truth residing in all Gracious hearts, so the Old Gracious can rest all her confidence on her obedient Lunatrixes."

"I shall do exactly that," Dragomira assured him.

"Nonetheless, the Old Gracious must have the information that Felony is on the prowl. Danger is not only situated within the interior of the picture, but also on the exterior. Friends are deceiving the Old Gracious and wish to take possession of the picture in order to lay hands on the Young Gracious when she emerges."

"Friends?" asked Dragomira in amazement, the blood draining from her face. "What friends?"

"The Old Gracious has the knowledge that her Lunatrix does not know. The Lunatrix does not know, he senses. The picture will sustain the violent covetousness of the Felons, it is imperative to protect it."

Dragomira directed a worried glance at the hidden alcove in the wall.

"No one will find this hiding place—no one!" she declared, trembling.

"The Felons possess cunning," replied the Lunatrix. "Cunning and cruelty which make them mightier than the Runaways and the Old Gracious."

Dragomira sank into a purple velvet armchair and began thinking hard, her head tilted to one side and her eyes half-closed. She groaned, upset by the Lunatrix's revelations. The creatures and plants in her private workroom stopped what they were doing and held their breath to avoid breaking the old lady's train of thought. Only the Ptitchkins—her tiny golden birds—flew over and perched on her shoulder, where they stayed without moving a feather. An hour later, Dragomira roused herself from her reverie and leapt up. The Goranov, which had been watching her all that time, jumped with a loud rustle of its leaves.

"I'd imagine we're in great danger if the Old Gracious is in this state," remarked the stressed plant. "We're all going to die!"

"Stop frightening everyone, you freak!" mocked a dishevelled creature.

"Be quiet, Getorix!" retorted the Goranov. "I'm the one in the front line!"

"In the front line for what?" sniggered the hairy creature. "In the front line for complaining, that's for sure!"

"You seem to forget that I'm a valuable plant!" said the Goranov, its leaves quivering with annoyance. "Without me, there'd be no Granok-Shooters, no Caskinettes, no Crucimaphila and no Werewall Elixir!"

Dragomira gave a start.

"What did you just say?" she asked eagerly, leaning towards the Goranov.

"Without me, there'd be no Granok-Shooters, no Caskinettes, no Crucimaphila and no Werewall Elixir!" repeated the Goranov, shaking its leaves harder and harder. "The production of that vile potion is what led to the largest sacrifice of Goranovs of all time, and don't you forget it! The Werewalls were nowhere near as careful as the Granokologists, who've always milked us gently and considerately. No!" screamed the Goranov, angrily flapping its foliage. "Instead of milking us, those Werewall monsters made incisions in our stems—deep incisions from which some of us never recovered! I don't want to go through that again. Ever!"

And the poor plant fainted, as all its leaves went limp and collapsed along its main stem. Dragomira went to find a small spray bottle which she used on each of the Goranov's leaves.

"Is that a new remedy, Old Gracious?" asked the Getorix, casually lifting a leaf which immediately sagged again.

"Yes," confirmed Dragomira. "Haltocollapsus, very effective in dealing with our dear Goranov's fainting fits."

"You look worried, Old Gracious," continued the Getorix, sticking its nose in the small bottle.

Dragomira nodded.

"I am, Getorix, I am. The Goranov isn't known for its moderation, but its extreme behaviour always has some basis in reality. And what it just said makes a great deal of sense: it's a key ingredient in all our secret formulas. And those made by our enemies, which is why we have a problem. What it said about the Werewall Elixir is also something I hadn't taken into consideration. The Goranov is the most powerful particle catalyst in existence. Do you understand what that means?"

"Absolutely, Old Gracious," replied the Getorix, the hair on its small head standing on end.

"In this house, we have four indescribably important treasures: the picture, the Lunatrix, who is the Guardian of the Definitive Landmark, Malorane's medallion and the Goranov. They possess great power, but they also make us extremely vulnerable…"

Saying this, she hurried towards the narrow staircase leading down to her apartment. She walked through the double-bass case, placed her hand against its plywood back and the case closed on the spiral staircase, hiding the entrance to her private workroom. With an impatient gesture, she swept all the clutter off the huge table at the back of the apartment and set to work.

22

TUMBLE-BAWLER REPORTING!

SETTLED COMFORTABLY IN HER ARMCHAIR OPPOSITE THE window, Dragomira was watching the square like a hawk, and it wasn't long before her wait was rewarded: three figures crossed the street and headed for the house. Night had fallen some time ago and the pavement was illuminated by the weak light of the street lamps, which left the façade in darkness.

"You didn't waste any time," Baba Pollock said softly.

She stood up, opened the double-bass case and walked in, a strange smile on her lips.

"Hoist with their own petard…" she said, closing the case behind her.

The three figures slipped furtively between the bushes dotted around the lawn in front of the small flight of steps leading up to the front door and flattened themselves against the wall.

"Are you sure Dragomira isn't in?" whispered one of the intruders, a tall, thin man.

"Absolutely sure!" replied a plumper figure. "She's with Abakum, and Marie Pollock is spending the night at Jeanne Bellanger's house with young Zoe. Don't forget my information comes from a reliable source."

"We couldn't ask for a better informant!" added the third person who, from her voice and curvaceous silhouette, was clearly a woman. "No one else could have got closer to them."

"If everything goes according to plan, Dragomira won't know what's hit her!" All three cackled with satisfaction.

"Come on, let's not waste time mocking poor Dragomira and her naïve friends for their imminent misfortune," continued the fat man. "It's time to go. Don't forget our future depends on this mission!"

The two men and the woman each drew from their pockets a small box from which they took a pearly white capsule, which they swallowed. A few seconds later they were climbing like spiders up the stone façade, hands and feet pressed firmly against the red bricks. When they arrived at the third floor, they stopped, and the thinner man crouched on the windowsill. Then, as if by magic, his body passed through the glass and disappeared inside the apartment.

※

Through a tiny chink, Dragomira exultantly watched the three figures break in. Her trap was working like a dream.

"Have you found anything?" asked one of the men.

"My mother told me the canvas would be rolled inside a wooden tube. As it's around fifteen inches long and four inches in diameter, it won't be easy to hide, so we should be able to find it..."

The three burglars snooped around the cluttered apartment, lifting cushions, opening drawers, feeling below and behind the furniture, until a particularly creaky floorboard attracted their attention.

"My friends, I think I've found it," said the woman triumphantly.

"Under the floorboards?" exclaimed the tall, thin man incredulously. "That isn't very original!"

"Yes, you'd have expected better from a woman like Dragomira. She must have had what they call a senior moment!" sniggered the sturdy man. "Come on, let's pull up this board and see what she's hiding."

All three grappled with the floorboards and, a few seconds later, pulled out a long wooden tube.

"Bingo!" whispered the woman, checking the contents. "Either we're very clever, or too much has been made of Dragomira's reputation!"

"Whatever the case, it's good news for us," concluded the tall man. "Anyway, let's not hang around."

The three intruders headed for the window and left the same way they'd come in, hands and feet adhering to the brick façade. From her window, Dragomira watched them disappear into the square and gave a sigh of satisfaction, pretending to clap.

※

Two days later, the Tumble-Bawler tapped at the skylight in his mistress's private workroom. The old lady pushed back her chair and got up to let the creature in.

"Back already, my dear Tumble?" she said, stroking it affectionately in welcome.

Although breathless, the Tumble-Bawler purred with obvious pleasure like a kitten.

"I'm so glad you're back," said Dragomira. "You must have so much to tell me!"

"I certainly do, my Old Gracious," confirmed the small creature. "But I fear the news isn't good."

"I was afraid of that, Tumble-Bawler, I was afraid of that…" nodded Dragomira, with a grave expression.

"Here's my report, my Old Gracious. The three intruders were two men and a woman. I was able to find out the men's names: the taller one is Gregor and the stockier one, Oskar. We left London by car and drove 387 miles, north-north-west, to reach the Scottish coast bordering the Sea of the Hebrides. We then boarded a boat to sail to an island eleven miles from the shore, latitude fifty-seven degrees north, longitude seven degrees west. I must remind my Old Gracious that I was shut inside the tube stolen by the intruders and that, as a result, I could only hear snatches of conversation between the three burglars. In addition, my Old Gracious knows I suffer from travel sickness. Such a long journey by car, followed by the boat trip over the Sea of the Hebrides with strong north-south currents, caused terrible bouts of sickness. I'm afraid I threw up in the tube, my Old Gracious."

Dragomira didn't seem unduly worried by this. She snorted with laughter and carried on stroking the Tumble-Bawler.

"So how did you manage to escape their notice?" she asked.

"When the pitching of the boat stopped at last," continued the small creature, "the villainous trio walked to a stone building standing 2,438 feet from where the boat had been moored. The woman, who was carrying the tube in which I was hidden, went up three steps, then crossed an entrance hall that measured twenty feet and one inch long by twelve feet and six inches wide. We came to a room and I sensed a fire burning in a hearth that was six feet and ten inches high by seven feet and six inches wide. Another woman was waiting for them there with three men. I couldn't hear clearly what they were saying, because I still felt sick. But they all seemed very pleased. They opened the tube and I was afraid my last hour had come, since everyone could immediately smell my vomit and they all complained about the stench. However, they were only really interested in the picture, which they extracted very carefully from the tube. They were so engrossed in what they were about to find that I was able to escape unseen from the tube that the woman had put on the table: I hid in a corner of the room, unable to see straight because of my awful travel sickness, and I must say I got out just in the nick of time because Oskar picked up the tube to see if he could work out how the picture could have become soiled. They immediately began looking around. 'There has to be something here! Look everywhere!' cried the woman. I stayed hidden behind a curtain where I could hear everything, even though I couldn't see much, all the while looking for a way out of the house. Suddenly there was a loud scream and one of the women said: 'What's the matter, Mother?' The other woman shouted: 'She's tricked us! Dragomira has played us for fools! This isn't the picture!' Oskar, who was standing just sixteen inches from me, although he didn't know that, roared: 'What do you mean?' The woman replied:

"'Look, it's a copy! It was obviously all too easy! That old shrew suspected something… She outwitted us… Aaargh!' Angrily, she took hold of the wooden tube and threw it ten feet and six inches towards the northern corner of the room. Suddenly the curtain concealing me was thrown open and I found myself face to face with Gregor, the tall, thin man. I mustered all my courage and flew towards the door, which was more than seventeen feet and seven inches away. 'Catch it! Don't let it escape!' yelled the other woman. They all came chasing after me. I flew away frantically, my wings aching badly, battling another terrible bout of sickness. I found myself in the entrance hall, where I detected a draught travelling thirty miles an hour, west-south-west, from another room. At the same time, my unwelcoming hosts fired Granoks at me and the woman who seemed to be their leader almost killed me with a Knock-Bong which sent me crashing against the south wall of the entrance hall. I think it was the fear of being caught and my loyalty to my Old Gracious that saved me. I swiftly flew into the room where the draught was coming from and found an air vent, around three inches in diameter, which was barely wide enough for me to crawl into. I had only just squeezed my whole body inside when I sensed an extremely violent blast of air travelling at a speed of at least 140 miles an hour: that hideous woman had just fired a Tornaphyllon Granok at me! Luckily I was already in the ventilation shaft, from which I emerged twelve seconds later. Then I took to my wings and flew back as fast as I could, my Old Gracious. I'm ashamed that I didn't complete my mission. Will you forgive me for not providing exact details, my Old Gracious?"

"Of course, Tumble," nodded Dragomira, a strange smile on her lips. "You've done excellently, absolutely excellently. Tell me, were you able to see who that woman was?"

"My Old Gracious, despite my nauseous condition, the identity of the Felon woman didn't escape me," confirmed the small creature.

"Will you tell me her name?"

The Tumble-Bawler looked around, gazed for a moment at all the creatures, which were hanging on its every word, and wobbled its plump body from side to side in embarrassment. It seemed to think carefully, narrowing its small bright eyes, and at last reached a decision. It flew over to Dragomira's shoulder, where it landed gently and murmured a single name in her ear. Baba Pollock went white and, placing her hand over her heart, gave a hoarse groan.

23

DRAGOMIRA'S OLD FRIEND

THE VALIANT TUMBLE-BAWLER HAD BARELY DONE TELL-ing Dragomira about its adventure in the Sea of the Hebrides when three people silently forced open the front door of the Pollocks' house. Dragomira wasn't surprised: she'd been expecting this visit, not least because, from her window, she'd seen people taking turns to watch Bigtoe Square since the middle of the afternoon. When it was dark, the spies had abandoned any attempt at discretion and three of them had taken up position near the front door to prevent anyone from going in or coming out. Since early evening, Dragomira had been alone in the house with Marie, who was asleep in her bedroom on the second floor below. It had been decided that Zoe would help Jeanne at the restaurant, so she was safe. Dragomira had turned out all the lights, so she could see the three figures on the pavement facing the house more clearly. Then she'd descended the narrow spiral staircase and carefully closed the double-bass case fixed to the wall. Lighting a black wax candle, Dragomira had then settled down in an armchair covered in old gold satin. With her legs crossed and her hands flat on the armrests, she'd waited, her resolve strengthened by her anger.

In no time at all, two women rushed into Baba Pollock's apartment, followed by a tall, thin man with a craggy face. All three blinked, surprised by the subdued lighting. The room was so cluttered with furniture, occasional tables, coffee tables, armchairs, pictures and knick-knacks that they didn't know where to look first. The unsettling effect of the chaotic décor was only emphasized by the dim, flickering light of the candle. The man took out his Granok-Shooter.

"I'll shed some light on this mess," he announced.

"Don't bother!" boomed Dragomira's voice, making them jump. The three visitors were bathed in the sudden light from the glowing tentacles of a Polypharus, while Dragomira remained in protective darkness.

"So it is you," observed Dragomira in a flat voice to the woman standing in the middle of the trio. "My dear old friend… I didn't want to believe it. I wanted to give you the benefit of the doubt, give you a chance to deny the incriminating facts. Why, Mercedica? Why?"

The tall, grim-looking woman with dark hair raised her chin even more haughtily and looked towards the back of the room, where Dragomira's voice was coming from.

"My dear Dragomira," she remarked drily. "You talk about facts, but do you know what they really are? You're so naïve sometimes… you still think life is all sweetness and light, don't you?"

"It's a long time since I lost my illusions, Mercedica," retorted Dragomira. "If you remember, I was thirteen when I watched Ocious murder my mother."

"Speaking of Ocious," said Mercedica spitefully, "allow me to introduce you to his grandson, Gregor—Orthon's eldest son!"

Dragomira's face crumpled in the darkness. Her hands tensed on her armrests and she shivered. In her mind's eye, she saw Orthon-McGraw again being vaporized in the cellar by the Crucimaphila and the memory reopened old physical and mental wounds. Gregor gazed at her with a cruel, chilly indifference, which didn't bode well for her. He looked very much like his father: the same frosty expression, the same tall, dark figure, the same impression of strength and power. The old lady flinched and tried to suppress a surge of resentment.

"Even if you haven't seen her for a long time," continued the formidable Spanish woman, "you must have recognized my daughter, Catarina."

Dragomira looked at the young woman standing next to Mercedica. She'd changed a great deal since they'd last met two or three years ago. Her hard, pitiless face was completely at odds with her feminine appearance—huge eyes fringed by thick lashes, luxuriant hair cascading over her shoulders and a natural elegance, clearly inherited from her mother.

"She's the image of you. In all respects, I should imagine," remarked Dragomira sarcastically. "Well, I can't for one minute believe this is a social visit," she added, speaking directly to her onetime friend, who was now her enemy.

"You can believe whatever you like," retorted Mercedica with a shrill laugh. "But I'm politely asking you to give me the picture, Dragomira!"

With these words she walked towards the back of the room, where Dragomira stiffened in her armchair, still shrouded in shadow. Baba Pollock was seething with rage at her former friend—and at herself. How could she have been so blind to Mercedica's treachery? How long had she been fooling her? Whatever the answer, the Spanish woman had clearly played her cards very close to her chest: no one had noticed anything. Not even cynical Leomido or intuitive Abakum.

"Why are you doing this, Mercedica? Why?" groaned Dragomira, filled with bitter disappointment at this betrayal.

Mercedica sighed in exasperation, which Dragomira found even more hurtful. Narrowing her dark, heavily made-up eyes, she replied defiantly:

"I chose the other side, Dragomira. The winning side."

"What do you mean?" asked Baba Pollock.

"I don't have the same ambitions as you and your friends, that's all!" said Mercedica scathingly.

"My friends were your friends not so long ago…"

"Can people be friends when they have so little in common?" retorted the Spanish woman. "My friends—my *true* friends, I should say—are the people with whom I share the same aims and the same world view. Which are nothing like those you and your cronies hold so dear. A case in point is the answer you gave our darling Oksa when she asked why the Runaways didn't set off immediately for Edefia, do you remember? She didn't understand why you were waiting and your main argument was that you weren't physically ready to leave because of your age. I'm sure you had something else in mind, something much more fundamental: all of you have such wild hopes for the future, but deep down you know how pathetic they are. You know hope isn't enough. You know you'll be completely out of your depth when you find out what's waiting for you in Edefia. And you're right! Me, I prefer to stick with the strongest side. That way I'm bound to win!"

"WIN WHAT?" thundered Dragomira.

"Win what? You still have to ask? Power and wealth, my dear Dragomira! Power, Dragomira, power! Do you remember what we left behind in Edefia? Do you realize our innate potential? Haven't you given any thought to our vast superiority?"

"You're like them..." murmured Dragomira.

"Of course I am!" cried Mercedica. "And I'm proud of it. I'm proud to belong to such a strong group of people!"

"But why do you want more? Haven't you got enough?"

"Life on the Outside has taught me never to be satisfied with what I've got," replied Mercedica curtly, sidling closer.

"While I feel exactly the opposite!" retorted Dragomira, standing up. "Don't come any closer, Mercedica!"

Despite this warning, the formidable Spanish woman kept advancing, her arm outstretched. Her fingertips crackled with thin, bluish sparks which she was about to hurl at the gold armchair. But Dragomira was faster and, to the great surprise of her three unwanted guests, she aimed an unexpectedly violent Knock-Bong at Mercedica, who was thrown against the wall at the far end of the room. The impact was so hard that the hairpins fastening her impeccable bun flew off in all directions. Long strands of black hair escaped, partially concealing Mercedica's face. Catarina rushed over to her unconscious mother, while Gregor launched himself with the supple grace of a cat at the dark corner where Dragomira was standing. Baba Pollock had no time to react and was hit head-on by Orthon-McGraw's son. His speed and weight sent them both flying backwards. Immobilizing Dragomira with his thighs, Gregor leant over to grab her wrists and, bringing his face close to hers, hissed:

"Mercedica is right, you're completely out of your depth and you know it! Give us the picture, the real one this time. Spare yourself unnecessary pain and, just maybe, a pointless death…"

Dragomira couldn't help trembling with fear as much as disgust at this cruel man who looked so much like his father. In her mind's eye, she saw young Orthon again. The memory of the affectionate, vulnerable boy he'd once been flashed before her eyes fleetingly, like a mirage, then disappeared.

"You wouldn't dare…" she ventured.

Gregor gave a frightening snigger.

"Why not? You dared order your flunkey to kill my father, didn't you!" he said, his voice even harder.

"How…" said Dragomira, sounding choked. "How did you know…"

"How did I know it wasn't you who killed him?" murmured the Felon, completing her sentence. "Why don't you guess? It's more fun like that, isn't it? Don't forget we don't need you. It's the girl we need, not an old witch whose powers are a distant memory."

Beside herself with rage, Dragomira made a superhuman effort to roll over despite Gregor's weight and strong grip. The surprised Felon suddenly found himself thrown against the work table, bringing a large number of glass jars and metal utensils crashing down on his head. Dragomira stood up quickly and, seizing her Granok-Shooter, fired a Granok at Gregor which caused him to whimper with fear: the Felon's hand had just been hit by a Putrefactio. He barely had time to realize what had happened before the flesh started to rot.

"Take that from the old witch!" snarled Dragomira triumphantly.

While Gregor was writhing on the ground in pain and Mercedica was gradually regaining consciousness, Catarina decided to attack, hitting Dragomira in the chest with a Tornaphyllon Granok. The tiny, powerful tornado imprisoned her and spun her around, causing her to collide with everything. The furniture, walls and even the smallest objects became weapons against her. Unable to halt the raging wind, she banged into the corner of tables, cut herself on shards of glass from the pictures she shattered as she whirled past and hurt herself trying to hold on to anything within reach. Mustering all her strength, she tried to counteract the violent wind by making her body spin in the opposite direction. "The human top," she thought, remembering Oksa's favourite manoeuvre. The effects of the Tornaphyllon quickly diminished but, unfortunately, Mercedica had been the first to notice: she pounced on Dragomira and slammed her against the wall with such force that Baba Pollock felt as though her body had left a dent in the plaster. Every bone hurt and she groaned at the excruciating pain and her helplessness. Mercedica pinned Dragomira's hands against the wall and pushed against her even harder, as if she wanted to crush her. Poor Baba Pollock saw Catarina coming, her expression even chillier than ever, along with a scornful, evil-looking Gregor. The sight of the latter made her panic even more: the wound caused by the Putrefactio a few minutes ago was disappearing! All that remained was a faint scabbed scar on the smug Felon's arm, which he waved under Dragomira's nose.

"Surprise, surprise!" he hissed and, as his dark eyes bored into hers, he added:

"I must admit that Granok was very painful, but it was worth suffering for a few unpleasant seconds to see such a look of confusion and panic on your face. Aha! Dragomira Pollock… don't tell me you've forgotten who I am! The blood of my ancestor Temistocles flows in my veins and you must know what that means and what an incomparable advantage it gives me and my family over every last one of you. In any case, you know now…"

His eyes fixed on Dragomira, he cackled jubilantly. Suddenly a creaking sound was heard. They all turned to look: the double-bass case had just opened, allowing the Lunatrix's little round head to peer out.

Dragomira stiffened under Mercedica's pressure and couldn't help crying out:

"NO!"

"Oh yes, my dear Dragomira!" retorted Gregor.

Seeing his mistress being held against her will, the Lunatrix rushed out of his hiding place, brandishing his little fists.

"The Old Gracious allocated an order, you do not have the power to bypass it!" he yelled, his face ashen.

By way of a reply, Gregor stretched his hand out in front of him and aimed a merciless Knock-Bong at the Lunatrix. The small creature was thrown against an occasional table, his head smacking violently against its steel base.

He gave a muffled cry and collapsed unconscious on the ground.

"We must take him with us, Gregor," said Mercedica. "He's the Guardian of the Definitive Landmark!" Dragomira struggled frantically, but to no avail—Mercedica's hold was too strong.

Gregor went over to the Lunatrix and was just bending down to pick up the little creature when the two tiny Ptitchkins flew out of the back of the apartment and swooped down on the Felon. Positioning themselves by each ear, they squeezed inside and began relentlessly pecking at his ear canals. Gregor put his hands over his ears, distracted by the terrible pain. Regaining consciousness, the Lunatrix leapt to his feet and, taking advantage of the prevailing confusion, fled the apartment.

"Aaargh!" cursed Mercedica. "That's too bad. We don't have time to go looking for him now, the Knuts will be here soon and I'd rather have finished before they get back... We might not have the Guardian of the Landmark, but we'll at least have this!" she said triumphantly, snatching Malorane's medallion from Dragomira's neck.

"It won't be of any use to you!" raged Baba Pollock, her face twisted in pain. Mercedica's face contorted in a small, cruel laugh.

"Don't worry, dear Dragomira, I'll use it advisedly. And now, I'll tell you one last time: give us the picture!"

"NEVER!" screamed Dragomira.

"We'll find it with or without your help, believe you me!" threatened the Spanish woman.

"You'll never find it!" continued Dragomira. "It isn't here."

The three Felons seemed taken aback by this possibility. Mercedica looked at Gregor with a frown. Then, brushing away a strand of hair with her manicured fingers, she challenged her captive:

"You're bluffing! We've been watching your every move since Impicturement. The picture hasn't left this house, I'm certain of it."

"There's no such thing as a definite certainty," remarked Dragomira, glaring at her.

"Dragomira? What's going on up there?" called a voice suddenly. "Dragomira?"

A wheelchair-bound Marie Pollock was calling out to her mother-in-law from the floor below. Dragomira caught a look from Mercedica and her face crumpled when she realized what the Felon woman had just decided.

"Catarina, would you please go and reassure our friend Marie, while Gregor finds what we're looking for?" asked Mercedica triumphantly.

Dragomira just had time to see Gregor disappear through the back of the double-bass case before a violent blow plunged her into darkness.

24

AN UNUSUAL HIDING PLACE

WHILE THE FELON GREGOR WAS RANSACKING Dragomira's private workroom, Oksa Pollock's friend Merlin Poicassé was glancing nervously at the hermetically sealed tube that Oksa's gran had given him. No one would guess that the ordinary-looking wooden object on his desk contained something so important or that the lives of several people, including Oksa, depended on the canvas rolled up inside! She was so amazing. His heart raced when she gazed at him with her slate-grey eyes... she was the prettiest girl he'd ever seen. The prettiest, fieriest and most magical—he probably wouldn't ever meet anyone like her again in his whole life. From the first day he'd seen her, looking uncomfortable in her school uniform, he'd realized she wasn't like everybody else. After observing her covertly for months, he'd become convinced that she possessed magic powers—which she'd eventually, and reluctantly, admitted. However, despite Gus's warnings, she'd never had any reason to regret telling him the Pollocks' secret: he'd never breathed a word to anyone. He'd never referred to it in public and had never dropped any cryptic hints. And, because of his discretion, Oksa and her family had come to trust him implicitly. He'd had clear proof of this a few hours ago when the phone had rung. He'd picked it up and had been surprised to recognize the voice of Dragomira Pollock, Oksa's extraordinary gran. The old lady had seemed very anxious, breathing very fast and speaking very quietly, as if afraid of being overheard. Not that they had said anything incriminating—they'd just made small talk.

"I was tidying Oksa's room and I found a few books belonging to you," Dragomira had said. "Could I pop over and give them back? You might need them over the summer and Oksa has already gone on holiday."

"Books belonging to me?" Merlin had asked, remembering that Oksa hadn't mentioned any planned holidays.

"Yes!" Dragomira had said urgently. "May I bring them over? I have to visit a friend who lives near you."

"Er… yes, if you like," Merlin had agreed, guessing that Dragomira had something important to tell him.

Half an hour later, the old lady was nervously drinking a cup of tea in the Poicassés' living room. Merlin's parents were at work, so he was alone with the accomplished apothecary, who gave him chapter and verse about what had been happening over the past few days, from Gus's disappearance and the information from the Tumble-Bawler to the Impicturement of Oksa and the valiant Runaways. Merlin had been terrified by this awful news, but had immediately agreed to hide the wooden tube containing the rolled Imagicon.

"You're the only one who won't be suspected, my dear boy," she declared.

"Are you sure no one followed you?" Merlin had asked, trembling at the huge responsibility he'd just been given out of the blue.

"Positive!" Dragomira had assured him.

However, a few hours after she'd left, Merlin couldn't help wondering whether he was as anonymous as she'd believed. He twitched back his bedroom curtain and glanced outside, towards the terrace of the tearoom opposite. The man was still sitting there, drinking endless cups of coffee, his eyes glued to the front door of Merlin's house. He hadn't budged an inch for the past two hours. It might be a coincidence or a figment of Merlin's imagination after hearing the Pollocks' latest secrets, but he didn't really believe it: that man was definitely watching his house. He knew Dragomira had come. So what was he waiting for, sitting there, sipping coffee? If he wanted to steal the Imagicon, it would be very easy! He'd just have to break into the house, come upstairs to his bedroom, bash him over the head, tie him to a chair or kill him and it was job done.

Aaaarghhhhhh!

Merlin jumped, barely able to stifle a loud cry: someone had just rung the doorbell, which had never before sounded so scary. Instinctively he glanced out of the window.

"Oh no—I don't believe it!"

The man was no longer in the tearoom. He was obviously *waiting behind the door*, his finger jammed on the doorbell! Merlin was sure of it. He crept out onto the landing and glanced at the frosted-glass front door. It was filled with a massive silhouette from top to bottom. Merlin's legs buckled and perspiration beaded his forehead. He had to get out! He whirled round, stuffed the wooden tube into his backpack and dashed into the bathroom at the back of the house. Standing on the edge of the bath, he opened the small window overlooking the back garden and climbed through, his jaw clenched with fear. He was terrified of the empty drop below, but he soon had a more pressing problem, more frightening than a few feet of empty space below him: the man had just got into his house. Merlin could hear heavy footsteps climbing the stairs. If he found him, he'd take the picture and Oksa would be lost for ever! Merlin grabbed hold of the drainpipe and, using the gaps between the bricks as footholds, scrambled down the back of the building.

❉

"My son? Are you sure, Meredith?"

"Yes, sir, he's here in the lobby."

"I'll be right down!"

Edmund Poicassé threaded his way through the crowds of tourists on the staircases in the famous clock tower of Big Ben. Merlin's father was an intelligent, imposing man. He loved London so much that, in the space of just a few years, he'd almost forgotten he was French and saw himself as a true Londoner. He spoke perfect English with only the faintest trace of a French accent, and this only increased his popularity with colleagues and friends. As a result, when he saw his son waiting in the reception area, he spoke to him in English, which didn't faze Merlin, who was bilingual.

"Merlin, what are you doing here?" asked Edmund Poicassé in surprise.

"I've just come to pay my dear old dad a visit at work!" replied Merlin with feigned cheerfulness. "Believe it or not, I was getting bored, and I suddenly had an uncontrollable urge to see Big Ben. I haven't been here for ages..."

"I'm hardly going to complain about that, am I?" chuckled his father, tousling his curly hair.

"Will you take me to see the clock?"

"Of course I will, young man!"

With a wide smile, Edmund Poicassé guided his son through the maze of staircases leading up to the great bell. Merlin was still a little shaken up after his narrow escape, which had left his heart feeling like it had been put through a lemon squeezer. The tall, thin windows showed glimpses of London, Parliament, Westminster and St James's Park in the distance. And somewhere in those streets a man was looking for him... He fingered the wooden tube in his backpack. Dragomira had given him a huge responsibility. He thought about Oksa, trapped in the Imagicon. Never had she been so close to him—and her fate depended on him! He felt dizzy for a moment. He stopped climbing the stairs and clung to the railing.

"You okay?" asked his father.

"Yes, thanks, Dad."

He was very proud of his acting abilities because, although he sounded relaxed and cheerful, deep down he felt really agitated. After leaving the house, he'd set off like a marathon runner, his pace steady and regular, his thoughts all over the place. Where could he hide the Imagicon? In St Proximus? No way! That was far too obvious for the Felons. In the left-luggage office at the station? Not bad… but still too easy, maybe. He couldn't take any risks. "Of course!" he suddenly thought to himself. He'd then retraced his footsteps and headed straight for the Houses of Parliament. When he'd arrived at the foot of Big Ben, he'd looked up with a satisfied smile.

"Don't worry, Oksa," he'd murmured, patting his backpack. "No one will find you here!"

Big Ben was certainly one of the busiest tourist attractions in Great Britain, but Merlin had an advantage over hundreds of daily visitors: his father was a master clockmaker and, a few months ago, had been appointed to the sought-after position of custodian. This meant that he had access to rooms that were off-limits to everyone except him and the two other custodians.

"Will you be all right on your own for a few minutes, Merlin? I just have to check something with James!"

"I'll be fine, Dad, see you in a mo."

Merlin was now in the clock room, which was filled with huge toothed wheels. The hands of the most famous clock in the world could be seen through the small, opaque glass panes. Merlin opened one and leant out: the minute hand wasn't far away. He stood on tiptoe to open the window opposite it. "Aaargh!" he raged. He was too short. And not only was he too short but he had to act quickly too. His father was going to come back any minute and the hand was moving too slowly. Merlin began trembling, feeling panicky. He leant out again through the window he could reach: the hand was almost level with him. Just a few more seconds… He took out the wooden tube and undid his shoelace. The enormous wrought-iron hand was about to appear in the little window. Merlin tied the tube to the hand as it continued its slow journey, knotting the lace as tightly as he could. Then, overwrought and breathless, he watched the tube move away as the seconds ticked by.

"There you are, Oksa, no one will ever find you there," he murmured, closing the window. "I can promise you that!"

25

THE EXTENT
OF THE DAMAGE

WHEN NAFTALI AND BRUNE KNUT PARKED IN FRONT of the house in Bigtoe Square, they immediately realized something was wrong because the Lunatrix was leaning out of the third-floor window, wailing so loudly that any passer-by could have seen him, which went against every safety rule he'd obeyed for the past fifty years. Naftali and Brune frowned and dashed up to the house. The front door was half-open, which was also very strange. Particularly in these troubled times…

"The Swedish friends of the Old Gracious make a much-awaited arrival!" cried the Lunatrix, rushing downstairs. "Impatience and alarm have invaded the domestic staff of the Old Gracious."

"What's happened, Lunatrix?" asked Naftali gravely. "You look upset."

Brune picked up the small creature in her arms. The Lunatrix was trembling and his teeth were chattering. He wrapped his long arms around the old lady's neck and clung to her.

"The Felons have made the institution of terror in this house!" he wailed shrilly. "They have provoked catastrophe in the apartment of the Old Gracious. Their determination to seize the Imagicon has been thwarted because the Old Gracious was overflowing with suspicions and organized its escape."

"Dragomira! Dragomira! What have you done?" muttered Naftali to himself.

"The hiding place of the Imagicon holds supreme safety since only the Old Gracious has knowledge of the identity of its custodian. But the tragedy of this household is complete, boohoohoo..." sobbed the Lunatrix. "The Felons have demonstrated the cruelty that has embraced their hearts, and the Old Gracious has encountered injury. Her Swedish friends must climb to the rescue!"

Naftali immediately ran upstairs. Brune followed at a slower pace, weighed down by the Lunatrix in her arms.

"What about Marie?" she asked the small creature.

The Lunatrix dissolved into tears and buried his round head in Brune's neck.

"The mother of the Young Gracious has sustained tragedy."

"What?" cried Brune in alarm. "Don't tell me she's—*dead?*"

"No!" cried the Lunatrix. "The mother of the Young Gracious has not encountered death. But the Felons have performed a kidnapping. The mother of the Young Gracious has been taken!"

Brune wailed in astonishment.

"That can't be true! Tell me it isn't true, Lunatrix!" she cried, gazing at the small creature in despair.

"My mouth only makes broadcast of the truth. If the Old Gracious gains knowledge of the event, her heart is at risk of stopping its beating. Boohoohoo... The Runaways are shrouded in tragedy... Thanks to the help of the Ptitchkins, the Lunatrix Guardian of the Definitive Landmark encountered success in performing evasion, but it was by the chin of his teeth."

"Skin... you mean skin of your teeth!" chirped the little golden birds, flying around Brune. Struggling to make sense of all this information, Brune joined her husband in Dragomira's apartment. The large living room was a complete mess—there was smashed glass and broken furniture everywhere. The frantic search by the Felons hadn't left a single object intact or a single armchair undamaged. Dragomira was lying on one of the ripped sofas with a nasty red welt around her neck, bruises all over her face and a black eye. She looked completely devastated. Naftali was sitting dejectedly beside her.

"Brune," murmured Baba Pollock, stretching out her arm towards her old friend. "Mercedica… it was Mercedica…"

Puzzled and concerned, Brune looked first at Dragomira, then Naftali. What did Dragomira mean? No way! Mercedica couldn't have had anything to do with this chaos. But Naftali nodded, confirming the awful truth.

"Mercedica de La Fuente belongs to Felony!" declared the Lunatrix. "With the company of her descendant named Catarina and the son of the Felon Orthon-McGraw named Gregor, they showered acts of aggression on the Old Gracious and committed theft of her medallion and the Goranov!"

Naftali buried his face in his hands and Brune, her head reeling, collapsed onto a wobbly chair.

"Those scumbags," groaned Naftali. "They had everything planned."

"If only I'd been more observant!" wailed Dragomira. "Mercedica has always been uncompromising, she'd never change her mind about things and I'd noticed she'd become even more inflexible over the last few months. She seemed tenser and, on several occasions, harsher than I'd ever known her to be. I should have paid more attention and listened to my doubts."

"You can't blame yourself, Dragomira," said Brune. "How could you have known she was a Felon? She was an old friend who'd been through so many hard times with you, a woman who'd sworn loyalty to your mother, Malorane!"

"That's true," agreed Dragomira bitterly, overcome with sadness. "But I should have realized. I should have noticed the signs!"

"Mercedica knew we were going to Abakum's house this evening to tighten security," added Brune. "She made the most of it to let her 'friends' in. She really pulled the wool over our eyes."

"If I ever see her again, I don't think much for her chances, I can promise you that!" thundered Naftali, his green eyes bright with fury.

"I'm so sorry, my friends," whispered Dragomira.

"This isn't your fault!" repeated Brune, hurriedly taking her hand.

"What about Marie?" asked Dragomira faintly.

Brune gnawed at her bottom lip and glanced despairingly at Naftali. She squeezed her friend's hand even more tightly in hers.

"They've taken her, haven't they?" asked Dragomira, her voice breaking.

Brune gazed at her mutely with tears in her eyes. Dragomira groaned and her face crumpled as her last shred of hope vanished. Baba Pollock's strength deserted her—she was physically and mentally spent. Her head lolled against Brune's arm and she began crying with worry and remorse.

"It's all my fault," she sobbed. "I thought I could tackle them alone… I'm just a stupid, pathetic old woman."

Holding back her tears, Brune interrupted her:

"The Lunatrix told me everything, your instincts were spot on: by hiding the Imagicon, you avoided a huge catastrophe. But you couldn't prevent everything. I would have done the same as you, you know."

"Where is it, Dragomira? Where's the picture?" asked Naftali as gently as he could, despite his fury.

"Naftali, Dragomira can't tell us," replied Brune. Naftali and Dragomira looked at her in amazement.

"She mustn't tell us," continued Brune. "It's the only way to make sure she isn't killed. If she's the only one who knows where it is, the Felons can't do anything to hurt her and, anyway, it's a good way of ensuring our own safety."

"You're right, my dear Brune," murmured Dragomira.

"On the other hand, I'm afraid that Marie will only be used as a bargaining counter now," said Naftali. "Those scumbags couldn't ask for a better way of putting pressure on us. And we know what they're going to ask."

"To swap Marie for Oksa…" groaned Dragomira, putting her face in her hands.

"They don't know us very well!" growled Naftali. "The Felons have an advantage over us today, a sizeable advantage, certainly. But so long as we have Oksa, the ball is in our court. This may have weakened us, but we're still in a position of strength. Oksa represents the supreme power and even the fiercest Felon can't match our Last Hope. Hold on to that thought, Dragomira."

26

CONFIDENCES IN THE CAVE

THERE WAS A DEATHLY SILENCE. THE MOUTH OF THE cave was now blocked by a dark, roiling mass. The Runaways stared at this frightening phenomenon, shocked by what they'd just experienced.

"If anyone had told me I'd be pursued by the Void one day, I wouldn't have believed them," whispered Oksa. "Brrrr, it gives you the shivers!"

She looked round for her father, who was crouching in the darkest corner of the cave, his arms wrapped around his knees, his face hidden. He gave a quiet groan, which all the Runaways heard. They gazed at Oksa, and Abakum put his hand on her shoulder, murmuring:

"Go to him, Oksa. Go to your father."

Oksa looked at him doubtfully, but walked over to Pavel. She slid down the rough wall of the cave to a sitting position beside him. Without looking at her, Pavel put his arm round her shoulders and squeezed hard, inviting her to lay her head on his shoulder.

"Dad, what's happening to you?" she whispered after a while. "That was your Ink Dragon, wasn't it?"

Pavel tensed, surprised at hearing Oksa speak openly about something he'd kept hidden for so many years. Then again, Oksa had a talent for uncovering secrets. She was a real expert, in fact... He sighed.

"My Ink Dragon has always been there," he said, sounding resigned as he tightened his embrace. "I suppressed it for years and, in the end, it took refuge deep inside me where it lurked, silent and unmoving. But I can't control it any more."

"Is it a real dragon, then?" asked Oksa.

"You've seen it with your own eyes," said her father. "You already know, don't you, that an elderly monk initiated me into the secrets of the martial arts when I was in China? I lived with him on the mountain for months. He was my master and I was his student. I realized from day one that he knew about my origins and the depth of my suffering. For ages, I wondered if he was a Runaway too, but we never felt any need to talk about it—it wouldn't have changed anything. After a difficult period during which I couldn't find any answers to the many questions that plagued me, that venerable monk offered to give me a tattoo. I was taken aback and I told him I wasn't keen. Naturally, this was a special tattoo—which was no big surprise given the magical nature of my master's teachings. Its purpose was to gather my worries in one place, instead of allowing them to run riot, as they'd been doing up until then, poisoning my heart and soul. In some respects, it was a way of dealing with my darkest thoughts and of staying in control by transforming my pain and suffering into a form of energy combining will with power. You, Oksa, are much stronger than I was at that age: you can handle your powers."

"Um… not always!" broke in Oksa, thinking back to certain episodes.

"The big difference between you and the young man I was," continued Pavel, "is that you're not afraid. Being a descendant of the Runaways doesn't frighten you. As far as I'm concerned, you know, it feels more like a problem than—how shall I put it—a *motivation?*"

This wasn't the first time that her father had mentioned how difficult it had been for him, but Oksa couldn't help asking:

"Are you afraid of what you are then?"

"I'm not sure I'm ready to talk about it," replied her father, looking embarrassed. "Let's just say that I'm growing less afraid as time goes by… the appearance of my Ink Dragon is proof of that."

"It also means you're becoming a great sorcerer, Dad!" added Oksa, nudging him.

"You mean a monster!" retorted Pavel with a bitter laugh.

"Oh stop it, I'm so proud I've got a father like you!" cried Oksa. "It means I can tell people: 'Yes, my father's a direct descendant of the Gracious of Edefia and has a dragon living inside him... you should see his *ma-gni-fic-ent* pair of wings! Yes, I know, he is pretty *extra-ordi-nary*,'" she continued, pretending to stick her nose in the air.

Pavel laughed openly this time and tousled his daughter's tangled hair. Oksa was delighted to see he was looking more relaxed.

"I certainly have to keep my end up with a daughter like you!" he said with a wink. "I can't let myself slide into mediocrity without running the risk of being disowned by my own child. I may have gone a little overboard, but you can't be afraid of making grand gestures if you want to keep up to the mark."

"Mockery is eternal in the mouth of the father of the Young Gracious," declared the Lunatrixa, clapping.

"Mockery is a method of survival," explained Pavel, whose smile didn't quite reach his eyes. "Each to his weapon of choice."

Saying this, he stood up, taking care not to look at anyone. Realizing the subject of Pavel's mysterious Ink Dragon was now closed, Oksa took her father's hand and they joined the group of Runaways standing at the centre of the cave. The black butterfly was fluttering frantically above their heads. As soon as it saw Oksa, it flew over, causing the girl to step back in alarm.

"Sorry, Wayfinder! I've never been very comfortable around insects," she felt obliged to explain.

"What the Young Gracious actually means is that she loathes and detests insects," said the Squoracle, being a good deal less diplomatic than Oksa. "They disgust her! She thinks they're repulsive, foul, sickening, despicable..."

"That's enough, Squoracle!" broke in Tugdual. "We already knew you have a very extensive vocabulary."

"Fine!" retorted the cross little hen. "Why don't you do something useful, like finding a way out of this horrible place. It's freezing—the temperature has dropped a good twenty degrees and it feels like we're trapped in a fridge!"

Oksa looked around: the dark cave was illuminated only by the bright tentacles of the Polypharus summoned by Abakum's Granok-Shooter. The grey, rocky walls rose to an irregular ceiling some seven feet above their heads. The turbulent Void seemed to be standing guard in the cave mouth while, opposite the opening, a narrow passage led into the unknown.

"It's certainly not very warm," remarked Oksa, agreeing with the Squoracle, which had taken refuge in Abakum's jacket. "Where are we, Wayfinder?"

The black butterfly fluttered in front of her and replied in its remarkably deep voice:

"We're in the Medius, Young Gracious."

"What's that?"

"Before you reach the Soul-Searcher and the Sanctuary which stores all historical data, you have to pass through several levels. I heard your Young Gracious's Tumble-Bawler referring to Russian dolls: it's the same principle. The Soul-Searcher is like the smallest doll, the one at the centre of all the others."

"Are there many dolls?" asked Oksa, frowning.

"I don't know, Young Gracious," admitted the butterfly, still fluttering. "You've already passed through two levels: the Forest of No Return and the Maritime Hills. Between every level there's a transit zone similar to this one: the Medius will lead us to the next level. You'll have to face an ordeal on every level."

"What kind of ordeal?" asked Oksa again, interested despite her concern.

"The ordeals existed to make the Impictured individual a better person. That was the original purpose of Impicturement. Unfortunately, the Soul-Searcher is in a coma and I'm afraid the ordeals may not be as meaningful as they once were. The Felon Orthon took an Imagicon with him during the Great Chaos. He informed it of his misdoings and breathed on it, so the Soul-Searcher received details of the crimes committed by the person we all hate, along with his breath. Given the serious nature of Orthon's misdemeanours, the Soul-Searcher had no choice but to Impicture him. However, as you know, Orthon had other plans and was careful not to place a drop of his blood on the Imagicon, which would have led to his Impicturement. As a result, his twin sister, Reminiscens, was Impictured in his place."

Leomido grimaced and put his head in his hands. Beside him, Reminiscens put her hand on his shoulder and looked down. Then, with great emotion, she carried on where the butterfly had left off:

"When Orthon realized I thought he'd become an unscrupulous madman and that I might give the game away about his monstrous aspirations, he saw me as a potential danger. He didn't care that I was his twin sister—brotherly love went out of the window! Everything happened so quickly but, quite frankly, he'd laid his plans very carefully," explained the old lady bitterly. "We were arguing again, when suddenly he unrolled the Imagicon. He breathed on it and the pale canvas immediately began shimmering with a strange dark light that gave it the appearance of a stormy sky. I didn't understand what my brother had in mind at first, but when he took out a knife and advanced on me with a steely gaze, ordering me not to fight him, I remembered all the stories about Impicturement I'd heard when I was a girl. That was when I realized what my brother was planning to do and I tried to run away. But an Arborescens Granok stopped me in my tracks, binding me hand and foot. Orthon grabbed my hand and cut my palm, making it bleed. I struggled, speechless with horror, but I wasn't strong enough to fight the Arborescens—or my brother. That monster looked me straight in the eye and said frostily: 'Goodbye, sister. It's a shame you couldn't understand.' And, even though these words sounded like a final verdict,

I was sure he'd change his mind. I gazed at him, hoping there might still be some shred of humanity or compassion left somewhere inside him. I saw something flicker in his eyes and a shadow of doubt passed over his face, making my heart lurch. For a few seconds, things might have been different, but then my brother showed his true colours: he grabbed my hand, dipped his finger in the blood pooling in my palm and allowed a drop to fall on the Imagicon, whose shimmering surface turned into a kind of vortex. Orthon pushed me and I was immediately sucked inside. The Soul-Searcher had Impictured me instead of my twin brother."

"This first mistake severely unbalanced the Soul-Searcher," continued the butterfly. "It had never made a mistake before. The main problem was how to adjust the ordeals: they'd been designed for Orthon, not Reminiscens, even though she was his twin sister. The task was further complicated by the fact that Reminiscens couldn't be accused of any wrongdoing punishable by Impicturement. In short, she wasn't Impicturable! And yet... The Soul-Searcher did what it could to correct its mistake and Disimpicture Reminiscens. But only a Gracious has the power to do that. And Graciouses aren't ten a penny, if you'll forgive the turn of phrase. When the Soul-Searcher sensed the Young Gracious's presence in the science room at St Proximus, it dared to hope again. It tried everything to attract her attention, but she was never alone, which made Impicturement impossible. However, one day, it sensed she was there, on her own and susceptible. It only took a few seconds to suck her in..."

"It's such a compliment to be mistaken for Oksa," muttered Gus, pulling a face. "Your Soul-Searcher must really have gone haywire!"

"It didn't detect you," explained the butterfly. "What it sensed were the Young Gracious's tools—you were played false, so to speak, by her Granok-Shooter and Caskinette. And that second blunder proved fatal to the Soul-Searcher."

The butterfly fluttered frantically, then landed on Oksa's shoulder. She shivered at the feel of the insect's rapid breathing against her neck.

"Here you are, Oksa, have your things back," said Gus, holding the small bag out to his friend. "I'm really sorry… this is all my fault!"

"Oh, you're impossible!" snapped Oksa, her eyes shining with anger. "It's been ages since we've been treated to your 'pathetic-loser-who's-to-blame-for-everything' routine! Perhaps you'd like a whip so that you can indulge in a spot of self-flagellation? If the Soul-Searcher could help you solve this problem and convince you that all this isn't your fault, it'd be doing everyone a big favour, that's for sure."

She cupped her hands either side of her mouth and shouted:

"Soul-Searcher, if you can hear me, please do something! We've had about as much as we can stand!"

Crimson with anger and embarrassment, Gus threw the bag on the ground and fled to the back of the cave. Pierre rushed after him, while Oksa, taken aback by her friend's reaction, gnawed her lower lip. Perhaps she'd gone too far… but Gus could be so infuriating sometimes. When would he get some self-confidence? Shaking with anger, she bent down to pick up her bag, avoiding Tugdual's amused—and exasperating—gaze, when a terrible cry echoed from the dark passage which Gus and his father had just entered.

27

THE AIRBORNE SIRENS

THE RUNAWAYS SWAPPED WORRIED GLANCES, THEN ran to the back of the cave in the direction of the cry, Abakum in front lighting their way with the Polypharus. They heard another terrified yell.

"Leave us alone! Go away!"

When Oksa recognized Gus's voice, her blood ran cold. "What's happened to him now?" she couldn't help thinking wryly. "That boy has a real talent for landing himself in trouble." But no amount of sarcasm could stop her worrying about her friend. Grabbing the Incompetent, which was still standing in the middle of the cave, she ran to join the group in the narrow passage. Tugdual was waiting for her.

"You mustn't ever be on your own!" he said disapprovingly. "It's very reckless. Don't ever stray too far from us."

Despite the dim light, Oksa made out an expression of concern on Tugdual's face. He held her gaze and she felt unable to break eye contact for what seemed like ages, although it was only seconds.

"Did you hear something?" asked the Incompetent, interrupting this silent exchange. "It sounded like a cry. A human cry..." it added.

Tugdual and Oksa apprehensively walked into the passage, which soon widened to the size and unappealing appearance of a railway tunnel. In the light from the Polypharus, they immediately spotted the Runaways standing around Gus and Pierre, about twenty yards away.

"Phew!" whispered Oksa, relieved to see her friend safe and sound. "But—what's that?" she asked anxiously.

She couldn't quite make out what was floating above the heads of the Runaways. Bats? Giant moths? She took a step forward, but Tugdual held her back by the arm.

"Wait," he murmured. "Don't go any nearer."

"What are they?" repeated Oksa.

"Incredible… I didn't think they existed! That's amazing," he said, staring at the swarm hovering in the air. "Have you got your Granok-Shooter, Lil' Gracious?" he asked, without taking his eyes off the strange cloud.

"Um… yes," mumbled Oksa.

"Maybe you could provide us with a small Reticulata?" he suggested.

"Yes, of course!"

Oksa took out her small, elaborately worked blowpipe and whispered the magic words:

Reticulata, Reticulata
Things far away look larger.

A bubble immediately emerged from the Granok-Shooter and turned into what looked like a large jellyfish. Tugdual moved closer to Oksa and, with his fingertips, lightly directed the girl's shaking hand to point the magnifying membrane at the mysterious swarm. The girl trembled at this unexpected contact, but when she saw what was hovering above the Runaways, she couldn't help grabbing Tugdual's arm.

"Aaarghhhh!" she screamed.

As soon as she cried out, everyone seemed to freeze. The Runaways, alerted by her cry, turned round and looked at her anxiously. Unfortunately, the horrible creatures she'd just glimpsed didn't seem to be either deaf or blind: they turned their terrifying eyes on her and were instantly hanging in front of her face. Startled, Oksa dropped her Granok-Shooter and the Reticulata burst with a soft pop as it hit the ground.

"Don't be afraid," murmured Tugdual, handing her the Granok-Shooter he'd just picked up.

Protectively he took a step forward, but they were surrounded by the creatures, which had formed a perfect, inescapable circle around them.

"They're... hideous..." said Oksa, fascinated by what she saw.

The scene was alive with terrifying magic. A few inches from Oksa, about fifteen bodiless heads were suspended in the air. Their long hair was gently floating around them, framing delicate faces which seemed totally at odds with their cruel eyes. One of the heads floated nearer to Oksa and stared at her. Oksa gazed at her with a mixture of fascination and nausea. She was extremely beautiful, with a flawless oval face and perfectly shaped mouth, but her eyes held a harsh cruelty and merciless ferocity which shocked Oksa to the core. It was making her feel sick to hold the creature's gaze so she lowered her eyes in confusion.

"Airborne Sirens," whispered Tugdual, unable to wrench his eyes away from the circle of terrifying floating heads. I've always thought they were a myth."

"Some myth!" retorted Oksa, pulling a face. "So what do these Airborne Sirens do?"

"Make us fall asleep, so they can carry us off and possess us for ever," whispered Tugdual.

"You're joking, aren't you," replied Oksa, turning to look at him.

But he didn't look as though he was joking. Pale and tense, he didn't move a muscle. Oksa touched his arm: it was rock-hard. Tugdual seemed to be in a state of shock.

"Tugdual? Tugdual? Can you hear me?"

Outside the circle formed by the sirens, the Runaways watched the scene fearfully. To everyone's surprise, Pavel came over. The silently floating heads parted to let him through, their eyes focused on every member of the group. Pavel began leading Oksa and Tugdual towards the others, not forgetting the Incompetent, which was gazing blissfully at the creatures.

"I can't help feeling they've got something missing," it remarked with its customary powers of observation.

Oksa gave a nervous giggle, glancing back anxiously at the heads, which were following them.

"Look at them, Gus!" she asked quietly. "It's mental, isn't it?"

"No kidding," the boy replied, looking scared. "I feel like I'm going mad. It's like I'm trapped in a nightmare."

"A nightmare that could last for ever if the sirens manage to send us to sleep," added Tugdual bleakly.

"What's he on about?" asked Gus.

"Tugdual is right," said Abakum. "The Airborne Sirens were spawned by a fallen Ageless Fairy, who'd been banished from the Island of the Fairies."

"Why?" asked Oksa.

"Don't go interrupting him again!" snapped Gus in annoyance, nudging his friend. "Why don't you try to control yourself for once!"

Oksa's eyes widened in surprise at Gus's authoritarian tone. This made him smile more than he'd have liked to admit, so he looked down, allowing a long strand of hair to hide part of his face. Abakum gestured to the Runaways to sit around him with the Polypharus in the middle providing warmth and light. The alarming Airborne Sirens continued to float soundlessly above their heads.

"The fallen Ageless Fairy was called Cremona," continued Abakum. "Her heart had been warped by greed and a lust for power—because even Fairies are not immune to such fatal flaws. Cremona had plotted a conspiracy to take leadership of the Ageless Fairies so she could reign over the Inside and force the Insiders to do her will. Her plans were thwarted in the nick of time and the Ageless Ones banished her from their community, after casting a spell to deprive her of her body. Feeling misunderstood and humiliated, Cremona held a bitter grudge against her former sisters from that time onwards. Over the centuries, she persuaded several corrupt Ageless Fairies to join her cause and they formed the clan of the Airborne Sirens."

"Are they dangerous?" asked Pierre.

Abakum looked at him gravely.

"Very," he admitted. "What Tugdual said about them is true: the sirens strive to make living things fall asleep so they can steal their souls. That's tantamount to killing us because, without our souls, we're nothing but empty shells. We've not yet had to fight their fatal attraction, but it's only a matter of time. We must remain on our guard and not give in to the temptation to fall asleep, which is what they're bound to try to make us do."

"Would you have the will to hear a substantial detail inscribed in my knowledge?" asked the Lunatrixa.

"Of course, Lunatrixa," nodded Abakum. "What do you know?"

"Sleeping isn't inevitably the state of slumber," announced the Lunatrixa. "Sleeping may be a mirage that pursues the aim of misleading the mind of the person who abandons his consciousness to follow it. The mirage is powerful and the sirens have hearts filled with cunning and seduction. They are the mistresses of traps riddled with illusion."

They all remained silent, paying heed to the Lunatrixa's warnings.

"The Runaways must protect themselves against the power of illusion!" added the small creature. "Illusion is a lure intended to bring sleep and spirit away souls."

"I understand exactly what you mean," declared Abakum, sounding worried. "It's much more ingenious than it appears, you did well to warn us, Lunatrixa."

"Are they listening to us?" broke in Oksa, looking at the long-haired creatures.

"Airborne Sirens do not have interest in the words that emerge from our mouths," explained the Lunatrixa. "They draw their information from the heart."

"My friends," continued Abakum, shaking his head, "we must be very vigilant. I suggest we keep an eye on each other and warn the group if anyone seems to be giving in to the attraction of the sirens. Let's keep going and stay together. I'll lead the way. Reminiscens will keep watch on me and Leomido on Reminiscens, Tugdual on Leomido, Oksa on Tugdual and so on. Pavel, I'll give you the Incompetent. Lunatrixa, you stay with me. You must all raise the alarm if anything seems to be wrong. Is everyone okay with that?"

"Oksa has to keep watch on Tugdual?" muttered Gus, annoyed. "Isn't that a little—"

"A little what?" added Tugdual, with a casual amusement that irritated Gus.

"A little dangerous!" spat Gus. "Because you're not exactly the sharpest tool in the box, are you?"

Tugdual's only answer was to flex his fingers and crack his knuckles with a mocking look at Gus.

"You two are a real pain," grumbled Oksa. "Shall we go?" she continued, looking at her father. "We're not going to stay in this tunnel for the rest of our lives, are we?"

Pavel nodded, with a wary glance at the sirens, who were still hovering in the air above the Runaways. Then he put his arm around his daughter's shoulders and, without saying a word, they all started walking down the dark tunnel.

28

No Mercy!

THE TUNNEL, WHICH SEEMED TO GO ON FOR EVER, GAVE the worrying impression that it was leading straight down into the centre of the earth. What was worse, the gently sloping terrain was strewn with sharp-edged pebbles which made walking very painful, particularly for Reminiscens, whose lightweight sandals had thin soles which afforded her sore feet next to no protection. Although Oksa was wearing sturdy, comfortable trainers, she soon became tired of turning her ankle and cursing with every step. She quickly proved her worth as a Young Gracious, though, by coming up with a clever solution: launching a Tornaphyllon Granok at the ground every twenty yards or so, she cleared all obstacles from the path. The violent wind sent the stones flying to the sides of the tunnel, where they clattered into piles with a deafening noise.

"Well, at least that solves the problem of those rotten pebbles," she declared triumphantly, putting her Granok-Shooter away.

Illuminated by the Polypharus and escorted by the threatening sirens, the Runaways forged ahead for quite some while. They had the strange feeling that time had ceased to exist. Their watches had stopped when they'd been Impictured, so it was impossible to know if they'd spent two hours or two days in the ill-fated picture. However long it had been, though, they were beginning to feel tired. They kept one eye on their friends, the other on the sirens, and it was exhausting to concentrate on two things at once. As the group walked down the tunnel, Oksa felt her resistance ebbing away. Her legs seemed to weigh a ton and she had an overwhelming desire to sleep. Tugdual was walking on her left with the supple gait of a cheetah and, unlike her, didn't seem to be flagging at all. Or if he was, he didn't show it... Suddenly he turned round and looked surprised at the tiredness etched on Oksa's face.

"I'll fire the Tornaphyllons if you like," he suggested, taking out his Granok-Shooter.

The Runaways kept walking, their silence broken only by the noise of pebbles colliding down the tunnel. Their pace was slowing, but they were all making it a point of honour not to show any weakness. Reminiscens was the first to give way: ashen-faced, she crouched down on the dusty ground with a sigh.

"I can't go any farther..." she gasped.

"Perhaps we could take a short break?" suggested Abakum, to his friends' great relief. "But we must remain on our guard."

They looked at each other, their faces drawn with tiredness and concern.

"Why are we so tired?" asked Reminiscens. "We haven't been walking all that long."

"Perhaps it's the sirens?" suggested Oksa. "Maybe they're trying to make us fall asleep?"

As she said this, one of the creatures floated nearer and hovered a few inches from Oksa's face. Filled with chilling cruelty, the siren's eyes bored into Oksa's, while her long, floating hair stroked the schoolgirl's face. Oksa shivered violently as a wave of unexpected images washed over her: she was no longer in the tunnel, but at the very top of something that looked like... the Glass Column in Edefia! From a balcony high above the city, she could hear a crowd shouting her name. Men were perform-ing acrobatics in front of her in the middle of the sky. She looked round, her heart spilling over with happiness. By her side, she recognized her father, despite the few extra years which had left their mark on his face. A man entered the room and Oksa gave a start. It was Gus! He also looked older, or rather *more grown-up*. His face had become more angular and his shoulders were broader, but he was just as handsome. He brushed his black hair away from his face, revealing dark-blue eyes that studied her intently. He walked over and she felt his lips against hers.

"Happy?" he murmured, holding her tight against him and stroking her back.

Oksa nodded rapturously, her cheek grazed by the stubble on the chin of the man Gus had become. She then noticed a woman walking towards her and smiling and, in an instant, she realized it was her mother. She certainly looked older… but what was more important, she was standing on her own two legs.

"Mum! You're better!" she exclaimed.

Immediately, Pavel leapt up and punched the siren so hard that she was sent flying against the wall of the tunnel. The subliminal image of Marie standing there vigorously on her own feet vanished from Oksa's mind. Astonished, Oksa looked at the anxious Runaways.

"I was hallucinating!" she exclaimed, frightened by the strength of her vision.

"Watch out, Pavel!" Pierre yelled suddenly, his eyes popping out of his head.

The Airborne Siren knocked out by Pavel had just regained consciousness. With her mouth wide open in a silent scream, she swooped down on Oksa's father. Pavel immediately adopted his fighting pose and struck the creature hard with the edge of his hand. But the siren was ready for this: she took the blow, but remained motionless a few inches from Pavel. Her eyes narrowed and she glared at him, before another identical and equally frightening head emerged from her mouth.

"What's going on?" muttered Oksa, aghast.

"I've missed you so much," said Abakum groggily.

They all turned in alarm to see a siren stroking the Fairyman's face with her hair. His vacant eyes showed the strength of the illusion.

"Good Lord!" cried Reminiscens. "I wasn't watching him!"

"My dear parents," drawled Abakum quietly. "It would have been so lovely… so lovely to *love you…*"

Acting on instinct, Oksa jumped up and grabbed the siren by her hair. Recovering his senses, Abakum saw her hurl the head with all her might at a pile of stones, yelling:

"Filthy creature! Leave Abakum alone!"

The head smashed open like a watermelon, causing the Young Gracious to pull a disgusted face. However, this only won them a very brief respite: two new heads, eager to avenge their sister, sprang from the pieces of shattered head. They flew over to the other sirens and the hovering circle advanced on the Runaways with a threatening gleam in their eyes.

"Get out your Granok-Shooters," instructed Abakum. "No mercy, my friends!"

In the next few seconds the sirens came under fire from a continuous stream of Granoks. Pierre, Abakum and Tugdual began pelting them with Putrefactios and Colocynthises. Pavel, who had opted for the martial arts, was running up the stone walls of the tunnel and smashing any heads in his way with massive kicks. Oksa tried the Arborescens Granok first, ensnaring the vile sirens in a net of sticky creepers, but the artful creatures found it too easy to free themselves so Oksa decided to use fire, like Reminiscens and Leomido. The three of them decimated the ranks of the sirens with their consummate mastery of Fireballisticos. The terrible stench of rotting and burnt flesh filled the air and soon the hovering heads were all lying on the ground. Some were decomposing, their skin rotting as the Runaways watched, while others, which had been sliced in two, were writhing wildly. The worst hit were the heads which had been hit by Fireballisticos: flames were sizzling in their hair, producing an acrid smoke that caught in the throat. It was a sickening, apocalyptic sight. A leaden silence descended on the tunnel, rooting the Runaways to the spot. Everyone held their breath. They had a nasty feeling that, despite their defeat, the sirens wouldn't let things rest there. Oksa, who couldn't wrench her eyes away from the slowly decomposing heads, took her father's hand and squeezed it. It wasn't long before they were proved right: from every head sprang two more identical heads with vicious, menacing faces. The Runaways couldn't help taking a few steps back from this frightening phenomenon, clutching their Granok-Shooters defensively. Oksa bent down, picked up a large stone and hurled it at one of the heads. The stone found its target, smashing the head with a loud splat. However, a few seconds later two new heads emerged from the previous one, increasing the number of sirens to around fifty.

"Don't do anything else!" warned Abakum, raising his hand. "Don't do anything else, my friends. Violence is only making things worse. We have to find another solution."

"It'll have to be quick," murmured Oksa, again targeted by a siren.

She was so tired… and the siren's hair stroking her face felt so good… it was impossible to resist the urge to sleep. Or the desire to experience that wonderful vision again. Her body went limp and she felt herself slipping into a delicious drowsiness, while feelings of intense happiness flooded her mind. How long had it been since she'd felt this happy? Suddenly she snapped out of it so abruptly that it took her breath away. In front of her, huge flames were decimating the sirens, including the one who'd just been guiding her towards that irresistible mirage. There was an agonizing cry: her father was writhing in pain a few yards from her, his Ink Dragon rising from his back, furiously belching long, ravaging flames.

"Dad! Don't! It's okay, I've woken up!" yelled Oksa.

Immediately everything stopped. The Ink Dragon withdrew, sinking back into Pavel's body, and he rushed over to Oksa.

"My darling—I thought they had you!"

The fear he'd felt made him hug her much harder than usual but, feeling shaken, Oksa didn't complain.

"I couldn't help myself, I'm sorry," Pavel said to the Runaways.

"No father or mother would have acted any differently, Pavel," said Reminiscens. "You followed your heart and none of us can blame you for that. But now look what we have to deal with."

The fifty charred heads had stopped burning, and the horrified Runaways were now confronted by a mass of about a hundred sirens, their cruel eyes even fiercer than before.

29

A Heart-breaking Sacrifice

"RUN!" BAWLED THE BLACK BUTTERFLY. "RUN AS FAST as you can!"

Frantically flapping its wings, the Wayfinder disappeared deep into the tunnel. Pavel grabbed Oksa's hand and raced after the butterfly, followed by the other Runaways. The sirens immediately pursued them, surrounding them at the rear and on either side. Although she was being pulled along by her father in a headlong rush, Oksa couldn't help glancing at them and instantly felt herself sinking into an irresistible trance. Her pace decreased, her legs seemed to be moving in slow motion and her heartbeat grew more sluggish. Pavel looked at her and growled angrily when he saw her vacant eyes. Oksa was caught between two worlds: the one where her mind was taking her—a world suffused with light where she was with her parents, in Gus's arms, free from pain or fear—and the dark, hostile one, where she was struggling against the baleful power of the sirens. She was finding it harder and harder to resist the power of the first world, even though it was just a glorious mirage. After all, how can you fight something you want so desperately, even if you're not aware of it? Realizing that his daughter was surrendering to the sirens, Pavel picked Oksa up and continued his frantic flight through the tunnel cradling her tightly in his arms.

"Listen to my voice, Oksa!" he said loudly. "Listen carefully to what I say! Focus on my words, okay?"

Slumped in her father's arms, Oksa nodded, concentrating hard on his voice.

"You're awake, Oksa!" he declared firmly. "You're with your friends in a tunnel somewhere deep inside a painting. We're being chased by malevolent sirens, who are trying to trap the most soft-hearted among us. Those ravenous creatures have no power over me, because my deepest desires are suppressed by my Ink Dragon and can't be used against me. You can't fight them, darling, because your heart is an open book. But you have to banish the sirens' lies from your mind. The sirens are deceitful, Oksa. What they're showing you isn't real—it's just what you want to see! You need to focus on the harsh reality of our situation. Look at the stones piled against the walls of the tunnel! Look at the pebbles flying around us! Look at the butterfly showing us the way! Think about your friends... think about Gus, about Tugdual... Tell me everything you can see! Come on, Oksa, tell me what you can see around you. Where are we, Oksa? Where are we?"

Despite the sirens' assault on her mind and the terrifying drowsiness that seemed about to claim her at any moment, Oksa tried even harder and followed her father's advice. Clinging to him, she looked around and, to prevent herself sinking into sleep again, she started loudly listing the Runaways, who were running together in a close-packed group.

"We're in a tunnel," she began, so loud she was almost shouting. "Vile heads are floating around us and we're running to escape them. I can see Reminiscens behind us, Abakum is holding her right hand and Leomido her left. Reminiscens looks exhausted and there's a strange expression in her eyes, as if she's finding it hard to resist the sirens. Tugdual is just beside her, he's carrying the Lunatrixa on his shoulders. Poor Lunatrixa... her eyes are closed and she's almost transparent, I think she's frightened to death. Tugdual looks okay, he seems to be keeping a very clear head."

Her voice suddenly tailed off. A siren had just stroked her face with her long, silky hair. Oksa's head lolled onto her father's shoulder.

"Don't stop, Oksa!" he bellowed, shaking her. "Don't stop! What else can you see?"

Oksa jumped, as if she'd just been woken from a deep sleep, and obeyed her father's order.

"I can see Pierre!" she replied, yelling as loudly as him. "The Incompetent is clinging to his back and he's carrying Gus in his arms. Oh no! Gus looks completely out of it."

She fell silent, horrified by what she was seeing. Pierre was racing along, his cheeks wet with tears, cradling Gus in his arms. Five sirens were gathered around them, their hair hanging over part of the boy's face. Oksa could only see his eyes, which were empty and devoid of expression.

"Mum!" he stammered. "I've always wanted to meet you *so* badly..."

"They've got Gus, Dad!" cried Oksa in alarm. "He's seeing his mother. It's awful! Aaarghhhh! Oh no, what's the Lunatrixa doing?"

Pavel immediately stopped, as did the Wayfinder, the other Runaways and the sirens. They all turned to look at the Lunatrixa, who'd just leapt from Tugdual's shoulders towards Pierre and his unconscious son, lost in the mirage created by the floating heads. There was an ominous silence and time seemed to stand still, until the small creature started speaking.

"Regret fills my heart to arrive at this extreme measure," she began, brushing the sirens' hair from Gus's face with her hand.

She sniffled and continued, fixing her large, protruding eyes on Oksa, who shivered apprehensively.

"The sirens will continue their hunt of hearts wide open until they succeed in their possession of one of them. The Fairyman has revealed a weakness which missed being fatal, but he has managed to make his mind as impervious as concrete. The Young Gracious, her friend and Reminiscens are the most accessible targets and their resistance weighs too little to withstand the virtuosity of the sirens. Great unhappiness is inevitable: the sirens will produce permanent perseverance until one heart yields. The young friend of the Young Gracious was unable to provide a fight and has begun the surrender of his heart."

"NO!" screamed Oksa, heartbroken. "NOT HIM!"

The Lunatrixa walked over to her and put her plump hand on Oksa's shoulder.

"The domestic staff of Your Gracious possesses the solution," she said, sounding sad, but determined.

"What is it?" spluttered Oksa, wiping the tears from her eyes.

The small creature edged even closer, and motioned to Oksa to bend down so that she could whisper a few words in her ear. Oksa blanched and put her hand over her mouth to stifle a cry, as tears streamed down her cheeks. She looked miserably at Gus, then at the Lunatrixa. As if they'd understood, Abakum and Leomido came over and each of them in turn hugged the Lunatrixa with great sadness and gratitude.

"The sirens desire a noble and loving heart," the small creature told the other Runaways. "The heart I possess is pulsing with a deep wish to perform the rescue of the friend of the Young Gracious. This wish contains a strength more fierce than any of the desires that each one of you may enclose within and the sirens cannot muster resistance to this attraction. I utter my determination and my farewells…"

Then, without waiting for any reaction from the Runaways, she bounded towards the swarm of floating heads and cast herself into their waving hair, which wildly engulfed her.

✳

Gathered around the small mound of freshly dug earth, the Runaways looked downcast as Abakum delivered a moving eulogy to the Lunatrixa.

"Our gratitude will know no bounds," he said, his voice breaking. "Never doubt that we'll remember you for ever: the memory of your devotion will last for eternity, like a precious stone."

Oksa gulped back a sob more noisily than she'd have liked. She felt exhausted and very sad. She blew a kiss towards the small makeshift grave and joined Gus, who was sitting under a tree a few yards away.

The boy looked heartbroken. His black hair hung over his tearful eyes, his face was pale and stricken, and he held his head in his hands. When Oksa sat down next to him, he turned away so that she was left looking at his hunched back. Oksa didn't say anything for a few minutes, then she placed a hand on his shoulder. Gus flinched and scowled even harder.

"It should've been me, not her," he muttered through clenched teeth.

Hearing this, Oksa saw red. She jumped up and went round to kneel right in front of Gus. Grabbing his chin, she raised her friend's head with a roughness that surprised her.

"When will you stop making such stupid remarks?" she raged. "You should be ashamed of yourself! Out of respect for the Lunatrixa—"

Her voice cracked and she turned away, gnawing at her lower lip. Then she stood up, her grey eyes fixed on Gus, and continued:

"Out of respect for *her*, you need to do everything you can to show that you deserved her sacrifice. If you don't, it's like she died for *nothing*!"

Shocked by what she'd just said, Oksa stood in front of Gus, her hands on her hips and her eyes defiant, despite her rough words. Gus looked back at her. The pain and anger in her friend's eyes unsettled her and she suddenly felt cross with herself for going too far. Again... Gus tried to speak, but nothing came out. He continued looking at her and the suffering in his eyes disconcerted her. She hesitated, then put her hand on his arm in a conciliatory gesture.

"Sorry, Gus," she whispered. "I can be like a bull in a china shop sometimes."

"Often, you mean," he replied, sniffling. "I didn't want things to turn out like this, you know," he added, referring to the Lunatrixa.

"No one wanted things to turn out like this," said Oksa. "And no one expected it. But we were trapped in that tunnel and it was a tragedy waiting to happen. One of us had to stay behind. And the fact that the tunnel and those revolting heads disappeared as soon as the Lunatrixa plunged into the midst of the sirens proves it."

As if trying to accept it, Gus looked around at the landscape that Oksa was showing him with arms outspread. The immediate effect of the Lunatrixa's sacrifice had, in fact, been to eliminate that hideous level and its malicious occupants. The Runaways had immediately found themselves in an oasis of lush greenery, a paradisiacal place filled with the sweet sound of birdsong and the murmur of a waterfall splashing into a clear lagoon. They'd looked at each other in amazement, stunned to find they were still alive. Reminiscens had collapsed onto the soft, fine sand, exhausted by the relentless battle with the Airborne Sirens. Her feet were red-raw and bleeding and there was a painful scratch on her cheek. Abakum and Leomido had rushed over to her and the Fairyman had taken from his bag a phial of Spinollias—those clever seamstress spiders—watched gravely by Leomido. Pierre had still been holding Gus who, a few seconds earlier, had been held in fatal thrall by the sirens. He'd fallen to the ground too, his eyes still gleaming with the profound despair he'd felt as he watched the life drain from his son. Pavel had laid Oksa on the soft sand and had immediately clapped his hands to his back, which seemed to be incredibly painful. He'd arched his spine as if to stretch it with a loud cracking noise. After making sure that her father was okay, Oksa had then looked around for Tugdual. The young man was kneeling beside the body of the Lunatrixa. His long fingers, adorned with silver rings, were sombrely stroking the colourless head of the small, valiant creature. They'd all stood there, in silence, gazing at the lifeless Lunatrixa until Tugdual had stood up at last. Without a word, he'd picked up a large, flat stone and used it to dig a hole in the earth under a tree with thick foliage. Now, numb with tiredness and grief, they were all anxiously waiting for the next leg of the journey to begin, taking care not to let their eyes stray to the Lunatrixa's grave. Only Oksa dared to do so, with a heavy heart and red-rimmed eyes. She swallowed her tears and looked away again, taking a deep breath to try to stifle the sob that was threatening to explode from her chest. It was then that she noticed some magnificent flowers blooming beside the lagoon. Their petals were such a bright red that it looked as though they were little flames. Oksa walked over, intrigued. The plants, which were tall and elegant like reeds, were swaying gently, even though there wasn't a breeze. Her first impression had been correct: sparks were flying from the petals as if a tiny fire were burning at the heart of every flower.

"Unbelievable," whispered Oksa in wonderment.

She edged closer and waited for the fire to burn itself out, but nothing happened: the petals forming the flamboyant corolla of those magnificent flowers weren't on fire, they *were* flames!

"I'm sure she'd love these," murmured Oksa, glancing sorrowfully towards the Lunatrixa's unadorned grave.

She stretched out her hand to pick one of the flowers—a perfectly natural reaction on Earth, but not in a bewitched painting, as she soon realized.

"What are you trying to do, wretched girl?" screeched the flower Oksa was trying to pick. "Let go, you're strangling me!"

Oksa did what she was told immediately, less taken aback by hearing the plant speak—she was getting used to that, after all—than by a puff of hot gas which burst from the petals and headed straight for her. Eyes wide in amazement, she took a few steps backwards as the small, glowing cloud came dangerously close.

"What is that thing?" she muttered, putting her hands out in front of her. "Ouch! That's really hot!" she cried, shaking her fingers, which the cloud had barely touched.

"It's an Inflammatoria," said Abakum informatively. "It's like a miniature volcano and I think you caused it to erupt. Look!"

After expelling the cloud which had hit Oksa, the plant was in the middle of a volcanic explosion, spitting out sparks and an orangey substance similar to molten magma.

"That plant seems very cross," remarked the Incompetent, watching this surprising sight. It took Oksa's hand and her burnt skin immediately felt soothed by a delicious cooling sensation.

"Don't think you can get away with anything you like, just because you're the Young Gracious!" spat the Inflammatoria, expelling a stream of burning lava.

"I'm very sorry," replied Oksa, brushing a spark from her T-shirt. "You're so pretty... I just wanted to pick you to put on the Lunatrixa's grave."

"Just pick me? Just pick me?" said the plant, working itself up into a temper again. "Haven't you learnt anything? Inflammatorias *aren't for picking*!"

"Sorry," repeated Oksa, pulling a face.

"Inflammatorias aren't for picking," repeated the plant, "but they do multiply. Huh, no one could ever accuse me of being mean-spirited!" it added, projecting a stream of lava over Oksa's head.

"Look, Oksa..." urged Tugdual, pointing to the Lunatrixa's grave.

On the small mound of earth where a drop of lava had landed, a magnificent Inflammatoria had just bloomed, accompanied seconds later by a cluster of others, each blazing more brightly than the last. Tugdual winked at Oksa, while the Incompetent murmured:

"Everything's going up in flames around here."

Oksa couldn't help smiling. She leant over to pick up the Incompetent, took one last look at the grave, covered in Inflammatorias, and turned on her heel.

"Well," she said, wiping away a tear. "Let's have a look at where we are."

30

BURNING QUESTIONS

THE SQUORACLE SCRAMBLED OUT OF ABAKUM'S JACKET, its little beak quivering with satisfaction.

"At last!" it exclaimed. "This is the perfect habitat for my ultra-sensitive constitution. I'm glad someone has finally listened. Thirty-one degrees centigrade, seventy per cent relative humidity, no wind, and a light that's bright but not blinding—ideal!"

"Where are we?" asked Oksa, turning to the Tumble-Bawler, which had perched on a rock overhanging the lagoon.

Nodding gently, the Tumble-Bawler concentrated hard, then replied:

"All co-ordinates within our current location have been obliterated by the spell cast on the Soul-Searcher because, as I said, none of the cardinal points exist here, nor is there any height and depth. All conventional methods of measuring distance and time have disappeared inside the picture. However, our external location has changed, Young Gracious. We're now in south-central London. The Thames is beneath us and we're 317 feet above ground, resting against an opalescent circular glass wall measuring twenty-three feet in diameter, facing south."

Abakum and Leomido blinked in astonishment at this revelation.

"Are you sure?" asked the Fairyman, aware that it was a pointless question.

"I'm absolutely certain, you can rely on my infallibility," replied the Tumble-Bawler, bowing respectfully.

"So the painting is 317 feet up from the ground?" asked Abakum, anxiously.

"That's right!" confirmed the Tumble-Bawler.

"But we don't live that high!" pointed out Oksa. "Unless London is at that altitude... Do you mean the height above sea level?"

"Not at all, Young Gracious. I mean the height above ground level."

"That's very strange... not even Baba's private workroom is that high. It can only be about thirty stairs up from the ground floor, no more."

"We've climbed exactly 437 steps," specified the Tumble-Bawler.

"Something must have happened," murmured Abakum, concerned. Reminiscens looked enquiringly at him, then turned to Leomido.

"There has to be a sensible explanation," said Oksa's great-uncle wisely. "I think we just have to trust Dragomira and focus on our immediate future."

"You're right," nodded Abakum. "Wayfinder, do you know where we are?"

The black butterfly fluttered closer to them and hovered in the air in the middle of the circle of Runaways.

"We've passed through three levels: that of the Forest, that of the Maritime Hills and that of the Sirens' Tunnel," began the Wayfinder. "We're in a Medius where we can recharge our batteries before entering a new level."

"Before *enduring* a new level, you mean," murmured Oksa bitterly.

"You're right, Young Gracious," nodded the butterfly. "Every level is an ordeal to be endured and, above all, overcome."

"And will the Soul-Searcher kill one of us every time?" asked Oksa angrily.

The butterfly flew over to her and hovered a few inches from her face.

"No, Young Gracious. You don't understand. The Soul-Searcher has nothing to do with this. It means you no harm for the simple reason that it's in such a bad way it's incapable of doing anything."

"Yeah, right," remarked Gus, shaking with rage.

"None of the tragedies that befall you are actually intended for you," explained the Wayfinder. "The ordeals you're encountering along the way were designed for someone else entirely!"

"Although, unfortunately, we're the ones who have to overcome them," added Reminiscens.

The butterfly gave a small sigh.

"The Airborne Sirens weren't for or against you: they're merely a manifestation of the Evil which now controls this picture. Don't forget that Orthon-McGraw was the person who should have been Impictured."

Oksa thought for a few seconds, then continued:

"And what were they supposed to do to him?" she challenged.

"Make him confront a past which he's blotted out and which has made him the man he is. The sirens explore what's buried deepest in us. They know how to extricate desires and regrets we're not even aware we have. That's how they lure us into their trap."

"But you talked about fantasies and illusions," remarked Gus. "That isn't the same!"

"Isn't making us believe that our desires—or regrets—have become a reality which we can control, the most powerful illusion of all?" asked the black butterfly, turning to him.

"It's devastating…" murmured Oksa.

So her innermost desires included her mother being cured, Edefia… and Gus. She glanced at her friend and immediately blushed, flustered by the thought that the others might have found out about a feeling that she herself didn't want to admit she had. She turned away and met Tugdual's no less unsettling and perceptive gaze. He looked at her enquiringly and she felt as though she was glowing as hot as an Inflammatoria and melting with embarrassment.

"What about you, Gus, what did you see when the sirens captured your mind?" asked Tugdual, without taking his eyes off Oksa.

Gus hesitated. He ran his hand through his hair and said in a low, breathy voice:

"I saw my mother. The mother I've never met."

Pierre jerked, as if stung by a wasp, and stared miserably at him.

"So did I, Gus," added Abakum. "I saw the mother I've never met and will never meet. My mother and father... those damned sirens knew exactly what they were doing: they went straight for the jugular."

Pierre clenched his fists and Gus looked timidly at him.

"Why?" muttered the Viking. "Why now?"

"I didn't even realize I felt like *that* inside, Dad," he mumbled, ashamed.

"This isn't your fault, Gus!" cried Oksa. "Why should you feel ashamed about wanting to meet the woman who gave birth to you? It's no big deal. Don't go making a mountain out of a molehill. That's all we need!"

"I'm sorry, Dad," continued Gus, still feeling shamefaced. "I didn't know... I didn't want... I love you and Mum so much!"

Pierre came over to his son and hugged him tightly with tears in his eyes.

"I know, son, I know," he murmured hoarsely.

"Where we come from is fundamental to our knowledge of ourselves," said Abakum diplomatically. "If we don't know our origins, we're nothing. We can't be complete if we only have a partial understanding of who we are—we'll always lack a vital part of our identity." Gus's father turned away and wiped his eyes with the back of his hand.

"It's completely normal for Gus to be seduced by that fantasy," added Abakum. "It's something he'll feel all his life, although it won't stop him loving you and Jeanne. Look at me, Pierre! I'm over eighty, I was raised by wonderful people for whom I had a deep and abiding love. And if I could have just one wish, it would be to meet the people who brought me into this world. No one can do anything about that desire. It's not a betrayal, because Gus loves you and Jeanne. He loves you more than anyone. We all know it. So don't spoil what you have between you."

Pierre gave a loud sob, roaring like a wounded bear. He hugged Gus even tighter and murmured something in his ear, which made Gus look up at him with a sweet, tremulous smile.

31

A PERFECT PARADISE

"WELL!" SAID OKSA, SOUNDING MORE LIKE HER UPBEAT self. "Are we going to explore this paradise or not?"

She jumped up and clambered onto the rock where the Tumble-Bawler was perched. Her heart felt heavy with grief. She turned her head away and her vision blurred with tears as she recalled the Lunatrixa's chubby face. She wondered what illusion the small creature had seen when the sirens had swooped down on her. The apartments in the Glass Column where she'd lived with Malorane? The fabulous forests of Green Mantle? Poor Lunatrixa... Oksa stifled a sob and took a deep breath to quell her tears. They couldn't afford to sink into melancholy—they had to keep going. She forced herself to look around. The tropical, dreamlike beauty of this place seemed to have come from the mind of some visionary creator and, after that gloomy tunnel, couldn't fail to raise their spirits.

"It's fantastic here!" she exclaimed, hoping her enthusiasm would be contagious. "Have you seen this water? How can it be so blue and so clear at the same time? It's really... magical!" she said with a nervous laugh.

Around the lagoon, the trees were bowed under the weight of enormous fruits that looked delicious. As if it could read her mind, one of the trees bent down until its most heavily laden branch was level with Oksa, who suddenly realized how hungry she was.

She reached out and picked the plumpest fruit she could see, a sort of huge apricot, and bit into it. Sweet nectar flooded her mouth, making her feel better immediately. Devouring it greedily, she peered into the lush foliage. Little golden birds were cheeping and darting between the shiny leaves, their tiny wings sparkling in the rays of the strange mauve sun.

"I don't believe it!" cried Oksa. "Ptitchkins!"

She held out her hand and one of the golden birds, a fraction of an inch big, landed tamely on her palm.

"Hello, Ptitchkin!" she said, stroking it gently.

"I hope the Young Gracious will accept my kindest regards," replied the remarkable bird, bowing its microscopic head.

Oksa burst out laughing, as usual, embarrassed at being addressed so verbosely.

She grinned at her father, then the other Runaways, Gus, Tugdual...

"You're so cute, Ptitchkin!" she continued. "Did you know that my gran has two of your kind? She carries them around on little perches which she wears as earrings."

"It must be a huge honour for my companions to adorn the ears of the Old Gracious, how fortunate they are!" exclaimed the small bird in a shrill voice. "Are they worthy of their lucky lot in life?"

"Um... not always!" replied Oksa laughing. "They do have a few issues with discipline, but they're so lovable they're always forgiven in the end."

"Hey, that reminds me of a certain Young Gracious," said Gus, with a meaningful glance at his friend.

"Oh, you!" growled Oksa, letting the Ptitchkin fly away. "You've really got it coming this time!"

She charged at him and they both fell backwards on the soft sand at the foot of the Inflammatorias, which gave off a few surprised sparks. They rolled down to the edge of the lagoon bellowing with laughter and ended up in the translucent water.

"Come on in!" cried Oksa to the Runaways, who were watching this scene in amusement. "It's lovely!"

"Why not?" replied Abakum, taking off his kimono jacket and ankle boots.

The Fairyman climbed onto an overhanging rock about six feet above the lagoon and dived into the warm, clear water. In a few strokes, he swam over to join Oksa, who was playfully splashing Gus.

"Talk about a Young Gracious! She's more like a young mad dog!" laughed the boy, his eyes shining mischievously.

"Argh!" growled Oksa, pouncing on him. "Do you want to know what this mad dog is going to do to you?"

Merrily she tried to duck Gus, but unexpectedly he foiled her every attempt.

"You won't sink!" she grumbled. "Are you refusing to bow to the will of the Young Gracious, you philistine?"

"Not at all, I assure you, Young Gracious," replied Gus, crying with laughter. "I'd love to obey and sink like a stone, but look—I can't! I just stay on the surface!"

"Look over here, youngsters!" called Abakum.

The Fairyman was standing right in the middle of the lagoon, where the water was at its deepest. He rolled over to dive below the water, but only managed to flip over on the surface.

"It's impossible to sink to the bottom," he remarked. "The water's too dense."

"You're right," remarked Oksa, floating closer to him, water up to her neck, her body vertical. "The water's at least thirty feet deep and I'm not moving at all so I should sink! That's insane!"

"Wow!" cried Gus in delight, walking over to Oksa. "Dad, come in!"

Pierre needed no urging. He threw himself into the water, leaving the Incompetent, which had picked him as its protector, on the sandy shore.

"I can't remember if I like water sports or not," it said with its customary nonchalance. "Will I get wet?"

"There's a high probability you will," replied Tugdual, pulling off his black T-shirt.

Oksa couldn't help looking over at his pale torso, gleaming in the light. Ignoring her, Tugdual dived in and swam over to the small group floating in the middle of the lagoon.

"All right, Lil' Gracious?" he asked in a deceptively casual tone.

"I'm more than all right, this place is wonderful!" she replied enthusiastically.

Then, to hide her agitation, she floated on her back in the water, her heart pounding, as Tugdual swum around her like a shark.

"He must be in a great deal of pain," he said, looking at Pavel.

Oksa returned to a standing position and watched her father crouching on the bank of the lagoon. He was trickling water over the Squoracle's feathers, making it cluck with joy. The tiny hen's delight made him smile, but she could see from his tense features that he was in pain.

"Dad!" called Oksa, upset to see how much he was suffering. "Come in for a swim! Come on!" Pavel stood up and stretched with his hands planted on the small of his back.

"I'm coming," he called, with a grimace.

He hesitated for a second, then decided to pull off his tattered T-shirt. No one looking at him face-on would have suspected the existence of the Ink Dragon, except for the tattooed talons appearing over his shoulders. Pavel walked into the lagoon cautiously, even though the water was warm and the sand at the bottom of the lagoon was soft. He carefully splashed the upper part of his body and Oksa could have sworn she saw a plume of white vapour rise from his back where the droplets had just landed. Her father pulled another face and gave an almost inaudible moan. Oksa couldn't look away and, not far from her, Tugdual was also watching with an intrigued expression. Pavel sank into the water. A dense cloud of steam rose from his sizzling back and he gave a scream, his eyes rolling back in his head. Oksa had obviously not been seeing things after all.

"Dad!" cried Oksa, rushing over to him.

The surface of the water was covered in plumes of steam evaporating around Oksa's father, who looked as if he might faint.

"Dad!" repeated Oksa. "Lean on me, I'll help you get out!"

"No, I'm fine, Oksa," Pavel reassured her shakily. "The water's soothing. It's extinguishing all the fire in me. It's such a relief... You have no idea..."

"Are you sure?" asked Oksa dubiously.

"I thought my back was going to catch fire," said Pavel, who seemed to be looking better with every second. "I felt like I was burning up."

"That's awful!"

"Seriously, I just need to learn to control my Ink Dragon so that I don't end up cooked to a turn," said Pavel with his customary wry sense of humour. "Unless you fancy 'barbecued dad'?"

"Dad!" exclaimed Oksa indignantly, punching his arm. "How can you joke about *this*?"

"Better to laugh, Oksa-san," he murmured bitterly. "Better to laugh."

Better to laugh than suffer? Better to laugh than die? These questions whirled round Oksa's mind as she kept her eyes on her father. They stood there, face to face, the water lapping around them, until Pavel took her hand and led her beneath the fruit trees.

"You looked as though you were having quite a feast just now," he said gently, indicating that the subject worrying Oksa was now closed. "Aren't you going to let me taste those juicy apricots? We should probably refuel and regain our strength, shouldn't we?"

Oksa didn't even have to stretch up: the tree she was standing beneath with her father bent down until it was within easy reach and let her pick its finest fruit. Everyone was resting beside the lagoon, relaxed by the swim and soothed by the idyllic setting.

"Look at Reminiscens over there!" said the girl, her mouth sticky with apricot juice. "Leomido is waiting on her hand and foot."

Farther off, Reminiscens was swaying lazily in a hammock woven by Leomido out of creepers from a spectacular banyan tree, while a large green dragonfly fanned her with its iridescent wings. The Spinollias appeared to have finished their work mending the cuts and scratches on her feet and she'd fallen asleep with her hands crossed over her chest, her exhaustion obvious from the purplish rings under her eyes. Leomido was leaning against a tree beside her, keeping watch while eating a piece of fruit similar to a large mango.

"It must be hard for him," murmured Oksa. "Being reunited with the woman he loved, after all these years…"

"Particularly after believing she was dead," added Pavel.

"Do you think Abakum was in love with Reminiscens too?" asked the girl suddenly, noticing the expression of the Fairyman sitting some distance away.

Pavel cleared his throat.

"I'm sure he was," he replied, following Abakum's gaze as he stared at Reminiscens. "But don't forget that Abakum has a strong sense of duty and is used to remaining in the background. From the moment he was born, he's devoted himself to the Gracious's family: first Malorane, then her children, Leomido and Dragomira. And now us, her descendants. Although he's stronger than the lot of us, he's always taken a back seat."

"That really is devotion!" exclaimed Oksa.

"That's what Abakum is like: he puts loyalty before anything else."

"Even before love…" rang out Tugdual's voice.

Oksa whirled round: the young man was stretched out on the lowest branch of the apricot tree.

"Now that's true strength!" he continued. "Dominating something that has the power to dominate you."

"What do you mean?" asked Oksa, bewildered, as her father looked on in amusement. Gazing at the sky, Tugdual scratched his head casually.

"Being dominated is a disaster waiting to happen," he replied. "If you can keep the upper hand over something that has the power to enslave you, you're stronger than anyone or anything." Oksa frowned.

"I get the impression that the Lil' Gracious would like an example," continued Tugdual, with a devastatingly mocking smile. "Take a feeling with great potential for domination like love. It's dangerous to surrender to it because it's so hard to control. If you can master it, in other words ignore it and go your own sweet way, that's quite a feat! That kind of inner strength makes you unbeatable."

"Perhaps," admitted Oksa. "But that must really hurt!"

"Of course it does!" nodded Tugdual, with a loud peal of laughter. "Otherwise it would be too easy. There's no such thing as a fairy-tale ending…"

"There's no danger of forgetting that with you," muttered Oksa, turning back to the black butterfly, which was fluttering closer.

"Young Gracious, Runaways, you should come and see this," announced the winged Wayfinder. "I think I've found the way to the next level."

32

RESERVATIONS

O KSA STOOD UP IMMEDIATELY, FOLLOWED BY THE intrigued Runaways. The butterfly flew along the bank of the lagoon, leading the small group to the waterfall.

"Here it is!"

Abakum walked over and narrowed his eyes, his nose almost touching the curtain of falling water.

"I can't see anything…"

"Poke your head through," advised the butterfly. "You're completely safe as long as your body stays on this side."

Firmly held by Leomido and Pierre, Abakum followed the insect's advice and put his head under the waterfall. Water pounded on his back, splashing the Runaways. A few seconds later he withdrew his head.

"Well?" asked Oksa, unable to wait a second longer.

Abakum wiped his face briefly and grimly replied:

"Well, my friends, I think we're going to need all our courage and strength to endure the next ordeal."

"May I see?" implored Oksa immediately.

"Of course," agreed Abakum, sounding resigned.

Gripped tightly by her father and Pierre, Oksa put her head through the waterfall. She soon forgot the water beating down on her shoulders when she saw the bleak landscape on the other side—a vast, hostile plain covered in greyish, almost black dust, and scoured by violent flurries of ash, stretched as far as she could see. Above it, a sky marbled with dark veins was split by flashes of pitch-black lightning which cast an unsettling glow over the deeply fissured ground. This frightening sight was accompanied by a deafening noise, which sounded like loud drum rolls interspersed with plaintive squealing. Horrified, Oksa withdrew her head from the waterfall and blinked, dazzled by the gentle radiance of their aptly named little paradise.

"What a horrible place…" she muttered.

"That's the Endless Barrens," explained the butterfly.

When they heard this, Reminiscens and Gus groaned apprehensively. Oksa looked at them in concern, aware that they were—for different reasons—the most vulnerable members of the group. It upset her to see that Reminiscens's fortitude had been so badly undermined by her solitary wanderings in the picture. The elegant woman looked so tired and drawn, clinging to Leomido's arm as if it were a lifebelt. How would she cope in the arid land waiting for them on the other side of the waterfall? And what about Gus? Despite being stronger and younger, he was actually more at risk than Reminiscens, who was still a Firmhand and a Werewall. Gus was just an Outsider and that made a huge difference: he possessed no magic powers and was entirely dependent on the others for protection from the continual dangers that beset them. Oksa's gaze strayed to the Lunatrixa's small grave. She shivered and, as if he could read her mind, Abakum walked over.

"We're in a very perilous situation," he said softly and sadly. "But we must do our utmost to avoid another tragedy and get out of this mess alive. It's perfectly normal to be afraid, but don't forget how many clear advantages we have: your father and his Ink Dragon, Leomido who has Gracious blood flowing through his veins, Reminiscens and Pierre with their Firmhand powers, Tugdual and his many gifts…"

"Not to mention a great big millstone around your neck," broke in Gus crossly.

"Not to mention Gus, who's proved time and time again how important he is in keeping Oksa on an even keel when she has a tendency to over-react," added Abakum firmly. "Everyone has their part to play."

"Particularly as we're all in the same boat," remarked Tugdual with a shrug.

"Exactly!" nodded Abakum. "And let me remind you, Gus, that you weren't the only one targeted by the sirens."

"That's true!" exclaimed Oksa. "Think about it. Even though Abakum is the Fairyman and I'm the Gracious, they didn't treat us any differently."

Gus agreed between clenched teeth, scuffing the ground with his heel.

"Hey, look at that! I just managed to shut Gus up!" announced Oksa, rubbing her hands together.

"That's quite enough from you, show-off," grumbled Gus, hiding a smile behind a strand of hair.

"And you, young lady," continued Abakum, placing his hands firmly on Oksa's shoulders, "mustn't forget the most important thing: you're the Young Gracious."

Oksa frowned and gnawed at her lower lip.

"Yes… maybe… but I don't feel like that's an advantage. I can't do very much compared to all of you."

"Uh oh, it looks like our Lil' Gracious has caught the 'acute Gussonitis' virus," remarked Tugdual sarcastically. Abakum's grey eyes looked deep into Oksa's.

"It isn't what you can do that's important," he said reassuringly. "It's what you represent, as well as your potential. You aren't always aware of it, but you're our biggest asset, Oksa." The Runaways nodded, looking thoughtful.

"Are you interested in any information about the next level?" asked the Squoracle suddenly, breaking the silence.

"See, Gus, that's what I meant when I said we all have our part to play," murmured Abakum with a wink. "Of course, Squoracle, we're all ears!" he said, turning to the tiny hen.

"This level boasts some very extreme, and therefore very unpleasant, weather conditions. The temperature is wonderful—around forty-five degrees centigrade—but when there is zero humidity, idyllic temperatures like this can cause intense suffering."

"What do you mean?" asked Oksa immediately.

"I mean there's no trace of water at all. It is totally, absolutely and utterly dry!" exclaimed the Squoracle. "I've never seen anything like it, but it doesn't bode well at all, if you ask me. From what I can make out, the air is clogged with particles of very fine dust, like soot. We'll have to protect ourselves from it, otherwise we'll suffocate. I hope one of you will offer me the protection of a pocket, as I have no wish to die…" Abakum agreed and invited the Squoracle to continue.

"Other than that, I should warn you about the ground: it's covered in bottomless fissures. If anyone falls into one, they'll be lost for ever."

"Great," muttered Gus.

"What do you mean by bottomless fissures?" again asked Oksa. The Squoracle rolled its eyes and fidgeted irritably.

"It's not rocket science!" it snapped. "There's no bottom! You fall and whoosh, infinity awaits. The void! Nothingness!"

"Okay," said Oksa flatly. "Well, we'll do our best not to fall…"

"If only it were that easy!" retorted the Squoracle. "Anyway, once you've got through this level—if you succeed—you'll reach the Sanctuary of the Soul-Searcher."

"The Sanctuary is an ordeal in itself," added the black butterfly. "The most important one too, because that's where you'll find out whether you will be Disimpictured or not."

"I've got a bone to pick with that lousy Soul-Searcher!" complained Oksa. "I've a good mind to present it with an Inflammatoria—a few flames might teach it a lesson."

"That's as may be, but it might be a good idea to gather as many provisions as we can," said Abakum. "We'll need fruit and, most importantly, water… As for the dust, I suggest we use the plants I spotted over there, under those rocks in the shade. If memory serves, they're Spongiphyles, a kind of sponge with thousands of tiny holes, which makes them ideal as air filters. I'll make some masks, which will come in extremely useful, I fear."

Gus looked at him in alarm.

"You mean we're going into that hellhole *now?*" he sputtered.

"What's the point of waiting?" remarked Tugdual.

"It's easy for you to say!" retorted Gus. "You'll be in your element. The creepier the place, the better you like it."

Tugdual shrugged and looked away.

"Contrary to what you might think, I'm not thrilled about what's waiting for us," he replied gravely.

"This is no time for arguing," said Pavel. "Tugdual's right: there's nothing to be gained by waiting."

"It's so nice here…" murmured Oksa.

"Yes, it is," agreed Pavel, grasping her hand. "But we want to get out of this picture more than anything, don't we? And we won't do that by staying here."

There was no disputing his logic. Pavel was right and everyone knew it. Backing up his friend, Abakum took out his Granok-Shooter and uttered in a ringing voice:

Reticulata, Reticulata
Things far away look larger.

He held the large jellyfish which had just emerged from the Granok-Shooter under the waterfall. Water surged into the Reticulata, filling it to the brim and making its transparent walls bulge under the pressure. Following his example, the Runaways each got out their Granok-Shooters and said the magic words, before plunging every Reticulata into the waterfall. Meanwhile, curbing his frustration, Gus had positioned himself under the trees, which were trying to outdo each other by lowering branches laden with fruit into his hand. When every Runaway's bag was full to bursting, he lingered a minute on the Lunatrixa's grave, overwhelmed with grief. He wanted to say something—a thank you? an apology? a promise?—but the words stuck in his throat, almost suffocating him. Then, eyes downcast, he rejoined his friends, who were waiting for him.

"Come on, son," said his father. "You can carry my bag of provisions—it's my turn to carry the Incompetent," he added, adjusting the harness for the creature.

Perched on Pierre's back, the Incompetent looked around with a dazed expression.

"Where's that nice lady who wears plaits around her head?" it asked. "I lived with her before moving here, and I haven't seen her for ages… I hope she isn't dead!"

Taken aback, Pavel rubbed his face, while Oksa looked at the Runaways, feeling a surge of panic at the thought that it might be a premonition. As if reading her mind, Abakum reassured her immediately:

"The Incompetent doesn't have hunches," he declared in what was meant to be a firm voice. "This creature has certain qualities and powers, but seeing into the future isn't one of them, so don't worry."

However, Oksa sensed that the Incompetent's remark had upset more than one of the Runaways, particularly her father. Even Abakum seemed rattled, despite his apparent confidence. Driving the nail of doubt deeper into their hearts, the Squoracle popped its tiny head out of the Fairyman's jacket, where it had taken up residence, and squawked loudly:

"The Felons are calling the shots and their power is increasing with every passing minute!"

Abakum stuffed the little hen back in his jacket and resolutely strode towards the waterfall. The Runaways, armed with their diaphanous balls of water shimmering in the sun, held hands and followed the Fairyman. Oksa couldn't help glancing once more at the small mound where the Lunatrixa had been laid to rest. She blew her one last kiss, before being pulled through the watery curtain by her father.

33

Two Minus One

AFTER BEING CONFINED TO BED FOR TWO DAYS, Dragomira was recuperating slowly from the violent attack by the three Felons. With her talents as an apothecary, she'd been able to treat her physical wounds, particularly the many cuts caused by Catarina's Tornaphyllon Granok and the devastating effects of Mercedica's hefty punch. However, no potion or balm could raise Baba Pollock's spirits. Nothing worse could have happened: not only had the Felons kidnapped Marie—which was a tragedy in itself—but they now also had the medallion and a Goranov plant.

"What a fool I am," she sighed for the hundredth time that day.

Lying on a sofa, she watched with tear-filled eyes as Zoe applied Spinollias to the deep gashes on her arms.

"The Old Gracious should not condemn herself with these reproaches," objected the Lunatrix.

"I was so rash," continued the old lady, patting her swollen eye. "You see, my Lunatrix, I just made things worse with my over-inflated pride."

"The domestic staff of your Old Gracious does not have understanding of this blame," added the Lunatrix. "Pride is not the cause of the tragedy: the Felons hold a responsibility which no one can ignore."

Dragomira sighed again. She struggled to sit up, aching all over. Quietly, Zoe hurried to prop her up against some cushions and looked at her sadly.

"Perhaps... Probably," continued Dragomira. "But if I hadn't been so sure I was strong enough to deal with those traitors, I'd have asked for help and none of this would have happened. I wanted to prove that I was stronger than them. But I have to face facts: I'm just an old woman way past her prime."

The Lunatrix came over and gazed at her with his big blue eyes. He looked heartsick, with bowed shoulders and colourless skin.

"Harshness is abusive," he observed. "The Old Gracious is first and foremost the Old Gracious."

"That's profound, that is!" said the dishevelled Getorix, jumping onto the back of Dragomira's sofa. "Bravo major-domo!"

"Sarcasm does not damage the heart of the Lunatrix," retorted the plump creature. "It does not even reach its periphery."

"Hey, servant, why are you looking so colourless?" asked the Getorix mockingly. The Lunatrix sniffled and slumped onto the carpet.

"The Lunatrix pair is shattered," he said hoarsely.

Alarmed, Dragomira sat up on the edge of the sofa and seized the small creature's pudgy hands.

"The female double has experienced the loss of her mind," continued the Lunatrix, curling into an even smaller ball. "Reunion is abolished."

"That isn't possible!" exclaimed Baba Pollock in horror.

"That's terrible news!" boomed Naftali in his deep voice.

The imposing Swede was standing with his wife at the door to Dragomira's apartment. They both walked over to the Lunatrix and knelt down in front of him to stroke his large, silky head.

"You mean that the Lunatrixa is..." ventured Zoe, without daring to utter the fatal word.

"Ageless Fairies banished from their community have subtracted the soul of the beloved Lunatrixa," confirmed the Lunatrix, letting fat, round tears flow freely down his cheeks.

"That can't be true," murmured Brune, gazing tearfully at the small, hunched creature.

"The risk of loss has accomplished its fusion with reality."

The sympathetic Getorix hurried over to hand the Lunatrix a hanky. Saddened by this revelation, it stood in front of him and hugged him.

"I've never thought you were just an ordinary servant, you know," it said abruptly to hide its sadness. "Hey, come to think of it, one of your delicious cheese and ham toasties would go down a treat!" it added, changing the subject.

The Lunatrix stood up obediently and headed for the kitchen, where he busied himself with a great banging and crashing of crockery. Anxious to make up for its tactlessness, the Getorix tried to make him feel better by telling him jokes of its own devising. But the Lunatrix's heart wasn't in it—he remained unresponsive, locked in his grief. Dragomira stood up with a groan and, leaning heavily on the arm Zoe offered, went over to the miserable creature.

"You knew from the start, didn't you?"

"The two Lunatrixes had the knowledge of the subtraction of their other half before the arrival in the picture," he said, looking at Dragomira. "Their heart was prepared for endless separation, but not for the pain."

"And neither of you said anything?" murmured Dragomira, taking him in her arms.

"The Old Gracious must not be forgetting that the Lunatrixes do not offer communication of what they know unless questioning is performed," replied the Lunatrix with a sob. "An absence of interrogation brings the consequence of an absence of broadcasting."

"Of course... it was unforgivable of me. I should have asked you what you knew before Impicturement."

"To know and to say what one knows does not prevent destiny from striking without mercy whomever it chooses..."

"But we wouldn't have made the Lunatrixa enter the picture!" exclaimed the old lady with tears in her eyes.

"My Lunatrixa received the appointment from destiny to practise the rescue of an Impictured Runaway. Her obedience was complete because choice has no existence."

"No one can escape their destiny," said Zoe softly, deeply moved.

"The friend of the Young Gracious possesses exactitude in her heart," agreed the Lunatrix weakly.

His head fell back onto Dragomira's shoulder and she staggered under the weight of her small steward. Naftali rushed over to help Zoe support Baba Pollock and all three took the Lunatrix over to a sofa.

"I do hope he'll get over this," whispered Zoe.

The Lunatrix turned to look at her.

"The friend of the Young Gracious has hope in her mouth and her wish will encounter satisfaction," he announced, sounding exhausted. "The heart of the Lunatrix will remain ripped to shreds until the egress of his life, but his longevity will experience continuation."

"I'm sorry to have to ask you this, my Lunatrix," continued Dragomira looking troubled. "But—"

"The Lunatrix has knowledge of the anxiety of the Old Gracious," broke in the creature. "The Runaways will make a return that is almost complete, that is a certainty."

"Almost complete?" repeated Naftali in alarm, while Dragomira's face fell.

"Eternal disappearance will occur again," replied the Lunatrix. Dragomira gave a heart-rending cry:

"WHO? TELL ME WHO?"

"An Impictured Runaway will make surrender of their life. But the Lunatrix does not have knowledge of the identity. The Lunatrix is not destiny," concluded the small, grief-stricken creature, huddled in a ball on the sofa.

❃

This thought came as a terrible shock to the five helpless Runaways in the house on Bigtoe Square. Dragomira tottered back to her sofa, took a deep breath and shut her eyes, losing herself in dark thoughts. Brune and Naftali sat opposite on the armchairs, still in tatters after the Felons' visit to Baba Pollock's apartment. The elderly Scandinavian couple's bewilderment could be read on their faces. Worn out with anxiety and hard work at the restaurant, Jeanne looked as haggard as her friends. Her large brown eyes, filled with panic, seemed to take up the whole of her face. As for Zoe, a strange feeling of emptiness came over her. A feeling she'd experienced a few months earlier when she'd lost her parents, then her gran Reminiscens and, finally, her great-uncle, Orthon-McGraw. They'd all disappeared so suddenly, taking a piece of her with them. There was no pain—she just felt numb. It was a highly personal defence mechanism that Zoe had created to cope with her profound unhappiness: survival by emptiness. Perhaps it was made easier by her Firmhand origins? Or the part of her that was descended from the Werewalls? Or the Graciouses? Maybe all three, she thought, surprised by her own cool reaction. Sitting to one side, she watched Jeanne, Naftali, Brune and Dragomira. She knew how worried they were. The Knuts had to be thinking about their grandson, Tugdual, and Jeanne about her husband and son. As for Dragomira, her son, granddaughter and brother were imprisoned in that picture. Who were the people she might think about? Her gran? Leomido, her brand-new grandfather? Gus? She forced herself to picture them, even though the pain might be unbearable. So bad she might never recover. This nudge to her memory brought her gran's face to her mind's eye…

※

She clearly remembered the last time she'd seen Reminiscens. It had been a Thursday and the weather had been glorious—only a few wisps of fluffy cloud in the sky. They'd walked briskly to school—Reminiscens always took her to school and met her afterwards. They'd kissed goodbye, wishing each other a good day, and Zoe had gone off to class. But that evening her gran hadn't been waiting for her after school. Orthon, her great-uncle, had been there. His black eyes had gleamed with a strange sadness when he'd told her that Reminiscens had drowned. This news, following hard on the horror of losing her parents in a plane crash a few months earlier, had stolen all the happiness from Zoe's heart.

※

After this tragedy, Orthon's family had welcomed her in. Everyone was very kind to her. Her great-aunt Barbara, who was a sweet-natured, affectionate woman, suffered from depression. She missed her native United States badly. Her cousin Mortimer was as protective and as kind as a real brother. And, despite his stern nature, her great-uncle Orthon made sure she lacked for nothing and she became accustomed to his brooding expression as he watched her with a strange curiosity. The three McGraws were her only family and her gratitude soon turned to deep affection.

Once she was living with them, Zoe reluctantly witnessed the arguments which often blew up between Orthon and Barbara over subjects which obviously had nothing to do with her—much to her great relief. It was always to do with something called Edefia and about Orthon going too far. It had been hard for her to understand everything then and she'd even thought that Edefia was a woman with whom Orthon might have had an affair! Now she knew all about the Pollocks and the Runaways—she was one of them now—she understood why Barbara and Orthon had fought so violently. But that hadn't been the case at the time… One evening she'd come home from school and had walked in on Mortimer and Barbara in tears in the living room. Barbara was yelling and Zoe hadn't understood what was going on. She'd simply realized that something serious had happened in the McGraw household.

That was the last time she'd seen them.

※

She thought about her gran again. She'd believed she was dead and now it seemed that she might be alive after all. The tiny possibility that she might see her again had been undermined by the Lunatrix's remarks. Then the image of her grandfather, Leomido, popped into her head—she hadn't known him for long, but she already loved him so much—followed by a string of other faces: Pavel, so tormented and yet so endearing; Abakum, the Fairyman who knew and understood everything; Gus... her confidant, whom she loved with all her heart. Unconditionally. Absolutely. He didn't even know and, anyway, he loved Oksa, she was certain of it. How could anyone not love Oksa? Suddenly, she heard the Lunatrix's words again. "An Impictured Runaway will make surrender of their life". Zoe caught herself wondering something awful: if she had to decide who should die, whom would she choose? Emptiness immediately flooded into the panicky part of her mind and caused it to snap shut, protecting her from the terrible answer. The girl huddled smaller in her armchair and tried to force herself to breathe normally.

34

The Island in the Sea of the Hebrides

"We're powerless to do anything to help!" roared Naftali suddenly, letting go of Brune's hand. "It's so frustrating…"

Dragomira jumped.

"Which is why we must focus on damage limitation here!" continued the imposing Swede, his emerald eyes shining with anger.

"But the harm has been done, my friend," remarked Dragomira, sounding resigned.

Naftali jumped up.

"Where's the Dragomira I know and love?" he thundered, towering over her. "Where's the fighter, the confident, spirited Gracious who's supposed to show us the way to Edefia? You're not the kind of woman who gives up so easily!"

Dragomira sighed in vexation, her eyes fixed on the hard-working Spinollias deftly stitching her arm.

"What can we do?" she asked, straightening up.

"First of all, we need to find out whether Marie is being well treated," said Naftali. "Has the Tumble-Bawler returned from its fact-finding mission in the Sea of the Hebrides?"

"Not yet…"

"It'll be here soon," said the tall man reassuringly. "But I already know what it'll tell us about Marie: the Felons can't risk mistreating her. I think we're bound to be contacted soon. Marie will be used as a hostage to demand certain things from us."

"The picture," murmured Dragomira.

"Think about it," continued Naftali. "What's most important for the Felons? What's their ultimate aim?"

Dragomira, Brune and Jeanne thought for a few seconds, then chorused: "Returning to Edefia!"

"Exactly!" agreed Naftali. "And what—or rather, whom—do they need to do that? Oksa! She's the only one who can open the Portal and that's the only thing they're concerned about: using Oksa as a key. Their attempts to kidnap her are proof of that. Let's face it: at the moment, the picture is only one way to lay their hands on our Young Gracious. Thanks to you, Dragomira, the picture is safe. And it must stay safe no matter what. Forgive me for asking, but are you sure it can't be found?"

"I'm sure," declared Dragomira. "To be honest, I don't even know where it is at the moment."

The four Runaways looked at her in amazement. Had she lost her mind? Was she becoming senile? Naftali narrowed his eyes, his forehead creased in a worried frown, then his face lit up with a broad smile as he grasped the meaning of his old friend's words.

"You secretly asked a third party to help!" he exclaimed in relief. "Do you know how glad I am that you're still in full possession of your wits, Dragomira Pollock?"

"That's very clever," added Brune. "There's no better way of keeping it safe than not knowing where it is. Well done!"

Dragomira smiled humbly and gave a disparaging wave of her hand.

"Here's my theory," continued Naftali. "The Felons, like us, have to wait for Oksa to be Disimpictured, which keeps her out of their clutches for the time being. But when she reappears, they'll use Marie to apply pressure on Oksa to lead them to the Portal and open it for them."

"You're forgetting that Oksa cannot open the Portal unaided!" remarked Dragomira. "We need the medallion and the Felons need the Guardian of the Definitive Landmark."

"That's true," admitted Naftali. "The ball's in their court because Marie gives them a serious advantage over us. Will we be able to withstand their demands? I fear not and you know that as well as I do. We'll be forced to capitulate at some point or other. Or at least to make some concessions."

"Unless we rescue Marie," said Zoe in a small voice.

"Unless we rescue Marie," confirmed Naftali, nodding.

"But we're in no position to do that!" exclaimed Jeanne. "We don't have the resources."

"You're right," agreed Naftali. "We must wait patiently until our friends are Disimpictured, so that we leave nothing to chance. There's strength in numbers, after all. In the meantime, we'll have to be extra vigilant, because there's no guarantee that the Felons will just sit and wait patiently. We need to be prepared for them to bring out the big guns to get hold of the picture before Disimpicturement."

"There's absolutely no danger they'll find the picture!" exclaimed Dragomira triumphantly. Naftali turned to her, looking far less convinced.

"Careful, Dragomira. Underestimating our enemies may be our Achilles heel and could weaken our position. Particularly as our worst fears have already been realized," he added sombrely.

Embarrassed, Dragomira looked down and nodded, without saying a word.

"Hey! Look who's here!" cried Zoe suddenly.

She rushed over to the skylight and opened it for the breathless Tumble-Bawler, which was tapping on the windowpane. The small scout fluttered over to a rickety occasional table, where it perched and gave a weary sigh. Zoe handed it a thimble-sized glass of water, which it gulped down in one, eyes half-closed, as it caught its breath. She stroked its tiny back, which was aching after its long journey.

"Mmm, what a divine massage!" it purred, rocking from left to right.

"Tumble, did you see Marie?" asked Dragomira, unable to contain her impatience.

"Tumble-Bawler of the Old Gracious reporting!" exclaimed the creature. "There are 398 miles between this house and the place where the Young Gracious's mother is being held captive on the island in the Sea of the Hebrides. I travelled nine and a half miles between the coast and the island of the Felons on a fishing boat moving at a speed of sixteen miles an hour, then one and a quarter miles on the back of a very helpful seal and the last half-mile swimming in water whose temperature was fifteen degrees centigrade. When I came to the island, I covered 2,438 feet to arrive at the building where Marie Pollock now resides. It is a very big house: seventy-two feet long by fifty-nine feet wide. It has a raised ground floor, an upper floor and two basements hollowed out of the stone in which I spotted at least four laboratories."

"Two basements?" repeated Brune in surprise.

"Yes," confirmed the Tumble-Bawler. "One basement the same size as the ground floor and a second basement beneath the first. It was hard for me to gauge the measurements of the second basement, because I couldn't get in there. But, from my calculations, it's twice as big as the first."

"That's huge!" remarked Naftali.

"The building is densely populated with human beings," informed the Tumble-Bawler. "I counted twenty-eight people living there, as well as the Young Gracious's mother."

Dragomira frowned.

"Twenty-eight?" she exclaimed, looking at her friends in alarm. "That means Orthon and Mercedica have put together quite a commando group... Would you happen to know, Tumble-Bawler, if they're all Runaways?"

"Yes, they are Runaways and their descendants," it assured her. "I spotted Mercedica de La Fuente and her daughter Catarina, as well as Gregor and Mortimer McGraw."

"Mortimer!" exclaimed Zoe, sounding upset.

"Yes, and also Lukas's two sons and three grandsons."

"Wait a moment," broke in Naftali, raising his hand. "You mean Lukas, Edefia's renowned mineralogist?"

"The same!" declared the Tumble-Bawler.

"Do you know him?" asked Zoe.

"Oh yes," sighed Naftali. "Lukas was a brilliant mineral specialist back in Edefia. If I remember correctly, he concentrated his research on the energy potential of stones from Retinburn, isn't that so, Brune?"

The tall woman nodded regretfully.

"He was also extremely interested in crystallochemistry," Brune recalled. "Lukas was an out-and-out Firmhand. In other words, he had all the typical personality traits of that tribe in spades. He was particularly known for that chilly arrogance which caused some of the Firmhands to join forces against the ruling Gracious. Of course, I haven't forgotten that I belong to that tribe too, as does my husband, and that you both have Firmhand blood," she added, turning to Jeanne and Zoe. "I'll respect the Firmhand tribe to my dying day, but I can't turn a blind eye to the part they played in bringing about the Chaos which destroyed Edefia. Because of men like Ocious. Or Lukas."

"Was he dangerous?" asked Zoe.

"Very!" replied Brune. "That's what we discovered, in any case, when the Chaos began. Lukas showed his true colours and there were some who paid for it with their lives."

Brune nodded, lost in her memories.

"He must be about ninety now," remarked Dragomira.

"Ninety-three, four months and fifteen days exactly," said the Tumble-Bawler. "His two sons are called Hector and Pyotr, and they are fifty-two and forty-nine respectively. Pyotr has three sons who live on the island, Kaspar, Konstantin and Oskar. Let me add that it was Oskar who visited your apartment with Catarina and Gregor, my Old Gracious."

"This new generation is certainly keen to follow in the footsteps of its grandparents," muttered Dragomira sarcastically. "Did you recognize any other Felons, Tumble?"

"I snooped around with the greatest enthusiasm, but the fear of being discovered and captured caused me to take certain precautions which prevented me from performing a more in-depth inspection. I did however hear the Goranov wailing in one of the rooms in the basement. Then I recognized the Abominari and a Long-Gulch who used to be in charge of the Memorary in the Gracious's Archive Department."

"Well, well!" said Naftali bitterly. "Don't tell me you're talking about Agafon?"

"You must be psychic!" replied the Tumble-Bawler. "It was indeed Agafon, who's now eighty-nine, eight months and twelve days old."

"So quite a few of us were ejected from Edefia," remarked Dragomira. "More than I thought."

"From what I found out," continued the Tumble-Bawler, "Agafon ended up in Finland after passing through the Portal. He now lives on the island in the Sea of the Hebrides with his twin granddaughters, Annikki and Vilma, who are both twenty-eight years and seventeen days old. I couldn't identify anyone else, my Old Gracious. As for Marie Pollock, I found her in the fifth room on the first floor to the left of the central corridor, starting from the southern end of the building. I took the liberty of slipping into her room to speak to her."

"How is she?" asked Dragomira eagerly.

"She is physically fine. The Felons are treating her well and her room is comfortable. Unfortunately, the Robiga-Nervosa continues to decimate her nervous system, but I saw Agafon's granddaughter, Annikki, who is a nurse, give her some injections of Vermicula, which seemed to make our dear invalid feel better. Annikki looks after her attentively, because she knows she's the mother of the Young Gracious and she respects that, despite being a Felon. However, the care she lavishes on Marie does nothing to relieve her anxiety: her imprisonment and the absence of news about those she loves are a continual source of suffering."

The Tumble-Bawler continued rocking from left to right, disturbed by these recent memories.

"When I saw how upset she was, I took the risk of approaching her," it continued. "I waited for two hours and forty-three minutes until Annikki went out and I entered the room. The Young Gracious's mother seemed extremely happy to see me. I told her where she was being kept and assured her that the Runaways were making plans to come and rescue her. She told me to beware the power of the Felons and not to take any risks. Then Annikki came back and sat down in the room. I had to hide under the bed, where I waited for one hour, eighteen minutes and three seconds before I could get out. I escaped by crawling over to the hearth and climbing up the smoke-filled flue for seventeen feet and nine inches at a temperature of fifty-two degrees centigrade. It took eleven hours and twelve minutes to get back to Bigtoe Square in London, taking various means of transport: seagull, pilot whale, boat, cattle truck, pigeon and tourist coach. I hope my report will be useful to my Old Gracious and her friends."

"No doubt about that, Tumble," said Dragomira reassuringly, leaning back against the armchair. "No doubt at all."

35

A Hazy Figure

Zoe's mind was racing after hearing the Tumble-Bawler's report, which made it hard to fall asleep. She was comforted by the thought that Marie was being well treated and the Felons were doing their best to alleviate her suffering. It was in their interest to do so, she reasoned. If Marie died, they'd lose their only means of exerting pressure on them. But what was really occupying her thoughts in the half-dark of this summer night was the news she'd had of Mortimer. The Tumble-Bawler might not have said very much, but the mere mention of her second cousin had unsettled her. For a few months he'd been like a brother to her and, despite his brusque manner and intense dislike of the Pollocks, he'd treated her with a kindness that made up for the affection she'd missed so much since the death of her parents and her gran. He'd shown her nothing but consideration and generosity since she'd arrived at the McGraws'. His behaviour had been the complete opposite of what she'd expected from his outward appearance... She'd even wondered how someone could be so different! "Go to your room, Zoe. Don't worry. I'll pop up and see you in a bit." Those were the last words Mortimer had ever said to her. He was crying as he said them. Naturally: his father had just been vaporized before his very eyes. But, despite his promise, Mortimer had never showed up. He'd run away, leaving her all alone, knowing nothing about what was going on. Was she angry with him? Yes, a little. He could have taken her with him; she could have made herself useful.

Instead, she was now living with the Pollocks. And fate had been very kind to her. The Pollocks had accepted her and she felt like she really belonged to this amazing new family. They were all so loving and warm, which was so much more than she could have hoped for when she arrived in Bigtoe Square. But despite their many qualities, they could never replace the family she'd lost. She thought about her gran. If, by some stroke of luck, she was reunited with her, how would Reminiscens react? Whom would she feel drawn to? Leomido, her lost love, one of the mainstays of the Pollock family? Or Mortimer, the son of her twin brother, Master of the Felons on the Outside? Zoe was more aware than ever of the dual heritage which made it impossible for her to be sure of her own feelings. The Gracious-Firmhand-Werewall mix weighed heavily on her, plunging her into an abyss of doubt. Which part of her was the strongest?

Everything was such a muddle. She thought about Ocious, the great Felon who'd instigated the downfall of Edefia and the Gracious's clan— that man was her great-grandfather. Malorane, the naïve Gracious, was on the other side of the family tree. The blood of those two illustrious figures flowed through her veins… She sighed, feeling unsettled. Did she have a role to play in this saga? And if she did, would she stand with Leomido or with Mortimer? Did she really have to take sides? She rolled over onto her stomach in bed and threw off her duvet. When the time came, she'd listen to her heart, which was now aching and silent.

Exhausted, she eventually fell asleep, her head spinning with night-marish images and tantalizing hopes. Gus's sad eyes kept coming back to fill her dreams. She half-opened her eyes and drifted, not quite awake and not asleep. She knew Gus was very much like her. Although their origins were different, they were similar in that they both had a darker side which caused them heartache and stemmed from the fact that they didn't know where they belonged. Struggling with feelings of low self-esteem, Zoe never stood up for herself and showed people what she was really made of. And she knew nothing would ever change until she could truly accept her origins.

A sudden shiver ran down her spine, like a draught of cold air passing through her body. She shut her eyes, upset by all these gloomy thoughts, and didn't see the strange figure, which had just risen from the surface of her back, pass through the wall and disappear into the night...

❋

A couple of miles away from Bigtoe Square, Merlin Poicassé suddenly sat bolt upright in bed. He had the nasty feeling there was someone in his room. He turned on his bedside lamp and looked around with a frown. There was nothing there. He turned off the lamp and lay down again. A second shiver ran down his spine, although not as strong as the one that had just woken him. He glanced at the alarm clock on the bedside table: ten past two. He sighed, stretched and pulled his duvet over him. A few minutes later he was in a deep sleep.

❋

The man passed through the wall and looked round the dark room. He silently walked over to the girl's bed, his hazy body floating above the ground. His fingertips lightly caressed the sleeping girl's arm and she shifted slightly at his cold touch. The man froze for a second, his senses alert. The girl turned over in bed and half-opened her eyes. She lay like this for a moment, gazing vacantly into space. The light from the street filtered through the curtains, bathing the room in the milky glow she liked so much. Her eyes wandered around the room before settling on an odd form standing by her bed. A human form with fragmented outlines which looked like a pixelated photo. Was it a ghost? A hallucination? She knew, logically, that she should scream and jump out of bed, but she wasn't afraid, which surprised her almost more than the blurred figure standing there. She narrowed her eyes, then opened them wide when the form came nearer and put his indistinct hand on her forehead.

209

"Sir?" she murmured in surprise. "Is that you?"

An icy wave washed over her brain, flooding every inch of her body. Before she sank into a dreamless sleep again, she could have sworn she recognized the malicious smile of the late Dr McGraw.

36

LIES AND SURPRISES GALORE

C LINGING TO DRAGOMIRA'S ARM, ZOE FELT VERY APPRE-
hensive about the new term. She wasn't as anxious as she'd been
last year at the same time when she'd just started her new school, but she
still couldn't wait for the day to end. She tossed back her blonde hair and
tightened her uniform tie, trying to ignore the butterflies in her stomach.
Dragomira was also unhappy: it would have been so much better if Oksa
and Gus had been Disimpictured in time to go back to school. She'd
waited until the last moment to tell Mr Bontempi, the Headmaster of
St Proximus. Officially, the two children were stuck on the other side of
the world, confined to bed by an exotic and highly contagious disease.
Bringing them back too soon might have serious implications for their
health… Fortunately, Mr Bontempi hadn't lost the open-mindedness
that seemed to develop magically as soon as Dragomira addressed him,
and he scurried over to greet her as soon as he saw her entering the
school's magnificent paved courtyard.

"My respects to you, my dear Mrs Pollock!" he exclaimed, kissing her
beringed hand. "How are you? And how are our two invalids?"

"Much better, thank you," replied Dragomira, favouring him with a
lingering gaze. "Although they're still not well enough to travel back to
England or join their class in the next few days."

"Let's hope they can come back soon," said the Headmaster. "Where
are they exactly? I know you told me, but it must have gone in one

ear and out the other. One of the pitfalls of old age," he added with a laugh.

"I know exactly what you mean, my dear Mr Bontempi," agreed Dragomira with a charming smile. "I have the same problem. So, before I forget your question—and perhaps the answer as well—let me remind you that Oksa and Gus are in a small hospital in Kota Kinabalu, in the Borneo archipelago. My son Pavel and Pierre Bellanger are with them."

"Good, good," nodded Mr Bontempi. Then, turning to Zoe, he continued:

"So, Miss Evanvleck, it will be your job to help your friends catch up."

"That's what I'm intending to do," nodded Zoe. "You can count on me."

"Excellent. Anyway, it's very good of you to bring this young lady to school today, Mrs Pollock."

Dragomira hesitated for a second, which only Zoe noticed, then announced matter-of-factly:

"Perhaps you didn't know that Zoe is my great-niece?"

Zoe Evanvleck? Dragomira Pollock's great-niece? But Mr Bontempi had thought she was Dr McGraw's great-niece! He looked surprised and spent a few seconds digesting this new fact, brow furrowed, trying to work out any ramifications he might have missed.

"No, I didn't know that," he replied, taken aback. "Does that mean that Dr McGraw was a member of your family?" he asked uncertainly.

He couldn't believe it had taken him this long to realize that the Pollocks were related to Dr McGraw. He'd never warmed to that sarcastic disciplinarian who'd terrorized students and colleagues alike. There was no denying he'd been an excellent science teacher who'd come with glowing references, but there was something disturbing about the man and he'd always made Mr Bontempi feel uneasy. No one had jumped for joy at the news of the car crash that had claimed his life a few months ago, but no one had been terribly upset either. The Headmaster looked again at Dragomira, who was startlingly beautiful in her garnet-coloured silk dress.

"That woman is the polar opposite of McGraw," he thought and, as if she could read his mind, she said:

"Yes, we were distantly related… but we didn't really have much contact with each other, as we didn't see eye to eye, you understand," she explained confidentially. "Oh, isn't that Miss Heartbreak over there?"

Mr Bontempi turned round and his eyes brightened when he spotted the smartly dressed young woman chatting to some students in the middle of the courtyard.

"She looks well!" remarked Zoe, pleased to see her history and geography teacher again.

"Thanks to your wonderful great-aunt's talents as a herbalist," added Mr Bontempi, leaning towards Zoe.

He straightened up and took Dragomira's hand, which he pressed warmly.

"I shall be eternally grateful for everything you've done for Benedicta, Mrs Pollock," he said, sounding choked. "I'll never question the healing properties of plants again. You see before you a total convert to alternative medicine!" he added with a laugh. "Well, it must be time for me to take my place on the rostrum. The students are waiting… My humble respects, Mrs Pollock. See you soon, Miss Evanvleck."

He saluted them briefly and headed over to the rostrum erected in front of the cloister bordering the courtyard. Before she followed him, Zoe glanced inquisitively at Dragomira.

"I didn't know you'd been called in to help Miss Heartbreak."

"I couldn't leave the poor woman in that state!" exclaimed Dragomira with a jingle of her intricate perch-shaped earrings. "I offered my help to Mr Bontempi, who accepted, although he was a little sceptical at first. As you can see, it didn't take long to win him over."

"Does she remember… everything?" asked Zoe, a little concerned that the sweet-natured teacher might recall Orthon's terrible attack.

"Good Lord, no!" cried Dragomira, her hand pressed to her heart. "Let's just say that she has selective amnesia about a certain episode."

Zoe gave her an amused smile.

"What's up with you, young lady?" asked the old lady, her eyes sparkling.

"I've never seen anyone—" Hesitating, she left the sentence unfinished.

"Lie as well as I do?" continued Baba Pollock. "I know, sweetheart, I know… Would you believe me if I told you it's not something I'm proud of? Unfortunately, though, lying is part of the survival instinct of all Runaways. If none of us had ever lied, our community wouldn't have survived for so long."

"Well done, anyway!" exclaimed Zoe. "You had all the answers ready."

"Another of our indispensable gifts is the ability to anticipate the questions we might be asked," concluded Dragomira thoughtfully. "Anyway, off you go, Zoe. Your friends are waiting for you."

꙰

Mr Bontempi had also done Zoe a good turn, putting her in the same class as her friends Merlin and Zelda, which made her feel much better— she felt so alone sometimes. Best of all, Gus and Oksa would also be in Year 9 Hydrogen when they'd recovered from their tropical disease. Unfortunately, Hilda Richard—Cave-Girl, as she'd been nicknamed by Oksa—was also on the list, which didn't please Merlin.

"Oh, that's such rotten luck!"

As he was muttering to himself, he noticed Dragomira standing to one side, leaning against a massive statue of an angel. Oksa's gran waved discreetly to him with a vague smile. Since she'd entrusted him with that hateful picture, they'd avoided talking to each other in order to keep their secret. Dragomira was being watched closely by the Felons, but they were also suspicious of Merlin. He'd known that ever since he'd found his house turned upside down just after he'd hidden the picture at Big Ben: every room had been ransacked, but nothing had been stolen—not even the brand-new computer or the twenty-pound note lying in plain sight on a side table. Merlin was convinced that this was no ordinary burglary. He shivered at the memory. He hoped Oksa came out of that picture soon...

"Hi, Merlin!" drawled a loud voice behind him.

He turned round to find himself face to face with Hilda Richard. Merlin couldn't get over how much she'd changed. The bully who'd spent her time terrorizing the other students had undergone a complete transformation.

"Have you grown your hair?" she continued, studying him closely. "It really suits you! Did you have a good break?"

Merlin looked at her in astonishment: she was still thickset, awkward and tall, but there was something much more feminine about the girl whom everyone avoided. Her small, close-set eyes gazed merrily at him from beneath lids covered in blue eye shadow, without a glimmer of malice.

"Er... yes, thanks!" replied the boy, taken aback.

Hilda smiled, which completely fazed him. She'd never been friendly to him before. She turned on her heels and walked away, swinging her hips so that the pleated skirt of her school uniform swayed with the motion.

"Wow!" exclaimed Zelda, loosening her tie. "Who'd have thought— Hilda Richard has turned into a real girl! The school holidays have certainly done her good."

Zoe and Merlin looked at each other in surprise at this mean remark from Zelda, who was usually so kind.

"Watch out! She's coming back," murmured Zelda, winking at Merlin.

Blushing to the roots of his hair, Merlin looked at his feet and studied the blades of grass growing between the paving stones.

"Hey, Merlin!" called Hilda, making a huge effort to soften her voice. "Did you see that we're in the same class and Miss Heartbreak is our form tutor? Isn't that cool?"

Zelda couldn't hold back a snort of laughter, which earned her a scornful look from Hilda. Merlin, on the other hand, seemed about to go up in flames.

"Yeah, really cool…" he muttered.

"See you soon then," murmured Hilda, darting one last challenging look at the two girls. Brusquely shouldering her backpack, she headed off towards the centre of the courtyard, leaving the three friends to recover from their surprise.

"Casanova!" said Zelda to Merlin.

"Give it a rest!" retorted Merlin, his eyes twinkling and his cheeks scarlet. "It's got nothing to do with me. Come on, we'd better get to class. We don't want to keep Miss Heartbreak waiting."

37

ZOE'S HEAVY HEART

A S THEY CLIMBED THE SPLENDID STONE STAIRCASE LEAD-
ing to the first-floor classrooms, the three friends remarked to each
other that this new term was full of surprises. Hilda Richard, who was in
front of them, was almost unrecognizable—gone were the vicious kicks,
shoves and insults which had made her the most feared girl in the school.
Her victims in previous years couldn't get over it. Everyone was relieved
that her belligerent behaviour seemed to be a thing of the past, but they
were still cautious in case the change was too good to be true. They were
all watching and waiting for conclusive proof, Merlin more than anyone.

※

It wasn't just Hilda Richard who was different from last year: the summer
break seemed to have done Zelda good too. The shy, clumsy girl who was
scared of everything had grown a few inches and gained a hefty dose of
self-confidence. When Miss Heartbreak said they could sit where they
liked, the students rushed to pair up with their friends and Zelda bagged
the desk next to Merlin's, after what he would have sworn was a great
deal of pushing and shoving. "What's got into them?" he wondered,
feeling puzzled. "Is that what puberty does to girls?" Only Zoe was the
same: reserved, placid and sad. He noticed her disappointed expression when she saw Zelda sitting next to him and awkwardly shot her a

resigned smile. She didn't seem cross with him, though, and smiled back indulgently. He saw her spot a seat in the front row and sit down alone, her shoulders hunched. Full of remorse, he was just about to pass her a note of encouragement when someone tapped him on the shoulder. He turned round to see it was Hilda Richard... of course.

"Do you know where the Russian doll and her bodyguard are?" she asked quietly. "People are saying they're ill. Is that true?"

"I'll have you know that the Russian doll, as you put it, is my best friend!" snapped Merlin, quick as a flash.

"Hey, I didn't mean anything by it!" protested the former Cave-Girl. "I was just concerned, that's all."

"Yeah, sure," muttered Merlin, suddenly less convinced that the school holidays had worked any kind of magic on her.

"What's wrong ? It's hardly unflattering, is it? Russian dolls are cute."

"May I have your attention, please!" called out Miss Heartbreak.

Merlin turned round, relieved to escape Hilda's attentions.

"First of all, I'd like to tell you how glad I am to see you all again," began their teacher. "Thank you for all your messages and gifts, which have been a great comfort to me, more than you can imagine... What I went through is still a mystery, but I'm determined not to let it hold me back, which is why I'm here today. I'll be your form tutor this year and I wish you every success with your studies. You can count on me to help you as much as I can."

A few students murmured their thanks, aware of the vast difference between Miss Heartbreak and their previous form tutor, sardonic Dr McGraw.

"Excellent!" she said gaily, to lighten the mood. "Let's get down to work then. We'll start with the roll call. Please introduce yourselves as usual and perhaps you'd also tell us something about your school holidays, if you wouldn't mind?"

Sitting in the front row, listening distractedly as the first students stated their names and introduced themselves, Zoe couldn't take her eyes off her teacher. Standing behind her desk, she was just as slender and natural in appearance as she'd ever been. Only her face showed traces of her ordeal: tiny wrinkles fanned out from the corners of her eyes and all the vivacity had gone from her gaze. Miss Heartbreak had come back in one piece, but Zoe couldn't forget the horrible image of the teacher with tangled hair and tattered clothes, frolicking about in the icy water of the fountain like a puppy, yelling songs at the top of her voice. Nor could she forget that it was her great-uncle, Orthon-McGraw, who'd attacked her so violently. Did Miss Heartbreak know they were related? Of course she did. But she didn't seem to hold it against her. Then again, why on earth would she? Zoe knew what had happened, but Miss Heartbreak would never know! She'd forgotten everything. As far as she was concerned, her surly colleague had died in a car crash and Zoe had lost her form tutor, full stop. It was so strange… Everyone hated her great-uncle, but he wasn't just despicable Dr McGraw or the ferocious Felon: he was also a generous man who'd taken care of her and had welcomed her into his home. Zoe didn't want to believe he could be responsible in any way for her gran's Impicturement. The Squoracle was wrong. They were all wrong. Lost in dark thoughts, she gnawed her lower lip until it bled, her eyes brimming with tears. Miss Heartbreak looked over at her again and Zoe shivered, sure that the expression on her face betrayed her inner turmoil. Their teacher gave her a quick, compassionate smile, which made her feel worse: once again, she was an object of pity to those who only knew the bare bones of her story. She smiled back, her fists clenched, feeling upset and frustrated.

"Your turn, Miss Beck!" continued their teacher.

As she said this, Miss Heartbreak went pale and a shadow seemed to dim her blue eyes. She gripped the edge of the desk, her knuckles white with the effort of holding herself up.

"My name is Zelda Beck," announced Zelda, sitting up straight in her chair and staring at their teacher. "I like reading and foreign languages, electro music and running. I'd also like to add that I visited the Space Museum this summer. It's a brilliant place for understanding all kinds of stuff about the history of the universe."

"It is fascinating there," agreed Miss Heartbreak, a little tensely. "Thank you, Miss Beck. What about you, Miss Evanvleck?"

If possible, Zoe would have preferred to give a totally honest introduction: "My name is Zoe Evanvleck, I like history, particularly the history of the Insiders, who are my ancestors. This summer, I saw my cousin and grandfather swallowed up by an evil picture which had imprisoned my gran, whom I thought was dead, and my best friend, whom I really miss. Other than that, I spend my days practising my powers, so that I can walk through walls, beat the 100-metre track record and levitate in my room." She was desperate to tell the world about the life she was living. Would the truth make her feel any better? Probably not and she knew it. She choked back her foolish desire to come clean, even though it was threatening to suffocate her.

"My name is Zoe Evanvleck," she answered Miss Heartbreak nervously. "I like history, imaginary creatures and plants, as well as fantasy books. I spent the summer with my great-aunt and was kept very busy taking care of the animals belonging to her best friend, who'd gone on holiday."

"Thank you, Miss Evanvleck," smiled Miss Heartbreak. "Your turn, Mr Forster…"

※

When the bell rang for break, Zoe shot off to the toilet, where she locked herself in a cubicle and leant against the door. Her nerves were jangled, although she wasn't sure why. Or rather, she had a hundred good reasons to be on edge today, but she didn't know which one was making her feel so uptight… She took a deep breath and rubbed her hands over her face, as if trying to erase her bad mood. When she came out, Merlin was waiting for her with Zelda in tow. He'd also changed. In the space of a few weeks, he'd matured. He was taller, broader and less chubby, and his luxuriant blond curls, which had made him seem so angelic, now formed a thick golden mass of hair, which did nothing to detract from his good looks.

"Are you all right, Zoe?" he asked, looking at her intently.

"I'm fine... I always get a little nervous on the first day back—you never know who you might run into..."

"Well, there's no denying that this year has got off to a pretty good start, hasn't it?" said Zelda cheerfully. "No more McGraw to terrorize us, what more could anyone ask for?"

Merlin nudged her as sharply as he could and glared at her. Zelda bit her lower lip, realizing—a little too late—how tactless she'd just been.

"Sorry, Zoe," she muttered. "I'm a prize idiot..."

"Forget it," answered Zoe with a sad smile. "You're always putting your foot in it, that's just the way you are. Shall we see if we can find somewhere to sit by the fountain?"

"Come on then!" said Merlin, relieved there were no ill feelings.

"Can I come with you?" rang out a voice behind them.

"Er..." replied Merlin, turning round.

He again found himself face to face with Hilda Richard, who was looking at him with unprecedented friendliness. He blushed again, as Zelda and Zoe struggled not to laugh.

"I'll take that as a 'yes'!" exclaimed Hilda.

"You've scored there!" Zelda whispered in Merlin's ear. "What have you done with your sidekick?" she said to the heavyset girl waiting for them. "Have you frightened her off?"

"You mean Axel Nolan?" asked Hilda, narrowing her eyes. "Oh, I've grown up since last year, and I don't just mean I've got taller!"

"We've noticed!" replied Zelda, mockingly. "Have you given up boxing and rugby?"

"I know what you all think of me," retorted Hilda. "And I don't care. I'll never be a girlie girl who loves ballet and cuddly animals. And I'm fine with that!"

The three friends looked at each other in surprise. With a shrug, Merlin changed the subject to their school holidays. Hilda chatted enthusiastically, devoting all her energy to being nice. The two girls were unimpressed and kept their distance during break while Merlin, trapped by his upbringing and sense of politeness, had a conversation with her which, against all odds, proved quite enjoyable.

38

The Endless Barrens

A TERRIFYING WAVE OF DIZZINESS SWEPT OVER OKSA as she was sucked into a blisteringly hot, dark corridor. A few seconds later she was standing beside her father and the other Runaways in the terrifying landscape buffeted by dusty winds that she'd glimpsed through the waterfall. Although the sight had been less than inviting, they hadn't reckoned on the sweltering heat and awful stench. She covered her nose with her hand to try to block it out. Abakum handed round the Spongiphyles and the Runaways pressed the plants over their noses to filter out the fine dust that filled the air and made it almost unbreathable. Tugdual looked around and, narrowing his eyes, spotted a large rock.

"Come on! Let's head for shelter!" he cried.

They followed the young man towards the makeshift refuge, their Spongiphyles pressed firmly to their noses.

"How can he even see that rock?" muttered Gus, drawing nearer to Oksa. "I can't see a thing in this pea-souper."

"Don't forget he can see like a hawk with his Optiview power," said Oksa, trying not to lose sight of Tugdual, whose slim figure she could barely make out.

She could hear Gus grumbling, despite the whistling wind. When would he accept who he was? She glanced at him in irritation, as she battled against the violent gusts that were hindering the group's progress.

They finally reached the shelter of the rock, appalled at how grim this new level was.

"What a revolting smell," said the Incompetent, raising its muzzle in the air. "It reminds me of something…"

"Bad eggs!" cried the Squoracle, emerging from Abakum's jacket. "Yuck!"

And, protesting shrilly, it buried its tiny head again in the folds of fabric.

"Do you think we're strong enough to get through this?" Leomido asked Abakum, looking anxiously at Reminiscens.

Abakum studied the old lady, whose face was pale and drawn with exhaustion.

"I'll answer you with a question, my friend: do we have a choice?"

Oksa glanced at Pavel in fright at this exchange, but none of the Runaways, not even her father, looked in a fit state to reassure anyone. Fortunately, the rock sheltered them from the billions of sticky, soot-like particles blown almost horizontal by the fierce wind, but it didn't stop the vile smell from working its way through the tiny holes in the Spongiphyles or lessen the heat that was sapping their energy. Even the Squoracle, a fan of high temperatures, appeared to be affected.

"We're going to burn to death!" it squawked, which was no great comfort to anyone.

"Thanks for that, Squoracle," replied Oksa. "I hope it's not a premonition!"

"Huh!" retorted the tiny hen. "We'll have to be very clever indeed to avoid being burnt to a crisp…"

It gulped loudly and crawled back inside Abakum's jacket.

"What a good idea it was to bring water!" declared Gus. "What? Why are you all looking like that?" he asked in alarm at the sight of the Runaways' ashen faces.

When he'd mentioned the water, they'd all turned to look at the Reticulatas which, a few seconds ago, had been full to bursting with the cool water they'd brought with them. Now, to their horror, the transparent jellyfish were flat as pancakes: their valuable contents had drained away. The Runaways no longer had a single drop of water—which, in this diabolical furnace, spelt big trouble.

"Oh no—where's all the water gone?" asked Oksa.

"Sorcery!" screeched the Squoracle frantically.

"We still have the fruit," remarked Gus.

He rummaged around in his bag and the blood drained from his face: he pulled out his hand, which was covered with wriggling maggots thick as broad beans from all the fruit juice they'd gorged on. He cried out in disgust and shook off the maggots, which disintegrated as soon as they hit the ground and mingled with the dust. The Runaways plunged their hands in their bags in the hope of saving just one apricot or banana, but decay had already set in and there was nothing to be done.

"Oh well," exclaimed the Incompetent languidly. "So long as we have water, we'll be fine. Don't they say where there's water, there's life?"

"But we don't have any water, you feather-brained idiot!" shrieked the Squoracle from its place of shelter.

"Is that so?" asked the indolent creature in amazement. "Well, in that case, we're all going to die," it said as casually as if refusing a sweet.

"Thanks for spelling that out," muttered Oksa, who was trying hard not to cry.

She clamped her Spongiphyle to her face in an attempt to hide her growing panic. She looked at the Runaways, who were all devastated by the harsh facts. Held up by Leomido, who seemed to have aged ten years in a few seconds, Reminiscens looked about to faint. Beside them, Abakum's eyes were fixed on the ground, his face expressionless. Gus and Pierre were clinging to each other in shock. Tugdual stood opposite and his eyes, which didn't leave Oksa's face, held such a strange expression that she wondered if he'd realized the true gravity of the situation. Pavel was also watching her from the edge of the group. Plumes of white smoke were rising from his back, which alarmed Oksa. She crawled over to him on all fours to stay within the shelter of the large rock.

"Are you okay, Dad?"

"Well, I've certainly been better... I have to admit that my customary unbridled optimism has taken a bit of a hit."

Oksa couldn't help smiling. Optimism wasn't a quality she'd ever associated with her father: it was completely foreign to Pavel's tormented nature—he was more likely to be caught in the grip of unremitting pessimism.

"You've certainly got a lot to contend with," confirmed Oksa, resting her hand on his arm. "I'm sure we'll find a way out of this though."

Her father retreated into a silence that spoke volumes.

"Anyway, I can't believe we won't!" insisted Oksa loudly, as if trying to convince herself. "Since we have no water and no provisions, we'd better not hang around here. We have to get moving."

"Do or die. Is that it, Lil' Gracious?" asked Tugdual, gazing at her with a faint smile.

"You can be sarcastic, if you want," she replied defiantly. "But there's no point waiting here to be reduced to a pile of dust, is there?"

"You're right," nodded Abakum, standing straighter.

"But which way should we go?" asked Leomido. "We don't know where we are!"

They gazed at the plain, which seemed to stretch as far as the eye could see. The wind had dropped, making the dust less troublesome, but the landscape before them did nothing to allay their fears: the soil was barren and cracked from the intense dryness and covered with a layer of swirling dust. It looked like an endless desert, a parched, scorching, hostile expanse. Oksa cursed through gritted teeth. Suddenly her eyes gleamed: she bent her knees as if about to Vertifly, then her face tensed, and she looked disappointed.

"Aaargh... I can't!" she said angrily.

"Vertiflying is impossible when the laws of gravity have been subverted, Young Gracious," informed the Tumble-Bawler.

"The laws of gravity? Subverted?" repeated Oksa incredulously.

"Yes," confirmed the Tumble-Bawler. "You may not realize this, but the laws of physics governing the Outside aren't the same as in here. The Runaways who can Vertifly can try if they like, then you'll see..."

At these words, Leomido positioned himself, straight as a poker, his arms flat against his sides. His friends could see how hard he was concentrating, but they were all disappointed: like Oksa, Leomido couldn't Vertifly. Pavel, Pierre and Tugdual also tried, but in vain.

"Where's the butterfly?" asked Oksa, looking around in annoyance.

The Runaways screwed up their eyes and studied the marbled sky, trying to spot the small insect. The fierce wind was now a more bearable breeze, despite the heat it brought with it, but the dark, threatening clouds continued to scud past at a terrifying speed, making it hard to locate anything in the sky.

"It must have been carried off by the wind," remarked Gus.

"But we need it!" exclaimed Oksa.

"It'll find us," said Tugdual reassuringly. "It can't miss us: we can be seen for miles in this desert."

"There's no such thing as miles here," corrected the Tumble-Bawler, crawling out of Oksa's bag, "because the unit of measurement here is way beyond human comprehension. This desert has no limits. We're in the middle of nowhere."

"If anyone has any other comforting information, then please go right ahead and tell us!" replied Oksa, tears in her eyes.

"Oh, Young Mistress, forgive me for speaking out of turn," apologized the Tumble-Bawler. "When I said this desert has no limits, I meant that it has none of the normal limits."

"What do you mean?" snapped Oksa.

"I'm talking about horizontal limits, which are the ones we know best."

"Does that mean there are vertical limits?" asked Oksa, her eyes gleaming with renewed hope.

"Affirmative, Young Gracious!" agreed the Tumble-Bawler.

"Above? Below?" continued Oksa.

"The way out may be up in the air or under the ground," explained the small creature.

"Do we have to dig down?" asked Abakum.

"No point!" came the voice of the Squoracle, muffled by the cloth of Abakum's jacket. "The passage will reveal itself when the time is right."

"I hope that's before we all die of thirst," said Gus bitterly.

"If you don't have any water left, you'll die, that's for sure," said the Incompetent. "Where there's water, there's life," it repeated lethargically.

"This affects you too, you know!" squawked the Squoracle. "Even large clumsy dolts like you need water to live."

The Incompetent waited for this information to make its way into its brain and reacted a good thirty seconds later:

"Are you sure of your facts?"

Gus turned pale, before giving a nervous guffaw. His body shaking with laughter, he dropped his Spongiphyle and immediately grimaced.

"Yuck! That smell is revolting!"

"It's sulphur, friend of our Gracious," explained the Tumble-Bawler, darting over to pick up his sponge. "Protect yourself, it's very dangerous."

"So we can choose whether we die of thirst, poisoning or despair, that's just great!" grumbled Gus, pressing the protective mask to his nose.

"You're forgetting hunger," added Tugdual.

"What do you mean, hunger?" yelled Gus.

"We can also die of hunger."

Oksa glared at the two boys, upset and exasperated. Then she stood up, eyeing the blistering, endless expanse, and said resolutely:

"Well, I don't want to die, and I don't want any of us to die either! So get up and follow me. We're going to find a way out of this horrible place, by hook or by crook."

39

A BLISTERING EXPANSE

THE RUNAWAYS MADE SLOW PROGRESS THROUGH THE scorching desert, particularly as there were no landmarks to show they were going the right way. The wind had dropped at last, but the dark incandescence of the sky gave the light a disturbing quality. The Barrens stretched away endlessly under the inky sky. The red-hot powdery soil on the ground was like sifted compost mixed with searing ash. Every step the Runaways took raised small clouds of black dust which stung their ankles like little sparks. They soldiered on, grimacing in silence, but the pain soon became unbearable. Oksa was the first to stop, her face dripping with sweat. With her hands on her hips, she breathed through her Spongiphyle, then bent down to undo her trainers so that she could use her laces to fasten the bottoms of her jeans around her ankles. She tied a bow then straightened up, feeling more positive. Tugdual smiled at her conspiratorially, then bent down to stuff his trousers into his ankle boots.

"How you can bear this revolting smell?" asked Oksa, noticing that he'd put his Spongiphyle in his pocket.

"Seems like my senses aren't entirely ordinary..." he replied, gazing at her.

"Too right," muttered Gus. "You've got the senses of a bat!"

Tugdual looked away with an amused smirk, which was at odds with the deep sadness in his eyes. Oksa stared at the two boys, her heart pounding. Why did they always have to wind each other up? It was so annoying and confusing! But she couldn't start trying to work out her feelings now. Their lives were at stake here in the Endless Barrens. "Get a grip, Oksa," reasoned the girl, glancing at her two friends again. "You'll have all the time in the world to think about this later—if you ever get out of this alive!" Then she turned round and continued walking.

☀

The youngest members of the party proved to be the strongest: Oksa took the lead with Pavel. Behind them, Gus made it a point of honour to keep pace with Tugdual, whose easy stride showed his tremendous stamina. The other Firmhand in the group, Pierre, also seemed to cope better with the harsh conditions in the Endless Barrens than the others. "What an enviable ability," thought Oksa, whose strength was failing with every step. But she was the Young Gracious, the heir to Edefia! She had to set an example and this thought, more than any other, motivated her. Bringing up the rear of the procession, Abakum kept his eyes on her. He could instinctively sense the girl's highs and lows, her fluctuating thoughts. He knew she didn't know what to do. Oksa often overlooked mundane details and didn't keep her eye on the main objective, but the Fairyman had complete confidence in her. He knew she'd save them, as did they all. It was not just a hope now, it was a deep-seated conviction—a fact. It was important to remember that the Ageless Ones were watching over her. The only question was whether, acting together, they could hold their own against the evil power of the Wickedesses… The Fairyman's eyes darkened. He straightened his shoulders, fixed his eyes on Oksa's slender frame and kept walking. Despite his great age, he was coping with the terrible conditions incredibly well, unlike Leomido and Reminiscens. The old lady was physically very weak. This was one ordeal too many after everything she'd been through with the Runaways and the harrowing years of solitude during which she'd thought she'd be trapped for ever in the picture. It didn't help that her feet were being scorched by the dust on the ground, since the straps of her flimsy sandals didn't offer much protection. Leomido hadn't lost any time in wrapping her feet in the sleeves he'd ripped from his thick cotton jacket, but Reminiscens was weakening and her spirits were at an all-time low. She wasn't even buoyed by the prospect of seeing her granddaughter Zoe again: exhaustion had the upper hand and hope was fading. She was leaning with all her weight on Leomido, who felt her weakening with every step. He also felt disheartened and was focusing all the courage and strength he had left on the woman he'd never stopped loving.

"I'll carry you..." he panted hoarsely.

Reminiscens didn't make any protest. She didn't even have the strength to answer. Leomido looked at her in despair, then looked away, unable to bear her sorrowful expression. Behind them, Abakum clenched his fists, feeling helpless and excluded.

"How long have we been walking?" Oksa asked her father.

Pavel shrugged to show he didn't know and stopped himself from asking another question: how long could they keep going in these hellish conditions? He held Oksa's hand, which was boiling hot. All the Runaways were burning up. They were trying not to think about it, but the lack of water was becoming critical. Only the Incompetent made no effort to banish the thought from its flabby brain.

"Could someone just give me a drop of water?" it said. "I'm dying of thirst..."

"We all are!" replied Oksa sharply.

"Just a small glass of cold water, if it isn't too much trouble," continued the creature, oblivious.

"With a straw and some ice, of course," snapped Gus in irritation.

"Oh, that would be lovely!" replied the Incompetent enthusiastically. "Thank you, friend of the Young Gracious."

"Don't mention it," said Gus, scuffing the dusty ground. "I'll bring it over in a minute—but only if you shut up!"

It took the Incompetent a few seconds to understand what Gus had offered: it watched him with its large, bulging eyes and covered its mouth with both hands to stop any words from emerging. Then it waited patiently for its glass of water… unless it had forgotten it. Which the Runaways hadn't! They were all suffering in silence and doing their best to conceal the panic that was starting to undermine their morale. A few more hours at this pace and they would die. They kept walking and walking, stopping just to doze on the baking, dusty ground. Their reserves of energy were becoming fatally depleted. According to the Tumble-Bawler's estimates, they'd been walking through the Endless Barrens for over three days in temperatures averaging forty-five degrees centigrade—or the equivalent on the Outside—which was an extraordinary feat. Reminiscens and Gus were the worst affected by this ordeal and were a pitiable sight. With dry lips and dark circles under their eyes, they were finding it increasingly difficult to put one foot in front of the other. Leomido had accepted Abakum's help and the two were taking turns to carry Reminiscens, who was struggling to catch her breath. Every time they did, though, the effort took more out of them. Pierre and Pavel were giving Gus piggybacks, since he was only a Runaway by inclination, not birth. This cruel ordeal had made them aware that descendants from Edefia had a distinct physiological advantage and they all tried to help the "Outsider". They didn't have much strength but, despite their extreme weariness, everyone agreed that Gus took priority. They began collecting the sweat pearling their foreheads and Oksa gathered the steam continually escaping from her father's back to obtain a few droplets of water through condensation, which she trickled into her friend's mouth.

"I'm so ashamed…" murmured Gus, hiding his head against his father's shoulder.

"Stop pretending you don't want it!" scolded Oksa, trying to hide her concern.

They kept walking, dragging their feet more and more, their eyes redder and redder, their feet covered in blisters. They were aching all over. Without any water to drink, they were perspiring less and less and becoming severely dehydrated. The desert stretched away around them, unchanged, although the foul, acrid stench had almost disappeared and the ground was now full of the cracks that the Squoracle had described, which made their advance even more dangerous for their exhausted bodies. Time dragged and the hours stacked up. Or was it days?

※

When Oksa stopped, they all silently followed suit, relieved at the chance to rest, even though it wouldn't do anything to alter their situation.

"I can't go on," groaned the Young Gracious.

Gaunt with weariness and hunger, the dusty Runaways gazed at her. Their clothes were just dirty rags, their hair was tangled and the soles of their shoes scorched by the burning earth. Filled with despair, Oksa raised her arms to the sky in a pleading gesture and shouted:

"Help us! Please!"

No one could avoid seeing her filthy T-shirt rise up over her stomach and reveal the magnificent Mark around her belly button. The eight-pointed star glittered with a thousand amber glints against Oksa's skin, drawing all eyes. Suddenly Abakum, who was bowed with exhaustion, began humming quietly, then the sound of singing filled the air:

Fairies and Firmhands, every Edefian tribe,
Sylvabuls, Lunatrixes and tiny Squoracles,
Incompetents, Getorixes and other animals,
Raise voices in harmony and sing with all your might!
When the Great Chaos came, we were forced to disappear,
Leaving Gracious Malorane and our homeland far behind.
Ocious and Orthon made the Runaways take flight
And we've waited since that time for the Mark to reappear!
Edefia will be ours again one of these fine days
For that is Oksa's will and this the Song of the Runaways!

"What's that?" asked Oksa, surprised.

"The Runaways' Anthem," replied Leomido, moved to tears. "We wrote it when the Mark was revealed to you."

And, to raise his spirits, the old man also began to sing along with Abakum.

> *Nothing could be better than to go back to our home,*
> *For since we were ejected from our war-torn Edefia*
> *Guided in our actions by our Gracious Dragomira*
> *And aided by young Oksa, our new ruler and Last Hope,*
> *We've been waiting for a sign that'll make us smile again,*
> *The light in the sky that marks the Portal to our land.*
> *When our wandering is over, we'll hold each other's hands*
> *And celebrate in style, one big family of friends.*
> *Edefia will be ours again one of these fine days*
> *For that is Oksa's will and this the Song of the Runaways!*

Pierre's guttural voice joined in with those of the two men, and then Pavel began singing along hoarsely too.

> *Across our regained kingdom, the crowds will cheer for miles*
> *To see peacetime restored and our prosperity return*
> *From the mountains of Peak Ridge to the waste of Retinburn,*
> *From the forests of Green Mantle to the Ageless Fairies' Isle.*
> *Throughout the realm, the courage and conviction of our friends,*
> *Their steadfast loyalty, as well as Oksa's strength and guile,*
> *Will go down in history and make this quest worthwhile.*
> *Everything is possible when our trials are at an end!*
> *Edefia will be ours again one of these fine days*
> *For that is Oksa's will and this the Song of the Runaways!*

The Runaways started to walk again in time to the beat of the song, its optimistic words filling their hearts with courage. Oksa was trembling with emotion. Her surprise had given way to embarrassment and she felt awkward at being honoured so highly. She strode ahead with crimson cheeks, feeling deeply moved. How many people could say they'd had an anthem written for them? But did she deserve that kind of respect? She didn't think so. She didn't dare meet anyone's eyes, despite feeling extremely proud.

"Edefia will be ours again one of these fine days, for that is Oksa's will," sang Tugdual softly, coming up alongside her.

"Oh, stop teasing me!" she said.

"I'm not."

"Well then, if you're any kind of a friend, you won't ever mention it again, okay?" she said.

"Whatever you say, Lil' Gracious... even if I'm not convinced that it's a good idea to pretend something isn't happening when it is."

Oksa had no time to think about Tugdual's enigmatic answer, as her attention was distracted by the dull thud of a body hitting the ground. She turned round to see that Gus had collapsed in the scalding desert.

"I can't go any further," he whispered, his eyes bloodshot.

Oksa looked at her friend. He was in a dreadful state and wouldn't be able to keep this up for much longer. Sadness washed over her. Above them, the marbled sky was covered with clouds that shimmered with metallic glints. Black lightning cut through the sky from time to time, startling them all, but it was those violent flashes that gave Gus the inkling of an idea:

"Oksa!" he shouted.

The girl jumped, surprised by her friend's vehement tone.

"It's a long time since you lost your temper," he croaked, hoarse with thirst.

She looked at him incredulously. What on earth was he on about?

"Er... sorry, Gus, but don't you think things are complicated enough already? I'm dehydrated, exhausted and desperate. And, if you really want to know, I'm also terrified at the thought of dying here in the next few hours... but I'm not angry. I don't have enough energy for that."

She fixed her slate-grey eyes on Gus, who gave her a faint smile.

"Do you remember what happened when McGraw sent you out of the classroom?" he said.

It took Oksa a few seconds to realize what her friend was getting at.

"Of course!" she exclaimed, her face lighting up. "Anger equals storms equals... RAIN!"

This last word caught the attention of all the Runaways and rekindled a spark of hope in their hearts—they might survive after all.

"Make me angry!" ordered Oksa, her eyes shining. "Come on! Wind me up! Make me lose my temper!"

40

THE HEALING POWER
OF ANGER

THE RUNAWAYS EXCHANGED GLANCES, DAZED WITH
tiredness. Oksa was already concentrating, trying to summon up
any memories, thoughts or scenarios that might make her boiling mad.
Although McGraw and Mortimer were the first to spring to mind, Oksa
was surprised to realize it was pity she felt, not anger, when thinking
of the Felon in the cellar a few seconds before he imploded and disappeared into the black hole of the Crucimaphila. Nor could she stop
herself seeing Mortimer as a boy who'd just lost his father. "Brilliant!"
she scolded herself. "Despite everything they've done, you still feel sorry
for them. Honestly, Oksa-san, you're incorrigible." While the Runaways
wracked their brains to think of a way to make her lose her temper, the
Young Gracious reviewed her other memories: the mental image of her
mother confined to her wheelchair upset her. Her nose began prickling
as if she'd breathed in mustard, but that feeling was a million miles away
from anger. A wave of sadness combined with intense anxiety made it
hard to breathe. This wasn't working… it was exactly the wrong way
to go about it. She thought about Zoe and her tragic past. She missed
her kindness and insight so much. Then Dragomira. Her Baba. She was
dying to be cuddled by her, watch her bustling around her private workroom and stuff herself with her delicious rolled crêpes. No good… Her

thoughts were just unachievable dreams filling her heart with sadness and terror. All hope was evaporating in this furnace, causing the images in her mind's eye to fade.

"Oksa!" called Gus weakly. "You know what? I'm a real loser. A girl like you deserves a better friend than me."

Still distracted by her memories, Oksa looked at him in bewilderment.

"Gus… this isn't the time…" she murmured, trying to chase away thoughts of her mother's face.

"Gus is right for once," added Tugdual, glancing coolly at her.

"If I need your opinion, I'll ask for it, okay?" retorted Gus, holding himself upright on his father's arm. "I'm sorry, Oksa. It's all my fault. I'm to blame for everything. I had to go and look at the picture. I should've resisted the temptation and run away, but I didn't. I wanted to prove how strong I was when I'm just a nobody! Do you hear: I AM A NOBODY! I'm the biggest failure on earth. The only thing I'm good for is handing my best friend, father and friends to a psychopathic entity on a plate."

"Ooohhh! You're starting to get on my nerves!" cried Oksa, trying desperately hard to ignore the fact that Gus might be laying it on thick just to annoy her.

"There's no denying that it wasn't a very bright move on your part," remarked Tugdual scornfully. "Then again… what else could we expect from someone like you?"

"Tugdual!" snapped Oksa indignantly.

"You'd better shut up!" replied Gus angrily. "After all, we know what you're capable of, don't we…"

Tugdual whirled round.

"Is that right? What am I capable of, then?" he asked curtly.

"Well, for starters, what about those daft rituals with your Goth friends sitting round a tasty bowl of soup made from rat and toad offal?" hissed Gus.

Tugdual went white, his eyes darkened and his lips tightened into a thin line. Oksa didn't know what to think. She was at a loss: were the

238

two boys just pretending? Had they joined forces to annoy her? Or had exhaustion caused them to drop their polite façades?

"You're disgusting!" continued Gus to Tugdual, who stood there unmoving, his hands balled into fists against his thighs.

"It's better than being mediocre," retorted the young man. "Anyway, some people around here don't seem to think I'm disgusting, if you get my drift."

"Well, I'd rather be mediocre than a lousy Werewall! An ally of tarry-nosed freaks who hoover up other people's feelings."

Tugdual glared at him haughtily. Oksa looked back and forth between them, her hand clamped over her mouth, horrified by this barrage of insults. Surely they didn't dislike each other this much? Gus wasn't like that and Tugdual was much too proud to be this nasty. Then again, could they be putting on an act because of their terrible plight? Oksa couldn't dismiss that thought, which stopped her from doing or saying anything. She just stood there helplessly, paralysed by doubt.

"Well, you said it," continued Tugdual, "you're a nobody. No one can say you aren't perceptive, at least."

"Aaarghhhh!" screamed Gus, mustering his last reserves of strength to fling himself at Tugdual.

Tugdual seemed to expect this reaction. Far from being surprised, he raised his hand and sent Gus flying to the dusty ground with a perfect Knock-Bong. Pierre cursed and rushed over to his son, while the other Runaways watched the scene unfold in amazement. Seething with anger, Gus refused his father's helping hand and struggled unsteadily to his feet. Hampered by extreme physical weakness, he launched himself again at Tugdual, who eyed him with cold indifference. Pavel made as if to stand between the two boys, but Abakum stopped him.

"Have I upset the nobody?" challenged Tugdual, stretching out his hand to perform another Knock-Bong.

"Shut up, you weirdo!" retorted Gus. "You may be stronger than me, but you're as despicable as McGraw and his clan. And, you know what,

239

I've always wondered if you weren't a mole, passing on everything you hear from us…"

Tugdual visibly paled. The veins on his neck stood out, pulsing with annoyance, and he looked on the point of exploding with anger.

"You're the one who got us into this mess," he retorted bitterly, "so what makes you think you have any right to add your two pennyworth? Have you already forgotten what you said a few minutes ago? You were snivelling because it's your fault we're all here, remember? Do I really have to you remind you who's to blame?"

Oksa couldn't think straight any more. She could see the two boys were heading for the point of no return and she was scared that one of them might say something unforgivable that would scar the other for ever.

"STOP IT!" she screamed, gasping for breath.

Tugdual turned to look at her, while Gus staggered with exhaustion.

"Why, Lil' Gracious?" he asked, sounding suddenly gentle. "Are you afraid your friend can't take the truth?"

Oksa met Tugdual's steely blue eyes, which stood out even more against his pale, drawn face. He stood motionless in front of her, his tall, dark figure silhouetted against the streaked sky, preparing to deliver the blow that would finish Gus off for good. Her eyes pleaded with him not to say the words she feared so much, the words he could never take back. Over their heads, an enormous black cloud was forming, sizzling with electricity that was discharged in brilliant flashes of lightning, black as onyx. She looked up and saw Tugdual do the same. Their eyes met again and, without knowing if he was driven by rage or an instinct for survival, Oksa realized that there was nothing she could do to melt his icy resolve.

"If you're so clever, perhaps you'd like to remind us all whose fault it was that the Lunatrixa died?" he sneered spitefully at Gus.

Oksa didn't see Gus faint with shock at these words, because she'd already launched herself at Tugdual's throat, roaring like an angry lioness.

"Why did you have to say that?" she cried. "WHY?"

Tugdual did nothing to defend himself and the force of Oksa's rage sent them both crashing to the ground. The Young Gracious began punching Tugdual's chest and scratching at his face, crying with anger. They were surrounded by clouds of burning dust but, lost in the heat of the moment, neither of them felt the pain.

"Why couldn't you just keep quiet?" yelled Oksa, sobbing violently and gasping for breath. "You're horrible! Do you hear? Horrible!"

Tugdual couldn't stand it any longer. He caught hold of her wrists tightly and then, with a swift movement, rolled Oksa onto her back and held her there. This only made her more angry.

"You're hurting me!" she screamed, as a flash of black lightning ripped through the sky. "I hate you! I HATE YOU!"

"No, you don't..." murmured Tugdual, bending down towards her.

She tried to wriggle free of this confusing and infuriating embrace, but she wasn't strong enough.

"No, you don't..." repeated Tugdual, his face so close to hers that she could feel his incredibly cold breath. His light touch was enough to send a bolt of electricity down her spine from head to foot. She froze for a few seconds, held by Tugdual's hypnotic gaze, feeling torn between two conflicting emotions: an uncontrollable urge to sink her teeth into him and an even stronger desire to pull him closer. Without really understanding why, she suddenly thought of Gus and this immediately refocused her mind on the matter in hand.

"Why did you have to say that to him?" she repeated. "It was so cruel. And unfair!"

She could hardly breathe, she was so angry. Tugdual sighed deeply and sat up.

"It was just a tiny wound to his ego. He'll recover, Lil' Gracious!" he said, smiling provocatively. "And look, it was worth it, wasn't it?"

A large drop splashed onto Oksa's forehead. She looked up at the overcast sky in wonderment. A few seconds later the heavens opened and the exhausted, dehydrated Runaways were drenched by heavy rain. Oksa propped herself up on her elbows with a tentative laugh. All around her, the Runaways were grinning and greedily holding their faces up to the downpour. Oksa looked around for Gus: he'd regained consciousness and his father was holding him up by the shoulders. Their heads were tipped back and they were both drinking. Oksa was struck by how fragile Gus looked—his ebony hair fanned out over the damp fabric of his shirt, which clung to the bony contours of his back. She lay down on the muddy ground next to Tugdual, who was sitting there with his forearms resting on his knees. She closed her eyes and let the miraculous rain trickle over her exhausted body, feeling it soothe away her tiredness. Her tears mingled with the raindrops. They'd survived by the skin of their teeth! But at what cost? She was too tired and too happy to think about it. She felt a hand take hers. She didn't need to open her eyes to know it was Tugdual. With an enigmatic smile on his lips, he'd stretched out in the mud beside her, his face turned towards the sky and the rain, which was still falling heavily. Surprising herself, Oksa didn't pull her hand away. Was it because she was tired? She didn't think so. And, although she should have enjoyed the providential shower with Gus, she shut her eyes and lay there next to the boy who was holding her hand so gently and so firmly.

41

REPTILIAN ATTACK

THE GIANT REPTILE OPENED ONE EYE AND LIFTED A LEG to brush away the water dripping on its crested head. The rain was streaming into the fissure where it had been asleep for ages, carrying with it small pebbles and a great deal of fine earth. Rain? The reptile hadn't seen rain for so long… not since the Wickedesses had forced the Soul-Searcher to do their evil bidding. Intrigued, it stood up on its short legs and stretched its head towards the opening of the fissure. It could hear human voices! It picked up some delicious aromas, confirming what it had dared not hope: there were people on the surface. With a little luck, they were young and tender. All its senses sharpened, the reptile licked its chops with a long forked tongue. Clinging to the earthen walls of the fissure with its talons, it began to climb, its nostrils quivering at the mouth-watering smells filtering down from above.

❋

Lying in the mud, surrendering to the rain falling over her body, Oksa gradually calmed down. Tugdual was still holding her hand and she'd done nothing to stop him. She had the nagging feeling that, for the first time in her life, she wasn't exactly being a good friend to Gus. Despite her forceful intervention on his behalf, there was no doubt she'd chosen Tugdual over him. Did she have any qualms about that? It felt so good lying there with Tugdual, raindrops bouncing off her body and quenching her thirst. But why was she so happy? Was it because she'd saved the Runaways or because she was close to Tugdual? Her forehead creased in a worried frown. This was not the time or the place to think about it, she decided, confused by the probable answer. She took a deep breath, focusing on the undulations of her Curbita-Flatulo, and let herself enjoy the moment.

※

"Oksa! Whatever you do, don't move!" Oksa opened her eyes.

"Stay very still!" continued Gus urgently. "Don't make a noise!"

The girl lay there, gazing at the rain falling from the dark sky onto the Barrens.

"What's the matter?" she whispered.

All she heard was a loud roar that sounded like a tiger growling.

"Pavel! NO!" shouted Abakum.

Oksa jumped up. Pavel, borne aloft by his Ink Dragon with its massive wings outspread, was fighting a hideous twenty-foot-long creature, which looked like a giant chameleon and was a sickening fluorescent green.

"It's a Leozard!" cried Abakum. "Quick, my friends! We have to help Pavel!"

The Ink Dragon's fire didn't seem to be having much effect on the Leozard, nor did it look afraid as Oksa's father blasted flames at the horny crest bristling along its spine; it kept swiping at the Ink Dragon as it drew closer and closer, trying to catch it in the air.

"Dad! Be careful!" screamed Oksa.

Her warning came too late: blinded by the dragon's flames, Pavel was unable to dodge a talon which raked across his stomach. He gave a hoarse cry as blood spurted onto the Leozard's muzzle. The creature greedily licked it off, while the dragon turned back to ink on Pavel's back, bringing him crashing down in the mud. Abakum brought his

Granok-Shooter to his mouth and fired an Arborescens, then two Colocynthises. But the Granoks just bounced off the Leozard's back like raindrops, as if the vile creature were Granok-proof. The Leozard gave a faint smile—Oksa could have sworn it—and its yellow eyes gazed avidly at the Young Gracious. Then, with surprising speed, it pounced on her. She toppled over backwards with the creature's body on top of her, although it was careful not to crush her. Oksa's face was only a couple of inches from the Leozard's filthy teeth, and she almost choked on its fetid breath. She heard the Runaways screaming and glimpsed Gus's tatty trainers frantically kicking the monster's flanks. The creature raised its head in irritation and sent the annoying human flying with a swipe of its foot. Oksa saw Gus's body land a few yards away. Then the Leozard turned back to its main concern—the girl who was about to make a tasty meal…

"Get off me, you filthy creature!" she screamed, struggling to free herself.

The Leozard's only answer was to treat her to another blast of putrid breath. Oksa launched a furious Knock-Bong at the creature, catching it in the jaw. The impact forced the green monster's head backwards and Oksa had time to glimpse Abakum's face between its forelegs.

"Hang in there!" he shouted. "Attack its abdomen with Fireballisticos— that's its weak spot."

Despite her terror, Oksa concentrated on the fire she felt rising up inside her—she was fighting for her life, after all. Raising her palms towards the monster's breast, she saw a flame begin to lick at the thick skin. It wasn't anywhere near enough though.

"Don't stop, Oksa!" screamed Pavel, attacking the Leozard's muzzle and eyes. "You're doing great!"

Struggling for breath, but with her heart full of hatred, the girl redoubled her efforts. The flames grew stronger, giving off a fearsome heat, and Oksa began to hope she might actually get out of this predicament alive. The monster's thick hide began to melt as if a blowtorch had been turned on it. Instinctively, she rolled to one side to escape the horrible creature as it collapsed with a groan, consumed by relentless flames.

"What was that thing?" she asked, after a few minutes of dazed silence.

"A Leozard," replied Abakum, his eyes riveted on the enormous pile of smoking ash that had been the monster. "The Leozard was the result of interbreeding between a lizard and a lion, centuries ago. It has the behaviour and appearance of a lizard and the dietary preferences of a lion."

"Great!" exclaimed Oksa. "Being devoured by a carnivorous lizard is hardly the most glamorous way to die. How do you know all this anyway?"

The Fairyman stroked his short beard thoughtfully.

"I've encountered Leozards before," he said with a frown and a distant look in his eyes. "In the territory of the Distant Reaches."

"You mean… in Edefia?" asked Oksa in amazement.

"I didn't mean anything particular by it, my dear," continued the old man.

"Edefia or not, we have to get out of here before we pay for it with our lives!" said Pavel briskly.

Oksa glanced over at her father. He was lying on the ground, where Reminiscens was applying Spinollias to his wound. He looked exhausted, but there was a steely determination in his eyes.

"Wait!" said Leomido, stopping them. "What Abakum has just said is very important."

"What?" exclaimed Pavel, his eyes wide. "You don't really think we're in Edefia, do you?"

"Why not?" replied Leomido defensively.

The Runaways were struck silent with amazement. Besieged by a host of conflicting thoughts, Oksa gazed at them in turn. Leomido, Reminiscens and Pierre looked hopeful; Abakum had withdrawn into his shell like an oyster, his face expressionless; beside him, Pavel's tense features betrayed his annoyance; Oksa could only see Gus's back. He was hunched over, probably from weariness and from being thrown through the air. The Incompetent was clinging to him and watching him admiringly. Everyone was considering this far-fetched theory, except for Tugdual. Oksa turned round, her senses alert. Tugdual wasn't far away—just a few yards behind her, crouched near the smoking skeleton of the Leozard.

"What about you, Lil' Gracious?" he asked. "What do you think?"

"We're not in Edefia," she said, louder than intended. The Runaways raised their heads and stared at her.

"What makes you say that?" asked Reminiscens kindly.

Oksa didn't even have to think about it:

"If we were in Edefia, I'd sense it."

"The Young Gracious is right," said the Squoracle, poking its head out of Abakum's jacket. "Edefia is still far away. Stop wasting time on foolish hopes and put some thought into getting out of here!"

For the first time since his argument with Tugdual, Gus looked at Oksa. She met his eyes and was surprised to see no resentment in them. Perhaps she'd been imagining things after all: Gus and Tugdual didn't really hate each other, they'd just joined forces to make her lose her temper so that she'd unleash the storm. At least, that was what she hoped...

"Oksa, you're turning into a master ninja!" exclaimed Gus, walking over to her, followed by the Incompetent. "You realize you totally flattened a giant lizard, don't you?"

"I didn't flatten it," replied Oksa, delighted at this suspension of hostilities. "I burned it to a crisp! That'll teach it to mess with me."

Gus roared with laughter, which set Oksa off. When he stopped suddenly and grimaced, rubbing his back, she was alarmed:

"Are you injured?"

"No... but it would be nice if certain people would refrain from propelling me through the air," he remarked, glaring at Tugdual.

So much for Oksa's theory that the two boys had been play-acting.

"It would also be nice if your bat would stop smirking at me!" added Gus, destroying any hope of a lasting ceasefire.

"Don't call him a 'bat'," retorted Oksa, as neutrally as she could. Gus sighed grumpily.

"I'll try… but I'm not promising anything. At all. I'm warning you now!" he snarled, brushing back his hair. "And I'll give you one piece of advice for free: don't trust that freak. He isn't what he seems. There's something really creepy about him."

"Have we arrived in Edefia?" asked the Incompetent suddenly, still clinging to Gus. "What excellent news! I know an old lady who'll be very happy to hear it. What's her name again?"

Glad that she and Gus were back on speaking terms and that the subject had been changed so hilariously, Oksa burst out laughing, followed by all the Runaways. The Squoracle popped out its little head and squawked:

"What a dimwit!"

"I agree," said the Incompetent, oblivious to the fact that the tiny hen had been talking about it. "Did you see how ugly it was? Such a spiny hide! Such a hideous green colour! Where's it gone, anyway?"

The Squoracle sighed, raising its eyes skywards, and nestled back inside Abakum's jacket. "Let me know when it manages to understand anything," it clucked in resignation.

"The dimwit is over there!" Oksa told the Incompetent, pointing to the pile of smoking ash.

"Oh. Is it playing hide and seek? What fun!"

Bent over double, Gus wiped his eyes with the back of his sleeve.

"I love it!" he snorted.

"It's very entertaining, isn't it?" added the slow-witted creature. "And, you must admit, the smoking camouflage is very clever…"

Despite the tense situation, the Runaways were all laughing. Even Pavel couldn't help crying with laughter.

"Now I know why we brought it along: it's a great morale-raiser!" giggled Oksa, holding her sides.

"And we certainly need it," said Tugdual gloomily. "Just look what's heading our way."

42

A Fight
to the Death

THE RUNAWAYS STOPPED LAUGHING WHEN THEY SAW some twenty Leozards advancing on them. Although the creatures were too heavy and dozy after their long sleep in the dry fissures to move very fast, the sight of their raised crests bristling threateningly made their blood run cold. Oksa felt weak at the still-vivid memory of the Leozard's stinking muzzle above her.

"Run!" she screamed, whirling round to take to her heels but, to her great surprise, her father held her back by the arm.

"There's no point."

"Why not? Surely we're not just going to stand here and wait for them?" she stammered.

"We'll stay and fight, Lil' Gracious!" exclaimed Tugdual, ready to attack. "We're Runaways, aren't we?"

"Didn't you see how hard it was to kill just one?" she screamed, panicking. "Granoks don't work, we can't Vertifly and we're all exhausted… We're going to die!"

"You don't usually give up so easily!" mocked Tugdual.

Oksa glared furiously at him, cut to the quick.

"Come on, Oksa, don't forget your inner ninja," murmured Gus.

Her friend's encouraging words—in striking contrast to his

panic-stricken face—instantly made her feel cross with herself for being so defeatist. She had a few powers at least—Gus had nothing. His life depended on his friends.

"Your Fireballistico was pretty effective, wasn't it?" he continued. "And maybe the Incompetent and its devastating humour could cause those monsters to die laughing!" he added, his sarcastic tone tinged with despair.

Oksa sniggered nervously, sick with worry.

"Stop it, Gus! That isn't funny. The poor Incompetent versus the Leozards! Can you imagine what an unfair fight that would be?"

"Many a true word spoken in jest, Gus," said Abakum. "Don't forget the Incompetent isn't just a harmless clown…"

The Fairyman turned towards the creature, which was still gazing at the charred remains of the Leozard, and whispered in its ear. The Incompetent raised its large eyes, then nodded before turning to face the army of Leozards advancing on the Runaways. Abakum and Leomido stood either side of the Incompetent, while Pierre and Tugdual took up their positions at the sides, forming a shield to protect Reminiscens and Gus.

"Oksa! Stand behind the Incompetent and use every single power you have in your arsenal!" advised Abakum, wand in hand.

A shadow fell over the group: Pavel's Ink Dragon had just spread its wide wings above their heads. Oksa raised her eyes and saw that her father had become part of the belly of the bronze dragon whose slowly beating wings had sprouted from his shoulder blades. Pavel looked her straight in the eye and gave her a sad, impenetrable smile. The sight radiated an impression of power and reassuring invulnerability that made Oksa's heart swell with courage. She assumed the ninja position, right leg bent in front and left leg locked straight behind. Then, with her arm outstretched, she fixed her gaze on the Leozards, which were now only about a hundred yards away.

"Throw everything you can at them, Oksa!" cried Gus. "I'll repay you one day, I promise!"

"You'd better," muttered Oksa between gritted teeth.

"Get ready!" screamed Abakum so that he could be heard above the din of the shrill, hungry cries from the approaching Leozards. "NO MERCY!"

※

If the green, crested monsters thought they'd soon be feasting on human flesh, they were about to be disappointed, because the Runaways had no intention of giving in without a fight. As soon as the Leozards were close enough for the Runaways to see the terrifying gleam in their baleful yellow eyes, Oksa and her friends showered them with powerful Knock-Bongs made all the stronger by their terror. The Leozards in the front line were propelled backwards and came crashing down on the heads of the Leozards behind.

"Watch out!" cried Abakum. "They're coming back!"

Some of the Leozards had struggled to their feet and were again lumbering towards them, furious at this unexpected setback, their appetites whetted by the promise of a delicious meal. While Oksa, Leomido and Pierre concentrated on attacking them with the most powerful Knock-Bongs ever seen, Abakum and Tugdual made intensive use of fire. The Fairyman used his wand like a blowtorch and Tugdual launched endless Fireballisticos at the creatures, aiming at their weak spots: eyes, ears, muzzle and abdomen. This was a fight to the death. A wave of energy flooded through every vein of Oksa's body, an unstoppable surge of strength and violence which made her powers seem endless. She'd never felt so brave or strong or invincible. She aimed the palm of her hand at the biggest Leozard and the monster flew nearly 300 feet through the air to come crashing down like a deadweight on another of its kind. The two creatures exploded on impact, their putrid guts spurting out through the remains of their green hides.

"Brilliant! Keep it up, Oksa!" yelled Gus encouragingly.

Oksa glanced at him and staggered, feeling weak and dizzy, as if the last Knock-Bong had drained all her strength. Gus noticed his friend swaying and looked at her warmly.

"Come on, Oksa! Concentrate! This is no time to go all wobbly on me. Give it some wellie!"

"It's all very well for you to say, but those monsters weigh several tons," she muttered.

She turned back to face the Leozards and Gus sensed she was mustering all her strength to continue fighting. With an even more powerful Knock-Bong than the last, Oksa sent two Leozards crashing into each other so hard that the monsters' razor-sharp teeth were knocked from their jaws. The Young Gracious bent over, hands on knees, to catch her breath. She soon straightened up, though, and renewed her efforts, despite her exhaustion. Above the small group, Pavel and his Ink Dragon were carrying out an effective air raid, dive-bombing the Leozards and blasting them with searing flames. The rearguard were doing what they could too. Gus was picking up all the stones he could find to pelt their attackers. "Pathetic," he thought in frustration, as the stone he'd just hurled bounced off the scaly hide of one of the Leozards. "Still, it's better than nothing." Beside him, despite her weakened physical condition, Reminiscens took everyone by surprise when she caused one Leozard to meet with an unexpected fate: holding out her arm towards one of the vile creatures a few yards away with her hand open wide, she hooked her fingers like the talons of an eagle about to seize its prey and turned her wrist as if trying to wring out a piece of wet material. The Leozard's head, which seemed to be in the grip of some invisible force, twisted round until it was at right angles to its body. The growling Leozard struggled futilely, then collapsed with a death rattle, head lolling to one side, its neck broken. Reminiscens, her forehead dripping with perspiration, gave Gus an exhausted smile in answer to his whistle of admiration.

"Wow, classy or what!" he said in wonderment.

"Thanks, lad," murmured the old lady, before sinking onto the dusty ground.

"Will you be all right?" asked Gus, kneeling beside her.

Reminiscens nodded and looked over at her friends' backs, tense with the huge effort of neutralizing the threat of the Leozards. Leomido's hunched shoulders clearly showed he was weakening, which seemed to worry Reminiscens. There were only five Leozards left, but they were the five toughest creatures. The Runaways' defences were crumbling, but the five monsters kept advancing, their gaping mouths stretched in hideous smiles. With the aid of Tugdual's Fireballisticos, Abakum pointed his wand at the largest Leozard, the one that, right from the start, had been able to withstand all the flames, explosions and knockout blows. This creature instinctively seemed to defend itself better than the rest: it arched its back and pulled its head into its horny hide so that only the thickest, toughest areas of its anatomy were visible. The flames licked over the creature's armour and Oksa's Knock-Bong only propelled it backwards five or six yards. Above the battlefield, Pavel seemed to be tiring: his Ink Dragon's wings were beating slower and slower, causing it to list drunkenly in the mauve sky like some immense bird in distress.

"Incompetent!" whispered Abakum, looking completely exhausted. "The ball's in your court!"

The Incompetent looked at him in surprise.

"Oh, I'm not very good at ball games, you know," it replied lethargically. "And that odd spiny creature doesn't look like much fun to play with."

"SPIT AT IT!" screamed Abakum.

Oksa looked at Abakum in amazement, while the information gradually sank into the Incompetent's brain.

"Stand back!" the Fairyman advised his friends.

"I'm spitting now!" the small creature informed them.

Without further ado, the Incompetent began projecting billions of droplets of saliva at the five Leozards, which were foaming at the mouth with rage and hunger. When the first drops landed on the largest Leozard, it started writhing in pain, its hide smoking as though attacked by a strong acid. Holes began appearing in its thick protective carapace, disintegrated by the corrosive spittle. Wide cavities formed, giving off an acrid stench and lumps of flesh, guts and muscle fell to the ground.

"I'm spitting again!" announced the Incompetent, as laid-back as ever.

This time, the shower of droplets landed on the four other Leozards, whose flesh dissolved in the fatal acid rain in a matter of seconds. When all that remained of the Leozards was a few skeletons bleached white by the acid, the amazed Runaways looked at each other.

"Wow, that was something else!" exclaimed Oksa, hands on hips. "Why did you wait so long to do that?" she asked the Incompetent, not sure whether she was furious with the slow-witted creature, or whether she wanted to throw her arms around it and smother it with grateful kisses.

The Incompetent looked at her.

"I don't know what I've eaten, but I think I may be suffering from acid reflux," it said in amazement.

"You don't say!" laughed Oksa. "Anyway, promise you'll never spit at me!"

"Spit at you? Why on earth would I do such a thing?" replied the Incompetent.

"Our friend may be a little slow on the uptake but, luckily for us, it's very obedient," explained Abakum, coming over to the Incompetent to congratulate it. "It only spits to order."

"That's a relief!" smiled Oksa happily. "Anyway, we didn't do too badly ourselves, did we?"

There was a general feeling of relief. Sitting on the drying ground, the Runaways looked at the impressive remains of the Leozards, which had been disembowelled, burnt to death or smashed to smithereens. They were soon joined by Pavel, whose Ink Dragon had retreated back inside him. He sat down beside Oksa.

"How are you, sweetheart?"

"Oh, Dad, that was some battle! Did you see my amazing Knock-Bongs?"

"I did indeed. This may well go down in history as one of the most heroic fights ever recorded," said Pavel, holding back a smile. "The brave

Runaways against the barbaric Leozards… It looked pretty impressive, particularly from the sky!"

Oksa snorted with laughter and glanced at Gus.

"You fought really well, Oksa."

"Thanks for all your encouragement."

"Don't mention it!"

Tossing back his long black hair, Gus winked at her. Oksa immediately felt more cheerful. She'd thought she'd lost her best friend, but he was back, and that was all that mattered. But she couldn't ignore Tugdual and the unsettling effect he had on her. She couldn't help turning round. When she met his steely-blue eyes, she flushed crimson, cursing her involuntary reaction and the pain she was causing Gus, who looked hurt. He stood up, kicking a stone and turning his back on them all.

"Right!" he said curtly. "I presume we don't intend to stay and rot here for ever. We ought to get moving."

He strode off into the Endless Barrens, leaving a trail of little clumps of mud behind him. The surprised Runaways were watching him walk away when, suddenly, he disappeared into the deeply fissured ground.

43

The Bottomless Pit

"**G**US!" screamed Oksa.

Pierre leapt up with a bear-like roar and ran towards the fissure which had just swallowed his son, jumping over others forming in the now unstable ground. The Runaways followed at a speed that nearly cost Reminiscens dearly. Despite Abakum's loving care, the old lady's feet were still very sore and, after leaping over a newly formed fissure, she landed heavily. She gave a moan of terror, waving her arms frantically to stop herself toppling backwards into a bottomless abyss. Leomido grabbed her waist in the nick of time and pulled her back from the edge.

"Gus! Are you there?" called Pierre, kneeling by the fissure.

He could just make out his son's frightened, muffled voice. It sounded so far away that every single Runaway paled.

"I'm here, Dad. Do something, please!" Pierre looked up at his friends in despair.

"Hang in there, Gus! We'll get you out!" cried Oksa.

Crouching or lying beside the fissure, which was barely three feet across, they tried to make out Gus's silhouette. They had no idea how deep he was because the crevice was so dark.

"Tumble, will you go and see where Gus is?" asked Oksa, taking her small scout out of her bag.

"Certainly, Young Gracious," said the Tumble-Bawler, plunging into the fissure.

The next few minutes seemed to last longer than any the Runaways had ever experienced and the absence of conventional methods of measuring time made the wait harder to bear. Oksa chewed off her last three remaining nails and tried to be patient. Soon after, the Tumble-Bawler reappeared, covered in dust. It shook itself and planted itself proudly in front of its mistress.

"The Young Gracious's Tumble-Bawler reporting!"

"We're listening," said Oksa impatiently.

"The Young Gracious's friend is on a narrow stone shelf which is twenty-two inches long by thirteen inches wide. It's fairly thin, barely two inches thick, but the Young Gracious's friend isn't heavy enough to cause it to give way. The Young Gracious's friend cut himself three times as he fell: twice on the face and once on the right hand. But there's no need to worry. They're superficial injuries and the Young Gracious's friend isn't in any danger."

"How deep is he?" asked Pierre, his face deathly white.

The Tumble-Bawler frowned and announced:

"By my calculations, the Young Gracious's friend is at a depth which equals 1,519 feet in Outside measurements."

"1,519 feet!" exclaimed Oksa, panicking.

"1,519 feet," confirmed the Tumble-Bawler.

Pierre swore and angrily kicked at the ground. Leomido looked at Abakum in concern: the Fairyman was deep in thought, his expression grave and his forehead creased with worry. Beside him, Pavel lay flat on his stomach on the edge of the dark drop and examined the crevice.

"My Ink Dragon won't get in there, it's too narrow," he muttered.

"And I can't extend my arm beyond 100 feet," said Abakum, putting his head in his hands.

Everyone thought carefully in anguished silence, fearing that they might not come up with a way to save Gus. Oksa shook her head to banish this unbearable thought. "It can't end like this!" she thought, feeling close to tears.

"What if I took my Ventosa Capacitors?" she suggested, opening her Caskinette. "I must have enough to get there and back."

Abakum looked worried.

"Getting back is the problem," he said. "With the best will in the world, you couldn't carry Gus back."

The girl looked down. Her heart was aching with anxiety.

"Help!" called Gus.

At the sound of this heart-rending appeal from the depths, Pierre gave a groan of misery. Tugdual, who was sitting a little to one side with his arms around his knees, looked up and gravely addressed the Tumble-Bawler:

"What are the fissure walls made of?"

"Limestone, grandson of the Knuts," replied the creature. "I spotted many cracks of varying sizes in the rock, ranging from a quarter of an inch to two inches. But the rock also has many sharp outcrops at more or less regular intervals, which makes descent dangerous."

"Perfect!" exclaimed Tugdual. "I'll go."

He jumped up and resolutely hurried over to the fissure.

"Wait a moment, lad!" said Abakum, holding him back.

"Why?" asked the young man, pulling free. "I'm the only one who can save him and you know it."

"Yes," agreed Abakum, looking resigned. "I know."

Feeling confused, Oksa couldn't help shouting:

"But how?"

Tugdual turned to her, put his hands on her shoulders and looked her straight in the eye with a faint smile.

"Alpinismus, Lil' Gracious."

"What's Alpinismus?" she snapped, her eyes full of tears.

"It looks like you've already forgotten some of the skills I inherited from my ancestors, as well as certain arachnidan episodes of my shady past!"

"Your Spiderman technique!"

"Got it in one!" said Tugdual. "The ordinary human saved by the power of the vile Firmhand Werewall, alias 'the bat'... How ironic is that? It'll make a pleasant change from the walls of morgues or medical faculties anyway," he added with a wry laugh.

He let go of Oksa's shoulders, murmuring quietly in her ear:

"See you later, Lil' Gracious…"

Then he turned to Pierre, who was watching him intently.

"Pierre, I know you have the gift of Alpinismus too. But, without wishing to offend you, my size and my recent experiences give me a substantial advantage."

"Very true," admitted Pierre sadly.

"I'm off, then."

"I'll be indebted to you for ever. Be careful, lad."

Tugdual disentangled himself from Pierre's embrace and knelt down by the edge of the pit.

"Tugdual?" called Abakum.

The young man turned round warily.

"You'll need these Arborescens and Suspensas—here."

The Fairyman turned his Granok-Shooter round several times in his fingers until it opened lengthwise. Then he emptied all but a few of the Granoks it contained into Tugdual's Granok-Shooter. He gave the other Runaways a look, urging them to follow suit.

"How do you open it?" asked Oksa crossly. "I didn't even know you could."

"Like this, Lil' Gracious," replied Tugdual, helping her. "Three turns to the left, two and a half to the right, then press twice a third of the way down the mouthpiece. Then say the word 'apriculum' in your head and you'll feel a notch forming under your fingers: that's the opening mechanism. Just slide your nail beneath it to open it."

"But I don't have any nails left!" wailed Oksa.

Tugdual chuckled and held out an index finger tipped with a filthy nail. When his Granok-Shooter was full to overflowing, he turned round and, gripping the edge with his hands, he lowered himself down into the fissure. A few seconds later he disappeared into the darkness.

44

RESCUE FROM THE DEEP

TUGDUAL DESCENDED STEADILY, USING THE TINY CREVices in the limestone wall as footholds, feeling more like a cross between a spider and a bat than ever. His eyes soon adjusted to the dark, allowing him to see as clearly as a cat at night, while his hands and feet easily found purchase in the rock. He moved steadily and gracefully, as if climbing down sheer walls barehanded came naturally. Most people would have felt increasingly nervous as the mouth of the fissure receded into the distance, but Tugdual wasn't like most people: his self-confidence grew the deeper he went, boosting his muscle power and strengthening his resolve. Although the mauve sky laden with metallic clouds was no more than a thin line above his head, he felt a mounting sense of exultation. He didn't hate Gus, even though everyone, including Gus, thought he did. He was exasperated by him, which was totally different—perhaps worse. Gus had certainly done nothing but cause trouble and lead the Runaways into all kinds of danger. And who was in the front line? Oksa, his grey-eyed Lil' Gracious. Oksa with her ninja skills and merry laugh. The Last Hope, protected by the Ageless Ones and the Runaways. Her deep bond with Gus also annoyed him. Tugdual was slowly realizing that their friendship, solid as the rock he was climbing down, was one of those things he'd never experience. He was too weird to have friends. Too different. Too much of a freak. The only friends he'd ever made had been weak, easily influenced kids who'd idolized him because they'd thought he was doing black magic. You couldn't even call them friends, really—they were more like puppets. Even his parents had washed their hands of him by sending him to live with his grandparents. He knew, too, that he didn't have the unanimous support of the small community of Runaways. He had no illusions about that: even though Abakum had agreed to take him under his wing, he was aware that many of the others put up with him out of affection for Brune and Naftali and not because they felt any liking for him. He'd decided he wouldn't let it get to him any more—he'd positively welcome other people's resentment, distrust or hostility. "What doesn't kill you makes you stronger," he often told himself, and it didn't really matter whether he was being deadly serious or sarcastic. He'd accepted who he was when he realized he couldn't be any different. Anyway, it hadn't stopped a certain someone from liking him...

"You're almost halfway there, grandson of the Knuts!" suddenly called the Tumble-Bawler shrilly.

"Hello! What are you doing down here?"

"The Young Gracious sent me to find out if you're okay."

"Cool!" replied Tugdual, half-smiling in a darkness so thick it could be cut with a knife.

"She sends her encouragement and this Reticulata filled with water to quench your thirst," continued the creature, holding out a grapefruit-sized jellyfish to Tugdual.

Tugdual jammed two fingers into a crevice and stood on an outcrop no larger than his big toe. He spotted the puffing Tumble-Bawler carrying the Reticulata and relieved it of its load, greedily gulping down the cool water.

"I needed that! Please thank the Lil' Gracious."

"Yes, sir."

The Tumble-Bawler flew back the way it had come, leaving Tugdual smiling with intense satisfaction.

❊

"You certainly fell a long way…" Gus jumped with a cry of surprise.

"Tugdual?" he stammered.

"In person!" Tugdual announced.

"You scared me half to death! I heard something moving and I thought it was another of those hideous lizards. You might have warned me!"

"I'll try to remember next time," said Tugdual, joining Gus on his tiny platform. "You really can't see in the dark, can you?"

"Ha-ha! Very funny!" snapped Gus bad-temperedly. "Neither can the five or so billion other human beings on Earth."

Tugdual smiled at this snub.

"What you meant was… hi, it's so nice to see you again!" he said cheerfully.

"Sorry," muttered Gus with bad grace. "Hi. And thank you."

"Whatever… Why don't we skip the niceties and get straight down to the small matter of rescuing you. Here's my plan: I'll fire some Arborescens above us to create a ladder of creepers which you can climb. The Croakettes will help by holding you up by your shoulders and you can follow me. Okay?"

"Um… there's just one small problem. As you so tactfully pointed out, I can't see in the dark."

"How about this?" asked Tugdual. He launched a Polypharus into the air, immediately filling the shaft with a dazzling light.

Gus looked round, blinking.

"Ugh… it's really scary down here!"

"Shall we go?" asked Tugdual impatiently, flattening himself against the wall, ready to start climbing.

"Um… there's another problem."

"What now?"

"I'm not very good at climbing."

Tugdual sighed and looked at him frostily.

"Is there anything you can do? Apart from getting on my nerves, I mean."

"You seem to forget that I'm only human," replied Gus crossly. "Not a species of bat!"

"Uh oh," sneered Tugdual. "His Lordship is bringing out the big guns. Come on, we don't have any time to lose. I spotted an enormous Leozard asleep in a hole and I wouldn't like to arouse his appetite, if you get my meaning."

"Is that true?"

"What do you think?" retorted Tugdual.

While Gus was seething with doubt, Tugdual took out his Granok-Shooter and fired an Arborescens at the rock face. A long, gleaming, yellowish creeper immediately shot into the stifling air of the fissure and floated there for a second before embedding its tiny tendrils in the stone. Tugdual grabbed the Polypharus and illuminated the dark shaft as best he could: the creeper had climbed about seventy feet while they watched. He whispered again in his Granok-Shooter and aimed it at Gus. This time, two tiny winged frogs shot out, flew over to Gus and grabbed him by the shoulders to carry him up to the creeper.

"We're off!" exclaimed Tugdual, climbing the wall with his bare hands.

※

The ascent seemed to last for hours, particularly for Gus, who was finding it harder than he'd have cared to admit. Tugdual had his work cut out too. Besides repeatedly firing Granoks, he'd made it a point of honour to make sure nothing happened to Gus and it was exhausting keeping an eye on every clumsy move he made. As Gus had warned Tugdual, he wasn't very good at climbing, particularly in such difficult conditions. It was much easier scaling the wall using the Arborescens rather than the rocky outcrops, but they were very slimy, which made them slippery as well as sticky. Fortunately, the Croakettes provided invaluable support, lifting him and preventing him from falling to his death. The Tumble-Bawler kept appearing at regular intervals to ask after their progress and bring encouragement from the Runaways.

"The Young Gracious says keep going, you're almost at the top!"

"Thank her very much from us," panted Tugdual. "How far now, Tumble?"

"A little more than 787 feet, grandson of the Knuts."

Gus groaned. Over 787 feet... His lungs were on fire, his muscles felt like lead and his eyes were burning from the dust, which was as hot as it had been earlier—not to mention that he was continually battling an overwhelming desire to sleep. In fact, his struggle to stay awake had taken priority over everything and he was more afraid of drifting off than falling into the bottomless depths below.

"Aren't you sleepy, Tugdual?"

The spider-boy turned round sharply and looked at him in concern.

"Not at all," he replied, thinking there was no point adding that he could go for several days without sleep. Tugdual wondered how long it had been since Gus had slept and felt a sudden surge of pity. He'd kept pace with them from the start and no one had seemed to question whether he was coping. Tugdual was surprised to catch himself feeling sorry for Gus.

"Can I tell you something?"

"Sure," muttered Gus.

"I think you're being really brave."

"Thanks," replied Gus seriously. "You wouldn't have something on you to wake me up, would you?" Tugdual thought for a moment and rummaged through his pockets, but to no avail.

"Sorry, I don't. But take a look at the wall opposite. That should stop you dozing off."

Gus turned round, holding tight to the Arborescens, and noticed a large hole in the wall. Deep within, the now familiar outline of an enormous slumbering Leozard was slowly rising and falling. Gus almost let go of the creeper in surprise. Tugdual obviously hadn't been joking earlier...

"We should probably get out of here sooner rather than later, wouldn't you agree?"

"Too right!" replied Gus, starting to climb again.

᠉

Tugdual and Gus were very relieved when they could glimpse mauve sky from inside the fissure. The Runaways waiting around the edge had been as quiet as they could after they'd learnt from the Tumble-Bawler that a Leozard was asleep in the depths, although they couldn't make out anything in the darkness. According to the Tumble-Bawler's best estimate, Tugdual and Gus only had about 130 feet left to climb, which was a good thing since Tugdual had just fired his last Polypharus. Luckily daylight was now filtering down and bathing them in a purple glow. Tugdual could see that Gus was battling tiredness and muscle fatigue, and continuing their ascent in total darkness would have endangered everything they'd achieved so far. It was a close-run thing...

"Almost there, Gus!"

He seized his Granok-Shooter to fire another Arborescens, but nothing happened. He tried again with the Croakettes—no joy there either. He was out of Granoks. Tugdual thought hard: he didn't have many options. He could either ask Abakum to help with his "telescopic" arms, or manage by his own devices. Pride won out and he chose the second alternative.

"Gus," he murmured. "We have a small problem."

Gus stopped climbing, clinging to the last slimy creeper.

"Let me guess... you don't have any Polypharuses left? Don't worry. We can see daylight now!"

"It's a little more complicated than that..."

Gus tensed.

"Oh, I get it... you don't have any Arborescens left either, is that it?"

"No Arborescens and no Suspensas either," announced Tugdual.

The still-vivid memory of the sleeping Leozard stopped Gus from crying out.

"What?" he hissed through gritted teeth. "You mean we're stuck here, so near the top?"

"You're stuck here," remarked Tugdual nastily.

"Thanks for clarifying that tiny detail. Much appreciated!" snapped Gus. "Well, go on then. Just leave me behind. I'm no use to anyone anyway."

Tugdual sighed.

"Are you always like this?"

"Like what?" retorted Gus. "Useless? Pathetic? A total loser? By Runaway standards, ABSOLUTELY!"

"Whatever. Your inferiority complex is getting to be a real pain," muttered Tugdual. "Just hang on tight to me and we'll get this climb over and done with."

Gus looked at him open-mouthed.

"You mean… you're going to carry me to the top?" Tugdual looked up. "What choice do I have?"

"But I'm too heavy!" objected the boy. "We'll never do it."

"I love your optimism," said Tugdual. "And your words of encouragement. They're so motivational."

"But—"

"No 'buts'," broke in Tugdual. "I don't look strong, but I can carry several times my own weight. Like ants… so if you think I'm worried about your seven and a half stone…"

"Um… eight…"

"HOLD ON TIGHT!" ordered Tugdual.

45

A VERTICAL WAY OUT

T HE TWO BOYS SCRAMBLED ONTO SOLID GROUND A FEW
minutes later as the Runaways clapped and cheered. Pierre was
beside himself with gratitude. Tugdual did his best not to show how
tired he was, but his gaunt face and deathly-pale complexion betrayed
his weariness. The last stretch had been the toughest part of the ascent
by far. It had cost him a superhuman effort to finish his mission and
his strength, like his Granoks, was gone. Even his intense pride at his
achievement couldn't change that. Cursing his weakness, he collapsed
onto the burning dusty ground.

"Tugdual!" cried Oksa, rushing over to him.

"I'm okay, Lil' Gracious," he said flatly, gazing up at the clouds rushing
past in the sky. "I'm okay. I just feel a little faint. Leave me alone for a
moment and I'll be fine."

"Tugdual, what you did was amazing!" continued Oksa, ignoring his
request. "I can't believe you succeeded. You're… FANTASTIC!"

Tugdual turned to look at her with an amused grimace.

"Did you doubt me?"

Oksa blushed, biting the inside of her cheek.

"Of course not! But I still think what you did is fantastic!"

"How about a kiss to thank me?"

"What?!"

"Forget it, I'm only teasing," said Tugdual, sitting up.

He looked away to hide a smile, his eyes sparkling, leaving Oksa covered in confusion.

"Does anyone know what's going on over there?" he said, his mood darkening suddenly.

They all followed Tugdual's gaze across the Endless Barrens. In the distance, an ominously dark tornado was forming. With a deafening roar, it raised clouds of red-hot whirling dust as it spun like a monstrous funnel reaching into the mauve sky.

"Wow!" exclaimed Oksa, fascinated by this spectacular weather phenomenon. "It's huge!"

As soon as she'd said this, the tornado swayed and then began speeding towards the Runaways, who couldn't believe they were having to face fresh danger. Hands on hips, Oksa gave a cry of anger.

"Enough is enough! How much more are we expected to take?"

❀

Oksa's father started running in the opposite direction to the tornado, pulling her with him. Abakum and Tugdual immediately did the same, snatching up the Incompetent, which was still examining the Leozard's remains. Summoning his last reserves of energy, Leomido picked up Reminiscens and raced after them. Gus, who was too exhausted to protest, was forced to accept a piggyback from his father, although he hated having to rely on other people yet again. His embarrassment faded, though, when he realized how fast his father could run. He knew Oksa was an amazing sprinter, but Pierre with his Firmhand blood was even faster than his friend.

"Dad!" he exclaimed, noticing his father's unusual ability for the first time.

"I know, Gus," broke in Pierre, leaping over a fissure with disconcerting ease.

"Your father and I could outrun a cheetah, you know," said Tugdual, again mercilessly targeting Gus's inferiority complex.

"That thing is a lot more frightening than a cheetah," remarked the Viking, glancing behind.

Gus looked round too: the tornado was catching them up and had now split into five, forming what looked like a terrifying wall of giant funnels advancing on them. Oksa screamed and concentrated on what had become a headlong race for survival over the burning desert—but no matter how fast they ran, the tornadoes drew inexorably closer.

"This way!" cried Abakum, swerving to the left.

They followed the old man's lead and, after a few hundred yards, turned round to see that the tornadoes were still following hard on their heels. Again they tried to evade them and again they failed. They stopped running, breathless and panic-stricken.

"We're done for..." wailed Gus.

"What, again?" said Tugdual sarcastically.

"Let's think about this," said Oksa. "If the tornadoes are following us, there's no point trying to escape. They must be doing it for a reason."

She thought hard, staring at the tornadoes.

"Hey!" she said suddenly. "Maybe they're the way out that the Tumble-Bawler said might be above us. Do you remember?"

The Runaways stared at her, impressed by her reasoning.

"You're right, Oksa!" exclaimed Gus. "That's brilliant!"

"There's just one small problem: which is the right one?"

To everyone's great surprise, Gus suddenly made a dash for the largest tornado and disappeared into the spinning vortex of burning dust.

"Follow him!" yelled Oksa, sprinting after him. "COME ON!"

❋

One by one the Runaways threw themselves into the heart of the tornado. Tossed about like a rag doll in the dreadful maelstrom, Oksa's terrified screams were drowned out by the deafening din. It was as if she were in a salad spinner, unable to control her movements, and she began to feel sick. She closed her eyes and mouth against the burning ashes. The dusty wind buffeted her face so violently that it felt like her skin was being rubbed down with sandpaper. It was terrifying to be so helpless, but she had no choice but to let nature take its course, convinced she was going to die. She felt her body rising through the turbulent column of air and couldn't help thinking: "Any minute now, I'm going to be launched into the sky and that'll be that! I couldn't have asked for a more spectacular death. Thanks a million!" To add insult to injury, her head suddenly crashed against something hard. A stone? A Leozard bone? Her head was throbbing as though it had been cracked in half although she couldn't feel anything with her hand. She now had a severe migraine on top of the nausea churning her stomach. Fortunately she'd reached the top of the tornado and was spat out into the mauve sky like a cherry stone. Oksa screamed with terror, frantically flailing her arms, before opening her eyes and realizing she was lying on moss-covered ground in the midst of a small clearing surrounded by giant trees.

⁂

"That was some ride, wasn't it?" came Gus's voice. Oksa looked at him, amazed she was still in one piece.

"Ooohhh, you!…" she growled, lunging at her friend.

"Easy now. Don't forget I'm the one who saved your life!"

Oksa was shaking all over with shock.

"Is anything wrong? You've gone a nasty shade of green," teased Gus.

Doubled up with painful stomach spasms, Oksa leant over and threw up. Gus put his hand on her shoulder, looking concerned.

"Are you all right?"

"Uh-uh," said Oksa straightening up, a wild look in her eyes. "I really thought I was going to die."

"You should trust me more!" remarked Gus.

"I have to admit you excelled yourself this time," she said, with an admiring, grateful glance. "How did you know it was the right tornado?"

Gus shrugged and, pretending not to be bothered either way, replied:

"You really want to know?"

"Of course I do."

"Well, I noticed that one of the five tornadoes was spinning anticlockwise, so I immediately thought it had to be the right one. Amazing, isn't it?"

"You're not kidding!" agreed Oksa. "And it proves one of your guiding principles: thinking before acting is the secret of success."

Gus didn't have time to reply: the other Runaways were falling out of the sky like human meteorites. They bounced on the carpet of moss in the clearing, terrified at their narrow brush with death. Even the unflappable Abakum looked shaken. Eyes glazed, he was bent over and retching with his hands on his thighs. Pavel and Pierre were recovering slowly, sitting on the ground with their heads between their knees, while a winded Leomido was trying to struggle to his feet to go to Reminiscens, who was crouched a few yards away. When Tugdual finally arrived, Oksa could at least breathe easily again. He lay unmoving on the moss, his skin chalky white, staring at the sky. Oksa was about to go to him, when Abakum stopped her.

"Leave him be!"

"But…"

"I don't think he'll want anyone to see him like this," explained the Fairyman quietly. Leomido walked over to them and murmured:

"Well, that was a close call! Well done, lad!" he added, patting Gus's shoulder.

The boy blushed and ducked his head, allowing a strand of dark hair to hide his face.

"It's nice to be useful for once," he muttered, as Oksa stared at him in exasperation.

"What a terrible storm!" remarked the Incompetent suddenly. "My hair must be a complete mess."

"But you don't have any hair, Incompetent!" remarked Oksa.

"Don't I?" it asked in amazement, patting itself all over.

Oksa smiled and turned again to look at Tugdual, who seemed to be rallying. Obeying her heart, she wandered over to him. He was rubbing his head with a rueful grimace.

"Are you okay?" said Oksa.

"Hmm… I've been better," groaned the young man. "I feel like someone hit me on the head with a brick. Here, feel."

He caught hold of her hand and placed it on a large, egg-shaped lump. Oksa snatched her hand back, flustered by his touch.

"I think that might have been me," she said, remembering the blow she'd received inside the tornado.

"If it was, you're really hard-headed, that's for sure!" remarked Tugdual, smiling. "Anyway, we're alive, that's the main thing… Good call, Gus!" he said to the boy, who was watching him out of the corner of his eye.

"Yeah, right," grouched Gus. "We're right back where we started."

They looked around and saw with surprise that Gus was right: they were exactly where they'd landed just after Impicturement.

"Oh, brilliant!" exclaimed Oksa. "I hope we didn't go through all that for nothing."

"Not at all," said the black butterfly, fluttering in front of her. "You've accomplished your mission."

"Oh, it's you! Maybe you can explain why we're here again," she said, looking around at the clearing.

"Do you see that rectangle flashing on and off in the sky?"

The Runaways looked up and nodded: the rectangle was shining brightly above them.

"Is that the picture?" asked Oksa hopefully.

The butterfly flew closer, fixing her with its tiny eyes.

"Not at all, Young Gracious."

"What?" chorused the Runaways.

272

"I'm sorry to disappoint you, but what you see isn't the picture," continued the butterfly. "It's the entrance to the passage leading to the Stonewall."

"Oh, for pity's sake!" wailed Oksa. "Is there no end to this?"

"Of course there is," replied the butterfly. "Everything comes to an end, here and everywhere else. Don't worry, Young Gracious, Runaways! The way to escape your Impicturement lies on the other side of that wall. So long as you manage to destroy the Soul-Searcher and foil the treacherous Wickedesses, of course."

"Oh, sure! Piece of cake," said Gus.

"Have confidence in yourselves," counselled the butterfly wisely. "Enter the passage and find the way out."

46

THE HOSTILE DEPTHS

The Runaways' first idea was to climb the trees to reach the flashing rectangle, but Gus soon talked them out of it. "It won't work."

"Why?" asked Oksa, who'd already begun climbing. "These trees are easily tall enough to reach it."

"Why won't you believe me for once?" snapped Gus. "I've already tried. You think you're climbing but you actually stay at ground level."

"He's right," confirmed the butterfly. "It's one manifestation of the hallucinogenic power of the Imagicon, which also brought you back to your starting point. Although you might have thought you were following a straight, horizontal path, you were actually moving in a vertical spiral. In the same way, although you think you're climbing these trees, you're really not getting anywhere fast."

"That's so weird," exclaimed Oksa, after giving it a try. "What are we going to do then?"

"I have an idea…" said Gus.

He strode into the dark forest and began poking around at the foot of the trees. Suddenly, the tiny heads with root bodies emerged from the ground, chattering shrilly.

"You found each other!" one said, inspecting the Runaways. "Congratulations!"

"Thank you," said Oksa.

"Have you crossed paths with the Wickedesses yet?"

"No, not yet," replied Gus. "Just their minions, the Airborne Sirens and the Leozards."

"And you managed to escape, did you? Congratulations again!"

"Sadly, not all of us did," murmured Oksa, seeing the Lunatrixa's plump face in her mind's eye. "But we definitely have a bone to pick with those Wickedesses. Can you help us?"

"Of course. What do you want us to do?" asked the little head, its dark eyes gleaming with impatience.

"We have to get up to that flashing rectangle, right up there…"

"You mean the trapdoor? The passage to the Stonewall?"

"WHAT?" cried Gus angrily. "You let us face all those dangers when you knew all along that the way out was up there?"

"You can only get to it once you've passed through all the levels," replied the head with the root body. "Don't forget that the purpose of Impicturement is to put individuals to the test…" After a short silence, Oksa turned again to the head-root.

"Well… We have a problem. We can't Vertifly or climb the trees and Dad's Ink Dragon appears to be dormant at the moment."

"I see what you're getting at, Young Gracious, and it'll be an honour to assist you," responded the half-human, half-plant creature immediately. "Reveal yourselves, my friends! We're going to help the Runaways!"

Forty or so heads with root bodies popped out of the ground, chirruping with excitement, and gathered in small groups of five or six around each Runaway. Opening their mouths, they took firm hold of everyone's tattered clothes with their teeth and, with supernatural strength, stretched up and up into the mauve sky until they could deposit their cargo on the trapdoor.

"Wow!" exclaimed Oksa. "That was amazing!"

"Sickeningly easy, you mean," remarked Gus.

"So this is the passage that leads to the Soul-Searcher," murmured Abakum, looking at the trapdoor.

"And the Wickedesses…" added Tugdual, feeling around the edge to locate the opening.

"Trust you to add something depressing!" grumbled Gus.

"Ah! There we are, it's open," said Abakum, crouching down. "We're on our way to meet our tormentors at last."

One by one, the Runaways dropped down into the dark shaft, which had the slimy walls and stale, foul-smelling air of a sewer. After sliding down the stone conduit, they landed in a room so low and narrow that they completely filled the cramped space. Above them, the shaft mouth closed and merged with the ceiling.

"We can only go in one direction," said the Tumble-Bawler, popping its head out of Oksa's bag.

"Which is?" enquired Leomido, before being swallowed up by the ground.

"Leomido!" cried the terrified Runaways.

"Stand in the middle of the room," advised the Tumble. "The passage is below."

They obeyed without delay, Oksa first. As soon as she stood where Leomido had disappeared, she suddenly felt herself being sucked down, as if someone had grabbed her ankles to pull her into the chilly depths. Despite her relief at being reunited with Leomido, this place gave her the creeps—it was scarier than anywhere she'd ever been: worse even than the Airborne Sirens' tunnel. The walls, which were poorly lit by torches, oozed a repulsive greenish substance whose origin didn't bear thinking about. Something dripped on her head, making her cry out in disgust. The other Runaways dropping down from the ceiling one by one felt just as intimidated as Oksa by these murky surroundings.

"Next, you have to go down there," said the Tumble-Bawler, pointing to a flight of steps in the ground.

"With pleasure!" exclaimed Oksa, who couldn't wait to get out of this gloomy passage.

The staircase felt endless. Fortunately, although the steps were high and narrow at first, they soon widened out and became easier to navigate as they descended in a spiral. The Runaways felt increasingly anxious. This level was supposed to be the way out and yet they felt as though they were descending into hostile depths where they'd be buried alive.

"This is horrible…" muttered Gus.

"Don't worry, it'll be fine," said Oksa comfortingly, although she didn't sound convinced by her own words. "How many more steps, Tumble?"

The little scout emerged from the bag and disappeared into the depths. A few long minutes passed before the results of its calculations rang out.

"You've walked down 2,549 steps, which means there are 7,451 steps left."

Oksa whistled.

"You're saying there are 10,000 steps leading down… to wherever we're going?"

"That's right, Young Gracious."

"10,000 steps?" remarked the Incompetent in amazement. "My calf muscles will be huge!"

"But you don't have any calves, Incompetent!" laughed Oksa. "Anyway, Pierre is carrying you."

"Really? I was wondering…"

"Come on, let's keep moving," sighed Oksa, gazing at the spiral staircase plunging into the darkness below.

※

The Runaways were doing their best to ignore the anxiety caused by this descent into the unknown. They had a nasty feeling they were walking into a trap, which strained their nerves to breaking point. It wasn't long before they had to take another break. Sitting on the steps, Oksa removed her trainers and inspected them dejectedly.

"It's about time we got to where we're going," she muttered, looking at the holes in her soles.

She pulled off her tattered socks and massaged her blistered feet, trying not to groan at the pain. She was beginning to feel discouraged. How was all this going to end? She didn't want to think about it, but she could sense death lurking in the shadows, ready to carry off her loved ones when the time was right. She shook her head to banish such awful thoughts and gently stroked the sleek head of the Incompetent. The Squoracle soon joined them, enthusiastically squawking:

"Happy birthday, Young Gracious!"

"What are you going on about?"

"It's your birthday!"

"That isn't funny, you know!" retorted Oksa irritably.

"I'm not in the habit of making jokes," retorted the tiny hen petulantly. "Today is the anniversary of your birth. You're fourteen."

The Runaways began doing the maths in their heads. Oksa was amazed.

"That means we've been in here for two and a half months…" stammered Pavel, thinking about Marie.

"I'm fourteen!" murmured Oksa.

Tugdual came to sit beside her. He leant over and whispered in her ear:

"Happy birthday, Lil' Gracious…"

His hair caressed her cheek and his lips brushed her neck. She quivered, unsure how to react.

"Anyway," rang out Gus's voice, "we'd better get a move on if we want to celebrate this special occasion in style!"

Oksa shot him a grateful look. He smiled sadly at her, which made tears spring to her eyes. Before she could break down completely she jumped up, exclaiming hoarsely:

"And when we're out of this hellhole, I want the biggest birthday cake on earth! And I do mean on earth! We've spent far too long in here already. Come on—let's go!"

∗

With a great deal of wincing and grimacing, the Runaways finally stepped off the interminable staircase.

"Phew!" exclaimed Oksa, rubbing her thighs. "I couldn't have gone down another step."

"I hope we don't have to climb back up to get out of here," remarked Gus.

"Horror of horrors! Don't even think such a thing!" said Oksa.

"Talking of horrors, I hope we haven't walked into a trap," said Tugdual. "Look! The staircase has vanished. We're well and truly stuck. If we were attacked by anyone or anything, I'm not sure how we'd get away," he added.

There was a deathly silence as the exhausted Runaways gazed helplessly at the immense wall which stretched into the distance as far as the eye could see.

"The Stonewall," whispered Gus.

47

THE
STONEWALL

A FTER TUGDUAL AND PIERRE HAD TRIED IN VAIN TO
climb the wall, which seemed vertically and horizontally endless,
the Runaways had to face facts: there was no getting over or around it.
Shrouded in a hazy half-light, they began walking along it, feeling the
stones in the hope that they might trigger some mechanism which would
reveal the way out of this trap.

"You won't find anything, even if you look for days!" screeched the
Squoracle after several hours.

"Thanks for the encouragement," muttered Oksa, her fingers sore
from the sharp stones.

"Huh," scoffed the tiny hen. "Why don't you use your memory?
Remember what the crow told the boy."

They all turned to look at Gus, who blushed with embarrassment. Pierre
walked over to his son and looked at him confidently. Gus cleared his
throat, frightened he might not remember the crow's message. Tiredness,
worry and pressure made it hard to concentrate. The Runaways were
depending on him, but everything was jumbled up in his head. Oksa
empathized with her friend's panic.

"Come on, Gus," she said. "Think! What exactly did the crow say
about this lousy wall?"

She put her hands on the boy's shoulders and looked at him hopefully. Encouraged by her support, Gus tried harder. A few seconds later, he triumphantly recited:

> *To leave the Forest of No Return*
> *Each traveller through it has to yearn*
> *For one thing—all else must be forsworn.*
> *Then every innocent heart and mind*
> *Must stop the Void from claiming life—*
> *Escape will depend on speed and might.*
> *Lives will again come under threat*
> *From creatures truly merciless*
> *Who descend on you with airborne death.*
> *Then you'll have to risk a rout*
> *In the realm of heat and drought*
> *Where cruelty crawls from underground.*
> *At last, the Stonewall opens wide*
> *When you locate the catch inside*
> *Bringing you closer to home Outside.*
> *But there's no escape if you don't beware*
> *The Wickedesses which, with lethal brawn,*
> *Hold sway over every creature born*
> *For the power of life and death is theirs.*

The Runaways stared at each other in amazement.

"Of course!" exclaimed Oksa, smacking her forehead with the flat of her hand. "The wall opens from the inside!"

"Oh great," said Gus, following his friend's line of reasoning.

"I'm confused…" admitted Reminiscens.

"The door must be inside the wall, I'd stake my life on it!" cried Oksa. "Which means that only a Werewall can pass through the wall and find the way out."

"I'll go!" exclaimed Tugdual.

He closed his eyes and concentrated, his body pressed flat against the wall. The veins in his neck turned blue with the effort of pushing against the stone. He pressed even harder with a groan of annoyance, but the wall didn't give.

"Some Werewall," remarked Gus sarcastically.

"I've already told you I'm still learning!" retorted Tugdual with barely suppressed anger.

"Perhaps I can help?" suggested Reminiscens.

The old lady walked over and passed through the stone with disconcerting ease, watched by the dumbfounded Runaways. Then her outstretched arms poked back through the wall, grabbed Tugdual's shoulders and pulled him through to the other side.

"Wow!" whispered Oksa. "That was something else!"

"Too right!" admitted Gus, fascinated by the miracle which had just taken place before his very eyes. "I'd love to be able to do that."

But their enthusiasm was soon curbed by frightened screams from the other side of the wall.

"What's going on?" asked Oksa in alarm, paling.

"I don't know," replied Abakum, visibly worried.

Oksa's anxiety mounted: this was the first time the Fairyman hadn't been able to answer her questions, which didn't bode well at all.

"Find the door and let us in!" yelled Pavel, close to the wall, his hands cupped around his mouth.

Oksa and Gus wrung their hands. This harrowing silence was even worse than the screams. Had Reminiscens and Tugdual been attacked by the Wickedesses? Were they still alive? Would the remaining Runaways be trapped at the foot of the Wall until they died? Panic began to set in.

"Where's Leomido?" murmured Abakum. They all looked around in concern.

"The last time I saw him, he was heading that way," said Pavel, pointing to the dark path running alongside the wall to their right. "I think he was looking for a way out."

"But there's nothing to be gained by that!" said Abakum crossly. "The Squoracle told us so. Anyway, it's far more sensible to stay together."

His words were interrupted by a sudden ripple of movement in the wall. Suddenly an opening appeared in the stone, revealing the way out they'd been told was there. Tugdual appeared, followed by Reminiscens and someone completely unexpected.

"Leomido?" chorused Gus and Oksa. The old man looked nervously at them.

"I found an opening in the wall, a little farther along from where we stopped," he explained flatly.

"But we looked everywhere!" remarked Oksa.

"Obviously not," retorted Leomido firmly.

"Oh well," said Abakum frowning, his eyes fixed on his friend. "The main thing is that we're all together again. But what happened? We heard screams…"

Tugdual came forward and they could see that there was a deep, bloody bite on his handsome face.

"We were attacked by some kind of bats with skull-like heads," he said groggily.

"Chiropterans!" exclaimed Gus, shivering at the memory of his encounter with those terrifying insects in the Welsh sky.

"I saw them heading straight for Reminiscens like wasps on jam and I tried to chase them away," continued Tugdual. "Which meant they turned on me. I was attacked by so many that I couldn't do anything to defend myself. Luckily Leomido arrived on the scene and dispatched them with a barrage of Fireballisticos. I think I may have a few singed hairs, but I escaped in one piece, so thank you, Leomido!"

The old man humbly bowed his head.

"Those creatures are hideous," remarked Tugdual, turning over his right hand to reveal two deep bites.

"Welcome to the club!" said Gus, delighted at being one jump ahead of his rival for once.

"How do you feel?" asked Abakum worriedly.

"A little woozy…"

"You have a remarkable constitution, lad. There aren't many people who'd still be on their feet after one bite from a Chiropteran, let alone three. You'd better allow me to give you something to ease the pain though."

The two of them walked away from the group and sat down beneath a torch. Abakum took a few bottles out of his bag and began smearing various ointments on Tugdual's injuries. As observant as usual, Oksa noticed how upset and tense Abakum looked, so she eavesdropped on the Fairyman's conversation with Tugdual.

"So you saw Leomido pass through the wall, did you?" asked Abakum, sounding surprised. "That's impossible! The Chiropterans must have affected your sight."

"You have to believe me, Abakum," said Tugdual, defending himself vehemently. "You know I'm telling the truth. I wasn't hallucinating: Leomido definitely passed through the wall."

"How could he have done? He's not a Werewall!"

"How do you know?" said the young man.

"I can't believe you…" murmured Abakum, sounding choked.

"You don't want to believe me!" retorted Tugdual.

Oksa put her hand over her mouth in bewilderment. She looked over at Leomido, who was staring stiffly at his old friend from a distance, and her heart turned over. Her great-uncle looked so miserable… She turned her head to hide her emotion and studied the huge circular room in which the awed Runaways were now standing.

48

THE DISPLACEMENT SPELL

A BAKUM WAS THE FIRST TO VENTURE FORWARD. THE ground was intricately paved with triangular stones that shone with a honeyed glow in the light of the torches fixed to the walls. Over the chamber was a gigantic dome supported by ten elaborately carved columns which widened at the top to provide better support for the vaulted ceiling. At its centre, a pool tiled with mosaics was bubbling with murky water whose acrid smell prickled their nostrils and made their eyes smart.

"Stay here," whispered the Fairyman.

He walked over to the edge of the pool and crouched down to peer into the pungent water. The only visible movement was large bubbles bursting softly on the surface, splattering the rim of the pool. Abakum brushed his fingers over the water. The pool seemed to come to life, as if his touch had woken it from a deep slumber: the bubbles swelled and exploded and a foul-smelling, yellowish mist filled the air. Abakum backed away in concern.

"I don't like this place at all," murmured Gus.

"You're not kidding!" agreed Oksa. "It feels like we're caught like rats in a trap at the centre of the earth! It gives me the creeps…"

"Don't worry, Lil' Gracious," said Tugdual, then added, looking up at a blurry form flying towards them: "Looks like we're about to find out our fate…"

The crow landed at Oksa's feet and bowed respectfully to her. She couldn't help admiring its huge wings—they had been so meticulously preened that the Runaways were reflected in their lustrous sheen. The crow opened its golden beak a fraction, releasing a plume of black smoke.

"You deserve high praise indeed, Young Gracious, and you've arrived just in the nick of time."

Oksa knelt down level with the crow, which seemed embarrassed beyond all measure by this gesture.

"No!" it exclaimed abruptly. "Please stand up immediately!"

Surprised and confused, Oksa did as she was told. The crow spread its large wings and hovered in front of her.

"I can't stay here much longer," it told her breathlessly. "The Wickedesses are after me. I thought I'd met my maker a thousand times before I managed to track you down. So I'll be brief: none of your powers can stop the lethal might of the Wickedesses. Only one thing can shield you from their power: the yellow mist spreading through this room. Despite its fetid smell, it's your last and final defence. You'll have to act quickly, though, because the mist is highly volatile and is only effective while it lasts, which won't be long. If it disperses, the Wickedesses will invade the Sanctuary and claim your lives and that of every living creature inside this picture. So please don't delay! I hate to say this, but you must destroy the Soul-Searcher. There's no other way," the crow said miserably.

"Where is this Soul-Searcher?" asked Oksa.

"There," said the crow, gesturing with its beak towards the pool, which was now bubbling furiously. "Mix your blood with the contents of the phial I gave the boy, throw it on the Soul-Searcher and you'll be freed by the Displacement Spell. I must get back to my family, or what's left of it... Farewell, Young Gracious, Runaways! I shall be eternally grateful to you."

Then the crow flew off swiftly and disappeared into the mist.

"Well, that seems straightforward enough!" said Oksa hoarsely. "Gus, would you give us the phial you're wearing around your neck?"

The boy carefully removed the necklace and held out the tiny bottle to Oksa with trembling fingers.

"I think the crow is right to insist we don't hang around," said Tugdual gravely. "Look! The mist is thinning and I'd rather not see what's waiting behind it…"

Apprehensively they studied the large round chamber and realized with horror that Tugdual was right: around the curved walls of the room the mist was gradually being replaced by wisps of dark vapour uttering hair-raising screams.

"The Wickedesses are coming," confirmed Abakum hurriedly. "Let's get a move on!"

"How do you open this thing?" cried Oksa in irritation, turning the tapering diamond-shaped phial over and over in her hands.

Abakum also examined the bottle, which seemed determined not to give up its secret. In the meantime, the hellish screams sounded like they were drawing closer.

"Perhaps you have to blow on it," suggested Gus. "Like a Granok-Shooter."

Tensely, Oksa blew on it, while the Runaways looked on, their eyes gleaming with a mixture of panic and hope. As if by a miracle, a small lid popped open at the top of the phial and a sharp point like the blade of a dagger emerged from the other end.

"Gus!" exclaimed Oksa, her face lighting up. "You know what? You're a genius!"

"Save the compliments till later," retorted the boy, blushing. "After we've escaped from this hellhole!"

"Hurry, they're getting closer!" said Pavel.

Strangely, the temperature in the chamber seemed to be rising as it grew darker and the ghoulish figures grew closer. The heat was becoming unbearable. The screams grew louder and they could see malevolent shadows moving in the yellow mist. The shield protecting the Runaways was evaporating before their eyes and it wouldn't be long before the Wickedesses closed in on them.

❊

Oksa was the first to prick her finger on the sharp point sticking out of the phial. The blood welled and she squeezed her finger so a drop fell into the bottle. The liquid turned a mysterious, iridescent colour and gave off a coppery smoke.

"Your turn!" cried Oksa, holding out the phial to the other Runaways. "Quick!"

The darkness was intensifying around them, becoming thicker and more ominous. Another few yards and it would all be over. For ever. Tense as drawn bows, Pavel and Pierre adopted a defensive stance around their children, ready to sacrifice their lives for them. Meanwhile the phial was hurriedly passed from hand to hand and enriched with drops of each Runaway's blood.

"We're good to go, Oksa!" cried Tugdual, brandishing the smoking bottle at last.

"Are you sure?" asked the girl, taking it from him.

"Absolutely!"

"Then let's do it!"

As soon as Oksa put her foot on the narrow mosaic rim, the acrid water was sucked towards the bottom of the pool to reveal a strange phenomenon: a formless mass began swelling until it filled the whole basin. With mauve veins, so dark they were almost black, this mass was beating like a heart. Oksa gulped, suddenly feeling unsure.

"It's alive!" she exclaimed.

"Of course it is, Lil' Gracious," retorted Tugdual, sounding unusually irritable. "And so are the Wickedesses, which are about to kill us!"

"You have to destroy the Soul-Searcher, Oksa!" yelled Pavel. "THROW IN THE PHIAL!"

The lethal breath of the Wickedesses was beginning to consume the last plumes of yellow mist. Suddenly, the shadowy tongue of the hungriest Wickedess licked around the calf of the Young Gracious and took hold. Oksa turned and saw the most hideous creature she'd ever encountered: puffs of pestilential vapour rose from its fleshless body, covered in strips of blackened skin, while its head could almost have been human but for eyes veined with black blood and a thick, endless tongue covered with toothed suckers. Oksa screamed. Beside her, Tugdual was rooted to the spot with horror. Surely none of the Runaways was strong enough to destroy such an abomination? But, at the sight of the foul creature reeling in Oksa with its tongue, he growled with rage and his determination to save her overcame his fear, spurring him into action. A thin trickle of electricity sizzled from his raised hand and exploded into a fireball when it hit the Wickedess. The creature released Oksa and fell to the ground, writhing in pain from the flames consuming it. Then the impossible happened: through the smoke and the flames, the Wickedess's body, which had been split in two, got to its feet as if nothing had happened and rushed at him with a terrifying roar.

"Why didn't it die?" railed Tugdual, his wrist caught by the suckered tongue.

The Wickedess, eyes contorted with pain, was determined to annihilate him and none of the defences used by the Runaways could counter its resolve. With horror etched on his face, Tugdual crashed to the ground, no match for the implacable strength of the creature dragging him mercilessly along.

"We've got to do something!" screamed Oksa.

Abakum fired his last Granok. The one he kept for dire emergencies. The Crucimaphila flew through the air like an arrow and time seemed to stand still. Everyone fell silent and everything seemed to move in slow motion as a black hole formed above the decomposing head of the

Wickedess. It looked up at the strange phenomenon and gave a loud, blood-curdling laugh. Its wide-open mouth allowed a glimpse of the hellish flames ravaging its body and its tongue coiled around Tugdual to drag him down into that blazing pit. Mustering all her courage, Oksa hurled the phial onto the pulsing Soul-Searcher as hard as she could.

49

HEARTS WILL BLEED...

THE RUNAWAYS WERE SUDDENLY SWEPT UP BY A GALE-force wind, even more powerful than the tornado that had transported them from the Endless Barrens. It roared furiously as it snatched them, helpless and screaming, from the ravening maws of the Wickedesses. A few seconds later they found themselves flung from the face of Big Ben into the rainy, orange-coloured sky of London at night.

"Daaaad!" screamed Oksa, flailing her arms.

Gus's scream echoed hers a few seconds later. None of the Runaways had expected to end up in mid-air and the relentless pull of gravity on the Outside was a shock to their systems. Not for Pavel though, who spread the broad wings of his Ink Dragon.

"Vertifly, Oksa!" he roared. "I'm coming!"

With two beats of his wings he reached Gus, who was plummeting through the air, and caught him in his talons before flying off to rescue Abakum and the Incompetent, who were still hanging from Big Ben's face. In the meantime, Oksa was doing her best to Vertifly and control her panic at the vast, empty drop below. Recognizing the famous clock tower, she was thrilled to realize she was in the middle of London and that they were all safe and sound. But she also knew that she was at the mercy of any pedestrian who chose to look up... When the Ink Dragon flew past and caught her, she thought her heart would stop. A girl floating 200 feet above ground was odd enough—but a dragon flying through the London sky was hardly something you saw every day! Pavel didn't seem concerned, though. Carrying Oksa, Gus and Abakum in his talons, he found Tugdual, Pierre and Reminiscens, who'd Vertiflown to a dimly lit square near Westminster.

"Tugdual! You're here!" exclaimed Oksa happily. "Are you okay?"

"Yes," replied the white-faced young man. "Another second and I'd have had it... Hey, where's Leomido?" he asked, looking around.

They stared at each other. No one knew where the old man was.

"Perhaps he was ejected from the painting farther off," suggested Reminiscens, trying to reassure them.

"Perhaps," said Abakum, not entirely managing to hide his concern.

"Let's get out of here," said Pavel. "All aboard. Next stop Bigtoe Square!"

Overwhelmed by exhaustion, the Runaways shrugged off their fear of being seen and climbed onto the back of the Ink Dragon which, in the blink of an eye, disappeared into the clouds.

※

At the very moment that Big Ben's clock silently witnessed the Runaways' Disimpicturement, the Lunatrix leapt to his feet, shouting:

"Success! Success!"

He bounded down the spiral staircase from Dragomira's private workroom to her apartment on the floor below. The Getorix followed hard on his heels, looking even more dishevelled than ever.

"What success are you shouting about?" he grumbled. "That of waking the whole house at three o'clock in the morning?"

The Lunatrix rushed to Dragomira's bedroom and flung open the door. Baba Pollock was already standing there, warmly wrapped in a thick dressing gown.

"The Old Gracious must receive the information that Disimpicturement has met with success!" he exclaimed.

"I know, my Lunatrix, I know," replied the old lady emotionally. "I felt it too."

"Should the household take delivery of this announcement?" asked the creature. "Does the Old Gracious give her domestic staff authorization to inform her friends?"

"No point, Lunatrix," boomed Naftali's guttural voice. "We already know!"

The towering Swede, Brune, Jeanne and Zoe were standing in the doorway, their eyes shining. The five Runaways had all instinctively awoken at the same time. They could hardly believe that the others had returned after almost three months. Overcome with relief, they hugged each other warmly, even though their happiness was tinged with regret. Their reunion would be wonderful, but it would also be the cause of many tears: Dragomira couldn't think of anything worse than having to tell Pavel and Oksa that Marie was being held prisoner by the Felons on an island in the Sea of the Hebrides. She also hadn't forgotten the Lunatrix's warnings: not all the Runaways would come back from their hazardous adventure inside the picture. The Lunatrixa had perished, and one of her friends would also be missing. Which one? Before daybreak, she would know the heart-breaking answer. Unaware of her worries, Brune placed her hands on her friend's shoulders.

"Isn't it wonderful!" exclaimed the statuesque woman joyfully.

Swept along by the general wave of euphoria, Dragomira didn't notice her Lunatrix huddled in the corner. He was finding it hard to share Brune's opinion.

"Success has not encountered plenitude," he murmured in a choked voice. "Joy will be marred by the subtraction of my half and the sibling of the Old Gracious..."

But the Lunatrix's warning was drowned out by their merriment, so no one heard the words of the little steward, who was weeping bitter tears. The five friends hurried out onto the steps in front of the house and stood facing the square, their eyes glued to the rainy sky. In the meantime, defying caution, the Lunatrix opened the third-floor window and leant out to watch for the arrival of the valiant Runaways. He kept brushing away his tears with his chubby hand. The Getorix perched on the windowsill and, unusually, rested its little long-haired head against the chest of the Lunatrix and hugged him tightly.

"The impatience to see the Young Gracious and her friends again is extreme," sniffed the Lunatrix. "But the reunion has experienced amputation and hearts will bleed…"

"Isn't everyone present and accounted for?" asked the Getorix, already guessing the answer.

"No," groaned the Lunatrix. "Not at all."

※

Drawing closer to Bigtoe Square, the Ink Dragon flapped its wings even harder. Hearts full to overflowing, the Disimpictured Runaways couldn't hold back cries of joy when they glimpsed the Pollocks' house.

"Good Lord!" exclaimed Dragomira, seeing the silhouette of the dragon in the night sky. "What on earth is that?"

"It looks like a dragon, my dear Dragomira," replied Naftali good-naturedly.

"An explanation may nourish your understanding," said the Lunatrix from his window. "Your gaze has encountered the Ink Dragon which was slumbering within the heart of the son of the Old Gracious."

"My goodness, Pavel!" murmured Dragomira in amazement.

That meant Pavel was alive… Baba Pollock took a deep breath to fight off a wave of dizziness. She'd been so afraid of losing her only son. The dragon circled Bigtoe Square for a while, waiting until the small square was empty. A car drove past, then disappeared down a side street, and the dragon could land at last. The Disimpictured Runaways lost no time in jumping down and running over to the five excited Runaways waiting for them on the steps in front of the house.

"Baba!" cried Oksa, throwing herself into her gran's arms.

"Dushka, here you are at last! Good Lord… what a state you're in!" exclaimed Baba Pollock, looking at her granddaughter's filthy face, gaunt with tiredness. "But what about your father?"

Despite her immense happiness, she couldn't help worrying about Pavel, who was gradually returning to human form. Oksa turned to look at her father, who was heading over to them.

"Dad's been so amazing. If only you could have seen him, Baba! He fought so well and I'm so proud of him. Without him, we'd have died several times over!"

Dragomira smiled and hugged her son and granddaughter tightly, while looking at her reunited friends. The magnificent woman hugging Zoe had to be Reminiscens.

"This is wonderful," she whispered, continuing her careful inspection. When she realized who was missing, Dragomira was suddenly deaf to the smacking kisses and ringing laughter on the front steps.

"Let's go inside!" she exclaimed, trying to hide her tears. "We wouldn't want to draw unwanted attention to ourselves."

"You're not kidding!" laughed Oksa. "Discreet certainly wasn't the word for it tonight!"

"You've got some odd ideas if you think a dragon is discreet!" said the Incompetent.

Thrilled to be out of the painting, Oksa snorted with laughter and followed Dragomira, who was holding her hand so tightly that it felt like she'd never let go. The emotional reunion continued in the living room, until Oksa said urgently:

"Where's Mum? Doesn't she know yet? Come on, Dad, let's surprise her!" And she raced upstairs to the bedrooms.

50

ABSENT FRIENDS

D RAGOMIRA STOOD ROOTED TO THE SPOT, WATCHING her granddaughter rush upstairs. Naftali and Brune, who were just as devastated as their friend, didn't move either, while Jeanne burst into tears. Gus gazed at her in bewilderment.

"Is there a problem with Marie?" he asked softly.

Jeanne couldn't reply. She just looked at him in despair, her large eyes brimming with tears. Although no one had said very much, the intensity of this short exchange hadn't escaped Pavel, who went white. He turned to Dragomira and, leaning against the wall for support, asked tentatively:

"Marie isn't here, is she? Is she in the hospital?"

Baba Pollock slumped into an armchair, her hand pressed over her heart.

"No…" she managed to whisper. Pavel went even whiter.

"Is she?…"

He couldn't get the fatal word out—it was trapped in his throat, suffocating him. Just then Oksa burst into the living room, wild-eyed with fear.

"Where's Mum?" she shouted, shaking. "Baba? Where's Mum?"

Dragomira closed her eyes to block out her son's and granddaughter's anguish. Contrary to all expectations, it was Zoe who spoke.

"It's not what you think," she said gently, going over to Pavel and Oksa. "Marie isn't dead. She's being well treated, and they're taking good care of her, so don't worry."

Hearing this, Pavel felt dizzy with relief, while Oksa yelled:

"Who's 'they'?"

Mustering all her courage, Dragomira replied in a rush:

"The Felons. Marie was abducted by the Felons."

The Disimpictured Runaways were all appalled, but Oksa's reaction was the most violent. After a few seconds of horrified silence, she collapsed onto the floor, screaming and crying. Immediately Zoe, Tugdual and Gus rushed over, hoping their affection would be some comfort, even though they knew she was inconsolable.

"Mum!" thundered Pavel angrily. "How could you let this happen?"

Dragomira gazed at him helplessly, unable to defend herself. The Lunatrix came over, his face puffy from crying.

"The Runaways have encountered great losses," he announced to Pavel. "Their hearts endure deep suffering. That notwithstanding, it is the duty and necessity of your heart to be valiant: the wife of the son of the Old Gracious and the mother of the Young Gracious is possessed of failing health, but treatment of her is kind. The Tumble-Bawler made confirmation of this fact in its report. Annikki, the granddaughter of Agafon the Felon, has mastery of the art of medicinal care and you can maintain hopefulness: the Felons have the understanding that their prisoner possesses great value. There is no risk that they will bring harm to her life. Your domestic staff will therefore offer the gift of advice: the drying of tears must be undertaken, because courage and strength are essential for the rescue of the captive of the Felons. Most important, do not generate an increase in your pain with the burdening of reproaches: the Old Gracious made the display of abundant resistance to the Felons. Her life ran the risk of being stolen! But her powers experienced a lack of impact, and the Felons made a show of cunning and cruelty. You must receive the knowledge that the fight was afflicted by inequality of strength. The fortunes of the Old Gracious endured weakness despite the sturdiness of her will."

On hearing the Lunatrix's explanations, the angry incomprehension in Pavel's eyes softened to a heart-rending look of anguish. Dragomira struggled to her feet and held out her hands to Pavel with a pleading expression. Pavel hesitated, then turned and put his arms around Oksa.

"The Lunatrix is right," said Naftali. "The Felons won't take any risks with Marie—she's much too valuable. I certainly wouldn't go so far as to say she's in good hands, but I do think that the Felons are taking care of her."

"This should never have happened!" accused Pavel, glaring at his mother. "I should never have trusted you!"

"Pavel…" groaned Dragomira.

"Stop it, Pavel!" said Abakum harshly. "Dragomira did her best to prevent this tragedy, as you can well imagine."

"Maybe she should have kept out of it, if this is how things turned out!" snarled Pavel.

"Stop arguing! We have to find Mum!" sobbed Oksa suddenly. "That's more important than anything!"

The Runaways looked at each other in an icy silence broken only by the sound of the Young Gracious crying.

"We have some first-class information about the place where Marie is being held," declared Naftali. "And don't forget that the Tumble-Bawler is an invaluable spy."

"At your command, friend of the Old Gracious!" declared Dragomira's little informant.

"As soon as you've all regained your strength, we'll set off for the Sea of the Hebrides," recommended Naftali. "I'm already working on a couple of plans—"

"You must redouble your vigilance," broke in the Lunatrix, "because your losses have already experienced heaviness. Take care not to descend into forgetfulness: the half of your domestic staff and the sibling of the Old Gracious abandoned their existence in the picture."

The Lunatrix's words were choked off by a sob, while the Runaways blanched, suddenly realizing that one of their number was conspicuous by his absence.

"Leomido? Where's Leomido?" asked Oksa frantically.

Until that second, Dragomira had been clinging to the faint hope of seeing her brother again. The Lunatrix might have been wrong… but now, her world was falling to pieces. The Lunatrix hadn't got it wrong. He was never wrong.

"Where's Leomido?" repeated Oksa.

"Leomido isn't coming back," announced Dragomira, her voice breaking.

"That can't be so!" groaned Reminiscens, hugging Zoe tightly.

Exhaustion and grief began to take their toll on the Runaways as they tried to come to terms with this terrible news. A devastated Abakum was in the process of walking over to Dragomira, who looked as if she might faint, when there was a deafening crash. The living room was lit by a powerful flash which illuminated their miserable faces. The air was wreathed in a strange light sparkling with gold dust and a hypnotic voice filled the room.

"The Ageless Ones…" murmured Oksa.

A dark form materialized and emerged from the halo of light. Spreading its large wings, it circled the living room and landed at Oksa's feet.

"Young Gracious, Runaways, creatures from the Inside, please accept my compliments and the everlasting gratitude of the picture's occupants," said the black crow.

The words evaporated from its beak in the usual black plumes of steam, which rose majestically towards the ceiling.

"Where's Leomido?" asked Oksa for the third time.

"The Werewall of Gracious Blood, son of Malorane and Waldo, brother of the Old Gracious Dragomira, half-brother of the Felon Orthon and Reminiscens has passed away," announced the crow gravely.

A ripple of shock ran through the room. The Runaways stared at each other in complete incomprehension, then turned to look at Dragomira and Reminiscens, who were wide-eyed with horror.

51

The Awful Truth

"WHAT DO YOU MEAN?" STUTTERED OKSA. "ARE YOU crazy? Have you gone as mad as the Soul-Searcher?"

Bending down, she tried to catch the crow, but it was as ethereal as a ghost. When the Young Gracious touched it, the bird disintegrated into a cloud of dark steam before re-forming a few seconds later.

"You may not be ready to accept it in your heart of hearts, but everything I've said is true," the crow declared.

With this, it took to the air and flew towards the half-open window.

"You can't leave us like this!" cried Oksa.

"The Ageless Ones will tell you everything," said the crow. "Farewell!"

Oksa gave a cry of anger and frustration. She looked around for her father and saw that he was sitting miserably on the floor with his head in his hands. Reminiscens seemed to be rooted to the spot with her hand over her mouth, as if she wanted to stop herself screaming. Zoe was standing next to her with the blank expression of someone in total shock. The golden halo of light crackled and intensified in the centre of the room, then they heard a pure, grave voice saying:

"We pay homage to the Young Gracious and our compliments to the Runaways, including the one who lost his life inside the picture. Accept his choice and do not hope for his return."

"His choice?" cried Oksa angrily. "It's hardly a choice when you sacrifice yourself!"

"Leomido did not sacrifice himself," corrected the Ageless Ones, heightening the Runaways' confusion. "He could have been Disimpictured at the same time as you, but he chose not to be."

Reminiscens and Dragomira groaned in anguish.

"What's all this about a Werewall of Gracious Blood and the half-brother of Orthon and Reminiscens?" said Zoe tonelessly.

The Ageless Ones didn't reply immediately. The golden halo grew dimmer and darker then, with a crackle, it filled the room with dazzling radiance. The voice was heard again:

"The father of Orthon and Reminiscens, Ocious, was a close friend of the Gracious's family and the children of both families were virtually raised together. However, when the friendship shared by Reminiscens and Leomido slowly turned to deep love, everything deteriorated. Gracious Malorane and Ocious did their best to keep the young lovers apart, but to no avail. Ocious was becoming ever more ambitious so he came up with the wicked plan to manipulate Orthon by telling him a secret that was bound to cause resentment. Malorane, who had no idea that this revelation would result in the Great Chaos, was forced to confirm what Ocious had told Orthon about his birth. She loved him and his twin sister, Reminiscens, with the love that only a mother has for her children."

"No!" gasped Reminiscens, looking horrified at this revelation.

"No one else had any inkling," continued the Ageless Ones. "The twins had been born in the greatest secrecy after the affair Malorane had, when very young, with Ocious. She then married Waldo and, two years later, Leomido was born. The twins, Orthon and Reminiscens, had been taken in by Ocious and his wife, who was unable to have children."

"Goodness..." whispered Oksa. "Then, if I understand this correctly, my gran, Dragomira, Leomido, Orthon and Reminiscens are all brothers and sisters!"

The golden halo trembled and crackled.

"Half-brothers and half-sisters, to be precise," said the Ageless Ones. "But that doesn't matter... they are related to each other. When Orthon heard this from his real mother, Malorane, his behaviour changed. He'd always lived in the shadow of his father, Ocious, who never missed an opportunity to run him down, often in favour of Leomido. Orthon was not strong enough to cope with the demands made by an ambitious father like Ocious. His unhappiness worsened the grudge he bore towards Malorane: the fact that his biological mother had refused to acknowledge him meant, to his mind, that she didn't consider him worthy of being a Gracious's son… Leomido was deserving of recognition, but not him. This belief turned him into a cold, hard-hearted man. There are some truths which can break men. Or make them unbreakable… Fuelled by resentment, Orthon's hurt pride grew into an insatiable lust for revenge. He started by conspiring in the Beloved Detachment of his sister, Reminiscens, just to show his father he could be equally uncaring, and to torment Leomido."

"Did Leomido know the secret?" broke in Zoe breathlessly.

"Orthon took it upon himself to tell him, just after Reminiscens was subjected to Beloved Detachment," replied the Ageless Ones. "It was a terrible shock for your grandfather—it almost drove him insane."

The magical golden light grew stronger and floated nearer to Reminiscens, who was grief-stricken.

"Leomido was not avoiding you because you had been subjected to Beloved Detachment," said the Ageless Ones. "He was avoiding you because he now knew you were related by blood. He had been devastated by the discovery. All the more because Malorane was unaware of one small detail which made her silence unforgivable in his eyes: you were expecting a child."

The golden halo returned to the centre of the room.

"Leomido felt as if the ground had opened and swallowed him up. Reminiscens, his half-sister, was pregnant by him. That would be enough to crush even the strongest and most stable of men: the same blood flowed through their veins! This was a terrible predicament for an ethical and honest young man and he began to thirst for revenge. When Orthon sought him out to persuade him to help the Secret Society of the Werewalls to cross over to the Outside, he rallied to their cause. The ceremony took place a few days later: the two feuding brothers put aside their differences to become Werewalls of Gracious Blood for ever. Supporting the same cause was just the first step for Leomido and Orthon. Their grievances were different, but they both wanted revenge on Malorane. This would allow Leomido to leave Edefia and Orthon to earn his father's respect. Their wishes were granted quicker than expected. Orthon suggested that his brother enter the Memory and steal the Gracious's Elzevir, which contained information about the Secret-Never-To-Be-Told, and things moved very fast after that. The Great Chaos plunged the people of Edefia into darkness, while the two brothers were ejected into the Outside. The only person who'd always suspected that Leomido's betrayal might be at the root of the Chaos was the Fairyman."

They all turned to look at Abakum, who was staring fixedly at the wall in front of him.

"Leomido lived in relative peace for fifty-seven years. He'd resigned himself to never seeing Reminiscens again. You all know what happened next: Reminiscens was Impictured by her brother, which allowed Leomido to be reunited with the woman he'd never really stopped loving. But what you don't know is how apprehensive he was at the prospect of seeing her again. They hadn't spoken since he'd found out the true nature of their relationship and he was beside himself with worry. Had Reminiscens been told? If she knew the secret, how would she react when she saw him? Would she reject him? He couldn't bear the thought of that... Or would she be as indifferent to him as the last time his eyes had met hers in the corridors of the Glass Column? The memory of that day was like a dagger thrust to his heart and he knew that her indifference would be as hard to bear as disgust. Memories flooded back, reawakening his shame at his betrayal. Soon all would be revealed. His beloved sister, Dragomira, would know that he'd sacrificed his family to take revenge on Malorane and to escape Edefia. Even before he was Impictured, he'd made his decision: he would enter the picture and see Reminiscens once more. Then he'd let the picture have him, so he wouldn't have to face either the woman he loved or his sister after they knew the shameful truth."

The Ageless Ones' golden halo faded and the voice fell silent, leaving the Runaways struggling to take in this extraordinary story.

"What about my gran?" asked Zoe miserably. "Did she know?"

"I didn't know anything about this," replied Reminiscens flatly. "Until today."

"What about you, Baba? Did you know?" asked Oksa, turning to Dragomira, who'd kept her eyes closed throughout the Ageless Ones' story.

"I found out quite recently," confessed Baba Pollock. "Orthon told me everything the day I went to meet him at his house."

"Now I understand!" exclaimed Oksa. "You couldn't fire the Crucimaphila at him because you knew he was your half-brother!"

"That's right..." murmured Dragomira. "I just couldn't do it."

"Do not forget that Orthon is a Werewall of Gracious Blood," reminded the Ageless Ones.

"Was," corrected Oksa.

"You're mistaken," insisted the Ageless Ones. "The Crucimaphila is very powerful, but it cannot be fatal for someone with the combined power of the Werewalls and the Graciouses."

"What do you mean?" asked Oksa.

The answer to this terrifying question was hardly unexpected in view of the Ageless Ones' words.

"You have understood correctly," rang out the voice in the gloomy silence. "Orthon is not dead."

Meanwhile, all over the world:

Iceland, 18th June: unusual volcanic activity was detected in the ice-bound region of Vatnajökull. The highest volcano on the island, the Hvannadalshnúkur

(Glacier of Disaster), erupted suddenly after lying dormant for three centuries. The southern half of Iceland was covered by lava.

Japan, 2nd July: a deadly typhoon wreaked havoc on the Japanese island of Hokkaido. International meteorologists could not account for its origin, which remained a mystery, reviving the myth of the divine wind or Kamikaze.

Four days later, the typhoon regained strength and scored a direct hit on Taiwan and the northern Philippines.

The State of California (United States), 24th August: the San Andreas fault widened by almost twenty inches, causing an earthquake measuring 8.5 on the Richter scale and igniting fears of the Big One. The region of San Jose was wiped off the face of the earth, leaving San Francisco trembling on its foundations.

Province of Anhui (China), State of Uttar Pradesh (India), Kharkov Region (Ukraine), Perth (Australia), 3rd September: a string of unusually fierce giant tornadoes devastated these four regions, causing heavy losses of human life and severe structural damage. Measuring devices recorded up to forty consecutive tornadoes hitting the same area in the space of several minutes.

Réunion Island, 14th September: the Piton de la Fournaise became active like Hvannadalshnúkur in Iceland, Vesuvius in Italy and Mauna Loa in Hawaii. Other volcanos, extinct for centuries, even millennia, soon also gave experts cause for concern: Mount Ararat in Turkey, Furnas in Portugal, Mount Kenya…

Yemen and Oman, 17th September: the tectonic plates in the Indian Ocean suddenly shifted and overlapped, causing a tsunami which destroyed the coastline of Yemen and Oman. The tsunami warning system in this region saved thousands of lives. The waves travelled an estimated thirty miles inland.

Greece, Albania and Bulgaria, 21st September: torrential rain fell over south-eastern Europe. In two days, the Vardar and Struma rivers burst their banks, causing heavy flooding which brought business to a halt across the entire region.

The Gulf of Mexico shoreline, 24th September: Mexico, Texas, Louisiana, Mississippi, Alabama and Florida received similar rainfall to that experienced in south-eastern Europe. Millions of people were left homeless. The Mississippi River burst its banks and flooded the northern states. The water rose over six feet in the cities of New Mexico, Houston and Baton Rouge. New Orleans was completely under water.

London, 1st October: the leading international climatologists, meteorologists, seismologists and volcanologists were summoned by the main heads of state to an extraordinary meeting on the exponential growth of natural disasters.

52

A Reluctant Return
to School

D RAGOMIRA WAS LOOKING OUT OF HER LIVING-ROOM
window with her forehead pressed against the cold pane. She
was holding Abakum's hand so tightly that her knuckles looked like
they might burst through the skin at any moment. Two floors down, in
the tiny garden in front of the house, Oksa was giving her father a hard
time. Dragomira listened carefully.

"Can't I go back tomorrow?" her granddaughter groaned. "Please,
Dad!" Dragomira watched Pavel move closer to his daughter. He looked
exhausted.

"Tomorrow won't be any easier than today," he murmured sadly.
"It might even be worse," he added, glancing up at the window where
Dragomira was standing.

Baba Pollock stepped back, shaking with shock. Her son's eyes were
filled with a destructive rage as if he were being consumed from within
by dark flames. Dragomira put her hand over her mouth and stifled a sob.

"You couldn't have done any more than you did," said Abakum, gently
putting his hand on her shoulder. "You did your best, but you didn't have
a chance against three of them."

"Did you see his eyes? He hates me, Abakum! My son hates me!"

"No, he doesn't, he's just upset."

They heard the low, wrought-iron gate clang shut. Dragomira shivered and slumped in her old crimson velvet armchair.

"It's too hard…" said the old lady, her blue eyes brimming with tears. "We're not strong enough. Sometimes I just want to give up."

"Even if we wanted to give up, you know we can't," retorted Abakum. "No one can change their destiny," he insisted, watching Oksa disappearing down the street. "The Ageless Ones have spoken and you know what that means. You can't escape your fate. No one can."

※

Oksa was striding along the damp pavement. Gus, who was struggling to keep up with her, kept shooting worried glances at his friend. She didn't look well—she had purple bags under her eyes, her skin was pale and she was breathing as if something heavy was pressing on her chest. She tried to kick a sheet of newspaper out of her way but it stuck to her shoe, which infuriated her. She shook her foot to dislodge it and, when she couldn't, she opened her hand and muttered a few angry words. The sheet of newspaper immediately burst into flames in front of some bemused passers-by.

"Oksa!" shouted Pavel, catching them up.

At the sight of his daughter's tear-filled eyes, he thought better of telling her off.

"All this rubbish lying around really gets on my nerves," she raged, then gave a despairing sob.

"Hey!" exclaimed Gus, elbowing her. "Don't tell me you're crying over a sheet of newspaper!"

Oksa gave him a miserable look and dissolved into tears. Her father hugged her tightly, stroking her dishevelled hair comfortingly with his hand.

"I don't care about that rotten newspaper!" she cried.

"I know, darling, I know…"

"And my tie's too tight!" she whispered, yanking at the knot. "I'm suffocating!"

Pavel looked at her sadly and loosened her navy and burgundy uniform tie.

"You've got to be strong. Like all of us," he murmured, glancing over at Zoe, who was silently standing a few feet away.

"Come on!" said Gus. "A ninja never shows her feelings, even in an uncomfortable uniform. Anyway, you look okay in a pleated skirt—it shows off your pipe-cleaner legs!"

"I'll give you pipe-cleaner legs!" she said, scrubbing her cheeks dry with the back of her sleeve.

Keeping her eyes fixed on Gus, she twirled her hand. Gus's jet-black hair immediately flopped over his face as if blown by a sudden gust of wind. Gus brushed it away with a menacing growl, promising to pay Oksa back. This brought a smile to Oksa's face and a light to her eyes. She looked gratefully at Gus and her father, but didn't feel brave enough to look at Zoe, whom she sensed was staring coldly at her. She felt a little embarrassed: Zoe had to be as upset as she was, but she wasn't showing it. Zoe hadn't shown any emotion since the revelations by the Ageless Ones. She hadn't shed a single tear or said a word about the secret they'd been told, even though it had far-reaching implications for her. Oksa was really bothered by this behaviour. How could Zoe be so dispassionate when she'd just found out why Leomido, her grandfather, had died? Picking up her bag, Oksa couldn't help glancing at Zoe. For a second, she thought she caught a look of indescribable pain, rage and fear in Zoe's eyes but she must have imagined it, since the next minute Zoe's face was as calm and unassuming as ever. Oksa blinked to banish this unsettling impression.

"We'd better get a move on, hadn't we?" she exclaimed, swinging her bag over her shoulder. "Or we'll be late because of all the fuss you've been making…"

Gus shot a glance at Zoe, pretending to look scandalized. She shrugged in amusement at Oksa's tendency to embroider the truth.

"Let's go, then," agreed Pavel dully.

53

Unsettling Comparisons

OKSA AND GUS PAUSED BY THE GATES THAT LED INTO the impressive courtyard of St Proximus. It had been three months since they'd walked under this arch.

"Ready?" said Gus, trying to sound enthusiastic.

"Ready…" sighed Oksa. "See you later, Dad."

"It'll be fine," said Pavel reassuringly.

Oksa tossed her head and walked in, followed by Gus and Zoe. They were immediately the object of intense scrutiny.

"Great…" sighed Oksa in annoyance.

"OKSA! GUS!"

A curly-haired boy rushed over to greet them, looking delighted.

"Merlin!" cried Oksa.

Before Oksa could do or say anything, Merlin gave her a resounding kiss on each cheek then, red as a beetroot, he declared joyfully:

"It's so fantastic to see you… both!" he added, flushing even redder. "How are you? You're—"

"—alive!" broke in Oksa, biting the inside of her cheek.

"You'll tell me all about it, won't you?" went on Merlin, in a confidential tone. "I'm dying to hear what happened!"

Oksa nodded gravely.

"I'm so pleased to see you!" repeated Merlin, his cheeks still scarlet. "I don't think I've ever been so happy in my life!"

Oksa smiled as Gus elbowed him in the ribs.

"What's happened to your voice?" he teased. "It doesn't seem to know whether it's high or low."

"Tell me about it!" replied Merlin, not sounding fazed at all. "It's like being on a vocal rollercoaster. I think I've hit every single octave!"

Oksa and Gus burst out laughing, temporarily forgetting their concerns. A few minutes later, Zelda and the other students joined them and began plying them with questions.

"What kind of illness did you have? Was it malaria? Or some kind of tropical disease?"

"Was it contagious? Were you delirious? Did you have hallucinations?"

"Someone said you were in Borneo? Is it nice there? Did you see any wild animals?"

To the two friends' great relief, the bell for class rang.

"Saved by the bell!" whispered Merlin, pulling them towards the cloister surrounding the courtyard.

Oksa pretended to mop her forehead and grinned at him. The boy cleared his throat and started walking through the paved arcade.

"Merlin?"

"Yes, Oksa?" he replied, turning round.

"Thank you. For everything."

At those whispered words, Merlin's heart burned as hot as his cheeks. Open-mouthed with surprise, he blinked at Oksa and leant against the wall, feeling suddenly light-headed.

"You... you will tell me everything, won't you?"

"Promise!" she murmured.

※

Their first morning back at school was much more enjoyable than Gus and Oksa had feared. They avoided morning break because they were kept inside by Miss Heartbreak, who wanted to help them catch up on their school work.

"You've missed a lot, but you can still make up for lost time if you work hard," she said reassuringly.

"I know someone who's going to stuff herself with Excelsior Capacitors, while her so-called 'best friend' has to slog to catch up," Gus muttered to Oksa.

"What are Excelsior Capacitors?" enquired their teacher.

"Oh…" replied Oksa, without batting an eyelid. "They're a stimulant to help the brain work more efficiently. It's one of my gran's secret recipes," she added, glaring at Gus who was staring at her in disbelief.

"Oh, I see…" replied Miss Heartbreak, smiling. "Nothing illegal, I hope?"

Oksa smiled back.

"They're completely natural, honest!"

Miss Heartbreak went through their course books, showing them the lessons they needed to cover. Listening distractedly, Oksa suddenly noticed Zelda standing by the classroom window that gave onto the balustraded corridor. Their classmate was staring solemnly in their direction and a wave of nausea and exhaustion suddenly washed over Oksa. Feeling that she was being watched, Miss Heartbreak turned round to look and Oksa saw her shiver. When Oksa glanced over at the corridor again, Zelda had vanished as quickly as she'd appeared. But the uneasy feeling remained… Gus looked at her questioningly.

"What's wrong?" he whispered.

Oksa shrugged that she didn't know, while Miss Heartbreak continued listing the classwork they had to do, as if nothing had happened. Only Oksa, observant as ever, noticed that their kind teacher was trying to stop her hands trembling…

This scene had set warning bells ringing in the Young Gracious's head. For the rest of the day, she watched Zelda out of the corner of her eye, trying to work out what it was about her friend that was worrying her. When she mentioned it to Gus between lessons during the afternoon, he looking around cautiously and exclaimed:

"Zelda? No, I haven't noticed anything strange. But have you seen Hilda the Cave-Girl? Now that's what I call a transformation!"

"I'll second that!" said Merlin.

"Are you talking about me?" asked Hilda, walking over with a slightly awkward but clearly flirtatious smile.

"Great," groaned Oksa, turning round. "Oh, Hilda, that's a bit of luck. We were just talking about the next women's wrestling match!"

Hilda recoiled and looked so hurt that Oksa almost felt sorry for being rude.

"You don't have to be nasty," she said, sounding more upset than Oksa would have thought possible. "Not everyone's lucky enough to be a Russian doll."

"What do you mean by that?" asked Oksa angrily, glaring at her.

"I mean that even girls who aren't Russian dolls are allowed to speak to the fittest boys in the school," retorted Hilda, with a defiant shove.

She straightened her jacket and sashayed slowly past Merlin and Gus who, at that precise moment, would have given anything to be a million miles away. Oksa watched her walk off in surprise and whistled between her teeth.

"Amazing, isn't it?" remarked Zelda, suddenly appearing. "Some people just can't hack adolescence!"

"Zelda!" scolded Merlin. "You've got to admit it's better than before, don't you think?"

Zelda looked at Hilda, sitting on a bench trying to look feminine, and then at Merlin, red-faced with embarrassment.

"You mean more absurd!" she retorted, then burst out laughing. "In fact, I think it's pretty pathetic…"

With this, she bent down and picked up a pebble which she tossed towards the fountain in the centre of the courtyard. With remarkable accuracy, the stone flew through the air, hit the edge of the fountain and bounced onto Hilda's shoe.

"Bull's-eye!" crowed Zelda.

Oksa and Zoe exchanged a surprised glance, both struck by the same impression.

"Are you thinking what I'm thinking?" whispered Oksa.

54

CHILLING EVIDENCE

ZOE DIDN'T HAVE TO ANSWER OKSA'S QUESTION. THERE was no point—one look had been enough. A few minutes later, they all filed into the science room for the first lesson of the afternoon. Perched on their stools at the back of the class, Oksa and Gus had an unobstructed view of Zelda's profile in the third row and Hilda's in the second. Merlin had once again been the subject of intense rivalry by the two girls. Hilda had managed to grab the seat next to him this time and was looking very pleased with herself.

"Sir!" Zelda suddenly called out. "Could you please ask Hilda Richard to be a little more discreet about her petty romantic triumphs? It's getting embarrassing."

All the students, including Oksa, gasped at her nerve. This was so unlike the timid Zelda she knew and loved! The turns of phrase and chilly arrogance sounded very familiar, though, and brought back some unpleasant memories... While Oksa was lost in thought, Hilda turned round, seething with rage, and squirted an ink cartridge at her rival.

"Aaarghhh!" screamed Zelda, jumping back, her blouse splattered black. "Look what you've done now, you idiot!" Their teacher, Mr Lemon, glared at the two girls.

"I didn't do it on purpose, sir," simpered Hilda.

"Yeah, right!" raged Zelda.

"That's enough, the two of you!" shouted the teacher. "Miss Beck, go to the school office and see if they can lend you a clean blouse. Miss Richard, come and see me after the lesson."

Zelda jumped up with a face like thunder and left the room. Oksa immediately put her hand up to attract the teacher's attention.

"Please, sir! Can I go and get my folder? I left it in my locker." The teacher sighed and nodded.

"What are you playing at?" Gus spluttered, glancing meaningfully at the folder Oksa had hidden under the desk.

"Shhh! I'll explain later."

"Sure you will," he muttered.

Once again, he felt sidelined. Zoe, however, knew exactly what Oksa was doing… and caught hold of her arm as she walked past.

"Don't go, Oksa!" she whispered.

Oksa met her worried gaze and shook her head. Miserably, Zoe hunched over her desk and watched her leave the room.

⁂

Concealed behind a statue in a dark corner of the cloister, Oksa waited for Zelda to come back from the school office. She appeared a few minutes later, wearing a spotless blouse. Stopping short in the middle of the corridor, she looked round, then headed straight for Oksa's hiding place. The Young Gracious felt a jolt of panic and flattened herself against the wall, holding her breath.

"What are you doing there?" asked Zelda sarcastically when she spotted her. "Are you spying on me?"

"Of course not!" retorted Oksa, feeling scared and annoyed in equal measure. "I thought I'd forgotten my folder, so I went back to my locker to get it…"

Zelda smiled as pleasantly as a starving boa constrictor, and jabbed her finger at Oksa's chest, making her take a step back in fear.

"I'm disappointed," continued Zelda, in a cold, sarcastic voice. "Someone as clever as you shouldn't be making such stupid mistakes!"

She continued poking Oksa with her finger for emphasis as she spoke. A wave of nausea washed over the panic-stricken Young Gracious.

"Then again, perhaps your legendary intelligence was impaired by your stay in Borneo..." remarked Zelda.

"I'm absolutely fine, thank you!" Oksa managed to declare.

In reality, she was feeling anything but fine. She'd found what she'd been looking for when she asked to leave the class. The Curbita-Flatulo was undulating wildly on her wrist to calm her down and bolster her courage. Oksa steadied her breathing in time to the pressure exerted by the living bracelet, which was also urging her to be cautious. Zelda stood facing her, eyes unblinking. Her nostrils were quivering and her eyes were clouding over with a spreading darkness that terrified Oksa. Above them, the sky became overcast with an ominous layer of cloud. For all her strength and courage, the Young Gracious hadn't been prepared to see her sworn enemy—Orthon-McGraw, the supreme Felon—staring out at her from those ink-black eyes. She staggered as large raindrops began falling from the mottled sky. Suddenly, Zelda's eyes regained their familiar, kind expression. Oksa thought for a second she'd been seeing things. Her exhaustion following Impicturement, the excitement of the reunion and the anguish caused by Marie's absence had made her very vulnerable. But, in her heart of hearts, she knew... Zelda dragged her by the arm towards the staircase.

"Come on, Oksa! Lemon will kill us if we take too long! I'll let you have the work you've missed, don't worry," she declared with her customary kindness.

Bewildered, Oksa let Zelda take her hand and lead her up to the first floor like a lost little girl. Just as the two students walked back into the classroom, a loud thunderclap made all the students jump.

※

The last lesson of the day was finally over. The students in Year 9 Hydrogen noisily took their usual route back to their classroom along the first-floor colonnaded corridor, then headed out into the courtyard, where a few of them clustered around Oksa and Gus. Zelda lost no time in joining them, her eyes darker than a moonless night. The blood drained from Oksa's face.

"Was Borneo really bad then?" asked Zelda provocatively. "You must have felt so alone… Was your family with you?"

Oksa did her best to keep up appearances.

"Some of them, but not my mother."

"Did you miss her terribly?"

Gus and Merlin glared at Zelda in indignation at such a tactless remark, but Oksa was ready for a battle of wits. So McGraw wanted to play cat and mouse, did he? Well, he'd never come across a mouse as tough as this!

"Why do you want to know?"

Zelda looked at her innocently.

"That's what friends are for, isn't it?" she replied. "Is your mum any better?" she added, her narrowed eyes boring into Oksa.

"Everyone's fine, thanks…" Oksa said quietly.

"Is she still in a wheelchair?" asked Zelda spitefully.

Oksa looked at her, making a superhuman effort to reply enthusiastically:

"Who, my mum? Oh, she's great, thanks for asking! She's going from strength to strength!"

Her mind was racing with the adrenaline and she wouldn't have been surprised to see smoke coming from her ears. The chilling evidence was staring her in the face. Oksa decided to strike a decisive blow to prove she was confronting the impossible.

"Since we're having a good catch-up, do you know what's become of that Neanderthal, Mortimer McGraw?" she asked, staring intently at Zelda.

55

The Cat Among the Pigeons

"MORTIMER? NO IDEA," REPLIED ZELDA, TURNING around and starting to walk in the direction of Bigtoe Square. "Shall we go?"

"But this isn't your way home!" said Oksa.

"I know, but I'd love to say hello to your parents. I haven't seen them for ages."

"Sorry, no can do!" snapped Oksa, striding off without her.

Gus followed, looking surprised, leaving Zelda, Merlin and Zoe on the pavement in front of St Proximus.

"What on earth is wrong with you?" he whispered. "Why are you being so rude?"

"I can't explain now," she muttered through gritted teeth. "But she can't come with us!"

"Why not?" whispered Gus.

Oksa gave him a beseeching look, before being interrupted by Zelda, who'd caught them up with a strange smile on her lips.

"I won't stay long, I promise," declared the girl warmly. "Just long enough to say hi to your parents and your gran!"

"It's just that…" began Oksa, scratching her throat. "It's just that I'm not sure they'll be in."

"I'll take the chance. And if they're not, well, tough!"

Oksa sighed, then looked around for Zoe. Her second cousin stared at her gravely, biting her lip, just as flummoxed. She knew exactly why Zelda wouldn't give up. Zelda was just a puppet and cruel McGraw was pulling her strings...

"Well, we can't stand here all evening!" exclaimed Gus suddenly. "Let's go."

He set off, followed by his friends. Oksa pulled a face and looked at Zoe one last time. Zoe nodded helplessly, ready to confront the unthinkable. Zelda was walking ahead with Merlin and Gus, while Zoe and Oksa walked behind them, their eyes anxiously fixed on her back.

"The cat among the pigeons," murmured Oksa.

"What do you think he wants?" asked Zoe.

"To show us he's still alive and stronger than any of us. He's trying to provoke us. Just think, while he's occupying Zelda's body, he can get as near to us as he wants and we can't do a thing about it! It gives him quite an advantage."

At that moment, Zelda turned back to look at them with a hard, brooding expression. Her eyes no longer shone with affection. Keeping her arm close to her side, Oksa opened her hand and hurled a tiny fireball at Zelda. The final test... Looking completely unsurprised, Zelda casually sent the fireball spinning off-course with a thin thread of electricity from her fingertips. The spiteful smile on her face proved she was no longer just a schoolgirl. Oksa and Zoe instinctively took out their mobiles to warn the Runaways, but both their batteries were flat.

❖

Zelda had set a fast pace, eager to get to her destination, so the five "friends" soon arrived in Bigtoe Square. Gus was chatting to her and Merlin, blissfully unaware of any concerns that Oksa and Zoe behind might have.

"Dragomira and Abakum will know what to do," said Oksa to Zoe quietly, trying to make herself feel better.

"Oksa, I'm worried about my gran," whispered Zoe. "I don't know if she'll be able to cope with this."

Oksa couldn't think of anything to say, so she just took her friend's hand and squeezed it tightly. What else could they do? She was frightened to death. Why was this happening today, when she felt so tired and fragile? Would it ever be over? The Curbita-Flatulo redoubled its efforts on her wrist and she kept her Granok-Shooter within easy reach. Though she could hardly fire a Granok at Zelda, could she? What good would that do? The deadly Crucimaphila might not have killed McGraw, but it could kill Zelda, who was just a victim. And an Arborescens or Tornaphyllon might make things worse and unleash hostile forces which none of the Runaways was ready to fight.

※

As if alerted by instinct, Abakum was standing on the steps in front of the house, ready to greet the small group coming down the street. This unusual welcome made Oksa and Zoe feel better: the Fairyman knew. What's more, seeing the old man at the front door, Zelda—or the thing inside her body—also realized it and paused before continuing to head towards him.

"Hello!" said the girl cheerfully. "Merlin and I wanted to ask after Oksa's parents and Drag—"

"Everyone's fine!" broke in Abakum, much to Gus and Merlin's surprise. "It's very kind of you to show so much concern. But please, do come in..."

Now it was Oksa's and Zoe's turn to look bemused. Abakum gave them a reassuring glance.

"Let's find out what he's up to..." he murmured.

"How on earth did he know?" wondered Oksa. Zelda went in first and stopped as soon as she stepped into the hall, startled by what she saw: Reminiscens was on the fourth step of the staircase, pale and motionless as a ghost. Dragomira was standing very straight beside her, looking haughty. Despite their emotion, the two women exuded a tremendous aura of power. Even Oksa felt impressed. Behind, Pavel towered over them with the stony gravity of an invincible statue. To their left, Tugdual was leaning against the wall, his arms crossed, a dark strand of hair concealing half his face. Opposite, blocking the entrance to the living room, Naftali and Brune stared at Zelda inquisitively while, behind them, they could just make out Pierre and Jeanne Bellanger. The small group of Runaways stood together in this confined space, challenging Zelda who, after a few seconds of confusion, arrogantly stared back.

"You see? Everyone's fine!" said Oksa.

The Young Gracious had regained her courage after she'd understood Abakum's strategy: use the element of surprise afforded by this welcoming committee to beat McGraw at his own game and try to get some information out of him in the hope that the Felon was harmless while imprisoned in Zelda's body. It was a high-risk strategy because they might injure—or kill—Zelda, but it was worth a try.

"Do come in!" continued Oksa, pushing Zelda towards the living room. "Baba will make us a nice cup of tea… won't you, Baba?"

The old lady nodded and slowly walked down the last few steps. Her face was drawn and her eyes gleamed with rage, while Reminiscens looked like a shadow of her former self. The two women went into the kitchen where Oksa could hear them talking quietly, although she couldn't concentrate hard enough to hear what they were saying. Anyway, she was much more interested in Zelda, who'd sat down at Abakum's urging in the middle of the living room, facing the Runaways. The atmosphere was frosty. They all knew why, except Merlin and Gus, who were trying without much luck to attract Oksa's attention.

"Well, Zelda. I hear you were worried about us?" began Pavel harshly.

"Of course!" replied Zelda cheerfully. "I'm very fond of your family."

"We don't doubt it," snarled Pavel.

"When I learnt that Oksa was ill on the other side of the world, I was shocked. I was afraid I'd never see her again. But I'm so relieved to see her back here safe and sound."

"I sympathize," sighed Naftali. "Losing our dear Oksa would be a tragedy. For us all," added the lofty Swede, stressing the last three words.

Oksa noticed Gus grumbling in the corner. "Poor thing, he doesn't understand what's going on," she thought, with a sympathetic sigh.

"Isn't Oksa's mother here?" Zelda said suddenly.

This question surprised everyone. Dragomira poured tea over the tray and Pavel closed his eyes and pursed his lips.

"She's convalescing," replied Abakum with admirable calm. "On a small island in the Sea of the Hebrides. We know the people looking after her are taking great care of her. Annikki, a devoted young nurse, is always at her side. We can't wait to see her again and she'll be back very soon—we're just making preparations."

It was now Zelda, alias Orthon-McGraw, who looked surprised. For a second, her dark eyes clouded with indecision. Abakum's eyes burned fiercely.

"It's important not to rush things," said Zelda, regaining her composure. "Coming back too soon might be dangerous for her health… And what about Leomido? I haven't seen him yet. How is he?"

Oksa flinched at these callous words. She sensed Dragomira clenching her fists and Reminiscens stifling a cry. The two women looked about to faint. Behind them, Pavel glared at Zelda, his hand over his jacket pocket. He was itching to pull out his Granok-Shooter… On the pretext of fetching some sugar, Oksa pulled her father into the kitchen.

"I'll murder him," he growled in an icy rage. "How dare he come into my house and make sarcastic remarks about my wife and Leomido?"

"No, Dad!" whispered Oksa. "You might kill Zelda and McGraw knows it. So long as he's inside her, you can't do anything. And nor can he. Come on, let's show him what we're made of."

When they came back to the living room, they found Abakum explaining to their guest that Leomido had gone back to the peace and quiet of his farm in Wales and that he was fine—thanks for asking. Oksa was full of admiration at the Fairyman's calm demeanour and wished she could emulate him. What she really wanted to do was to charge at Zelda and shake her until McGraw relinquished his hold. Instead, her impulsive nature got the upper hand.

"Since you're here, I've got some exciting news to tell you," she said defiantly. Zelda turned to look at her, intrigued.

"We're all going on a very long journey," announced Oksa.

Each of the Runaways reacted very differently to this remark. Dragomira choked on her tea, Reminiscens dropped her cup on the carpet, Pavel and Abakum looked at each other in shock, while the Knuts and Bellangers seemed rooted to the spot in surprise. Gus and Merlin had the distinct feeling they were missing something. Only Tugdual and Zoe seemed to realize what Oksa was doing. They both watched her intently, Tugdual with his usual half-smile and Zoe with an encouraging gaze.

"Everything's ready," continued Oksa. "We're leaving in a few hours!"

"But…" stammered Zelda. "Aren't you going to wait for your mother to come back? You can't leave without her!"

"She'll join us later. You said it yourself, we mustn't rush things. It's much better if we go on ahead and get everything ready. That way, she can arrive in the best possible condition."

Zelda's pupils turned even blacker. Oksa glanced at her father, who looked miserable, then at Abakum, who gave her a discreet smile. She was sure the Fairyman could see what she was up to.

"But you can't… do that!" shouted Zelda, a tremor in her voice. Abakum slowly walked over to her and replied coldly:

"Why can't we? Why not… Orthon?"

56

An Icy Vacuum

The Runaways saw Zelda give a start. Her dark pupils dilated, then her eyes narrowed like those of a cat about to pounce. Abakum was standing a few paces from her, waiting with a quiet determination that seemed equal to anything, even the maelstrom that was unleashed in the centre of the room. Everything went flying—the shutters banged against the windows hard enough to break them and ornaments and pictures shattered on the floor. The flames in the hearth roared so high that they threatened to set light to the carpet. The Runaways didn't appear to be impressed by this show of strength. Or, if they were, they were hiding it well... They stood there watching, alert but motionless. Only Pierre and Pavel reacted: the Viking pushed Gus and Merlin behind a sofa to protect them from flying debris and Pavel stood in front of Oksa to shield her with his body. In the midst of this commotion, Zelda—who'd stopped pretending to be an innocent schoolgirl—stood up and growled some incomprehensible words in a low voice. Bluish lightning bolts suddenly sizzled from her hand, only to be sent back by the Fairyman with the flat of his palm. Oksa screamed:

"Mind Zelda!"

The warning came a second too late: the lightning hit Zelda head-on and the storm stopped abruptly as the lifeless girl fell to the ground. Oksa pulled away from her father's protective embrace and rushed over to Zelda.

"No, Oksa!" shouted Abakum. "It isn't over!"

Oksa had just enough time to jump back to avoid the strange cloud billowing from her friend's mouth. The initially formless particles coalesced into a fuzzy human figure, as indistinct as a blurred-out face on TV. The pixelated form floated closer to Oksa, who was speechless with horror. Pavel and Abakum rushed forward, Granok-Shooters in hand, attacking with all the Granoks they possessed, but it was no good—they bounced off what seemed to be an invisible force field over the figure's heart. Tugdual threw himself between Oksa and the human shape. Brune gave a shrill scream. The silhouette stopped briefly, then edged dangerously close to Tugdual, who looked completely unfazed and ready to do battle.

"Why don't you join me?" rang out Orthon-McGraw's cavernous voice.

"Thanks, but no thanks," sneered Tugdual.

"You'd make an excellent recruit," continued the Felon. "There's still time, you know. My offer won't last for ever…"

"I said 'no thanks'!"

"Pity. Such a waste… Don't come crying to me when you realize you've made the wrong choice. I'll crush you like the arrogant young whippersnapper you are!"

Saying this, the form unleashed a pitch-black wave which smashed Tugdual against the ceiling. He hung there for a few seconds, suspended by the black smoke, which seemed to be hurting him badly, then he fell to the floor with a cry of agony. The shape headed straight for Oksa, who put out her hand to stop it. It was no use—it kept coming at her and, the minute it touched her, a terrible chill spread through her body, as if she'd been turned to ice. She could hear a commotion going on around her. Panicked shouts from her father and Dragomira, which sounded clear at first, grew more muffled as the freeze set in. Then everything disappeared.

*

She tried to open her eyes, but it hurt far too much, so she gave up. She tried to say something instead.

"Dad…"

Had the word crossed her lips? There was no way of knowing. She couldn't hear anything, see anything or feel anything. Was she dead? Surely not. Not now. Not already!

⁂

The Runaways clustered round the two lifeless girls. Pavel looked devastated. Cradling his daughter's head in his lap, he glared at Dragomira with barely contained fury.

"If she's dead, I'll kill you…" he raged.

"You won't have to," said the grief-stricken old lady.

Abakum took Oksa's pulse. Staring into space, he waited a few seconds, then his face darkened and his shoulders slumped. Pavel groaned in anguish. Abakum leant forward and listened to Oksa's chest.

"She's alive!"

Pavel gave an animal whimper.

"There's no time to lose! Dragomira, do you still have the Extrichasmic Elixir?"

Dragomira looked at her Watcher in astonishment, then her face brightened. She whirled round and ran towards the staircase to her apartment.

"I refuse to let that woman anywhere near my daughter!" burst out Pavel. "She's done enough damage already!"

The Runaways flinched at his vehement tone, while Dragomira stopped at the foot of the stairs and gave a heart-wrenching sob, which echoed in the heavy silence.

"That woman is your mother, Pavel," said Abakum gently but firmly. "And things would have been a lot worse if she wasn't here."

"Oh, really?" snapped Pavel. "Marie abducted, Leomido and the Lunatrixa dead, my daughter and her friend in a critical condition and, if that isn't enough, we're at the mercy of forces which are too strong for us. How much worse can it get?"

"Stop right there!" shouted the Fairyman, surprising everyone. "Stop it and start fighting! If you even know what that means…"

Pavel looked shocked. Abakum's words had hit home. With his lips pressed in a tight line, he gazed miserably at the Fairyman.

"None of this is your mother's fault and you know it!" continued the old man. "The big difference between her and you is that she'll never give up, even if she's sorely tempted to. Your mother isn't perfect, but she's a fighter and a survivor, so please show her some respect. By insulting her, Pavel, you're insulting us all. Starting with your daughter."

Pavel held his gaze for a few seconds before he had to look away as tears flowed down his cheeks. Abakum put a comforting hand on his shoulder; Pavel was grief-stricken and they were all suffering with him—and the Runaways' solidarity was their greatest strength.

※

Dragomira soon hurried back from her private workroom, clutching a crystal bottle. She knelt down beside Pavel to be as near to Oksa as possible and broke the wax seal on the bottle, which gave off a pungent, marshy smell.

"Are you sure this won't poison her?" grumbled Pavel sceptically.

Dragomira tried to glare at him, but her eyes were soft with love and sadness.

"The Extrichasmic Elixir can bring pure spirits back from the depths when they aren't strong enough to escape unaided," explained Abakum.

"Son, will you open Oksa's mouth a little?"

Pavel did as ordered, startled that Dragomira had called him "son". The apothecary-cum-sorceress poured a drop of the bronze liquid into Oksa's mouth, waited a few seconds and repeated the gesture, holding Oksa's head up. The elixir seemed to spread through the Young Gracious's frozen body, warming her and breathing new life into her. Spluttering and coughing, as if rescued from drowning, she spat out huge quantities of water, which cleared her lungs and enabled her to breathe properly again. When her coughing fit had stopped, she looked around wheezing, her throat sore.

"Darling!" exclaimed Pavel, hugging her.

He squeezed his eyes shut tight to stop a fresh wave of tears. When he reopened them, he gazed at his mother in silent thanks. Dragomira smiled back, visibly moved.

"Where is he?" asked Oksa, gazing around in a panic.

"Don't worry. Orthon isn't here any more," murmured her father.

"I'm freezing..." stammered the girl, her teeth chattering.

Pavel pulled a thick mohair car rug over her and hugged her even tighter.

"Are you trying to smother me?" she spluttered with a grimace. "I can just see the headlines: 'Girl miraculously cheats death to be suffocated by her father!'"

Pavel couldn't help laughing. She was obviously feeling better. He looked at her tenderly and she smiled back. She felt a little light-headed, particularly when she thought about her brush with death. That strange figure had only touched her and it was as though she'd been plunged into an icy vacuum. It had been horrible... She shivered. Everything was fine now, or almost. Her eyes strayed to Zelda lying on a sofa.

57

SOME STARTLING
EXPLANATIONS

"WE'D BETTER SORT YOUR FRIEND OUT NOW," SAID Dragomira, heading over to Zelda.

The powerful concoction soon brought her round, to everyone's great relief. She sat bolt upright with a wild look in her eyes, and gazed at the ring of faces around her.

"What… what happened? What am I doing here?"

"You fainted, that's all. Nothing to worry about, my dear!" replied Dragomira hurriedly with what she hoped was a reassuring smile. "Here, drink this, it's a special blend of herbs that will have you back to your old self in no time at all."

Holding out the steaming bowl to Zelda, Dragomira produced her Granok-Shooter from the folds of her dress and, while Zelda's face was hidden behind the upturned bowl, she fired a Granok, freezing her in position like a statue.

"BABA!" protested Oksa.

"Memory-Swipe," whispered her father, signalling to her not to make a fuss. Oksa remembered Dragomira using this tactic before—last year, when the police had "benefited" from the combined effects of Memory-Swipe and Thought-Adder. Oksa couldn't wait to master the astonishing power of persuasion that only the Graciouses could use! In the meantime, she could do nothing but sit back and admire her gran's talent. The old lady closed her eyes to concentrate and, a few seconds later, a thin line of blue smoke entered Zelda's right ear and, in no time at all, emerged from her left. Granok-Shooter in hand, Dragomira uttered:

By the power of the Granoks
Think outside the box.
Particles of wiped memory
Remember the words I told to thee.

Then she murmured a few words right by her ear. Zelda woke up at last, a tranquil expression on her face.

"Wow! I don't know what you put in that drink," she exclaimed, gesturing at the large bowl she'd just drained to the last drop, "but I feel… on top of the world!"

"Excellent!" exclaimed Dragomira happily. "Now, my dear, it's getting late. Might I suggest that Tugdual takes you home? Your parents will be worried."

Tugdual came over, a smile playing over his lips, amused by Dragomira's verbal manoeuvres. When she saw him, Zelda shivered and glanced enquiringly at Oksa.

"He's a family friend," she explained.

"You could put it like that," he said sarcastically, scraping his tongue piercing noisily against his teeth.

They said goodbye to Zelda in relief and accompanied her to the front door.

"Is it wise to let him go like this, without keeping an eye on him, after what just happened?" asked Pierre, frowning.

The Runaways stood on the doorstep, watching Tugdual walk down the street with Zelda.

"Are you afraid he'll be tempted to accept Orthon's offer?" asked Naftali, looking as concerned as his friend.

"I didn't want to imply anything but—"

"—but you think my grandson is unstable and could easily be seduced," continued Naftali sadly. "He's certainly different from the rest of us, but you forget that he proved his loyalty inside the picture on numerous occasions."

Pierre looked down in embarrassment.

"I'm sorry, Naftali."

"Don't upset yourself," said Abakum. "It's perfectly natural to be wary when you don't know Tugdual as well as Naftali and I do. There's little doubt that Orthon's offer will have unsettled him, but I have complete confidence in him. Still, I'm happy to prove to anyone who still isn't sure that our trust isn't misplaced…"

The Fairyman immediately turned into a velvety black shadow and hurried off in pursuit of Tugdual.

※

"Are you going to wipe my memory too?" asked Merlin tremulously, as soon as everyone had filed back into the living room.

Dragomira turned round in concern.

"Is that what you'd like?" she asked.

"Um… I don't know," he mumbled. "I… I don't mind," he added, closing his eyes and spreading his arms wide with a resigned expression.

Baba Pollock burst out laughing, followed by the rest of the Runaways.

"I don't believe it's necessary! You've proved we can trust you. I'd even go so far as to say that you're a valuable ally, so there's absolutely no reason for us to take that… precaution."

Merlin sighed with relief and grinned at her.

"Now it's just us, can someone please explain what happened?" asked Gus in a small voice.

No one had taken any notice of the two boys since protecting them from Orthon's violence. Pierre and Jeanne jumped at the sound of their son's voice and the Runaways glanced at each other: the Squoracle had told them what was happening before Zelda had even set foot in Bigtoe Square. Gus and Merlin, the two "Outsiders", had been the only ones not in the know. When the Runaways had stood in a circle around Zelda and the battle of wits had begun, they'd been taken aback by the tone of the conversation. Until then, everything had been fine. The situation had become incomprehensible when a fierce storm had begun raging in the centre of the living room. Not to mention the strange cloud rising from Zelda's body... They hadn't been able to believe their eyes.

"Could someone please explain how Dr McGraw could possibly inhabit Zelda's body?" asked Merlin hesitantly.

Everyone stared at him, but no one said a word, which was unlikely to resolve the two boys' confusion. Surprisingly, it was Zoe who replied.

"Seeing is believing," she said, without getting up from the corner where she was sitting against Reminiscens, her arms around her knees. "Orthon, or McGraw if you prefer, has inhabited Zelda's body for quite a few weeks. Probably since the summer holidays."

Dragomira looked at her in amazement.

"I had my suspicions from the first day back at school," continued the girl, hoarse with emotion. "Zelda had really changed. She was very confident, sarcastic and not at all clumsy—completely different to when we saw her last. She made me feel uncomfortable and, on several occasions, there was something very familiar about her expression."

"Why didn't you say anything?" asked Dragomira, trying hard not to sound critical. Zoe hunched against the wall.

"It was too unthinkable to be... true. I thought I was seeing things. You'd have assumed I'd gone mad. And I didn't want you to worry about me."

Dragomira knelt down beside her and put her arms round her.

"You poor thing," she murmured in her ear. "I'm sorry if I didn't take enough notice of you..."

"Is... is he still here?" asked Oksa hoarsely.

"No," said Pavel reassuringly. "As soon as he touched you, the particles flew in all directions. They then coalesced to form a new mass, followed by a hazy figure that was still recognizably Orthon. We tried to stop him, but he disappeared through the wall."

"Unbelievable..." said Oksa. "But... why Zelda?"

"Look what happened when you came into contact with Orthon," said Pavel. "He probably didn't realize that he'd almost kill himself as well as you when he touched you. Zelda was an easy, harmless and docile host. I'm sorry if that sounds harsh, but it's true. What's more, she was one of your friends, which was a crucial factor. I think Zoe is right: he must have taken control of her body this summer to get closer to Merlin and the picture, because I'm positive he knew our young friend was involved. He didn't manage to lay his hands on the picture but, by staying close to Merlin, he made sure that he had a front-row seat when you were all Disimpictured."

"Of course!" exclaimed Merlin. "That's why Zelda has been all over me since we've been back at school! But I was too taken up with Hilda Richard's strange behaviour to suspect something fishy was going on... I thought it was just my irresistible charm!" added Merlin, pulling a face.

"It is where Hilda is concerned!" snorted Gus. "Lucky so and so!"

Merlin grimaced and shook his fist at Gus, laughing.

"Poor Zelda," he continued. "Does that mean she'll go back to being as bad at maths as she was before?"

"You can use Thought-Adder selectively and only erase what's necessary," replied Dragomira with an enigmatic smile.

"Hmm... I see," replied Merlin, smiling back at her. "You know, thinking about it, I had a strange feeling when I woke up one night this summer, as if someone was in my room... I suddenly felt really cold but when I turned on the lamp, there was no one there. The feeling lasted for a while though."

"I'm sure that was Orthon!" cried Oksa.

"The same thing happened to me…" said Zoe tremulously.

Everyone looked at her, which made her feel even more embarrassed. Trembling, she explained what had happened.

"You mean Orthon tried to inhabit you and Merlin before he 'found a home' in Zelda?" rephrased Oksa.

"That's my view…" murmured Zoe, turning pale.

"It's perfectly believable," added Abakum, who'd just returned from his "stroll".

"But why did he give up?" continued Oksa.

"Maybe he couldn't see it through… for emotional reasons, which would surprise me, because Orthon isn't soft-hearted. Or for physiological reasons, which seems more likely. Let's not forget that Zoe is a Werewall: it's possible that her DNA was too unstable to accommodate Orthon in his departicularized state. But I wonder what could have stopped him inhabiting Merlin: you were the perfect target, lad."

Merlin frowned, listening hard to the Fairyman.

"You mentioned an unstable DNA… I don't know if it counts, but I have a blood coagulation disorder. I'm a haemophiliac."

Abakum nodded.

"That would explain why he went for Zelda. Orthon obviously tried everything! Anyway, well done, Oksa, for bluffing that we might be going back to Edefia. That really threw Orthon. You made him unsure of himself, which is a very good thing."

"Maybe… but we didn't get much information from him about Mum."

"And we don't know whether that lowlife will try to take possession of one of us again," growled Pavel.

"He knows we're on the lookout now," replied Dragomira.

"And we've seen how well that turned out!"

"Thanks for the vote of confidence," murmured the old lady in an injured tone.

"I'm sorry I'm not jumping for joy, mother dear," continued Pavel, placing sarcastic emphasis on the last two words. "I'm just a little upset by the losses we've sustained."

Saying this, Pavel stalked out of the room with a face like thunder and ran upstairs. A door slammed, leaving the Runaways looking at each other in tense silence.

58

LITTLE BUBBLES OF WARMTH

LYING ON HER BED WITH HER ARMS BEHIND HER HEAD, Oksa was thinking back over everything that had happened in the past few hours when she heard three light taps on her door.

"Yes?" she murmured, without moving an inch, lost in thought.

"Can I come in?"

Hearing Tugdual's voice, she sat up.

"Er... sure."

Tugdual didn't bother to open the door—he just walked through it.

"That's one way to make an entrance," she remarked, going over to perch on her windowsill. Tugdual slid down the wall to a sitting position and fixed her with his steel-blue eyes. Unsettled by his gaze as usual, she looked away as a wave of embarrassment washed over her.

"Glad you liked it!" said Tugdual. "I can't do it every time, but you can usually get what you want if you believe in yourself."

Oksa sighed, exasperated as much by his oblique remarks as by the effect they had on her.

"Anyway, how are you, Lil' Gracious?"

"Surviving..." she muttered.

"That was some first day back at school!"

"Well, I'm an expert at starting a new term with a bang," she remarked, remembering her dreadful first day at school the previous year, when she'd crossed swords with McGraw for the first time.

"Anyway, you came through with flying colours, so well done."

"Yes… except that I really thought I was dying when McGraw touched me," she admitted, pulling a face.

Tugdual looked at her even more intently.

"What did it feel like?" he asked, getting up from the wall and coming to stand a couple of inches from her.

Oksa swallowed hard, suddenly short of breath. She closed her eyes and tried to get a grip on her emotions. Why did she feel so stupid when Tugdual spoke to her? Was it some kind of curse?

"It felt like I was dead," she said, kicking herself.

"Is that all?"

She took a deep breath, trying to keep her composure, and forced herself to meet his eyes.

"You're fascinated by anything to do with death, aren't you?" she surprised herself by asking.

Tugdual studied her seriously for a long time, his head on one side, then an unsettling cold gleam appeared in his eyes.

"Yes!" he admitted warmly. "I'm fascinated by all types of power, and death is one of them."

"What do you mean?"

"The power of life and death is stronger than anything, isn't it?"

Oksa thought hard for a second, giving their conversation her full attention.

"You're right…" she admitted.

"That's the game you and Orthon were playing."

"It didn't feel like a game to me!"

"Everything's a game, Lil' Gracious. Life is Russian roulette, a lottery, a toss of the coin. And fate is the puppet master, the one calling the shots. Fate puts weapons in our hands and then pulls the strings. Ultimately, though, it still decides how things will turn out. It's just that we aren't ordinary puppets."

"Why not?" retorted Oksa.

"Simply because no one else on this planet has a greater power of life and death. And you, Lil' Gracious, have even more power than that!"

"Thanks… That's just brilliant," she said, pulling a face.

"You have even more power because the future of the whole world depends on you."

"That's where it starts to get confusing…"

"You'll soon understand what's at stake and the part everyone has to play," said Tugdual as enigmatically as ever. "But you still haven't answered my question. What did it feel like when Orthon touched you?"

"You're not going to let it go, are you?"

"I never let things go…"

Oksa gnawed at her lower lip. Once again, she'd just given Tugdual an inch and, of course, he'd flashed one of his irresistible smiles and taken a mile.

"Well?"

"Well, if you must know, it felt like the kiss of death. As soon as I touched Orthon, I felt as though I'd fallen into a freezing lake… I've never actually fallen into a freezing lake, but I imagine that's exactly how you'd feel: you're surrounded by ice, you can't move and you can't feel anything any more, no more pain, sadness or fear."

"No fear?"

"No, it was weird. I knew I ought to be afraid, but I wasn't! It was as if I'd been turned into a statue or a robot. It's only now I feel shaken up…"

She broke off, a lump in her throat.

"About that and about everything else…" she struggled to say in a choked voice.

Turning away, she closed her eyes to hold back more tears. When Tugdual gently ran his finger down her cheek, she didn't push him away. His soft caress felt so comforting.

"Don't ever forget you're stronger than all of us," Tugdual murmured.

Oksa felt a mix of emotions—dark despair when she thought about Leomido, her mother and the fate of the Runaways, and exhilaration, which was like hundreds of little bubbles of warmth fizzing inside her, when Tugdual caressed her. Experiencing these two contrasting emotions simultaneously was strange and unsettling, yet intensely pleasurable. Keeping her eyes closed, Oksa took Tugdual's hand and entwined her fingers with his.

"Lil' Gracious…" whispered Tugdual, resting his cheek against hers.

He coaxed her to lay her head on his shoulder with his other hand and stroked her hair. Oksa buried her face in the crook of Tugdual's shoulder and gave a muffled sob. She nestled against him, shaking but unable to pull away. Tugdual tightened his arms around her and buried his face in her dishevelled hair.

❋

"Oksa! You've got to come and see this! Ooops! Sorry—"

Gus skidded to a halt, shocked at the sight of Oksa in Tugdual's arms. He stood rooted to the spot with his hand on the door handle.

"Don't you ever knock?" yelled Oksa, her face crimson.

"Sorry… sorry," he muttered, his lips trembling. "I'm really sorry."

"Go away!"

Oksa's violent reaction cut Gus to the quick and made tears spring to his eyes. Mortified, Oksa stared wide-eyed at her friend, whom she'd hurt so unfairly. Trembling with anger and shame, she tried to pull away from Tugdual, but he just tightened his embrace. Her last ounce of strength drained away and, giving an angry groan, she buried her face in Tugdual's neck as if trying to disappear. She heard the door slam and Gus's footsteps disappearing down the hall.

"What have I done?" she murmured.

Tugdual didn't say a word. He just took her face in his hands and tilted it up. There was a strange smile on his face, as if he was amused. Oksa felt completely lost and closed her eyes. She didn't have to wait long—a few seconds later, Tugdual's lips came down on hers, throwing her into a state of complete confusion.

59

DANGER FOR THE WORLD'S HEART

OKSA STOOD ON THE FIRST-FLOOR LANDING, LISTENING to the sound of voices from the living room. If she heard Gus's voice, she wouldn't go downstairs. Oksa couldn't believe how hurtful she'd been. She'd wanted so badly to be alone with Tugdual... but that was no reason to speak to Gus like that. She'd apologize. Gus would understand. She had to stop feeling so ashamed, though. She really hadn't done anything wrong.

Mustering her courage, she ran downstairs and walked unnoticed into the living room where everyone was staring at the apocalyptic images being shown on the TV. The presenter was gravely explaining that the storm had hit southern France with tremendous force. Lightning had struck in so many places that all measuring devices had exploded. The devastated Côte d'Azur was unrecognizable, the death toll was in the hundreds and it would take years to repair the damage. Oksa silently walked closer to the television, shocked by what she was seeing. Pavel immediately turned round, as did Dragomira, Abakum, Reminiscens, Zoe, the Knuts and the Bellangers—everyone, that is, except Gus, who kept staring fiercely at the screen. Oksa looked back and forth between the TV and the Runaways, but their eyes gave nothing away. Why were they staring at her like that?

"What?" she demanded with a helpless shrug. "I haven't a clue what's going on!"

"As usual," muttered Gus.

"What's happened?" asked Oksa.

Abakum stood up and turned off the TV. A heavy silence descended on the room.

"Things are speeding up…" he said seriously.

"What do you mean?" asked Oksa.

Abakum slumped into an armchair and stroked his short beard, looking worried.

"The Outsiders haven't been taking care of the earth properly for several decades now, even though it's their most valuable possession," he continued. "The damage, although bad, is not irreversible. However, the cause of all these anomalies over these past few months—all these volcanoes, storms and earthquakes—goes much deeper than man's irresponsible behaviour."

The old man frowned anxiously.

"Abakum?" asked Oksa impatiently.

"All this upheaval is coming from the inside, my dear."

"I don't understand…" confessed Oksa, after a few seconds' confusion.

"The upheaval is coming from the World's Heart," said Abakum sadly.

"The World's Heart?"

"The World's Heart… is our world, Oksa. Edefia."

The Runaways looked down and Oksa felt an icy chill spread through her bones. Abakum's reply had answered all her doubts. Edefia was the World's Heart. Their two worlds were indivisible and interdependent.

"It suggests that Edefia is in a really bad way," explained Abakum miserably. "It might even be dying… and all these natural disasters are being caused by the death throes of our lost land. Lunatrix, can you tell us anything more about it?"

The Lunatrix came over looking despondent. He stood in front of Oksa and fixed her with large, bulging eyes full of emotion.

"Two people have the capacity to cause an interruption in the process."

"Two?"

"The Young Gracious and the Old Gracious will have to perform the mixing of their powers. The disorder will encounter a halt if they both apply obedience to the instructions."

"What instructions?" said Oksa, not attempting to hide her agitation.

The Lunatrix looked at her.

"Obedience must be absolute."

"Obedience to what?"

"The Ageless Ones will make the gift of instructions and no one will have the power to make a diversion. Edefia and the Inside are experiencing the final wait: the Return has never encountered such proximity."

"The Return…"

"The Return, yes, my Young Gracious."

Oksa was finding it hard to catch her breath. The Lunatrix turned slowly and sadly walked back into the kitchen.

*

The adults had gone up to Dragomira's private workroom for a summit meeting, leaving the four teenagers reeling at the Lunatrix's revelations. Gus hadn't moved since Oksa had come into the living room, which only increased the girl's embarrassment. There was a horrible silence, which Tugdual was the first to break, making everyone jump.

"We'd better start packing," he said sarcastically.

"Very funny," muttered Gus, getting up to leave the room.

"It wasn't meant to be," retorted Tugdual, with a smile that didn't reach his eyes. "But take it like that if you want to. There's no way you can appreciate what's at stake here, after all."

Gus stopped dead, his face frozen in an expression of sheer disgust. Oksa reacted before he could:

"That's out of order!" she told Tugdual, sounding shocked.

"Why?" he retorted defiantly. "I'm not saying anything that isn't true: our friend Gus can't possibly grasp the full extent of what's coming."

"Stop it!" beseeched Oksa with tears in her eyes.

"I don't need you to defend me!" yelled Gus. "Why don't you just go and save the world with your superhero and forget all about me?"

Gus's words were like a slap in the face for Oksa. He stalked out of the room past her, his face white. She wanted to hold him back, but her courage failed her when she met his eyes: there was no anger or humiliation in them, just a deep sadness. Gus was about to stop, but Oksa's anguished expression only made him feel worse. All she felt for him was pity—it was sickening. He stomped out into the hallway and angrily kicked the wall, frustrated that he couldn't leave the house like any other fourteen-year-old boy. He knew the Runaways had good reasons for forbidding the teenagers to go out alone in London, but it was more than he could bear: he had to get out of the house. He wrenched open the front door and ran out, slamming it behind him.

60

SOME DIFFICULT
HOME TRUTHS

"WHAT A MOODY GIT," SIGHED TUGDUAL, FLOPPING into an armchair and draping one leg over the armrest.

"Are you happy now?" said Oksa miserably, her fists clenched.

Tugdual laughed. Oksa refused to look at him, feeling uncertain: she really liked him, but he got on her nerves too. She didn't know how to react. She could hardly give him a well-deserved slap while she was still replaying the memory of his kiss! Everything was so complicated... He was impossible to read—he could be sensitive then cruel, comforting then intimidating. And, what was worse, she felt a connection to him which was stronger than any feeling she'd ever experienced. Stronger than her deep friendship for Gus—she'd just proved that.

"You know what they say," continued Tugdual. "Nothing hurts like the truth."

"That's easy for you to say," Oksa muttered with a shrug.

"Are you cross with me, Lil' Gracious?"

"I've every reason to be, haven't I?"

As fast as a snake, Tugdual caught her arm as she was about to leave the room. He jumped up and turned her round without letting go, his face close to hers.

"No, you haven't..." he whispered, brushing her lips lightly with his.

Instinctively she tried to pull away, but Tugdual was holding her too tightly. A deep, uncontrollable rage swept away her uncertainties and she sent Tugdual flying to the other side of the room with a heartfelt Knock-Bong. Zoe, who'd been lying on her front by the fire and who'd witnessed the scene, gave a scream of surprise as a vase and a lamp smashed to the floor. The knowing look in her eyes was too much for the Young Gracious to bear, so she whirled round and ran upstairs to her room, her thoughts in turmoil.

❉

About ten minutes later, someone tapped three times on her door, so quietly she almost didn't hear it.

"Leave me alone!" she shouted, convinced it was Tugdual.

"It's me, Oksa," said Zoe.

Pushing down the handle, Zoe opened the door and slipped in, silently as a cat. She looked so fragile with her honey-coloured hair tied back in a ponytail... She tentatively walked over to Oksa.

"I'm so confused, Zoe," wailed Oksa, sitting at the foot of her bed with her head in her hands.

"I know... we all feel the same. It's a difficult time."

Zoe spoke softly, her voice sad and tremulous.

"It's awful," Oksa went on. "Everything's such a mess and I don't know whether I'm coming or going! We've just learnt some really important things about Edefia, the world's on the verge of destruction, my mother's in the hands of the Felons and I'm doing my utmost to make things worse! I'm not good enough—" She was trembling with annoyance.

"Not good enough for Gus?" asked Zoe pointedly.

"Do you think I've lost him?"

"You can't lose him. He loves you." Oksa looked at her in bewilderment.

"Why is it all happening now?" she said softly. "I'm sorry, Zoe," she added, seeing her friend's miserable expression.

She'd always suspected that her cousin was in love with Gus. If she was, then Zoe had to be finding the situation, and her confidences, unbearable. Oksa admired her courage and composure so much.

"What about you? How... how are you holding up?" she asked awkwardly.

"Not very well," replied Zoe quietly, looking down, which made Oksa feel even more guilty.

"Can I give you some advice?" continued Zoe, turning the conversation back to Oksa. "Be careful with Tugdual."

"He's not who people think he is!" protested Oksa, blushing.

"And what if he's not who *you* think he is?"

"He isn't a Felon..."

"No one said he was. But he's older than you... he's just playing with you. Look at how he makes you act. Look at how you've been behaving since you got... closer to him."

"But I haven't changed! I'm just the same! You're only saying that because you don't think I'm paying you enough attention, aren't you? I really want to help you, but I don't know how," snapped Oksa, losing her temper.

"That isn't the problem, Oksa, don't deliberately confuse the issue," replied Zoe, lowering her large brown eyes. "No one can do anything to help me. I may come to terms with all this in time. But, for now, just leave me alone, that's what I want."

"That's a horrible thing to say," whispered Oksa, feeling upset.

Zoe stood up, her expression unreadable.

"Don't you realize that Gus went out on his own, even though we're not allowed to, and you didn't do anything to stop him? You'd never have let him to do that, before..."

Oksa went white: her friend was right.

"Don't be a fool," murmured Zoe.

She walked out of the room and shut the door quietly behind her, leaving the Young Gracious battling with her feelings.

61

FAMILY OR FRIENDS?

Z OE KNEW THEY WEREN'T ALLOWED OUT ON THEIR OWN. Her gran Reminiscens reminded her of that several times a day... but this wasn't the first time she'd disobeyed. On two occasions already she'd gone over the wall—or walked through it, to be more precise. After her unpleasant conversation with Oksa, she headed for the storeroom adjoining the kitchen which overlooked a secluded courtyard at the back of the house, and disappeared effortlessly through the red-brick wall. Outside, night was falling and the sky was bluish-grey verging on smoky black. Zoe took a deep breath to slow her heart, which was thudding against her chest. She thought about Gus and she felt miserable. She might as well give up now... Gus didn't belong to her and never would, she knew that. The best-case scenario would be to stay his confidante, as she'd been over the past few days. He'd been wary of confiding in her at first, just dropping awkward hints about his unhappiness. Things had become easier and more natural as time went by and she'd been promoted from schoolmate to close friend. That was when everything had changed: her hopes had faded the better they'd got to know each other. Now her disappointment had given way to a deep, gnawing pain. Just one more reason to be unhappy. She looked up at the sky again and pictured Gus's face. She imagined him sitting miserably in his room at home, a serious expression on his face. Nevertheless, she turned to walk in the opposite direction—towards

Hyde Park, where someone was waiting for her, someone who could change her life.

⁂

The park wasn't well lit and the shadows of trees loomed over her, but Zoe wasn't afraid. She wasn't frightened of anything now—everything that had once scared her had already happened in the past few months: the thing she'd dreaded most was losing her loved ones. As she walked through the dark, she groaned softly as she remembered her parents. Her heart had been ripped to shreds when she'd realized she'd never see them again. She'd walked stiffly into the church for the funeral, her head held high, numbed by the pain and it had felt as if the service was nothing to do with her. It was as though none of it was true. She was going to wake up, open her eyes, hear her mother discussing the news on the radio and her father trying in vain to make her stop talking. She'd see them smile when she came into the kitchen. She was going to wake up and nothing would have changed. She'd believed that so fiercely... But nothing had gone back to the way it was before. Reminiscens had disappeared in her turn and the endless pain had taken hold, making her act like some kind of zombie. Gus and Oksa had been the only ones who'd managed to break through her shell. She loved both of them so much... in her own way and despite the McGraws and their relentless hatred. Then the Pollocks and the Runaways had taken her in, no questions asked. She'd discovered that happiness wasn't completely out of reach—she could sometimes touch it with her fingertips. These brief interludes of affection had eased the pain and helped her to survive. It was because of the Runaways that she'd been reunited with her gran, whom they'd rescued from the clutches of the Soul-Searcher. Seeing her again had been the strangest experience of her life and also the most educational: it had shown her that, although blood ties are powerful, in the end your heart decides which side to take and who deserves your loyalty. Reminiscens, despite her family bonds, had an enduring affection for those who'd saved her life and not just because of her Disimpicturement. Her attachment to them went deeper than that: Reminiscens was a Runaway by conviction and nothing in the world could make her go over to the Felons, led by her brother, who was so similar to her and yet so different. Zoe had understood that in the first few hours after the Ageless Ones' terrible revelation. She'd been worried that her gran would choose family over friends, but Reminiscens had made it perfectly clear where she stood, which hadn't surprised anyone. She hadn't wavered for a second.

None of this had dispelled Zoe's doubts about herself, though. In her heart of hearts, she felt ambivalent—torn between two camps—and the revelation about her strange and horrible origins had done nothing to help matters. Abakum and Reminiscens had tried their best to make her see that she shouldn't feel ashamed about something that wasn't her fault, but it was stronger than her: she owed her existence to the relationship between Leomido and Reminiscens. They were related to each other and the fact that they didn't know at the time didn't make it any less shameful in Zoe's eyes. That was how Leomido had felt too... Still, Zoe knew how wrong her grandfather had been: nothing would have changed the way the Runaways felt. The revelation had simply fuelled their desire to fight the Felons and Ocious. It had never lessened their respect for Leomido. Had it been so hard for him to trust them? That was what Zoe had believed before. But now that she also knew what it was like to be unhappy in love, she understood him better. Some people aren't strong enough to deal with the shame of being a helpless puppet in unscrupulous hands, and that had been the case with Leomido. Despite the passing years, despite all his strength, he chose death rather than risk seeing the expression in the eyes of the woman he loved when she found out the truth. He'd held his resolve to the end, humbly enjoying their emotional reunion. Leomido and Reminiscens had unwittingly starred in their own tragedy, but what Zoe felt now was worse than that: she saw herself as a piece of perfectly ripe fruit, tempting at first but rotten to the core, squirming with maggots when you took a bite. A Firmhand-Werewall-Gracious who didn't belong anywhere—or rather, who belonged to two sides.

※

She walked towards the dark coppice, where tall grasses were swaying. It was in a more natural, unspoilt area of the park that was not so heavily landscaped. An unusually fierce wind was blowing, as if a storm were brewing, and Zoe thought briefly about the chaos unleashed on the world. Above her, the cloud-streaked sky looked ominous. She shivered, then continued pushing through the agitated undergrowth. She scrutinized the foliage carefully. At last she spotted him leaning against a tree. They walked towards each other and hugged warmly.

"I was afraid you wouldn't be able to get away," he said quietly.

"Nothing would have stopped me," replied Zoe. "You've changed so much!" she added, taking a step back to examine her second cousin.

Mortimer McGraw no longer looked anything like Oksa's Neanderthal: the thickset boy with coarse features was now much more athletic in build, conjuring up the powerful muscles of the jaguar rather than the brute strength of the rhinoceros. In seven months, he'd grown a good four inches and his body was leaner and more brawny, while his face was thinner and tougher. He looked a lot like his father. That's what Zoe had thought when she'd seen him again four days ago. Zoe and her class had been on a school trip to the British Museum. Mortimer had boldly approached her when she'd been standing in front of Cleopatra's mummy. Zoe had been amazed to find herself face to face with the boy who'd been like a big brother to her. Until he'd decided to abandon her... She'd been so surprised that she'd forgotten all the bitterness and incomprehension of the past seven months. "Meet me in Hyde Park on Tuesday evening in the trees to the west of the Albert Memorial," he'd whispered, before disappearing into the museum's corridors.

The next four days had felt interminable. She was wracked with uncertainty. Why had Mortimer come back? Did he want to take her back to the Felons? After all, she was pretty strong… Or did he intend to ask her to take over from Mercedica as a spy? Had he come back because he needed something or because he cared about her? She hadn't heard from him for seven long months. Not a word. So why now? But, despite all her questions and doubts, her heart was pounding with fierce hope mingled with profound sadness as she met Mortimer's eyes in the cold moonlight.

"How are you?" he asked, leading her under a large oak. Zoe didn't know how to answer, because she wasn't fine, but she wasn't all that bad either.

"How about you?" she asked, sidestepping the question.

"I'm good! My dad… isn't dead, you know…"

"Yes, I know. And my gran's home too."

Mortimer lightly stroked her cheek with his fingertips.

"Are they taking good care of you?"

"The Pollocks? Yes, they're very kind. I'm part of the family now."

"Do you get on well with Oksa?"

"She's my best friend."

Zoe looked down, surprised by the spontaneity of her answer. She'd said it without thinking, which only proved how sincere she was. Yes, the Pollocks were taking very good care of her and, yes, Oksa was her best friend. In spite of everything.

"How are things on the island?" asked Zoe in her turn. Mortimer's eyes darkened.

"You know about that?"

"I think we know as much as you do."

"Sounds like it…"

There was another silence. Buffeted by the fierce wind, the two cousins studied each other a little defiantly.

"Why did you come?" said Zoe. "Did your father send you?"

"You may not realize this, but my father loves you like a daughter."

Zoe felt sick.

"Your father doesn't love anyone, Mortimer," she retorted, trembling. "He used me the way he uses everyone."

"And you think your friends, the Pollocks, aren't using you too?"

"Whatever, they never forced me to poison an innocent woman..."

Zoe couldn't forget about the poisonous soap which had caused Marie Pollock's illness. She'd feel guilty about that for the rest of her life.

"Come with me, Zoe."

Her eyes filled with tears.

"I'm begging you. Please."

Zoe couldn't speak. Mortimer watched her gravely; he seemed so sincere.

"You're not like them, and you know it," he continued. "You're like me, a Firmhand and a Werewall. The blood of Ocious runs through our veins."

"—and of Malorane," broke in Zoe.

"Malorane was weak. She chose the wrong side. Without pressure from her family and the High Enclave, we wouldn't be in this mess today. It was her foolish opposition to our clan that caused the Chaos."

Zoe stared at him in bewilderment.

"You... you can't possibly believe that!" she whispered. "The Chaos was caused by the Felons and their power-mad ambitions, no one else!"

"Why not face facts, Zoe? Why deny the obvious? The strongest always win, that's been the way of the world since the dawn of time."

"And you think you're the strongest?"

"Of course! And you know it. That's why I'm here and why you're going to come with me."

Zoe shrank into herself miserably.

"I don't want anything to happen to you and, if you're with us, you won't be in any danger."

"It's too late, Mortimer," she whispered.

"Why?" he protested.

"You shouldn't have abandoned me. I was afraid, I didn't know what was going on and you left me behind on my own in that freezing house. You promised you'd come back and I waited for days and days. But you didn't. You lied to me! You didn't give a damn if I was in danger then, I was the last of your worries… I could have died of sadness, on my own like a prize idiot, and you couldn't have cared less!"

Zoe screamed those last few sentences with all the pent-up anger she'd felt during one of the toughest times of her life.

"Your father took my parents away from me, Mortimer," she raged. "And he didn't think twice about taking my gran, his own sister. Was he the one who gave her back? Were you? Was it one of your powerful friends? No! It was the people who've accepted me as one of their own. You're right, though—I'm not like them. I have a dark side like your lot. I'm not pure like the Runaways. My heart is as black as my blood. It's a fact, I can feel it inside me, eating away at me like acid. But I'm not coming with you. Seven months ago, I'd have followed you to hell and back, if you'd asked me. I loved you like a brother, Mortimer. Now, it's too late."

Mortimer gazed at her fiercely, looking smug.

"You're like us, Zoe… your place is with your family."

Despite her firm words, Zoe felt like a tightrope walker. She was treading a thin line between two worlds, balancing above a sheer drop. She was burning to ask one last thing—a question that could be the deal-breaker.

"Why didn't you take me with you seven months ago?"

Although she spoke coldly, she felt as though she was on fire. Mortimer watched her carefully, never taking his eyes off hers for a second, his hands on her shoulders. Zoe held his gaze. She was about to hear the verdict. She'd had high hopes of this meeting and knew how disappointed she would be if her hopes were dashed. She mentally prepared herself, knowing the wrong answer wouldn't hurt any less.

"We didn't have a choice," replied Mortimer.

Zoe paused, before saying:

"If, as you say, you still care about me, then please don't lie. Not today... Why didn't you take me with you?"

A strong gust shook the trees and some branches crashed down around the two cousins, as if to symbolize the inevitable outcome of their meeting.

"Why?"

Mortimer hesitated, then told Zoe what she'd dreaded hearing:

"We needed you to stay. We wanted you to get close to the Pollocks!"

Zoe broke away from his grasp and took a few steps back. Devastated by the truth, she staggered over to a large tree and leant against it, feeling winded. A few yards away, Mortimer was watching her apologetically. It was the sadness she saw in his eyes which stopped her from giving vent to her anger at him.

"Go now!" she cried. "And remember: your father doesn't care about anyone! No one at all!"

She turned to face the tree, put her hands against the trunk and pushed with a heart-rending scream. The tree trembled then, with a sinister creak, crashed to the ground.

62

FEATHERED INFORMANTS
AND HAIRY MESSENGERS

"MY YOUNG GRACIOUS IS GIVING A DISPLAY OF GREAT elegance in her attire, my appreciation is dressed in honesty."

"Thank you, Lunatrix, you're very kind!" replied Oksa, studying her reflection in the mirror.

"Kindness is not the motivation of your domestic staff," said the Lunatrix with a loud sniffle. Oksa glanced at the small, plump creature standing beside her. Grief-stricken at the loss of his mate, the Lunatrix looked as pale and tense as all the Runaways.

"How... do you feel, Lunatrix?"

"The survival of the body is tantamount to an involuntary reaction, my Young Gracious, because the heart of your domestic staff has the steadfastness of a muscle that commands automatic beating. But this heart prolongs survival while suffering the unbearable absence of she who assured his accompaniment for decades."

Oksa hung her head, overwhelmed by emotion. She crouched down and hugged the Lunatrix. For some strange reason, as soon as she touched the small, plump body a feeling of well-being came over her, as refreshing as a sip of cold water trickling down a parched throat.

"Does the Young Gracious experience restlessness?"

"I can't wait to see Mum again," she sighed. "You know a great many things, Lunatrix, so is there anything you can tell me about that?" she went on, remembering that the Lunatrix only provided information when asked.

"The mother of the Young Gracious is experiencing the agony of being kept apart from her loved ones, but is not suffering from a worsening of her state of health. The nurse named Annikki distributes treatment filled with efficacy owing to the medical skills of some of the accursed Felons."

"You mean they have some Lasonillia?"

The Lunatrix shook his head.

"The accursed Felons do not possess the supreme remedy because, in alignment with the information delivered by the Fairyman, the supreme remedy is encountered only in Edefia, in the territory of the Distant Reaches where its growth is profuse. But the accursed Felons have alighted upon the mastery of certain medications which produce the stabilization of feverish conditions such as the one endured by the mother of the Young Gracious. And your domestic staff can communicate the declaration that the mother of the Young Gracious will soon encounter a reunion with the Runaways, the assertion is absolute."

"You're not just saying that to make me feel better, are you?" said Oksa.

The Lunatrix gazed at her sadly.

"The domestic staff of the Gracious is exempt from a capacity for untruths. The Young Gracious should be overflowing with certainty and possess permanent confidence in her Lunatrix."

"You're right, I'm sorry, Lunatrix," continued Oksa, patting his head. "I'm just so worried..."

"The Young Gracious has the disposal of explanations from the Tumble-Bawler, which presented reports stuffed with comforting details from the Sea of the Hebrides. But has she encountered the idea of tendering questions to the Squoracle?"

"No!" exclaimed Oksa, smacking her forehead with her palm. "Thanks, Lunatrix, you're right, the Squoracle is bound to know something!"

She raced upstairs and burst into her gran's apartment.

"Can I see the Squoracle for a minute, Baba? Please!"

Dragomira nodded, motioning with her eyes to the open double-bass case. Oksa disappeared inside and ran up to the private workroom. She was welcomed by the Getorix, feather duster in hand, tossing its mane of hair.

"Hello, elegant Young Gracious!"

"Hello, Getorix! Do you know where the Squoracle is?"

"Who is that person?"

Standing in the middle of the room, the Incompetent was staring at Oksa in bewilderment. The Getorix sighed, raising its eyes skyward.

"And who's that talking hairball?"

"Hey, Incompetent!" shouted the hairball in question. "Take a good look: I'm the Ge-to-rix."

"Getorix? What a delightful name. Have we met?"

"Yes! A trifling eighty years ago!"

"Oh! That explains it then," said the Incompetent in relief.

Oksa burst out laughing, as she did every time the Incompetent opened its wide, toothless mouth.

"It doesn't get any better," she remarked, laughing even louder at the soft-headed creature's joyful expression.

"It never will," grumbled the Getorix in exasperation. "You wanted to see the Squoracle, didn't you? It's over there, by the fire."

Oksa walked over to the hearth and spotted the Squoracle snuggled under a tiny blanket, just inches away from the still-glowing embers from the night before.

"Squoracle!" she whispered, gently rocking the tiny hen with her fingertips.

The Squoracle jumped as if on springs. Its eyes bulging, it surveyed the room, turning its head like a radar.

"I sense a draught from the north-north-west," it remarked severely. "I suspect that the window over there isn't insulated and is allowing heat to escape from the workroom!"

It shot a black look at one of the skylights, then crawled back under its blanket. Oksa crouched down level with the miniature hen.

"Squoracle, I need your help."

"If you've come to tell me that, at long last, we're leaving this country with its inhospitable climate to move to the tropics, then I'm more than ready!" it squawked, waggling the feathers on its head.

"Um... you do know that England has a relatively temperate climate, don't you?" remarked Oksa.

"You must be joking!" retorted the Squoracle. "This wind-blown country with its appalling level of rainfall?"

This discussion was hardly new, but it amused Oksa every time. She stifled her laughter to avoid upsetting the tiny hen, while the Ptitchkins dive-bombed them from above.

"Snow flurries have been forecast for the middle of the day," chirruped one.

"... accompanied by a spectacular drop in temperature!" continued the other.

Oksa shot them a merry glance and bit her lower lip to prevent a snort of laughter. The Squoracle tucked its blanket snugly around itself, squawking shrilly in protest.

"I'll protect you, Squoracle!" said Oksa.

"Promise?" asked the hen, popping its beak out of the blanket.

"Of course! You can count on me: I'd never let you freeze. But before something awful like that happens, I wanted to ask you something..."

"Yes?"

"Do you know... what's in store for us? And for my mother?"

"I can't predict the future but, as the Tumble-Bawler told you, your mother is on an uninhabitable island—climatically speaking, of course. She is being treated very well, though. The Felons have a vested interest in keeping her healthy: if something happened to her, it would immediately put paid to any possible negotiation."

Oksa frowned.

"Your mother is the Felons' only guarantee of returning to Edefia when the Runaways have decided at last to leave this frozen land. She's the key that will provide access, if I can put it like that."

"Are you saying that I won't see her again before we go to Edefia?" Oksa's face fell and a wave of panic washed over her. "Please explain."

"What I'm saying is that I'm dreading this expedition, which is bound to be horrible from a climatic point of view, but a showdown between the Runaways and the Felons is inevitable. That's why you'll see your mother again soon. She has a vital role to play in the return to Edefia, for the Runaways and for the Felons. You do realize that, don't you?"

"Is she... okay?"

"She's much better," declared the Squoracle. "Thanks to Mercedica, the Felons know some of the secret formulas devised by the Old Gracious and the Fairyman to treat your mother. They've adapted these and have used them successfully."

Oksa gave a long sigh and stared into space for a moment, not sure whether she felt relieved or even more worried.

"What about Orthon?" boomed a deep voice behind her.

Oksa turned round and realized in surprise that the conversation had attracted quite an audience: all the Runaways were there, listening attentively.

"The hated Felon Orthon is now completely reconstructed," informed the Squoracle. "He regained his strength as a result of the months spent inside young Zelda's body, profiting from the warmth and vigour of her blood—with the emphasis on warmth, which is in such short supply in this frozen land. The Goranov plant stolen from the Old Gracious was an essential ingredient for his reconstruction—large quantities of sap were extracted to permit cellular reformation."

"I can't even begin to imagine what a state the Goranov must be in," said Oksa. "I hope the Felons at least took the time to milk it."

"It's in their interest to do so if they want the Goranov to survive!" retorted the Squoracle, shivering. "The brutal incisions performed at one time were the primary cause of death for the Goranovs. Just as exposure to abnormally low temperatures is extremely dangerous for hypersensitive creatures of my species… Is that a blizzard I can hear howling outside?"

Oksa tucked the blanket tighter around the tiny hen and settled it nearer the embers, before turning to the semicircle of Runaways.

"It's still hard to take…" she said with a lump in her throat.

"Remember, Dushka," said Dragomira, "the Squoracle can only tell you what's true now. Things are constantly changing and what might be true at one moment may be false the next. Everything hinges on the circumstances, the people involved and how they react: some provoke change, while others maintain the status quo. One thing's certain though: we must be very careful, whatever we decide to do."

"Are we going to rescue Mum?" ventured Oksa, her voice trembling.

"We can't wait for ever!" added Pavel angrily.

"You're right, Pavel," confirmed Abakum. "We're in a weak position, even though the ball is in our court. At the moment, the Felons have no reason to take action and expose themselves to attack: they know you've been Disimpictured, they have a Goranov plant and Malorane's medallion, there are quite a few of them and they can lay their plans in the utmost secrecy on that island. Most importantly, Marie represents an invaluable advantage. I'm with the Squoracle on that point: any return to Edefia depends on Marie—both for us and for the Felons."

"Unless Orthon believed me when I said we could leave without her…" said Oksa, paling.

An awful thought had her struggling to catch her breath.

"If he believes we don't need her to go back to Edefia, he'll kill her! Why on earth did I tell him that? Why?" she cried.

The Runaways stared at her, startled by a logical argument that could have such serious consequences. After a second of sheer panic, Dragomira and Abakum exchanged approving glances.

"What you say makes sense, Dushka," declared the Old Gracious. "But Orthon doesn't think like that."

Oksa looked up, her eyes brimming with tears.

"Orthon knows we're incapable of abandoning one of our number to achieve our goal," continued Abakum. "When it comes down to it, we could have continued without Gus, but we chose to be Impictured to rescue him, didn't we? Orthon knows what dangers we've faced and the risks we've taken. Would he have been able to do what we did? It's doubtful and, in his heart of hearts, he knows it."

Oksa considered what Abakum had said for a few seconds—the Fairyman could be very persuasive.

"I know Orthon well," broke in Reminiscens, her voice sad and serious. "He's my twin brother and the kind of people he surrounds himself with are no different from the ones who hung around my father, Ocious. They're powerful men and women, but they're only motivated by their own ambition. They join forces to achieve their ends and use each other to succeed. The strongest will climb to the top of the pyramid and anyone who's helped them will earn a place at their side."

"Are we any different?" asked Dragomira quietly.

"I think you're underestimating the spirit of the Runaways. It's a powerful force," replied Reminiscens, "which has nothing to do with the Gracious's powers, Pavel's Ink Dragon or the Fairyman's talents. I'm talking about the spirit that governs the Runaways' hearts and minds, the natural goodness that makes us all unusual. What unites us is totally different from what brings the Felons together: we regard power as a way of achieving harmony while the Felons see it as something they can use to rule. Don't worry, Oksa: you certainly gave Orthon something to think about when you bluffed about returning to Edefia without Marie, but he won't touch a hair on her head. She's a trump in the game that will finally allow him to be reunited with the man who's his greatest weakness and his greatest strength: our father, Ocious."

63

THE ULTIMATE WEAPON

"ORTHON SOON REALIZED THAT OUR FATHER HELD HIM in low esteem," continued Reminiscens. "He admired, respected and feared Ocious, and was terrified of disappointing him. Everything he did was assessed, criticized and judged, but rarely appreciated. I never heard our father say anything favourable to Orthon, but he lavished praise on others, particularly Leomido."

"The son he would have liked…" murmured Dragomira.

"I was in the same position as Orthon when it came to you, Dragomira: Ocious would have preferred you for a daughter as soon as it became clear that I wasn't going to succeed Malorane as the next Gracious. There was an outside chance I might have been the Gracious, which is why he seduced her. When you were elected Gracious, I suffered the consequences of his disappointment and contempt. I was no more use to him and, in the space of a few days, I went from being the daughter he'd pinned all his hopes on to a worthless nobody. It was only Leomido's love and support which helped me cope with his behaviour. It was different for Orthon. My brother found it very hard to bear Ocious's scorn and he tried his utmost to earn our father's respect. Every day, I watched him struggling desperately to do better and every day our father greeted his efforts with indifference or, worse, showered him with sarcasm and belittled him. Everyone else was always better. Always. I don't know why Orthon kept trying. It was a type of masochism. He should have escaped. Cut all ties. Nothing he ever did measured up to Ocious's expectations. Except for the day when he became an accomplice in the Beloved Detachment ordered against me. That was a turning point: Ocious finally opened his eyes and saw his son as an ally who might deserve a place at his side. After years of hard work, Orthon had finally earned his reward. But evil had already taken root in his heart: resentment and a hunger for revenge had already caused irrevocable damage. Years of being deprived of affection had made Orthon desperate for recognition."

"I remember him when we were in Edefia," said Brune. "He was always trailing behind Ocious, blinded with admiration and fear. It was disturbing."

"And that admiration and fear ended up breaking him," continued Reminiscens. "As time went by, they developed into a strong feeling of hatred and destructive love. There's nothing worse. It's a feeling that makes men merciless."

"Or psychopathic," added Oksa.

"Orthon's severe inferiority complex has now become devastating pride. All he wants to do is show Ocious that he's stronger than anyone—that the student has outgrown the master. That's his sole ambition. Nothing else counts."

This statement was greeted by worried silence.

"What happens if Orthon learns that Ocious is dead when he gets to Edefia?" asked Tugdual. Oksa looked at him in concern, while Gus gave him an irritated glare.

This question seemed to have occurred to Reminiscens already. Sadly she replied:

"I think he'd feel that his lifelong dream had been shattered. It would probably kill him, because proving Ocious wrong has been the only thing keeping him going."

"That's terrible!" exclaimed Oksa, surprised that she felt sorry for the Runaways' sworn enemy.

"Yes," agreed Abakum. "But we mustn't let ourselves be blinded by compassion…"

"…or else we'll be defeated," said Reminiscens, finishing his sentence.

"Why don't we just let him see his father again? Once he's shown Ocious how strong and superior he is now, he'll leave us alone," suggested Oksa.

"It's more complicated than that," replied Abakum. "Orthon has reached a point of no return."

"I don't understand…" wailed the girl.

"There are three types of power, my dear: balance, domination and destruction. If they do meet again, and if Ocious doesn't acknowledge his son's strength, Orthon won't hesitate: he'll choose the third option."

"It's the ultimate form of power," remarked Tugdual, winking at Oksa. "The power of destruction and death."

"But that's suicidal! Why do the Felons support that?"

Abakum looked at her miserably.

"Because they have no idea what Orthon went through," he replied. "Tugdual's right: total destruction is the ultimate weapon. If he has to use it, he won't hesitate for a second."

"Knowing Ocious, I think we have to fear the worst," added Reminiscens. "Assuming that he's still alive, I doubt he's changed and being trapped inside Edefia—when others were able to escape—will have done nothing to improve his vicious nature. If Orthon is reunited with him, he's likely to be severely disillusioned: Ocious is bound to run him down again."

"If Ocious had been able to escape Edefia, he'd have conquered the world," remarked Dragomira, going pale.

"Yes, he would… Orthon could have done that too, but the darkness inside him makes him more likely to destroy it. That's the trump up his sleeve. Because who's stronger? The dominator or the destroyer? What do people fear most? Subjugation or death? Only fanatics choose death and they're a tiny minority."

"What about us? What's our role in all this?" asked the Young Gracious with a shiver.

"The World's Heart is in chaos. We must return to Edefia as soon as possible so that we can restore harmony," announced Abakum in a choked voice. "Lunatrix... help me, please."

The small creature shuffled over.

"If death is successful in conquering the Heart of the World, the Outside will meet annihilation. The end will descend on the two worlds after showering them with countless disasters. The danger has experienced commencement since the season of summer when you, Young Gracious and Runaways, endured the ordeal of Impicturement."

The Runaways looked at each other in silent amazement. Oksa knelt down so she was level with the Lunatrix and whispered:

"What can we do?"

The Lunatrix gave a loud sniff. Everyone waited on tenterhooks. Oksa squeezed the small creature's podgy shoulder as he blew his nose on a checked tea towel, before continuing:

"The Ageless Ones will grant the gift of their instructions when the right time meets opportunity: make preparation for their relaying, because chaos is spreading and the rescue of the two worlds is growing imminent. Accomplish the merging of forces. The Cloak Chamber surrounds the Heart of the World with protection and this protection is experiencing a weakening that is spreading havoc over the lands and seas of the Outside. The preservation of harmony on the Inside and on the Outside is located within the walls of the Chamber, and the powers of the two Graciouses must enter union to win victory over the submergence of the two worlds. The two worlds will then achieve survival."

"Unless Orthon decides otherwise..." said Reminiscens fearfully.

"The reasoning by the sister of the hated Felon is shrouded in accuracy," agreed the Lunatrix.

"Great, so we've got a choice!" exclaimed Oksa. "Either the balance of the two worlds is destroyed and we die a painful death, or Orthon prevents us from restoring the balance between the worlds to show his father that he's stronger than him and… we die a painful death!"

"The only difference is that it'll be quicker with Orthon," remarked Tugdual.

"Very funny," muttered Gus.

"Why don't we kill Orthon then?" said Oksa. "If only to guarantee the survival of mankind!"

"You're forgetting he has Marie…"

Pavel's mournful voice was like a cold wind. Oksa put her face in her hands, alarmed by the danger they faced and by what was at stake. She felt her father put his strong arms around her.

"We'll sort it out," he reassured her. "I promise."

She looked up at him in surprise. She recognized the gleam in his eyes. She was seeing a determined Runaway with an Ink Dragon slumbering inside him as well as a strong, steadfast father bent on reassuring his daughter. Dragomira walked over to them.

"My son…" she murmured, gently stroking his shoulder. Pavel turned. There was no anger in his eyes.

"Let me make one thing very clear, Mum," he announced. "Once we've saved Marie and the two worlds, you're going to let me live my life the way I want, okay?"

Dragomira simply gave him a relieved smile. Pavel was clearly a Runaway at heart and, despite their ups and downs, no one could doubt his allegiance.

64

Escape through a Downpour

T HIS CRUCIAL DISCUSSION RESULTED IN A RESTLESS
night. Given the urgency of the situation, all the Runaways had
moved into the house on Bigtoe Square, where the mood was gloomy
and somewhat hysterical. The only two Runaways who weren't there
were Naftali and Abakum. When the decision had been taken to travel
to the Hebridean island as soon as possible, the two men had set off for
Abakum's farm and Leomido's home to gather all the creatures in the
Fairyman's Boximinus. Their return to Edefia was imminent, so they
had to be ready.

The prospect of an uncertain, and dangerous, future wasn't the only
reason for the uneasy atmosphere in Bigtoe Square. In the middle of
the night the city was filled with the sound of sirens, which woke the
Runaways as well as everyone living in London and the suburbs. The sky
throbbed with helicopters, while the armed forces walked through the
streets with loudspeakers, ordering inhabitants to take shelter immediately on the upper floors of their houses and to listen to the newsflashes
on the TV and radio. Oksa rushed out of her room in a panic and came
face to face with Zoe and Reminiscens, who were in the room next door.

"What's going on?"

"The level of the North Sea has risen by ten feet in just a few hours," said Tugdual, joining them. "The area around Greenwich is flooded and the Thames is about to burst its banks."

"Youngsters, come up here!" cried Dragomira from the top floor.

Gus came out of the guest room. He shot a frightened look at Oksa, then pulled himself together, adopting a frosty expression which wasn't like him at all. Oksa sighed.

"Come upstairs!" ordered Pavel, leading the way.

When the Runaways were all in Dragomira's private workroom, Pavel turned on the TV and they stood there, riveted by the images on the screen.

"Good Lord," murmured Baba Pollock, her hand over her heart.

"It isn't possible..." whispered Reminiscens, sounding shocked.

Aerial pictures showed the full extent of the disaster: the east coast of England and the north coast of France had disappeared due to the unpredictable movement of underwater currents, which had exceeded all imaginable limits. Instead of running into the sea, the waters of the Thames were flowing back inland and had flooded the entire river mouth. The water was now surging back towards London, the river level was rising by several inches per hour, and the pace didn't seem to be slowing. Riverside areas had already been affected and the Houses of Parliament were ankle-deep in water. But what made it worse was that no one knew why these underwater currents were behaving like this or how far inland they would travel. Evacuation of inhabitants in the most exposed areas had started, but it would be hard to move the entire population of London to safety, particularly as it was still dark and heavy rain had begun to fall. So instructions were kept simple: head for higher ground in the city or the upper floors of houses and... wait.

"We're all going to die!" gasped Gus in a panic.

"Speak for yourself!" retorted Tugdual, walking over to the window.

"I warned you!" screeched the Squoracle. "We should have left this inhospitable country while we still had time. Now it's too late and we're trapped by icy water!"

"Come and look!" exclaimed Oksa, peering out of the skylight in the workroom.

The Runaways gazed out and were rooted to the spot with horror. The rain was falling so heavily that it formed a thick curtain of water. Despite this downpour of biblical proportions, they could see that Bigtoe Square and the surrounding streets were under a good eight inches of water. They could hear people screaming and there was general panic.

"I hope Abakum and Naftali haven't got caught up in this," said Reminiscens anxiously.

"They should be at Leomido's place by now," said Pierre reassuringly. "His house is several yards above sea level and there's no river nearby. Anyway, the west coast of Britain seems to have escaped unscathed."

"What are we going to do?" wailed Oksa.

"Time's short," said Dragomira, looking at the water rising almost visibly in the square. "I suggest we join our two friends as soon as we can. They'll find it very hard to get back into London."

"We can't just leave!" cried Oksa.

"What are the journalists saying?" Pavel asked Tugdual, who was tapping on the keyboard of his mobile.

"Nothing good," replied the young man with a frown. "Similar freak currents have been observed in Europe and elsewhere, causing water levels to rise suddenly by around ten feet in the cities of Lisbon, Canton and Seattle."

Every single Runaway went white. The Squoracle gave shrill little squawks of anxiety.

"We've got to leave…" said Dragomira, gazing at Pavel with tear-filled eyes. "Now."

Baba Pollock and her son had been forced to make some hasty departures during their years of exile, but this was by far the hardest. However, despite the pain it caused them, they had to go. Pavel took a deep breath, his forehead creased in concentration, and announced:

"I'll carry you all to Leomido's house."

Oksa looked at him gravely.

"You mean… on the back of the Ink Dragon?"

"We don't have a choice," said her father. "Unless one of you has a helicopter hidden in their garden, I can't see any other way to leave a city under water."

"How many of us are there?"

"Ten, including you," replied Dragomira, looking concerned. "Not to mention the creatures… Do you think you can do it?"

Pavel slowly nodded, looking at his mother.

"If I don't, we'll have to swim to Wales," he said, with a thin smile. "Although you'll have the advantage of staying dry, Mum," he added, referring to Dragomira's gift of Aqua-Flottis.

The old lady smiled back at him.

"I suggest that anyone who can Vertifly should take turns to spare Pavel," said Pierre.

"You haven't Vertiflown any kind of distance for years," objected Pavel. "Anyway, it's bucketing down!"

"We have to try… Let us help you as much as we can." Pavel nodded, looking concerned but grateful.

"Okay, but there's no way that Oksa is going with you."

"But Dad—"

"I said there's no way you're Vertiflying in the middle of the night, in this weather," repeated Pavel flatly. Oksa looked upset.

"You don't think I can do it, is that it?"

"Oksa, for pity's sake, please listen to your father," begged Dragomira.

Faced with her father's severe expression and her gran's entreaty, Oksa gave in.

"It's vital that I don't get a single feather wet!" suddenly screeched the Squoracle, staring at the skylight in terror. "It will kill me!"

"Could I just remind you that feathers are waterproof?" retorted the Getorix, rolling its eyes.

The Incompetent, seized by a sudden doubt, began to run its hands sceptically over its body. Oksa went over to the creature and reassured it that, contrary to any doubts it might have, its hide was waterproof. The Incompetent immediately looked blissfully happy again.

"I'll leave now to inform Masters Abakum and Naftali of your imminent arrival," said the Veloso, jumping onto the windowsill of the skylight.

"Excellent plan!" exclaimed Dragomira, congratulating the small creature. "But I think it might be a good idea if the Tumble-Bawler went with you. It's been a long time since you set off on a mission."

The small creature agreed and began stretching while the Tumble-Bawler gave it all the details of their route: longitude, latitude, temperature, altitude, humidity... When the Veloso had finished limbering up, the two creatures raced out onto the slippery tiles of the roof. The Runaways watched them leaping from roof to roof until they disappeared in the lashing rain. They noticed that the water in the square had risen a few more inches. An army truck drove noisily past, followed by an ambulance.

"Let's not waste any more time. We should go!" said Dragomira, shivering.

"Why don't you just leave me here," grumbled Gus, looking at Oksa. "Since I can't be any use, I'd rather be rescued by emergency personnel like any other boringly normal person."

Oksa studied him, looking dismayed and exasperated.

"You're worse than the Squoracle!"

"It's obvious that I'm the only one who doesn't belong here!" he retorted angrily. "Don't tell me the thought hasn't crossed your mind."

"That's ridiculous!" gasped Oksa, tears in her eyes.

"No one here thinks there's anyone who doesn't belong," said Reminiscens. "You're one of us and I think everyone here has already proved how much you mean to them, haven't they?"

"Everyone has their part to play," added Brune.

"And I suppose mine is as court jester to the Young Gracious?" growled Gus.

Oksa sighed miserably. She'd done her best... Zoe glanced sorrowfully at her and walked away from the group.

"Gus, that's quite enough!" thundered his father. "I don't know what's going on between you and Oksa at the moment, but you can stop trying to score points off each other right now. We've got no time to lose—we have to get ready."

There was a short silence after the Viking's rebuke, which was soon broken by the comings and goings of the three elderly ladies, who'd methodically begun gathering together everything they had to take with them. There was no way of knowing if the Runaways would ever come back to London. They were all trying not to think about it, but this might be the last time they had to run away. Following the example of the three women, they all sadly bustled about, collecting essentials.

"One bag per person!" reminded Dragomira, filling a small case to overflowing with bottles of Granoks and Capacitors.

Oksa dashed up to her room. A few minutes later, she groaned in despair: her bed was covered with a heap of things she absolutely couldn't do without.

The bare minimum...

"Think 'survival', Oksa-san," she tried to reason with herself, rummaging through the huge pile of books, knick-knacks, clothes, shoes and gadgets scattered over her bed.

She pulled out her favourite belt—the one with the skull-shaped buckle—studied it and tossed it over her shoulder.

"Ouch!" came Tugdual's voice.

Oksa looked round in annoyance. He was standing by the door, a tiny bag slung over his shoulder, Oksa's skull belt in his hand.

"Sorry," she said, resuming her difficult task.

"If I were you, all I'd take is this!" he said, unearthing a jumper, some warm socks and a waterproof cape. "You should be able to survive with those."

"As sentimental as ever..." she muttered, examining a small statue made of volcanic rock which was one of her treasured possessions and which she was intending to pack.

Tugdual smiled at this remark. He took the statuette from her hands and put it back on the bed.

"Why don't you take a few photos?" he suggested. "They're great for the occasional hit of nostalgia and they're light so they're easy to carry around, which is a bonus…"

"You're so cynical!"

"Lil' Gracious, you'll never manage to be rude to me. You'd do better to hurry up… Mmm, you looked good enough to eat in that one!" he exclaimed, catching sight of one of the many photos Oksa was stuffing into a plastic wallet.

Oksa growled between clenched teeth and snatched the photo from his hands. At the same time, she noticed Gus walking past in the corridor and her heart turned over.

"He'll get over it," said Tugdual, as if he'd read her mind.

He looked serious again… which did nothing to lessen his irresistible charm. Rattled, Oksa gave up trying to sort through her things. She fastened her bag and glared at Tugdual, before going back up to the private workroom where the Runaways were waiting.

※

Pavel gave a low growl, which seemed to come from deep within: the Ink Dragon writhed, then spread its wide wings. Helicopter searchlights swept across the sky in the pouring rain as the Runaways climbed onto the dragon's scaly back.

"Fasten that against my side!" Pavel shouted to Dragomira, who was carrying the case containing her Boximinus with the creatures and her stock of Granoks, potions and herbs.

Dragomira obeyed, slipping the strap of the precious bag around the dragon's neck.

"It's now or never, I think!" exclaimed Brune, scrutinizing the deserted streets leading into the square.

"It'll be even better like this!" said Pavel, snapping his fingers.

Immediately, the pale lights of the street lamps winked out, plunging the square and surrounding streets into darkness. Oksa gave a small cry of admiration.

"I love it when you do that, Dad," she murmured in her father's ear.

He turned his head to look at her, before shouting hoarsely:

"Hold tight!"

Flanked by Pierre and Jeanne, who were Vertiflying beside them, the dragon began beating its wings slowly and powerfully, with such implacable strength that they soon took off. The Runaways, pressed together on the enormous creature's rugged back, watched the trees and roofs recede below them. The Pollocks' house grew smaller, then disappeared, creating what felt like a hole in Oksa's stomach. Soaring through the heavy rain, the dragon soon flew over St Proximus, its courtyard under a foot of water, and Oksa felt even sadder. Were they leaving for good? Would she ever see her house again? Her school? Her friends? How much she was going to miss them all… It was awful leaving like this, without any guarantee that they'd come back. For the first time, she understood how the Runaways must have felt when they left their lost land. It was a horrible wrench—it was like having part of yourself amputated, or a wound that would never completely heal.

The dragon climbed higher, reaching the dark clouds, and Tugdual and Reminiscens both slid off its back to Vertifly at its side. It was a surreal sight. The dragon suddenly gave a loud, sorrowful cry as Pavel, who was finding it harder than any of them to leave, gave vent to his anguish. Gradually the lights of the ravaged city vanished. The Runaways were starting a new chapter which looked set to be as turbulent as the murky night into which they were flying.

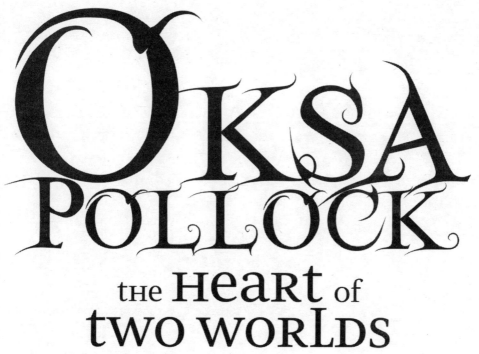

OKSA POLLOCK

THE HEART of TWO WORLDS

1

FLIGHT INTO THE UNKNOWN

PAVEL POLLOCK'S INK DRAGON FLEW THROUGH THE driving rain and wind with loud, powerful wingbeats. The only light in the almost total darkness came from an octopus—the Polypharus with its eleven illuminating tentacles—held out at arm's length by Dragomira like a beacon in the gloomy night skies.

"Keep going, son!" shouted Baba Pollock, leaning forward over the dragon's crested back.

The Runaways were trying to lighten the dragon's load by taking turns to Vertifly alongside it. Brune Knut, their stalwart Swedish companion, was the next to launch herself into the air, joining Pierre and Jeanne Bellanger, who were doing their best to brave the howling wind.

"The conditions are too treacherous," warned Pavel, his voice hoarse with exhaustion. "Let me carry you!"

"No way!" retorted Pierre, his hands shielding his eyes from the torrential rain lashing their faces.

With her arms wrapped around her gran's waist, Oksa was feeling extremely miserable. The sudden violence of the weather seemed to mirror the terrible wrench of their departure. In just a few minutes, their lives had been turned upside down: London had been flooded when an unprecedented tidal swell had caused the Thames to burst its banks. Fate had forced the Pollock family and friends to make a run for it—they'd had no choice but to embark on a headlong flight through the turbulent darkness into the great unknown. Looking back at Gus, Oksa met his terrified gaze. Her friend was clinging with all his might to Reminiscens and his face was wet, although Oksa couldn't tell whether it was with rain or tears. Frowning, she held on tighter and caught a glimpse of Tugdual and Zoe drawing closer to the dragon, their faces strained with effort. Vertiflying in a storm was no easy feat by any stretch of the imagination… Slipping between the dragon's beating wings, they both collapsed onto its back, making the creature groan in spite of itself and slow its pace, causing a sudden loss of altitude. Oksa couldn't help screaming.

"DAD!"

Pavel was growing weaker by the minute, as were the Runaways Vertiflying alongside him. Wanting to help her father, Oksa began to slide off the dragon's back to Vertifly, but the dragon gave a roar that seemed to come from the very depths of its soul.

"NO! Stay right where you are!" ordered Pavel.

"Then we'll have to stop for a while!" yelled Oksa. "You've got to land somewhere, Dad. We'll all die if you don't!"

It only took Pavel a few seconds to face up to harsh reality.

"Mum, put the Polypharus away so that no one can see us, and sit tight, my friends!"

The Vertifliers took firm hold of the dragon's scaly hide and the creature plunged groundward through the icy downpour.

*

The dazzling beam of light nervously scanned the darkness, but the four soldiers in the helicopter were convinced they hadn't imagined it: as incredible as it might seem, they'd just come face to face with a huge winged monster in the sky. Some kind of dragon, escorted by human beings who were flying too! They'd gazed at each other in disbelief, paralysed by the shock of this unlikely encounter. The pilot's jerk of surprise had almost caused him to lose control of the helicopter.

The aircraft had yawed for a few seconds before stabilizing and the Ink Dragon had taken advantage of the brief confusion to soar to a safer altitude. Hearts pounding, the Runaways were now anxiously looking down on the searchlight, which was trying to locate them. Suddenly the beam landed on them and their blood froze. They'd been spotted! The air was filled with the din of the helicopter engine as it headed straight for them.

"They're going to shoot us!" screamed Oksa, seeing one of the soldiers positioning himself behind a big machine gun.

Instinctively, she held up her hand, palm forward, to stop the bullets. As she'd discovered before on several occasions, extreme feelings of panic tended to produce an incredible surge of power. The helicopter's engines were no match for the blast of wind that sent it spinning several hundred yards off course.

"What have I done?" exclaimed Oksa in alarm.

"You've just saved our lives!" replied Dragomira.

"Come on, let's make the most of this temporary reprieve!" rang out Pavel's hoarse voice.

The dragon spread its huge wings, banked steeply and glided wearily towards the ground.

2

TREK OVER THE MOORS

"THE DWELLING OF MY OLD GRACIOUS'S BROTHER IS eight miles from here as the crow flies, heading north-north-west," remarked Oksa's Tumble-Bawler, a small creature which looked remarkably like a bumblebee without legs. "There are two routes available to us: the main road and a footpath over the Welsh moors. The footpath is more secluded, but it will take longer than the main road, which is quicker but much busier," it continued, gazing towards the horizon.

As if to illustrate the diminutive creature's information, the Runaways became aware of the noise from the road. Even though it was barely dawn, it sounded like the traffic was already heavy, with cars moving nose to tail. In the headlights, they could see birds taking flight in flocks, frightened by the blare of horns. The floods that had submerged part of England were driving people towards Wales and Cornwall in panic-stricken droves.

"Let's go over the moors," decided Dragomira with an anxious glance at Pavel.

Oksa's father was bent over with his hands on his thighs, trying to recover from the punishing night flight. He was a sorry sight. Although his Ink Dragon gave them a huge advantage, it was physically draining for him to share his body with another creature. He'd used up his last ounce of strength flying through the blinding rain to carry his family and friends to safety while ignoring the burning agony of his body and the anguish of leaving their home. He groaned through gritted teeth. Recent events had brought his dreams crashing down around his ears. Gone was the possibility of living a *normal* life one day. It was as if everything Pavel had done to achieve this had been built on sand. He'd started out with such high hopes and so much faith in the future... The restaurant he'd opened with Pierre in the centre of London had been a last-ditch attempt to put the past behind them and it had failed. In his mind's eye, he pictured the kitchen which was his pride and joy. Right now, it was probably knee-deep in mud as black as the misfortune about to descend on the world. *"We've got to leave... now,"* Dragomira had insisted. It wasn't the first time she'd said this, but her words had sounded so much sadder this time round, reawakening fleeting memories that filled their hearts with bitterness. Pavel shook his head as if to banish these dark thoughts. There was nothing to be gained by dwelling on the past. The most important thing now was to save his wife, Marie. She'd been a prisoner of the Felons for far too long. He straightened up as Dragomira came over and took a metal phial from her bag.

"Drink this, son," she said gently.

"Your famous Elixir of Betony?" he croaked.

"Yuck, that's revolting!" Oksa couldn't help exclaiming. "Revolting, but brilliant! You'll feel like a new man in no time."

Pavel smiled weakly at his daughter's enthusiasm and gulped down the contents of the phial in one.

"Blergh... it tastes like swamp water," he said, pulling a face. "It's just as well I trust you, Mum, otherwise I might think you were trying to poison me. You've really got to find some way of flavouring that disgusting concoction!"

Oksa sighed with relief. No one could match her father for sarcasm. But then, as he always said, mockery was simply a survival strategy for him.

"I'll give it some serious thought," promised Dragomira.

"Right, we've wasted enough time!" Pavel exclaimed suddenly, sounding much more like his old self. "We ought to get going."

It was growing lighter and the Runaways' shadows stretched over the heather as they followed the footpath through the deserted, hilly countryside. Wisps of mist clung to the bushes and leaves, creating a ghostly atmosphere. Above them, the sky was filled with British army helicopters which roared like enraged lions and made it impossible to work any magic. They had no choice but to keep walking in silence, still dazed by the cataclysmic sights they'd witnessed in London, where they'd left behind a piece of their history.

❋

"How are you bearing up, Lil' Gracious?"

Oksa glanced over at Tugdual. He was loping along with feline grace, tapping continually on his mobile, his wet hair hiding part of his pale face so that Oksa could only see the bottom of his jaw. She wouldn't have been able to tell if he was handsome or not, but that really wasn't the issue—more than anything, he reminded her of a black panther with his supple gait, keen intelligence and the brooding magnetism which played havoc with her emotions.

"I'm fine," she said without a great deal of conviction. "I just feel a bit… washed out. Literally as well as figuratively," she added, wringing out her soaked cotton scarf.

Tugdual gave a faint smile.

"How's the world doing?" asked Oksa, glancing at Tugdual's mobile.

"It's seen better days," he said, pocketing his phone. "Let's just say that you'll have your work cut out if you're going to restore order to this chaos!"

Oksa frowned. Today more than ever, she felt burdened by the responsibility. She was the Young Gracious, and the future of the world—of the two worlds—depended on her. She alone had the power to restore harmony to the Outside, where she'd been born, and to the Inside, her family's native land of Edefia, and she had no idea how she was going to go about it.

"Don't forget we're here too," whispered Tugdual intuitively. "You aren't alone."

That was true: she wasn't alone. She could always call on the strength and support of the Runaways. The Pollocks, Bellangers and Knuts—as well as Abakum, Zoe and Reminiscens—were all nearby. But she missed her mum so much: the future would seem a lot less uncertain when she could cuddle her again. As if to illustrate her anxiety, a fierce gust of wind buffeted the walkers, driving swollen clouds over the moor. It wasn't long before the heavy rain began again.

"I'd give anything for a bit of sunshine," grumbled Oksa, turning up the collar of her jacket.

As Tugdual matched his steps to hers, she took a deep breath and fixed her gaze on the Runaways walking along the narrow footpath in front of her, two by two. Dragomira was completely hidden beneath a long canary-yellow cape, which could be seen from miles away. "That's Baba all over!" thought Oksa with an affectionate smile. The Old Gracious was leaning on Pavel's arm. They were at the head of the small group, their shoulders bowed, but their pace resolute. Oksa was proud of her father. Proud of his strength and courage, and of the decision he'd finally taken to join forces with the Runaways and support them heart and soul. He'd been very firm in his own way: "*Let me make one thing very clear, Mum,*" he'd announced to Dragomira. "*Once we've saved Marie and the two worlds, you're going to let me live my life the way I want, okay?*" Just behind him, Gus and Zoe were walking in silence, their heads hunched down into the collars of their coats. Gus was the only one who had no magic powers and he seemed to be finding this forced march along a sodden path in the storm totally exhausting. Brushing her blonde hair out of her eyes with the back of her hand, Zoe kept glancing anxiously at her friend and Oksa's heart constricted. It should have been her by his side, not Zoe. It should have been her encouraging him. She clenched her fists, feeling furious and frustrated. She desperately wanted to do something. But what?

"Gus?"

No one was more surprised by Oksa's shout than Oksa herself—she hadn't even realized she'd called out. Her cheeks flamed as Tugdual looked at her with a half-smile. Gus turned round, just as startled as she was by her impulsive cry.

"What?" he snapped with bad grace. Caught unawares, Oksa didn't know what to say.

"Are you okay?"

"No better than anyone else…" he replied, his features drawn.

Before he turned away, Oksa caught a glimpse of the deep pain and resentment in Gus's dark-blue eyes. He was fuming about her growing closeness to Tugdual. From the minute they'd met, an intense rivalry had developed between the two boys and they'd made no bones about it, even though Tugdual tended to resort to mockery, while Gus was just downright rude. The moody Scandinavian teenager's appearance on the scene had aroused what Oksa felt might be the stirrings of love. Tugdual now occupied a special place in her life and her heart. The downside of this, though, was that it had undeniably broken something between her and Gus. Things just weren't the same—their deep bond seemed to have been replaced by an explosive hostility which Oksa found really hard to take.

"Why did I call out to him?" she fumed half-heartedly.

"Because you're an impetuous Lil' Gracious who acts before she thinks and who gets a kick out of putting herself in impossible situations," murmured Tugdual confidingly.

Oksa clenched her fists. "I don't want to lose him!" she thought as she watched Gus's thin frame labouring along the muddy path. She shoved her hands in her pockets and kept walking with a scowl on her face. With the toe of her laced ankle boot, she kicked a pebble into a ditch. The distant hills disappeared under the violent downpour, and the horizon—like their future—was hidden from sight.

✻

The Runaways had been walking for over two hours in exhausted silence when Oksa suddenly exclaimed:

"Hey! Look!"

They all looked up to see a hare bounding over the moor. Dragomira gave a long sigh of relief and her eyes immediately regained their sparkle.

"Abakum…" she whispered.

The hare rapidly drew nearer, escorted by two bizarre companions: Baba Pollock's Tumble-Bawler, which was wheezing as it flew, and the Veloso, which was leaping nimbly over the vegetation with its long striped legs. When the hare finally reached them, the Runaways greeted it with unbridled delight.

"It really is you, my dear Watcher!" crowed Dragomira joyfully, kneeling down and burying her face in the animal's thick greyish-brown fur. "I was so afraid…"

They all knew that Baba Pollock had hardly ever been separated from her loyal protector. Dragomira didn't like living without Abakum by her side and their emotional reunion showed the depth of that affection. The hare allowed her to stroke him for a few minutes, then, to the amazement of the younger Runaways who'd never seen this marvel before, he changed back into Abakum the Fairyman. The old man gave himself a shake, smoothed down his grey hair, then looked at the small group, as if mentally carrying out a roll call of everyone present. His eyes lingered gravely for a second on Oksa, then brightened, as though a huge weight had been lifted.

"You're all safe and sound, thank God!"

"We are, but only thanks to Pavel!" boomed Pierre Bellanger. "We wouldn't have got out of that mess without him."

Pavel looked away, embarrassed at being pushed into the limelight.

"Naftali and I saw what's been happening in London. What a terrible situation," continued Abakum, respecting Pavel's modesty. "And things can only get worse in this torrential rain."

As if to confirm his words, there was an alarming din as ten helicopters came hedge-hopping over the moorland. One of them hovered in front of the Runaways and they trembled with fear. Dragomira just had time to hide her Tumble-Bawler and the Veloso under her cape before a soldier popped his head out of the aircraft, megaphone in hand.

"Is anyone hurt? Do you need any help?" he boomed.

Abakum signalled that everything was fine, thanks, and the helicopter rejoined its squadron heading for the roads out of eastern England and London, which were chock-a-block as thousands of disaster victims poured into the area.

"How did you find us?" asked Oksa.

Abakum tapped his nose in amusement.

"Leomido's house is only a couple of miles from here."

Oksa sniffed at the air and exclaimed:

"All I can smell is mud, it's so unfair!"

"I do have an uncommonly good sense of smell, sweetheart," said the Fairyman. "And it's not as if you don't have a great many talents yourself, is it?"

"Fat lot of good they are! With these stupid helicopters popping up unexpectedly, we can't even Vertifly for short distances!"

Everyone smiled except Gus, who turned his back on them with a brusqueness which upset Oksa.

"Excellent... Let's go and find Naftali then!" suggested Dragomira. "It's high time we were all back together."

They set off again, their backs bowed under the beating rain but their hearts filled with renewed purpose.

May thanking filled with gratitude overrun the hearts of those who love Oksa and who have belief in her destiny.

May Estelle accept receipt of a special mention for bestowing the gift of the Song of the Runaways.

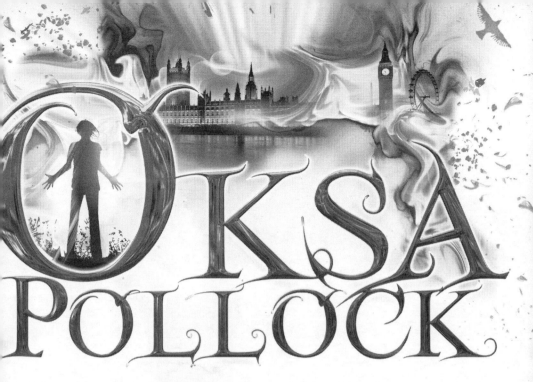

PUSHKIN CHILDREN'S BOOKS

Just as we all are, children are fascinated by stories. From the earliest age, we love to hear about monsters and heroes, romance and death, disaster and rescue, from every place and time.

In 2013, we created Pushkin Children's Books to share these tales from different languages and cultures with younger readers, and to open the door to the wide, colourful worlds these stories offer.

From picture books and adventure stories to fairy tales and classics, and from fifty-year-old bestsellers to current huge successes abroad, the books on the Pushkin Children's list reflect the very best stories from around the world, for our most discerning readers of all: children.